Black Wings Dark Fate

Evie Craigie

CONTENTS

CHAPTER 1

Soft strong fingers brushed across my hand and traced slow circles up my arm. Warm breath teased across my skin, causing goosebumps to follow in its wake. Heat wrapped around me. Soft gentle heat that seemed to cocoon my entire being. It was as protective as it was carnal, and promised a world of pure, serene, pleasure.

There was something else though, something dark lurking beneath that strong, numbing haze those touches always sent my mind to.

"Come to me..."

That voice called endearingly—commandingly. There was no hesitation in the darkness as it wrapped tightly around my body and turned my mind to mush. Those soft fingertips brushed along my bare shoulders, tracing my collar bone before dipping lower. Heat flamed in my veins, running deeply through my being, and making me crave things that no dream ever should.

"Need... you..."

"Lark."

The sharp sting of my name pierced through my skull like a knife, and weakened that embrace. The warmth slowly grew cold until it was no longer enticing against my skin, but an icy glacier creeping through my chest. I wanted to cry out as those tender touches disappeared.

"Larkin!"

I shot away from the window gasping for air. My head was pounding like millions of tiny hammers were nailing away at my skull. Waking from one of those dreams was always the same. Like drowning when you can't get to the surface in time to breathe.

"Are you okay?" Raffie was staring from the front seat of our 2005 Chevy SUV. Her dark, blue, doe eyes were wide as saucers.

Why the hell did we let a nine-year-old sit in the front anyway?

I sucked in a deep breath and leaned back against the old comforting leather of the vehicle's interior. I held my thumb up and rubbed the other against the pain in my chest. "Just peachy, Raf."

She blinked again, her tiny hands clutching the arm rest as that worried frown caused guilt to weigh heavily on my shoulders. "You were having another nightmare."

"Not really." I grumbled more to myself than her as I felt those identical eyes of her brother's pierce the side of my face through the rearview mirror. Adriel Marko was the most observant, concerned, pig-headed man I have ever met, and he never let shit go.

"You sure you're good, Lark? We can stop for a break if you want." His words were concerned enough, but I knew that look in his eyes was far pass meager worry. It was calculating, like it always was whenever he thought something was sketchy. That man was many things and oblivious was definitely not one of them.

"No, no. I'm good, Dri." The nickname did little to turn that dagger gaze away, but it did take that scolding frown from his lips. Not that he had any reason to scold me. I couldn't control dreams.

"Good. We're almost there anyway."

Almost there. Great.

I kept my disgruntled thoughts to myself as I gazed at the barren landscape. There were some trees scattered here or there with a lone house in the distance, but the area was mainly grassy hills as far as the eye could see.

I hated it.

"Explain to me why you're dragging us here again?" I grumbled and kicked my feet out until I could rest them against the other window. My head was still a little foggy and all warmth seemed to have left my body, and yet all I wanted to do was fall right back into that dream. I had some serious urges that needed to chill.

"I don't understand why you're still complaining." Adriel sighed with a shake of his head rather handsome head. "You applied to this school anyways."

"Because you told me to."

"I did not."

I scoffed and shot him a bewildered look as those sneaky lips of his tried to hide a smirk. "You said, and I quote, 'You better apply to Deshua University, Lark, cause we're moving there'. And I said," I cleared my throat for dramatic effect, "'What if

I don't want to go to that piss poor school?' and you said 'don't care, it's happening'. So, I applied and here we are."

He didn't try to hide his chuckle, and let me tell you a laughing Adriel was not common. "That does sound like something I would say."

"Because you did say it."

He rolled those bright blue eyes, his grip casual though it never left the steering wheel. "Our great aunt passed away and left us her house. I got a job here, there's a good school system, and it's cheaper than California. Simple as that."

"Simple as that." I mocked with a sardonic laugh. Yeah right. It's not like they were lacking for money. The Markos family was loaded, and their parents left them a shit ton that Adriel controlled. Not that I was legally allowed to any of it, but he still provided for me.

I had been in foster care for as long as I could remember, always bouncing from one home to the next. Until the Markos came into the picture. I was sixteen when they put me with their family, and lucky enough to stay there until my eighteenth birthday. They had been the nicest people I had ever been with, and I had been with a lot. In a lot of crummy places too. The Markos' paid for my extracurriculars in high school, my senior class trip, they even put money away for me for college.

They were the closest thing I had to a family in my entire life, and when I turned eighteen, I tried to run away. Run as far and as hard as I could, but Adriel wouldn't let me. Even though I got his parents killed.

"Are you excited for college?!" Raf asked for the thousandth time since I got accepted into that stupid university, and I tried not to let her see my eyes roll.

"Just beyond elated." I didn't bother hiding the sarcasm. I knew she wouldn't get it, and even though I was one-hundred percent sure her brother did, he didn't say anything. I didn't give one rat's ass about college, besides the fact that their parents had wanted me to go.

I was perfectly fine finding some mediocre job and living my life as best I could until I died. But then Dri decided he was not about that, and no matter how many times I told him to shove what he wanted up his ass, I ended up applying anyway.

"Why don't you major in art? You like that stuff."

I give the intrusive male a small shrug and went back to staring out the window.

He sighed. "You're not going to hate it as much as you think, Larkin. I loved college." Adriel tried to encourage though the sneaky glint in his eyes did little to make me feel better.

"You never left your room when you were in college. You isolated loner." I grumbled at the annoying man.

"Some things are more important than partying."

"Like being a normal, sociable person?"

The smile he shot me through the rearview mirror was almost wicked. "Exactly."

I closed my eyes against the stare in his and tried to ease the quickly brewing headache away. Conversing with the arrogant male was pointless. It usually always turned into an argument, ones he had a serious knack for winning. It made me beyond irritated.

"Don't fall back asleep we're almost there."

"Bite me."

The brakes on the car suddenly engaged and jerked the whole SUV in one hard motion. "Ah!" I screeched and toppled over onto the floor. Raf's elated giggles only made the sudden fury pounding behind my head worse. I snapped my gaze over to the siblings, who were staring at the road like nothing had happened—except I noticed Adriel slip his arm away from the protective shield it held in front of his sister.

"Brake-checking is for ass holes." I spat at the twenty-two-year-old as I climbed clumsily back onto the seat.

"No idea what you're talking about."

"Whatever." I kept my eyes glued out the window after that, silently fuming. He could be such a fucking dick sometimes.

I didn't want to start an argument though, not in front of Raffie at least. She didn't need to see fighting, no matter how much I enjoyed trying to annoy the living daylights out of the man. I would never admit this out loud, but I found him way more than a little attractive. He had dark, nearly black hair that was cropped short at the sides and slightly longer on top. Deep ocean blue eyes shown in stark contrast against toned tan skin, and he stood a good seven inches taller than myself.

It wasn't only his appearance either that drew me in like a moth to flame. Adriel was strong, smart, confident, and he actually cared. Even after what I did to his family. But when I started to irritate him or make him mad, those blue eyes would blaze with fire, and the muscles in his arms would ripple with tension. It was one of the sexiest sights I had ever seen, and I had no shame in admitting I tried to pull that out of him as much as possible.

I crossed my arms grumpily over my chest and watched the rolling hills give way to large houses. Then, like someone literally decided to just drop a bunch of buildings in the middle of freaking nowhere, we were suddenly driving through a medium sized town.

"This place is—"

"So cool!" Raffie cheered from the front, her wide blue eyes gazing adoringly at all the buildings.

"I was going to say old." I grumbled under my breath but didn't bother trying to kill her mood.

If I wasn't being such a brat about the situation, I could have probably seen the beauty in the town. Each building we passed seemed to be carved from ancient stone and brick with vines covering more than a few of them. The streets even turned to pristine cobblestone the further we drove.

School hadn't started yet and I watched as teenagers and college-aged kids cluster in and out of the many shops surrounding the area. I was too proud to admit that I was excited about exploring those stores and that little ice cream place we passed on a corner. Adriel would take way too much pleasure in it.

I had to force down a surprised gasp when we finally reached the center of town. Sitting smack dab in the middle of Deshua was a large beautiful cathedral. It appeared to be made of solid white marble. Each step leading to its grand entrance was smooth and glistened in the morning sun. Strong pillars held a massive archway over the crowd. It reminded me of one of those churches in Europe left over by ancient Romans.

"Whoa... I didn't even know there were churches like that in America."

Adriel glanced briefly over at the large building before that dark blue gaze flickered back to the road. "Yeah, there's a few. Usually in large cities like Boston and New York. I'm not too surprised to find one here though." I rolled my eyes. Nothing could ever really surprise Dri. Besides, his degree was in architecture and he was probably used to seeing those kinds of buildings all the time.

Each building seemed to have been built purposely around the cathedral in an encompassing circle—like beautiful little ornaments. Though I wouldn't call many of those houses little. They all looked like old manors, or the houses you see on TV dramas. "You guys inherited one of these?" I asked incredulously as we passed one house that had large, iron gates with gargoyles resting on top.

"Yes, though ours is nowhere near as big as these."

I was relieved by that. Living in a huge mansion would have been cool and all, but we didn't really need all that space. I don't even think they owned enough stuff to fill a house that big. Besides, Adriel was all about 'bonding', especially after the accident. He probably would have only let us use like five rooms out of a house that big, leaving the rest abandoned.

Like an invisible magnet was pulling my gaze back to the church, I turned away from the mansions to gaze admiringly at the marble. There was a large cemetery stretching lengths behind the cathedral, and it took up most of the town square. "What a weird place to put a cemetery." I mumbled under my breath as my eyes scanned the many gravestones. Though, I guess it was behind a church.

I glanced to the side and found what looked like a large construction site in the middle of what must have once been a park. A bunch of benches, slabs of cement that was apparently a sidewalk, and playground equipment were pushed far off to the side. Like they couldn't bother taking the time to remove them properly. A large lake sat untouched a few yards away from the upturned dirt and construction equipment.

"What do you think they're building?" I asked as we drove carefully by a bunch of teenagers eating ice cream and laughing in little clique clusters.

Adriel glanced briefly towards the park. "I'm not sure, but it looks like they're digging, not building." He shrugged like he wasn't all too concerned with the completely overturned area. "They might be trying to fix a busted pipe or something. But Avid is the construction agency that signed me, so I'm sure I'll find out soon." He nodded towards the large, bold name pressed into the crane and dirt removal machine-thingy.

"Are you going to be working with them?" I gestured to the guys, and a few women, wearing hard hats and protective gear that were climbing over large piles of dirt and rock.

"Probably." He sounded nonchalant as he turned the blinker on before driving us down a side street. The park, cemetery and church disappeared from view. I tried to shove aside the unease that had built in my stomach. It was ridiculous to worry about him doing his job. He knew what he was doing, and he always played everything by the book. He would be careful.

Chapter 2

"Is this it?" Raffie asked eagerly when we turned onto Haniel Drive and pulled to a stop in front of an old Victorian house.

"Obviously." Even though my voice was a little snappy, I gazed up in awe at the two-story manor. Adriel let out a dramatic sigh, but besides a warning look, he didn't say anything. Raffie and I followed as he stepped out of the SUV.

The manor was on the corner of the street, and lush green grass swept the front yard and around the side. Gray, stone steps lead from the driveway to the wooden front door. The porch was quaint, and rather small for the size of the house with a few stone pillars holding a terrace above it. The giant outcrop of bay windows running its length made up for it. The outside alone took my breath away, I was almost too afraid to look at the interior.

"Alright," Adriel quickly took on his 'get down to business' tone and began untying the thick rope holding down the boxes on top of the SUV. "Let's start getting this stuff into the house then we can figure out room situations-"

"Raffie and I are going for a walk." I cut off his orders with a loud yawn and stretched dramatically for effective. Dri's dark blue gaze instantly snapped to mine, and his strong jaw grit together. Sigh, I loved it when he did that.

"Don't argue, Larkin. The faster we get this done the-"

"Yay a walk!" Rafael cheered happily as she came bouncing around the vehicle and slipped her little hand into mine. The expert manipulator beamed excitedly up at her older brother. "Please, Adriel? I want to explore, and we'll be quick!"

Yeah, we weren't going to be quick, but I wasn't going to correct the kid. I knew the minute she turned on those puppy dog eyes he was a goner. No one could say no to the little twerp for long. Adriel's gaze was like icy stone until let out a long sigh.

"Fine. Whatever. Make it quick though."

"Yay! Thank you! Love you, bye!" With one last beaming smile, her little hand tightened around mine and she nearly dragged me away from the over-packed car.

"Be careful, Larkin."

"Always am, Adriel." I emphasized his name like he did mine and shot him a smirk over my shoulder as his sister continue to drag us down the sidewalk.

"This place is so cool!" Raffie exclaimed excitedly. There weren't many trees, but the few that rested in the yards we passed were tasteful and beautiful. The sidewalk dipped below foundation lines and ran along stone ledges that kept people's yards from the street. It really was a beautiful area, but I wasn't going to admit that out loud.

We were probably walking for about twenty minutes, staying strictly on the side streets, and avoiding the crowds at the center of town, when we stumbled upon another large, encompassing, open area. It was like an extra little town in the town. Massive, vine-covered buildings stared back at us, a courtyard with a water fountain sat directly in the middle, and a giant, granite sign reading 'Deshua State University' flashed brightly in the light of the sun.

"Oh wow! This must be your school!" Raffie's voice was as astounded as I felt.

I never thought a school this size would be found in the middle of nowhere like this. Then again, I didn't think a cathedral like the one in town square did either. What looked like dorms ran the length of the area, and little shops sat sparsely between the academic buildings. They were all made of the same red brick as the buildings in town, and looked just as old.

"Maybe you will like it there." She smiled up at me, her little head barely reaching the height of my chest.

"Maybe, but I'm not going to put much stock into it."

Her smile fell away, and that adorable pout she wore whenever she was confused pulled at her lips. "What does that mean?" I laughed as she tugged harshly on my hand.

"It just means that I doubt I'll like it."

"You could have just said that." She grumbled, but that pout fell away as she pointed towards the cobblestone road that led into campus. "Do you want to go explore?"

I weighed that question a lot more heavily than I needed to. A part of me felt guilty for leaving Dri to unpack the car all by himself—even though when I tried to help load it, he made a big fuss that I wasn't doing it right and took all the junk out to put it back in himself. Another part of me felt that same irresistible pull as I did with the cathedral. I couldn't look away, couldn't walk away either.

"Yeah, alright. Let's go."

She beamed happily before her hand tightened and started dragging me once again. "See! I told you this place was cool!"

I was too busy staring at the intricate designs that were carved into the bricks to pay much attention to what she was saying. They looked like prehistoric words, or symbols from a dead language. My fingers traced softly over the delicate designs, shivers running down my spine.

That's when I heard it.

Well, I wasn't really sure what it was, but it sounded like a soft, gentle lull brushing against my ears. I turned fully expecting to see someone standing behind us, but there was no one there. The noise came again, though this time it was more of a pulse pushing against me than a sound. I stepped away from the building, Raffie's hand still gripped in my mine as I walked towards the noise.

"Larkin? You okay?" I barely heard the kid ask as I started pulling her in the completely opposite direction from where we were heading. "Larkin?"

"Do you hear that?"

"Hear what?"

But I didn't answer her, I couldn't. My mind had completely focused on that sound. We were headed towards an outcrop of trees, a large bouldering face pressed behind them that I hadn't noticed before. My gaze zeroed in on the rocky mountain the school seemed to be pressed up against. Was that there the whole time?

"Larkin? Larkin, you're scaring me. I don't want to go in there—"

"Hey, you two!" A voice shouting across the courtyard finally pulled me from that sound pulsing through my brain. My eyes snapped over to the well-in-shape blond jogging quickly towards us, a small smile pulling on a pair of full lips.

I instantly shoved Raffie behind me and pulled out my regular 'fuck-off' attitude I used on random strangers. "Can I help you?" The guy, who looked around my age if not a year or two older, raised a blond eyebrow at my tone but didn't drop that charming smile.

"I was just going to warn you about going in there." He nodded towards the small patch of woods I had been making a bee-line towards. "Some people were saying they spotted cougars in there a few days ago." His eyes, that peaked briefly at me over the tops of dark sunglasses, were a dark, warm, brown that tried to melt away at my insides. Tried to, at least.

"Oh... Okay, well thank you for the warning." The noise had completely disappeared, and I instantly felt like a moron for trying to drag myself and Raffie towards it. Who just endangers a kid like that?

The guy's pleasant smile grew, and I was suddenly very aware of how white and perfect his teeth were. That must have taken years of braces and whitening treatments. No one's teeth were that flawless. "Yeah, no worries. I'm Luke, by the way." His hands stayed buried in his jacket's pockets and didn't reach out to shake mine, which I was actually pleased about. I hated shaking strangers' hands. You never know what they have been touching.

"Um. I'm Larkin—"

"And I'm Raffie!" Rafael peaked around my waist with that beaming smile and squeezed my hand tightly.

The guy, or Luke, or whatever, turned that same smile on her and nodded his head. "Nice to meet you, Raffie." She giggled and immediately went back to hiding behind my back. I rolled my eyes.

"She's not really shy, she just pretends to be." She pinched me hard, but I ignored it. Luke just laughed, and the action was all that unpleasant. He really wasn't a bad looking guy. Actually, he was pretty damn attractive, and if it wasn't for the unnerving feeling he shot through my entire system, I would have been laying the flirt on thick. In front of Raf and all.

"You two just move here?" Luke asked casually enough, but I knew better than to ignore my instincts, and all of them did not want us around the guy. No matter how nice he was.

"Yeah, how did you guess?"

He shrugged casually enough, but I noticed how his sunglass covered gaze flickered briefly towards the mountain. "Deshua is a pretty small town. Everyone has been here their whole lives. You get to know who's new and who's not pretty quickly."

"What about the college? I'm sure you get a bunch of new people here for school all the time."

That charming smile fell slowly until it resembled more of a smirk. "School doesn't start for another week, and most out-of-towners don't stay long."

I raised my eyebrow in disbelief. "It's a pretty big school for just townies."

He laughed. "Townies. It never occurred to me to call us that. Some people do stay, just not all ten thousand that flood in every year. Do you plan on attending?"

"Yeah, I start this semester."

That smile was back, delightful as ever. "Awesome, I'm a junior, but I'm sure I'll see you around."

Don't count on it, bud. No matter how charming and attractive he was, I wasn't going to let that override my senses. Besides, boys were just boys. If anything growing up on my own has taught me, it was how to play the game and come out on top. I never got flustered. No matter how attractive the guy was.

"Listen, I got to go get some stuff together for my apartment. It was nice to meet you though." He nodded, before leaning slightly to the side to shoot a smile at Raffie. "Nice to meet you too, Raffie." She giggled and pressed further into me. "See you around." He called over his shoulder as he turned and walked away. I breathed out the bubble of tension that had swamped my chest.

First the dream, then the weird noise dragging me to those trees, now this guy? I had enough excitement for one day. "Let's head back now. I'm getting hungry."

"Yeah, okay!" Rafael sang happily as she came back around to my side, all that scared fear from before gone. "I want some food too. Do you think Adriel finished unpacking the car?"

I let out a rugged sigh as I steered her away from the woods and back towards the street. "Knowing him, he probably left all the big stuff for me to get." My eyes flickered back to the trees, with its weird, commanding noises, and hidden man-eating cats. I had a sick feeling this place was going to have a lot more excitement than I thought.

Adriel actually didn't leave me the big stuff to unpack, but he did leave all my stuff. "Fucking moron. Stupid, piece of crap..." I grumbled viciously under my breath as I heaved my heavy boxes off the top of the car and placed them on the green lawn.

I didn't really have a lot of stuff, and besides a few worn out, raggedy clothes from my childhood, everything in those boxes had been giving to me by the Markos's. Adriel and Raffie were sitting casually in the manor's living room as a I lugged a few more boxes into the large foyer, ice cream stuffing their stupid mouth-holes.

"Ass." I hissed under my breath as I plopped a heavy box labeled 'Larkin's books' down. I didn't even like to read, but their parents had bought a bunch anyway.

"Watch your language." Adriel snapped from the old purple sofa left over by his great aunt and uncle. I rolled my eyes but was too tired to argue.

I sat on the cool wood floor just inside the front door and gazed around the grand interior. There was a large staircase that lead to the second floor, a living room that ran the length of the left side of the house, and the dining room with its large, mahogany table and connected pristine kitchen on the right. I hadn't been upstairs yet, but I had a feeling it would be full of the same old Victorian furnishings as they rest of the place.

"Are we going to keep all this stuff?" I called into the living room without moving an inch off the floor.

"Try to be more respectful, Larkin. They just died and gave us their house." Dri sighed as he stood to his feet. "If you guys want to get rid of their things, we can probably sell them. But its staying until we can get our own."

"I'm fine with their stuff..." I mumbled as I climbed back to my feet and headed for the door. I still had five or six boxes to bring in, then I had to figure out which room Adriel deemed me worthy enough to have.

"Fucking hell!" I shouted when the cardboard box I had pulled off the car collided with the moron who decided to make my life difficult. He raised one dark eyebrow, his lips pulling into a small smirk. "You scared me." I snapped as I side stepped around his athletic body.

"Sorry." Adriel chuckled, which automatically threw his apology in the trash. He wasn't sorry. He enjoyed scaring the shit out of me. I was surprised though when he started to help carry the rest of my stuff inside.

"Thank you." I mumbled when all the boxes were finally out of the car and covering the floor of the foyer.

"Hm." He didn't say anything else, though those blue eyes were sparking in amusement.

"Which room is mine?"

He shrugged and ran a heavy hand through his dark hair. My eyes lingered briefly on the muscles moving in his arm as he did before I forced them away. I wasn't going to risk getting caught staring at him. He would never let me live it down.

"Which ever room you want. I told Raffie you can have first pick."

"Really?!" I didn't bother hiding my excitement, and the soft smile that grew on his lips made it worth it.

"Yeah."

"You're the best. Thanks!" I wrapped my arms around him in a quick surprise hug before taking off for the stairs.

The steps fell away to a small balcony overlooking the foyer, with a metal railing keeping people safe from toppling over. The second floor was one long hallway with two doors on either end and two facing the balcony. I checked behind each one and found four bedrooms, a full bath and a tiny linen closet I hadn't noticed. There was a master bedroom with a master bath that I almost took, but then my too-damn-nice-self decided to let Adriel have it. He deserved that more than I did.

I took the room at the far-right end of the hallway. It was bigger than the other two and both outside walls had casement-style windows. There was a beautiful, wooden, bedframe and mattress pushed against the back wall. I let my fingers brush against the dust on the shelf nailed into the drywall and smiled at the room. Yeah, I could make this mine with no trouble.

"Pick one yet? I want to start bringing stuff up." I turned to see Adriel leaning casually against the doorframe, strong arms crossed over his stony chest.

The afternoon light streamed through the window and washed over his handsome frame, those blue eyes flashing in its soft rays. My heart clenched when he looked like that. A slow, burning anger—at myself—pushed the fire starting to spread through my veins away. I turned back to stare at the walk-in closet.

"Yeah, this one's good."

"I was almost certain you would pick the master." He chuckled and stepped over to one of the sliding windows to test the frame.

I shrugged and turned back for the hallway. "Yeah, well, you're the old one. Don't adults get the masters?"

His laugh followed me as I started walking towards the stairs. "You're eighteen, Lark. You're an adult too."

My smile disappeared as he followed behind me. I had always felt like an adult, being eighteen meant nothing to me. I knew how to take care of myself by the time I was ten, and I knew that the real monsters were just people pretending to care. The only time I ever felt my age, or like a kid at all, was when the Markos came into the picture. They took that burden off my shoulders, and slowly convinced my heart that I could trust them. That I could be a kid.

And I killed them.

"Hey. You okay?" I hadn't realized I was shaking until Adriel's hand was suddenly wrapping around my wrist and steading my grip on the box I had bent down to grab. I shook those dark thoughts away and shot him a reassuring smile.

"Yeah, yeah I'm okay. Can I have ice cream now?"

"Sure..."

But I didn't wait for the chocolate dessert. I just turned for the stairs and started dragging the box up with me. A shot or two of vodka was what I really needed. Anything to make unpacking more fucking bearable.

CHAPTER 3

Three hours later I stood in my unpacked room with a wide smile. This was the first time I ever got to decorate something. I felt way giddier than I should have. I didn't have many decorations except a calendar hanging on one wall and pretty star lights hanging from the other. It was enough to make me happy.

"I can get you a desk tomorrow." I turned to see Adriel walking through the open door, another bowl of ice cream in his hands. "You're going to need it for school."

"Thank you." I gave him a large smile as he handed over the way too sugary snack. I wasn't really into junk food, but occasionally I caved for ice cream.

"I'll get you a new laptop too." He added and bent down to adjust the corner of my fluffy throw rug.

"I already have one." I mumbled around a mouth full of icy deliciousness. Adriel could be the biggest ass sometimes, but just as sweet and caring in others.

He raised a dark eyebrow and turned those blue eyes to the computer sitting on my freshly made bed. The beautiful dark green comforter with black intricate designs and matching sheets had been an eighteenth birthday present—from him. I wasn't expecting one at all really. No other foster family had ever gotten me anything, and it was so soon after the crash. I didn't deserve gifts. Yet, there it was, all wrapped up nicely in black ribbon when he foiled my running away scheme.

"This thing is ancient. You can't even download Microsoft Office." Adriel scoffed and flipped the computer over easily.

"It has Notepad. I think that's all I really need, right?" I finished off the rest of the dessert and set the bowl on top of the dresser bureau by the door.

"No, not for college. You're going to need everything."

Ugh. I didn't even want to go college. I only agreed for him, and because his parents had wanted me to. "Fine, whatever, but I'll buy it. I have money."

He chuckled and reached for the empty dish. "Not as much as I do, and I take care of my girls." Adriel leaned forward and pressed a quick kiss to the top of my head before turning towards the door. I tried to ignore the way that simple action, meant to be endearing, made heat stream beneath my skin. I refused to admit it was a blush though. Adriel Marko would not be the one male on this Earth who could make me blush. Absolutely not.

"I'm getting take-out for dinner. Help Raffie with her room while I'm gone."

I sighed and followed him as he stepped out into the hallway. I hated when he wasted money on me, especially for things I didn't need, but arguing with him was useless. He always won. "They don't deliver?" I grumbled with a glance into Raf's room.

It was painted in shades of yellow and pink, and she already had the walls covered in Nightmare Before Christmas posters.

Adriel shot me a smug smile over his shoulder as he stepped onto the first floor. "You can handle being without me for a few minutes, Lark." My gaze narrowed angrily at the infuriating man.

"I know. That's not why I want delivery." I snapped and refused to say anything else as he turned into the dining room, that stupid chuckle filling the air instead.

In all honesty though, I didn't like being away from him for long. From either of them really. Ever since the accident, the siblings were the only ones that made me feel safe. When they weren't around the world seemed colder, and far more dangerous. Raf made everything brighter and more loving. And Adriel... Well, he kept the bad things away. Nothing could hurt me with him there.

"How's it coming, Raf?" I called into her room.

"Good!" She hollered excitedly, her little head poking out from around the dark wooden door. "I'm almost done, want to see?"

I let out a small sigh and leaned off the stair's railing. "Sure, kid. Do you need help with anything?" I peeked into the room to see the dark mayhem that exploded everywhere. There were blue and purple glittery blankets thrown across the floor, stuffed animals scattered around and her clothes stuck out oddly from her dark blue dresser.

"Um, yeah! Can you help me with my canopy?" She stood on top of her twin four-poster bed, the black and glittery shimmer canopy clutched in her tiny hands. The thin metal bedframe was made to look like a carriage from Cinderella. I eyed it suspiciously as she held the sheer material up with a beaming smile. "Isn't this bed cool?! It's like the old owners knew I was coming!"

I gave her a small smile and reached for the canopy. "Yeah, Raffie. It's really cute." Not really my style, but it was cute. I flung the thin material over the top of the frame and started tying down all the little ribbons. "So, you and Dri really never met your aunt and uncle?" I asked lightly as she started tucking her blankets into the bed frame.

"No, but I think Adriel said something about them being close to mom and dad." Then she bent down into one of her boxes and held a photo up to me with that large, beaming smile of hers. "Look what I got!" She sang happily, and I jumped down from the bed to grab the photo.

"When was this taken?" It was a picture of the three of us sitting around the kitchen table in Sacramento eating pasta. My mouth was stuffed with noodles, but Raffie was laughing and Adriel had that amused smile on his face as he watched me.

"Oh, I don't remember." She mumbled and turned back to the box. "But I think I remember mommy taking it. Adriel gave it to me a while ago and I kept it on my shelf." She gave up picking various things out of the box and lifted the cardboard to dump onto her freshly made bed. I tried not to roll my eyes. That kid always made a freaking mess.

"Do you care if I borrow this for a little while?" I asked as she threw the empty box in the corner with all the others. "I want to make a copy or two."

"Sure!" She beamed before tugging on my shirt until I took the hint and turned around. "Thanks for helping with the canopy,

Lark. But I want to finish the rest of the room by myself." Her tiny hands pressed against the small of my back and pushed my body towards the door.

"You still have a lot to do, Raf. And your brother wants me to help—"

"But I want it to be a surprise!" She exclaimed loudly even though the little terror had wanted me to see her room in the first place.

"Alright, but if Adriel gets mad, I'm blaming you." I laughed as she shoved me into the hallway.

"Okay, bye!" Then she closed the door in my face. Well then. Children these days, I swear.

"She kicked me out too." I turned to see Adriel walking back up the stairs with a small smile on his lips and his cell phone dangling from his hand.

"Then why send me in?" I raised an eyebrow as he leaned against the railing of the balcony and shrugged his strong shoulders.

"Figured you would have more luck, being a girl and all." I rolled my eyes before glancing back down at the photo. Dri stepped closer, a sound of approval came deep from his chest. "I remember that day." He murmured and reached up to tap the picture. "You were so cute, stuffing your face with pasta."

My gaze snapped to his as my rib cage suddenly squeezed tightly over my heart. Did Adriel just call me cute? It took a lot to make me flustered, but that one simple comment made my pulse race. "Food will be here in twenty." Then he turned to walk towards the master bedroom.

"It's getting delivered?"

"Yeah, Lark. I just drove for eight hours straight. I'm not planning on going anywhere tonight."

"But you said—"

He paused at the entrance of his room, and turned to shoot me that arrogant, pig-headed smirk of his. "I'm almost finished unpacking. Want to help?"

"No." I snapped and turned on my heels to stomp angrily down the stairs. Freaking ass. He just loved fucking with my head. Well, fine, he can shove that smirk up his ass and talk to my back. Just because I felt more comfortable being around him all the time didn't mean that I needed him.

Maybe I would like this college thing.

Maybe it was from the move, or just sleeping in the old creepy house for the first time, but my dreams were plagued with nightmares. I had hoped they were finally gone. I guess not.

There was no hint of those sensual images from the morning before, no matter how hard I tried to conjure them. It might not have been healthy, or sane, but those dark intense touches of the man in my subconscious were comforting in the moment. Now I only dreamt of fire and blood.

I stared blankly at the sleek marble of the cathedral town's square. My hands coated in dried blood. There was a darkness thrumming through the air, surrounding me, embracing me, whispering soft words that only I could hear. It spoke of pain and death, and told me not to fear the sharp blade pressing against my back.

"You want to be free, don't you?" The voice whispered against my ears. "Free of your fate..."

My fate... I had no idea what my fate was, or why the voice chose to care.

Something slid between my feet and I glanced down to see black fire creeping through the grass. It wasn't hot, but a slimy cold that crawled up my bare legs and tested the frayed edges of the white dress I was wearing.

"You're here."

My gaze snapped to the new voice. It wasn't dark and disembodied like the mist still wrapping around me, but I couldn't find the source of it either. "Hello?" I asked into the surrounding darkness.

"What a dream you are having." The voice said again, and I spun quickly around to find its owner. There was a man at my side, or at least, I thought it was a man. Any defining features were hidden by shadows and I only saw two pitch black eyes staring curiously through the darkness.

"I'm scared." I don't know why I admitted that to the man, but I knew it wasn't him I feared. I wasn't so sure I trusted my insides anymore.

"I can imagine why." Those black eyes tore from mine to glance around at the desolate town. His gaze landed on the cathedral. "Don't worry about the church. It is nothing."

"What does that mean?"

The man smiled. It was the only facial feature I could see peeking out through the darkness. I didn't step away like I probably should have when he raised a shadowed hand to my cheek. "Don't listen to the voices, Larkin. Their only goal is to destroy you."

Then he was gone and the nightmare faded into blackness.

I gripped the pristine new touchscreen laptop in my hands, refusing to look over at that beyond satisfied smirk pulling on the devilish man's lips. "Just because some random person agreed with you, doesn't make you right." I grumbled but kept my gaze locked on Raffie as she chased some birds in the middle of the courtyard a few feet away.

"Don't get pissy because I won."

"It wasn't a freaking competition." I snapped and my fingers curled tighter around the brand-new cardboard box. It was noon the next day, and I had pushed the weird nightmare aside to try and enjoy the day with them. We had been shopping around town all morning. Adriel bought a new bed since the master didn't have one, a nice sectional for the living room and got me a desk that was way too big for what I needed.

Then we got into a very heated argument, in the middle of an entertainment store packed with people, over which fucking laptop to buy. I wanted a simple Dell that looked sturdy enough in case I dropped it—which I probably would—and could download Microsoft Office. Adriel wanted me to have the newest one they had. It could flip from a computer to a tablet instantly and had a bunch of built in features I was never going to use. I refused to let him buy it. It was well over a thousand dollars and I didn't need it. But like always, he refused to listen to me and it didn't help that the worker—who was just trying to make a sale—kept agreeing with everything he said.

"Just say thank you and move on, Larkin." His blue eyes were locked on his sister as well, like the gaze alone would keep her from running off.

"Thank you." I grumbled, even though I wasn't happy about it. Then a sneaky thought crept into my mind and I had to force down a pleased smile. I still had the receipt in the bag. I would just wait until he started work tomorrow, sneak down to the town without him and return it for a cheaper one. I could just stuff the extra money in his nightstand for him to be mad about later.

Oh yeah, totally doing that.

Dri gave a pleased nod and a "you're welcome" before letting the subject die away. "There's something we need to discuss, though." His tone was nonchalant enough, but I could hear the underlying concern there. I shifted uneasily. Usually whenever Dri said we needed to have a discussion it wasn't something I was going to like.

"Okay..." I muttered disdainfully.

"I'm starting work tomorrow, and I'm expecting it to be a full-day thing."

Alright, I already knew that. It was impossible for Adriel to not work. If he wasn't locked in his room doing school work, he was doing part time jobs for some construction company back in Sacramento. Now that he was done with college, I was fully expecting him to be at work 24/7. Even though after the accident he did quit his part-time job to finish school quickly, become Raf's guardian, and move us up here. It was the longest I had ever seen him not working.

"I just..." He let out a sigh and eased further back against the bench. "I just want to make sure you're going to be okay while I'm gone." I hadn't realized how close we were sitting until his arms dropped heavily onto my shoulders and he gripped my upper arm endearingly. I hated how the gesture sent warmth shooting through my veins.

"I'm not a kid, Adriel. I can handle being alone with Raffie for a few hours." I snapped and refused to feel guilty about my tone. Even if the actual thought of him not being near made me nervous I wouldn't admit that to the guy. They hadn't left me alone since the crash, so I wasn't sure how well I would handle their absence. I didn't really want to know.

"I'm not worried about Raffie." The look in those dark eyes as they flickered to mine made my stomach flutter. It did that a lot around him.

"I'll be fine." I spoke softly, trying to reassure myself more than him.

"It's the longest you're going to be alone since—"

"I know. I'll be fine. Stop stressing out." It was only making my own anxiety go through the roof. I could handle a day away from him, more even. Besides, it wasn't like he could go to college with me. I would have to learn how to function without them at my side eventually.

Adriel didn't say anything, but that hand squeezed my shoulder gently and his thumb rubbed against my skin. I tried to not pay too much attention to him. He was just trying to be comforting, and completely oblivious to how my body reacted to him. I already found him way more sexually attractive than I should have, but add on those recent sultry dreams of mine, and I was a live-wire ready to snap. Every single touch from the guy, no matter how simple, made my body crave things it couldn't have.

God. I really needed to find a distraction soon, or poor Dri was going to have to deal with my hormonal grumpy ass. No matter how hot I found the guy, there was no way I would ever try to do anything with him. That would just fuck everything up. He was Adriel—pig-headed, arrogant, cocky, caring, endearing Adriel. That would all change if I made even one move on the man. No matter how badly my body wanted me to.

"Did you sign up for your classes yet?" Dri asked casually a moment later as Rafael started to skip towards us. He let go of my arm to drape his where it was originally against the back of the bench.

"No, registration is in two days. The email said to wait for that." I muttered as I tried to shove down the electricity that was shooting through my skin. He nodded and gave his sister a small smile as she came to a halt.

"I'm hungry, can we go get tacos or something?"

He raised a dark eyebrow, amusement lighting those blue eyes. "Tacos, huh?" Raf beamed brightly up at him with those big blue puppy eyes she adopted whenever she wanted something. The kid was a hustler, and a smart one at that.

I rolled my own before running my hand through the tangles in my hair. I didn't like wearing the long dark curls down much, messy buns and ponytails were my go-to, but Shelby had gushed more than once about how beautiful she thought my hair was. I wore it down for her, like that small action would make up for what I did to her and her husband—to their family. I would never be able to make up for that. Not in a million years.

"Yes please!" Raffie cheered happily, her small hands reaching up to pat his strong shoulders. Ugh, strong shoulders. I really needed to stop thinking about him like that. All strong, hard, and stony. It wasn't good for my sanity.

"What do you say, Lark?"

"Huh?" I tore my eyes from the sight of those very shoulders, straining against the fabric of his t-shirt. Adriel's lips pulled slightly at the corners.

"Tacos. You want some?"

"Um, yeah, sure." I refused to feel embarrassed at that smirk. If I just pretended like he hadn't caught me gawking at him, then he would pretend to.

We spent the rest of the day unpacking and waiting for the delivery truck to bring the recently bought furniture. There was a rather large storage shed in the backyard where we put all their great aunt and uncle's things. The more we moved stuff around and took things to the shed, the more relaxed I became. It was starting to feel like our home, and never having had that before, it made me more than a little excited.

"Careful or I might think you're actually starting to like it here." Adriel's chuckle completely wiped the smile from my face.

"It's not horrible." I grumbled and bent down to finish adjusting the sectional how I thought it looked best.

"Give it a chance, Angel. You might actually like it here."

My eyes snapped to his as that name passed his lips, but he was bent over a side table polishing the dust away. That stupid nickname came from Raf the first time we met and she had said that I looked like an angel. Her parents had laughed, they thought it was cute. Adriel just smiled before giving me a polite 'hello' and disappearing into his room.

I didn't think he really thought anything of me back then. He was always at school, or locked away in his room and despite polite greetings in passing, we hardly ever spoke. He would occasionally call me Angel though—on the rare moment we were in the same room longer than five minutes that is. I had liked it. Boys called me pretty and beautiful all the time, but none of it compared to how it felt when Adriel said something as simple as 'Angel'.

Now it was just a sick reminder of what I took from them.

"Whatever." I muttered just to show him I didn't care what he thought. Which was a complete lie.

He sighed, but I ignored it and turned to walk up the stairs. "Lark?" I groaned and tightened my hand around the banister. I really was not in the mood for some long reprimanding speech.

"What?"

"If you really didn't want to come here all you had to do was say so. I wouldn't have made us move." The look crossing those blue eyes tore at my heart.

"I know. I know, I'm sorry. I'm just being a bitch, ignore me." I eyed those strong shoulders of his that I seemed to have a hard time not drooling over earlier. Would it be a little obvious if I threw my arms around them right then?

Probably.

"I really do think this will be good for us." He gripped gently onto my forearm and that steady gaze made heat pool in my stomach.

"I know you're probably right." I admitted disdainfully as his hand fell away, the touch leaving a hot mark against my skin.

"Does that mean you're going to try?"

"Yeah, yeah, sure." I waved away his amused look and turned back towards stairs. Even if I didn't want to, it's not like I would fight him about it. I didn't like going against what he wanted, and I always caved.

CHAPTER 4

"Come to me..." That voice was whispering in my ear again, murmuring sweet words and dark promises that always made me ache. I could feel strong fingers brushing over my collar bone and down my arm. It sent fire soaring through every ounce of my being. So—so—much better than a nightmare.

"Stay with me."

Come to me, stay with me, the man really needed to make up his mind about where I was. Even if he was only my imagination. He chuckled and the sound was like a slow burning fire against my skin as it chased the sassy thought away. I tried to reach for dream-guy, desperate to feel him as he did me, but my hands came up empty. There were shadows surrounding him, allowing him to touch but never be touched. It was maddening.

A hand pressed against my stomach, his palm hot and heavy despite the fact I couldn't see it—or him. He rubbed my skin soothingly, as if he could sense my growing irritation. I didn't bother hiding a sultry moan as lips pressed just below my ear and nipped lightly at my skin. "Need You." His voice teased my mind, though his mouth never wavered from its determined path.

"Come to me."

It wasn't until my bare foot stepped in a puddle that I woke.

What the hell? I stepped away from the murky water with a frown. Cold, bitter, wind blew against my shoulders and I wrapped my arms tightly around myself to hold off a shiver.

Where the fuck was I?

I glanced up at the abandoned street, a lone road lamp flickering in the distance. Haniel Drive's street sign loomed a few feet above my head. Oh my God—was I sleepwalking?! Panic pooled in my chest and I whipped around to make sure this was, in fact, real. Sure enough, the cold biting my skin through the thin material of my tank-top and short-shorts that I had worn to bed was very real.

I didn't bother lingering on the street any longer. Being careful to avoid sharp rocks and stones, I rushed across the road and ran straight towards the Markos' manor. I tried not to slam the door shut when I rushed into the foyer, but fear was gripping my chest and I pushed it closed a little too loudly. I locked the deadbolt and door knob before pressing my back against the smooth wood and sliding down until my butt rested against the cold floor.

That did not just happen.

The grandfather clock in the living room chimed three times and stopped. 3 a.m. It was only 3 a.m. I hugged my knees to my chest and tried to force upset tears from my eyes. In all my crazy erotic dreams and creepiest nightmares, I have never slept walked. I didn't want to think of where I was going, or how far I would have gotten if I hadn't stepped into that puddle.

I would have to tell Adriel in the morning. That thought alone made me groan in contempt. The last thing I needed was his overbearing ass breathing down my neck. He was already upset about the nightmares, and I couldn't even control those. Not that I could control this, but he had become ridiculously over protective since the car crash and this would not sit well with the control-freak. But I was nervous about it happening again, especially if the dreams were getting so bad that I ended up on the opposite end of our street.

I just hope he wouldn't try to send me to a looney bin.

"Ugh, no!" I grumbled as the juice went everywhere. "Fucking great." I hissed and jumped to grab a bunch of paper towels.

"What's this?" My eyes snapped over to the dark blue pair flashing in sheer amusement. I ignored the scowl that wanted to pull on my lips and gave him a bright smile instead.

"I wanted to make you breakfast!"

Adriel arched his brow and set his work-belt down heavily on the countertop. It was five-thirty in the morning, and I had been up ever since the sleepwalking incident. I was terrified that if I went back to bed, I would wake up in the middle of town dancing on a light pole or something crazy like that. I figured I could spend the time preparing and making breakfast for the guy. I hoped it would butter him up for the upcoming conversation—and maybe lessen the blow about me returning the laptop later.

"It looks like you're wearing it more than making it." Those blue eyes washed over my entire flour and juice-soaked pajamas, taking in every awful inch. He chuckled and I shot him a glare instead of lingering on how that sound made my insides flutter.

"Yeah, well, I can't help it if stuff keeps flying out of my hands." I set a fresh glass of orange juice, and the plate of pancakes I was able to make, down in front of him with a 'hrmph'. We didn't have much food in the house yet, besides a few groceries from the day before, but there was pancake mix and syrup and that's all he ever needed.

That amused smirk didn't leave his lips, but he did sit down on one of the kitchen island's bar stools with a knife and fork. "So, what is this really about?" Dri asked around a mouthful of pancake.

"What?" I asked with an innocent shrug. "I just wanted to do something nice for you. Is that so hard to believe?" His eyes slowly flickered from the food to lock with mine. He didn't say anything, just held my gaze for a solid moment until I caved. God I fucking hated when he did that.

"Okay, alright, it's kind of embarrassing." I admitted on a heavy sigh and rubbed my palms nervously against my short-shorts. "But I—I slept walked last night and it kind of freaked me out."

He put his utensils down and leaned against the island with a frown. Oof, he never stopped eating when there was food left. That was worrisome. "What do you mean you 'slept walked'?"

I resisted the urge to roll my eyes at the question and pressed my hip against the other side of the counter. "Just that. I apparently sleepwalk now. I woke up at three this morning at the end of the street—"

"You left the house?" The dark look passing over his beyond handsome face, and the fact that his voice dropped a smidge, was a clear sign that his unhappiness was growing.

"Listen, it's not my fault, Dri. It's not like I did it intentionally." I held my hands up in mock surrender, not at all concerned about the angry tint to his tone. I knew he wasn't mad at me, just at the situation. Adriel didn't get mad at people, he got mad at circumstances. He was a strange one. A hot strange one, but still.

I wanted to away when he stood to his feet, the stool scraping against the floor as he did, but I told myself to be a brave bitch and stand my ground. "Are you okay?" I wasn't necessarily surprised at the concern in his tone, but the worried look flooding those blue eyes as he grabbed my chin and turned my head in different directions—like he would find some unseen injury if he did—was surprising.

"Y-Yeah, I'm fine." His touch was doing funny things to my insides. "It just spooked me, that's all..." Adriel didn't look all that convinced, but he did let go of my chin and took a step away after a moment. I didn't want to admit how much I liked his hands on me, but every time he stepped away from me a little part of my heart hurt.

"It won't happen again." He announced confidently and walked back around the island to his original seat. Fork and knife already in hand.

I didn't bother hiding my eye roll. "You can't know that. I don't even know the next time it will happen. I could end up in town square or—"

"There won't be a next time, Lark. I'll handle it."

I crossed my arms over my chest, pressed my hip against the counter and raised an eyebrow at him. "And how, pray tell, do you plan on doing that?"

Adriel shrugged, like he wasn't at all concerned, before sticking the fork back into the pancakes. "Motion sensors in the yard that I can hook to my phone, bells on the doors, hell I can probably lock you in your room in all honesty—"

"Adriel!"

"Joking, joking. That last part was a joke." His laughter filled the kitchen despite the flames of fire I was shooting at him through my gaze. "But seriously don't worry about it, Angel. I'll take care of it." Just hearing him say those words made the tension in my shoulders ease. I could do all that stuff myself, but just having him there to care about getting it done made me feel a thousand times better.

"What are your plans for today?" Adriel asked a few quiet, but peaceful, moments later. He had already down three of the pancakes and was making quick work of the rest.

I shrugged and grabbed the now cold cup of coffee I had been nursing for the pass hour. "I'll probably wake Raffie up around eight and go buy actual groceries." Amusement flashed across his handsome face at my scolding tone. Straight sugar was not real food, no matter how often the siblings argued that it was. "I'll make sure to get her all her school supplies, then I guess we can just explore the town for a bit—"

"I need to get you a car." My mouth dropped open, but the arrogant man continued to happily stuff his face. "These are really good."

"You are not buying me a car!" I practically exploded; the sleepwalking conversation completely forgotten. "The laptop was already overboard—hey! Don't roll your eyes at me! I'm being serious!"

"I am too." Adriel grunted and stood from the barstool once his pancakes were gone. "How else are you going to get around everywhere? I don't want you walking for miles carrying a bunch of shit, and what about school? You plan on walking back and forth every day?" He scoffed and placed the empty dish in the sink.

"If I have to! And I can carry bags just fine. It's not that far from the town center, and—"

"I'm not arguing with you about this, Larkin." He sighed and walked back over to where he dropped his work-belt. It was one of those hardcore tool-belts that had only god-knows-what in its deep pockets. "I'm not letting you walk around everywhere. We'll go get you one this weekend."

"Adriel—"

"If you're not going to think about your own safety than think about Raffie's." His words had my mouth snapping shut instantly. God, I hated when he was right. I didn't really care about walking everywhere, but I wouldn't be able to help Rafael quick enough if something did happen.

That didn't stop contempt from boiling inside my stomach though. I grit my teeth together and glared at the kitchen counter. "I'll pay for it."

Adriel grunted and I glanced up long enough to see him drag one of those strong hands through his dark hair. "You don't even have enough to buy a shitty one."

"Then I'm paying you back."

He chuckled and shook his head before grabbing the SUVs keys. "Whatever you say, Lark." He spun the keys around his finger, paused and glanced over. "Take me to work, and you can use the car for the day."

My eyes narrowed, and I crossed my arms grumpily over my chest. "You never let me drive."

"Because you're not that great at it."

"You taught me how! So, whose fault is that?" I snapped but that only made his booming laughter echo throughout the kitchen.

"You want the car or not?" Dri dangled the keys in front of my face, those blue eyes alight in sheer amusement. I snatched the hanging metal from the air and pushed pass him, that chuckle following my every step.

"Stupid jerk." I grumbled as I shoved my fluffy sock covered feet into the rainboots at the front door. After the whole sleep-walking-puddle incident, I had taken a steaming hot shower and pulled on a thick pair of socks like that would erase the memory. I stared at the infuriating man as he strolled out of the dining room, that arrogant, pig-headed smirk pulling on his lips.

"You're going like that?" He eyed the complete and total mess by pajamas were in, and the totally unneeded boots on my feet. Add onto the fact that my hair was a bird's nest in its messy bun. The fuck was he talking about? I was ready for Cinderella's ball.

"It's not like I'm getting out of the car."

"Okay, sorry, my bad." He held his hands up in surrender at my tone.

"Oh, shit, what about Raffie?" The thought hit me just as I was going to open the front door.

Those blue eyes widened, and he let out a disgruntled sigh before glancing up the stairs. "I can go grab her. Maybe she'll sleep through it." He dropped his work belt and bag to the floor before hurrying up the steps. I could hear him murmuring softly to his sister, who didn't sound at all happy about being woken up, but she came sluggishly out of her room anyway.

"She didn't sleep through it." He sighed and bent down for his stuff as they reached the bottom of the stairs. Raf walked over to me with a stuffed animal in one hand and reached for mine with her other.

"I don't want to go, Lark. I'm sleepy." She grumbled around a big yawn. I smiled.

"You can sleep in the car, kiddo. We're just going for a short ride. You can go back to bed when we come home." She didn't say anything else after that but pressed her face into my shirt as I opened the front door for her infuriating brother. He found the whole thing amusing.

I was impatiently waiting for him to walk pass us, Raffie attached to me like a koala bear, when he suddenly leaned down and pressed a feather soft kiss against my cheek. "Thank you for breakfast, sweet girl."

Freaking jerk.

"What do you mean, you won't take it back?" I snapped at the poor worker who stood behind his computer with wide and nervous eyes.

"I'm sorry miss, but our store policy says that we can't take returns without the receipt." The guy was young, probably a college kid trying to save up for the semester, and definitely not used to talking with the opposite sex. He was flustered from 'hello' and wouldn't look in my eyes the entire time. He was thin, with skin paler than mine, and bright carrot colored hair. His face was a mix of freckles and adult acne. Not my type, but he was tall though. I'll give the guy that.

"There is a receipt! It's in the bag!" I ripped the plastic back from his hands and tore the handles apart. I angrily lifted the unopened laptop box and stuck my hand inside like that would find the receipt my eyes couldn't see. "Well, there was one!" I shoved the box and the bag back onto the counter. In the past I wasn't above flirting with someone to get what I wanted, but that all changed when I moved in with the Markos. It didn't feel right using people like that anymore.

"I really am sorry, but we can't accept—"

"Listen, buddy, I was literally in here yesterday with that little girl," I threw my hand towards Raffie who was busy playing with a Nintendo Switch hanging on the wall. "And her idiot brother who bought this stupid thing. Just take it back and give me a refund and I'll be on my way."

"Without the receipt I really can't take it back, even if I wanted to. I have to scan the barcode and put it back in the system." I felt bad about the nervous terrified look in the kid's eyes, or Kyle, as his name tag read, but that didn't mean my anger was going anywhere.

"Okay, but I had the receipt! It probably fell behind your counter or something—"

"Is a receipt that long paper thingy you get when you buy something?" I hadn't notice Raf walk up until her voice was chirping up at my side. I tried to shove away the fury brewing behind my eyes as I glanced down at her.

"Yeah."

"Oh... Well, I saw Adriel grab something like that from your bag yesterday and put it in his pocket. If that's what you're looking for." She reached for my hand and her tiny fingers squeezed my palm as those big blue eyes widened.

"Are you fucking kidding me?" Of course, that asshole would take the damn receipt! Now I would have to go snoop through his room to find it. Damn it!

Raf's lips fell into a pout and she squeezed harder on my hand. "Adriel doesn't like it when you say bad words."

"I don't care what he likes." I grumbled as I let go of her hand to shove the laptop box back into the bag. "We'll be back." I snapped at poor Kyle who looked ready to hide in a janitor's closet and never come out.

"Can we get ice cream?" Rafael asked cheerfully as I dragged her out of the entertainment store.

"I have to get the groceries home before the food goes bad." And then I have to rip through your brother's room. But I kept that little tad-bit to myself.

"Can we go drop the stuff off and then get ice cream?" I ignored that doe-eyed gaze and opened the door of the SUV for her.

"That's a waste of gas, Raf." I sighed as she hopped into the passenger seat. I wasn't sure why the hell we let a nine-year-old sit in the front, but the car did have an automatic airbag shut off for a certain weight and the kid was old enough based on California law. I hadn't checked Oregon's, but I doubted it would be much different.

"Please, Larkin!" She begged once I climbed into the driver's seat and started the engine.

"Kid—"

"I'll tell Adriel that you're trying to return your computer."

My gaze snapped across the vehicle and narrowed at the devious evil look that had replaced those puppy eyes. "You. Wouldn't. dare." I enunciated each word, so she knew what I thought about that little comment. Rafael stuck her nose in the air, crossed those little arms of hers and 'hrmphed'.

Damn, she really was spending too much time with me.

"Yes, I would."

My hand was on the gear shift, ready to put the car in reverse, though my eyes glared daggers at the nine-year-old. We were suddenly locked in a competitive stand-off, neither of us blinking since that would mean defeat. I caved first. "Fine. But we're going now, and you better eat fast." Get a brain freeze, you little jerk.

That evil look left her eyes and her wide smile was suddenly beaming up at me. "Yay! Thank you! You're the best!"

"Yeah, yeah. Whatever."

Fifteen minutes later I was staring anxiously at the giant construction site across the street, my fingers tapping repeatedly against the plastic tabletop. "You okay, Lark?" Raffie asked at my side, our argument in the car long forgotten. She was back to being that perfect little angel she had everyone convinced that she was.

"Yeah, I'm just worried about your idiot brother." We were sitting at that little ice cream shop on the corner, our groceries and her school stuff locked safely away in the SUV. I had been staring at the large piles of dirt and rock for a solid five minutes, worry raging through my chest.

I had dropped Adriel off at some large metal building on the other side of Deshua that morning, the word 'Avid' flashing boldly against its side. I figured he was filling out a bunch of paperwork and going over the regulations since it was his first day, and he was hired as an architect, not a construction worker. I wasn't really sure what the difference was, but I hoped he didn't do any of the dangerous work.

"Adriel isn't an idiot." Raf's lips pulled into a pout, and she crossed her little arms over her chest all grumpy-like. I tried to hide my smile.

"I know he's not. I just say that sometimes to make myself feel better."

"How does calling him mean names make you feel better?"

I finally tore my gaze away from the overturned park and played absently with the plastic spoon in my empty ice cream cup. "Because I'm a jerk, and that's what jerks do." That, and if I was calling him an asshole, or an idiot, it was less time I spent calling him sexy and oh-so-handsome in my head.

A little hand was suddenly gripping mine and I raised my gaze to those dark blue doe eyes. "You're not a jerk, Lark. You're always nice to me." She gave me a large smile and squeezed my hand.

"Just you, kid. Even when you're manipulating me into buying you sugar."

Rafael let go of my hand to finish shoveling ice cream into her mouth, that sneaky glint lighting her eyes. I rolled mine. After today I was putting them both on a healthier diet. I mean, I loved ice cream as much as the next guy, but they were eating sugar twenty-four seven. They needed healthy carbs and vegetables. Hence all the groceries in the SUV that I just knew Adriel was going to grumble about. They could thank me later when their hearts won't explode.

Laughter from the corner of the shop caught my attention, and my gaze shifted towards the group of four guys crowding one tiny table. Their laughter seemed to carry effortlessly around the room, trapping anyone who heard. I shifted uneasily in my seat. Usually, I was all for hot guys, and I wasn't shy either. But recently I've been finding it easier to avoid eye contact with everyone. It wasn't that I doubted myself, I just didn't have the want to mess around anymore. Which, in retrospect, I really needed to start again if I wanted to stop thinking about jumping Adriel every other minute.

There was something wrong though. Something about those guys that made the hairs on the back of my neck stand on end. It was that same feeling I got on our first day here, when that Luke guy warned Raffie and I about going into the woods. It wasn't a good feeling, and it made my chest clench uneasily.

"Do you think they're cute?" Raf's voice pulled at my attention, and I forced my eyes to hers.

"Do I think they're cute?"

She nodded her head and glanced at the group before back at me, her spoon hanging expectantly from her mouth. I shrugged and reached over for her empty bowl as I tried to find the right words to say. "Sure, they're cute, but they give me a bad feeling."

"A bad feeling?"

"Yeah, like when you eat something gross and it makes your stomach feel weird." Raf nodded almost viciously as I threw our bowls into the trash. "It's kind of like that." I gave her a small smile as she stood from the table and brushed out the wrinkles in her black and pink skirt.

"Oh, okay." She reached for my hand, her lips pulling into a smile again as she squeezed my fingers tightly. "Then we should go."

I laughed as she began dragging us to the shop's door. "If you say so, kid."

I made the mistake of glancing back at the group, and my heart stopped beating in my chest. Two of the guys were staring after us and their gazes caused ice to spread like thunder through my veins.

Red. Their eyes were red.

CHAPTER 5

Contacts.

It had to be colored contacts. I tried to convince myself for the thousandth time hours later. I couldn't even think straight while I was tearing apart Adriel's room looking for that damn receipt—to no avail might I add. That jerk either threw it away or had it hidden really well.

I groaned and leaned my forehead against the steering wheel. It was five in the afternoon, the exact time Adriel specified to be there, but he still wasn't ready to leave. Raf was playing on her Nintendo Switch in the backseat with headphones glued to her ears, completely oblivious to the fact that I had been losing my mind all afternoon.

"Hey—"

"Fuck!" I nearly jumped out of my skin when the driver-side door suddenly open. Adriel's brow raised questioningly and his lips pulled at the corners. "You scared the hell out me!" I snapped and urged my fingers to let go of their death grip on the wheel.

"Hello to you too... Hey," His amused look gave way to a worried frown and he reached for my arm as I jumped out of the seat. "Are you okay?"

"No, you freaked me out." I yanked my arm out of his grasp and walked quickly to the passenger's side before he could say anything else. I was afraid, but not because of him, and deep down I knew I shouldn't have taken that fear out on him. He just made it so darn easy to be mad at him.

"Hi Adriel!" His sister beamed as Dri climbed into the driver's side. He shot her a small smile in the rearview mirror as I buckled my seatbelt. "Hey kiddo, how was your day?"

"Great! Lark and I did a bunch of shopping, and we got ice cream! Except she bought a lot of gross healthy food and says we have to eat it." Raffie stuck her tongue out at me and I rolled my eyes.

"You excited for school tomorrow?" Adriel asked as he pulled out of the awesome parking job I did. I couldn't drive well, my ass. I backed this beast into that spot like it was nothing.

"Oh yeah! I got this really cool backpack and it has a bunch of—" I tuned out the long explanation of everything we had bought her and rested my head against the cool glass of the window.

Colored contacts. There was no question about it. But why did they look so real?

I hadn't realized my leg was bouncing anxiously until one large, and insanely warm, hand covered my knee. Adriel's blue eyes stayed glued to the windshield as Raffie rambled on, but squeezed my leg when he noticed me glance his way. "How was your day?" He asked carefully once Raf finished her in-depth analysis report of all her school supplies.

I dragged my gaze away from his hand and shrugged. It took all I had not to rub my palms nervously down my skinny-jean covered thighs. He was still touching me, and I could feel heat radiating from his palm into my skin. Was it hot in here? Or was that just the mental image of him running that hand up my thigh? I forced my leg to stop bouncing.

"It was fine. Nothing to report, General." Adriel rolled his eyes before—thankfully—letting go of my knee. I released a shaky breath. "What about you? Did you like your first day?"

He gave me a shrug of his own and a lopsided grin. "Yeah, it was alright. I'm not building skyscrapers or anything, but I'm in charge of a few teams so we'll see what happens."

"That's good." I mumbled and turned back towards the window. "Are you going to be working on that site in town?"

"Yeah, on and off... But I'm telling people what to do, not actually doing it, Lark." The low, soft, tone that overtook his voice hinted that the jerk knew a little too much about my worrying.

One good thing about obsessing over those creepy red eyes all day, was that it took my mind off being away from him. Now with Adriel sitting beside me and Raf behind us, tension eased from my shoulders. One day down, a million more to go. I hadn't realized my eyes were closed until they snapped open when a soft touch brushed across my skin. I glanced over to the beyond handsome man, the one who had decided to reach over and lightly squeeze the back of my neck.

"I'm sorry I scared you earlier."

I let out a small sigh so he wouldn't see how that simple touch affected me. "It's fine. I'm over it."

"Then why are you acting like you're about to jump out of the car?"

"It's just been a long day. For everyone. Don't worry about me." His face pulled into a frown, but he didn't say anything else as his thumb rubbed softly along my skin. The gentle touch sent shivers straight down my spine, into my stomach, and lower. Not good.

I wasn't sure why I didn't tell him about the red eyes. Maybe because I was still trying to convince myself it wasn't real, or maybe I just didn't want to make him worry. He already knew about the nightmares, the sleepwalking, and now I was seeing people with red eyes while I was awake. None of that added up to mental stability. I didn't think mentioning the incident was a good idea.

Adriel was quiet as he let go of my neck, though his strong jaw clenched shut. "You know you can tell me anything, right?" He spoke a moment later, his voice low so Raffie couldn't hear.

I ran my hand roughly through my loose curs and kept my eyes glued to the sunset beside us. "Yeah, Dri. Yeah, I know."

"Okay, and you have your pencil bag and lunch, right?" I asked the sleepy, and rather annoyed child the next morning. Thankfully I didn't have another sleepwalking incident the night before. I didn't dream of anything really. It was the first time in a long time I was able to sleep through the night. Is it sad that was strange to me now?

"Yeah, Lark. I have everything, promise." Raffie reassured me for the fifth time. I was crouched down in front of her, making sure her backpack straps were even as Adriel stood patiently by the door. I let out a small sigh and brushed the invisible wrinkles out of her Corpse Bride t-shirt. The kid had a thing for Tim Burton films.

"We need to get going, Larkin." Dri spoke softly, and I could have sworn there was something warm filling those blue eyes as he watched us. I stood slowly to my feet and tried to erase the frown pulling at my lips.

"You have our numbers memorized in case of an emergency, right?"

"Yes, stop freaking out." Rafael rolled her eyes, and I felt a small bubble of laughter build in my chest.

Adriel was dropping her off at her new school on the way to work, and I had gotten up early—despite enjoying the first soundless sleep I had in weeks—to make sure she had every-thing she needed. But I was finding it a lot harder to let her go than I expected. It was the first time since their parents died that she was going back to any kind of school setting, and I was nervous that it might be too much. Though, in all reality, it really might have just been too much for me.

"Are you going to be okay today?" Adriel watched me intently as Raf skipped down the stone steps and headed straight for the waiting SUV.

"Yeah, Dri." I reassured the worry in his gaze as I turned towards the front door.

"You have everything you need for registration?"

"Yup."

"Hey," He spoke softly and reached up to flick my chin, a small smile pulling at his devilish lips. "She'll be alright. It's the other kids you need to be worried for."

Those dark eyes seemed to flash as I laughed. "You're telling me."

He grew serious again as my laughter faded away. "I'm going to get some motion detectors while I'm out today, okay?"

Great, back to the fact that my subconscious was clearly losing it. I let out a little sigh. "Okay, thank you."

Adriel had found a few Christmas bells in some random box the night before, and had wrapped it around my door's handle just in case. He even slept with his door open so he could listen for me. I tried to ignore how that caring action made my heart plummet straight to my stomach. No one ever cared for me like that before. It was terrifying.

"Have a good day, Larkin." He spoke softly before turning for the car, his tool belt and lunch box swung casually over one arm. "And my room better be spotless before I come home."

I let out an irritated groan and rolled my eyes skyward. "Just give me the receipt and I will."

"Not happening, that laptop is yours, and you're going to deal with it." Adriel's tone turned into that steely command I wasn't supposed to argue with.

"I told you it's broken."

"You haven't even taken it out of the box yet."

I crossed my arms in defiance. "No receipt, no clean room."

"Larkin."

My teeth grit shut in aggravation. "Yeah, fine, whatever." I grumbled and turned back into the house to slam the door shut. So, what if I hadn't cleaned his room after I tore it apart the day before? I was irritated about that damn laptop, and the sleepwalking and creepy red eyes didn't leave my mind in its best state. Despite that, guess what I spent the rest of the morning doing?

Cleaning his freaking room.

I did steal one of his flannels and t-shirts though, those things were damn comfortable.

After I made sure the jerk's room was spotless, I ate a quick breakfast and hopped in the shower. I wasn't expecting to meet anyone worthwhile during registration, so I pulled on a pair of black leggings, a dark blue tank and Adriel's flannel. I did decide to toss my hair into a messy bun instead of leaving it down though. I had a feeling I was going to be sitting all day listening to old guys talk about the school, and I wanted to be comfortable over sexy.

Dri's flannel stopped just below my butt, and the faint hint of sawdust and his aftershave clinging to the fabric made it seem like he was there with me.

I could do this. First day completely by myself since the accident.

I could do this.

It wasn't a far walk to the college, and I was glancing at the large sign supporting the universities name by nine o'clock. I was glad Raffie and I already came here before, otherwise I would have gotten so totally lost following the damn map on my phone. I had my plain, black, North Face backpack thrown across one shoulder, with that stupid new laptop zipped safely inside. I'm pretty sure Adriel bought a warranty on the stupid thing just in case I 'accidentally' threw my bag into oncoming traffic.

I held my breath as I crossed onto campus. The last time I was here there was that—that noise that pulled me towards the mountain. I was terrified something like that would happen again. With everything that's been going on lately, I wouldn't be surprised if my brain just decided to shut off and force me to follow some creepy disembodied sound into an uninhabited forest. Maybe I deserved to get eaten by giant man-eating cats.

"Hey, Larkin!" My gaze snapped to the familiar voice calling my name as I walked into the courtyard. Just fucking perfect. I grumbled to myself as that Luke-guy from the other day came jogging over. His wide, perfect, charming smile on full display. At least there was no creepy noise—yet.

I paused just outside the steeple-styled brick building with the sign reading Admissions pinned to its side. "Oh, hey, Luke. What are you doing here?" I tried to sound casual as he pulled to a stop a few feet away, but the guy still skeeved me out and I was never good at hiding what I was thinking. Adriel could always ready my facial expressions like a book, and it was maddening.

"I work for the school part-time and they wanted me to help run registration. You know, help all the freshmen find their way around?" His smile was beaming, as if he didn't know what the word 'frown' meant.

I nodded politely, even though I really didn't care. "Yeah, that's cool."

Luke laughed, and the sound was way too cheerfully for my pessimistic mood. "Not really, but it's a paycheck. Hey, listen, me and a couple of friends are planning on hanging out later up at Uriel Point. We usually have bonfires there and it draws a pretty big crowd. It'll be a lot of fun! Do you want to come?" His voice sounded almost hopeful, and although those dark sunglasses were covering his eyes, I could almost see their warm brown depths gazing down at me.

Oof. Hanging out with some strange guy that gave me the creeps and his buddies? Yeah, no thank you.

"Um, thanks but I have a lot to do today." It was the politest thing I could say without blatantly telling him to fudge off. Honestly, I didn't care about hurting his feelings, but I promised Adriel I would 'try', and starting off on the wrong foot with the townies wasn't necessarily trying.

That beaming smile faltered, but only for a moment before he shrugged and pulled a hand out of his jacket pocket. "Okay, well if you change your mind here's my number. Text or give me a call." I reluctantly took the small piece of paper with neatly written numbers from his hand. I had no intention of putting it into my phone, but didn't want to come off as completely rude. Despite the uneasily feeling in my chest Luke had only ever been pleasant.

"Thanks, I'll let you know." I raised the paper in acknowledgment before stuffing it into the water bottle holder of my bag. "I have to get to registration now. So, uh, um have a good day?" It came out more of a question than a statement, but that didn't seem to bother him.

"Yeah, I got to get going to. It was nice to see you! And I really do hope you change your mind about later. It'll be a lot of fun."

I didn't bother using the muscles it took to smile as he turned to walk away. There was just something off about that guy.

"How was your first day, Raf?" I asked that afternoon as we all sat on one end of the large dining room table eating Chinese food. It didn't matter that I had bought us a bunch of stuff to cook with. Oh no, savior Adriel to the day with take-out. Whatever.

"It was good! The teachers were all really nice and someone gave me their candy at lunch!"

"Did they give it to you, or did you take it?" Those dark, blue, all-seeing eyes of her older brother shot to the small child in a pointed narrowed glare. Raffie's lips pulled into a pout.

"He wasn't eating it." She grumbled and stuck her fork into her pork roll. I rolled my eyes, which I seemed to be doing a lot of lately. And here I was upset that she ate candy. Now she's stealing it from other kids.

"I'm not going to have this discussion with you again, Rafael." That strict tone ringing through Adriel's voice made my back arch straighter in my chair, and it wasn't even directed at me for once. "Stop taking other people's things without their per-mission."

"Okay, I'm sorry." She mumbled and pointed those puppy eyes down at her plate. Oh, so the little twerp can manipulate me all she wants but the minute big bad Adriel gets involved she's a terrified kitten. Right.

"How was your day, Lark?" Adriel asked a quiet moment later after the tension between the two Markos fell away.

I shrugged and twisted the Chow Mein noodles uselessly around the ends of my chopsticks. "It was alright." I didn't tell him about my conversation with Luke. I wasn't sure if he would scowl at some strange guy asking to hang out, or encourage me to go make "new friends". Either conversation wasn't one I wanted to have.

"Did you sign up for your classes?"

"Yeah."

"Pick a major?"

"Undecided."

"Hm." He hummed around a mouthful of Orange Chicken. "That's fine, you still have plenty of time."

My gaze flickered towards him as silence settled over the table. Adriel looked more—gruff than usual that day, and it was doing funny things to my head. Stubble brushed along the sharp edge of his jaw, his olive-toned skin was darker from working in the sun, and his hair had started growing slowly from its short crop-cut. I didn't realize it was possible for that man to get any more attractive, and I was beyond frustrated at being wrong.

"Yeah, I guess." I flipped the noodles over in their box. "I signed up for a few art classes though."

I was never good at school, but not because I didn't understand. I just didn't see the worth in it. I was never going to use Calculus or Chemistry in the outside world, even if I had wanted to go to college. The only subject I ever saw value in was art and history, but I wasn't any good at remembering the latter.

One of my charcoal drawings had even made the Regional showcase my last year of high school, and Shelby and Dave had been so excited they bought me a special frame for the piece. I glanced over at the black and white image of the Golden Gate Bridge. Adriel had hung the picture up in the foyer the day we moved in.

"Oh, good. I know you'll like those." He mumbled around a mouthful. It didn't really matter if I liked them or not. Adriel wanted me to find a career with college, and unless you had connections in high places, an art degree didn't get you anywhere.

"I took tomorrow off." The annoying man announced a while later. Raf was still pouting down at her food, but that didn't stop her from digging viciously into the crab cakes.

"Already?" I asked with a raised eyebrow. "It's only, like, your third day." Those deep-set blue eyes flickered to mine, and their gaze made my insides flip upside down. It was really not fair how attractive he was.

"Yeah, but they can go one day without me and you need a car." A smug smile pulled at his lips as a groan ripped from my chest. Not this again. "This weekend is still too far away for you to be walking around everywhere—"

"No—"

"So," He cut off my protest before the words could pass my lips. "We're going tomorrow."

"Adriel, I don't need you to buy me a car."

"You're getting one."

"Then I will pay for it." I slapped my chopsticks down for emphasis. "Stop wasting your money on me."

"It's not 'wasting my money'." He leaned back heavily in his chair; those dark eyes unwavering in their determination. There was no winning when he got like that. "And we've talked about this. You don't have enough saved up to buy a vehicle that actually works, and you need to be able to get around quickly for Raf." I hated that he knew how to hold the kid against me. I didn't care about my 'safety' or walking, but Rafael wouldn't be able to rely on me if I couldn't get to her fast enough.

"Then I'm paying you back." The smirk taking over his handsome features was one of victory. I had to press my hands against my thighs to keep from grabbing a chopstick to shank him with. "I'm being serious, Adriel."

"Oh, I know. I just keep adding up all the money that you plan on 'paying me back'. You don't even have a job."

"Then I'll get one."

"Nope. Not while you're in school, you agreed."

"I didn't agree to anything! Just because you tell me to do something doesn't mean I agree with it! That requires a verbal or written acknowledgment!" I could feel my temper rising and I didn't bother keeping my chair from scraping across the floor as I stood angrily to my feet.

"You need to focus on your classes, Lark." By this point I knew he was messing with me, I could see it in the clear amusement shining through those dark blue eyes. It only made my blood pressure rise.

"I can focus on classes and work. People do it all the time—you did it!"

Rafael was watching us with wide eyes, a little bit of crab cake hanging forgotten from her lips. I never wanted her to see us argue, though this was obviously becoming a one-sided argument. When Adriel had his mind set on something he made it happen, regardless of my feelings on the matter. In a way I respected that. I wanted to be like that. Except when it was directed at me, then it was just beyond infuriating.

"That's different. I was dedicated and actually tried, and—" His eyes flashed and his words cut off—like he realized a little too late what he had said.

"And what, Adriel? Intelligent? Driven? Everything I'm not, right?" The anger simmering in my chest disappeared to something far worse. Pain.

Thinking those things about myself was one thing, but knowing that he of all people thought them too was... disappointing? Heartbreaking.

It was heartbreaking.

"That's not what I meant, Angel." He leaned forward to reach for my hand, remorse shining in that blue gaze, but I pulled away and turned for the stairs.

"I'm going to bed." I didn't want to hear anymore. I had hit my emotional quota for the day, and I just wanted to curl under my covers and try to fall asleep.

"Larkin wait—" I hurried up the stairs before he could say another word and closed my door with a resounding 'smack'. The Christmas bells attached to the handle jingled loudly as I did.

I hated that his opinion mattered that much to me. I really did.

CHAPTER 6

Rafael was sledding down the snowy hill, her big blue eyes shining in the light of the sun. I smiled as she reached the bottom and jumped to her feet quickly. "Again, Lark! Again!" She cheered before dragging the sled up the hill.

"Have you gone yet?" Adriel's voice was closer than I thought, and I glanced over my shoulder to see him at my side. Our gazes locked and he smiled, a smile that shook me deep to the core. He really was too beautiful for his own good.

"No, Raf wants me to keep pushing her."

He glanced down at his sister. "Tell her it's your turn next."

"No, really its fine. I don't mind—" Jingling caught my attention and I turned to look for the noise.

"Larkin?" Adriel asked softly, that dark gaze I loved so much turning worried.

"Did you hear that?"

"It's your turn, Angel. Want to go with me?"

Rafael was suddenly at our side, and Adriel was holding the sled up with a smile. "It's small, but you'll fit in my lap just fine."

I almost forgot about the sound as he climbed into the small blue sled, looking completely ridiculous until he turned those blue eyes on me and patted his thigh. "Come on beautiful, the sun is setting soon."

My eyes blinked open as the Christmas bells went off again. My first good dream in months and it had to be rudely interrupted. I groaned and narrowed my eyes at the opened door. Whichever damn Markos opened that better have a good freaking reason.

There was no one there.

I frowned and leaned up on my elbows. "Raf? Dri? You there?" That's when I saw it—him. A dark outline in the shape of a man stood at the foot of my bed. Two glowing red eyes staring down at me through the darkness.

I screamed.

The terror ripping through my chest nearly made the high-pitched noise soundless. "Adriel!" His name came out much louder. I ripped at my bedsheets, trying desperately to disentangled myself and ended up falling hard onto the ground. I scrambled desperately to my feet, not caring about the slight pain ricocheting down my side.

"Larkin!"' Adriel's voice filled the hallway as I ran out of my room, right into his stone wall of a chest. "What's wrong?!"

"There's someone in my room!" My heart, that felt like it was beating a thousand miles a minute, jumped as strong arms wrapped around my waist and held me tightly against Adriel's chest. I clung to him almost desperately.

"What? What are you talking about?"

"There's someone in my fucking room! They opened the door, those stupid Christmas bells went off, and then there was some-one standing over my bed!"

Something close to horror flickered across his handsome face and his hands tightened around my upper arms as Rafael's door open. "Larkin? Adriel? What's going on?" The nine-year-old mumbled sleepily as she rubbed her fist into one of her eyes.

"Rafael, come here." Adriel all but barked. He gripped onto her free hand, pulled her into the hall way, then pushed us both against the wall. "Stay here." He ordered as I let go of him to wrap my arms tightly around Raffie, who now looked as terrified as I felt.

"Dri don't! They could be dangerous—"

"Stay here, Larkin." The look crossing his dark eyes made my stomach flutter for a whole new reason. That gaze stayed locked with mine until I nodded in agreement. He squeezed my arm tightly before turning back for my room. "I'll only be a moment." He swore before disappearing into the darkness of my room.

I let out a shaky breath and held on tighter to Rafael. I've never seen Adriel fight before, but I knew he could take someone down if he had to. Though, those muscles were nothing com-pared to a gun. "L-Larkin?" Raf stuttered against me, those big blue eyes so much like her brother's it was unnerving, blinked up at me in fear. "What's happening?"

"Sh, it's okay Raffie. Everything will be okay." I muttered softly and resisted the urge to rock her as we huddled together against the wall. I had no idea what was happening, but I knew Adriel would take care of it. He always did. She clung to me with her face buried into my stomach and her fingers gripping tightly at my shirt.

It wasn't long before Adriel reappeared, but the look crossing his face made me uneasy. "What? Did you find him?" I stepped closer to him, Raf still clutched desperately tight in my arms. He didn't say anything as he walked towards his sister's room, did a quick check, and then came back to our huddled bodies.

"Go back to bed, Raf. Everything's okay."

She pulled her face from my shirt and turned those big eyes to her older brother. "But Adriel—"

"Now, Raf. I'll check on you in a little bit."

I frowned as she nodded and pulled away. I stayed silent as she walked slowly back into her room and crawled into that carriage-framed bed. Adriel closed her door until the soft 'click' resounded like thunder through my ears.

"Adriel..."

"Come here, Lark." His tone was far too soft for my liking, but I didn't argue as his arms wrapped back around waist and pulled me into his solid chest.

"There was no one there, was there?" Though I already knew the answer. I felt tears prick my eyes, tears of self-pity and anger. Anger at myself for not knowing the difference between dreams and reality.

"I looked everywhere." His voice was a gentle murmur in my ear as his cheek pressed against the top of my hair. Those arms kept me cradled against him. "Your windows were all locked, there was nothing in your closet—I even looked under your bed."

I buried my face into his chest, not caring one bit that water from my eyes was probably dripping onto his bare skin. I was too distraught to enjoy the fact that he was shirtless. "I-I'm so sorry." It was all I could think to say.

"Sh, stop. You don't have any reason to be sorry." He was too understanding for his own good. Too caring and far too gentle.

"I thought it was real. I could have sworn it was real..."

The tears stopped, though a few hiccups followed their wake. I hated crying, hated it more than anything. It was weak. It revealed too much of yourself to the world. Made you vulnerable. But the nightmares weren't stopping, and Adriel made me feel so safe, so secure. Made me feel like it was okay to be vulnerable with him because he would take care of everything. He wouldn't let anything hurt me. It was a false hope, but one I would hold onto until the end of time.

"That's what makes nightmares so horrifying. It's okay to be afraid." His hands left warm paths across my back as they trailed slowly over me. "I will be here to fight off every one." His lips pressed into my hair and I closed my eyes as the tender action made my heart ache.

"Promise?" I mumbled against him.

His chuckle rumbled from his chest and shook through my entire being. I could feel its effects all the way to the tip of my toes. "I promise, Angel."

"See? You look cute behind the wheel."

"I look cute all the time." I snapped at the beyond amused blue-eyed idiot leaning against the open window of the little yellow Volkswagen Beetle. He was already visibly gloating about the whole situation and I didn't want him knowing how much I enjoyed the fact that he called me cute.

"I'm not arguing."

My gaze snapped to his, but the infuriating man was already leaning away from the car to speak with the salesman. Which was probably a good thing. I could feel a slight heat tint my cheeks and seep down my neck. I never blushed. I never really had a reason to, but lately he was pulling it out of me without even trying.

After the nightmare fiasco the night before, we stayed awake watching cheesy rom-coms in the living room until I fell asleep against him on the couch. He let me stay like that for the rest of the night, and I vaguely remember my head lolling on his strong shoulder as his fingers ran through my loose curls. At one point I could have sworn he whispered sweet nothings into my ear, but with the dreams I had been having lately I couldn't be sure. At breakfast everything had went back to normal, like the night before never happened. I wasn't so sure how I felt about that.

"We'll give you twenty-five hundred." I heard Adriel say as I climbed out of the cute little bug. I wasn't huge on the color yellow, but the paint was cool and I liked how it made the car look. It was a color I would use to paint soft sun rays with if I had the right canvas.

"Oh no, son." The salesman—Rick something—was an older guy, probably mid-forties with a more than obvious toupee. You could tell immediately he didn't get many customers when we pulled into his used car lot and climbed out of the old SUV. Two kids, for lack of a better term, coming to a buy a car all on their own? Dollar signs had lit the guy's eyes. I nearly laughed at the sight. He's obviously never met Adriel. "This car is worth at least seven grand."

Without blinking, and without hesitation, Adriel stared down the short, sweaty, little man. "We'll give you twenty-five hundred."

I did oh-so-love it when he got all firm like that, especially when that look wasn't directed at me. The excited light slowly left Rick's eyes, and he reached up with a silk handkerchief to dab at the sweat dripping from beneath his toupee. Yuck.

"You kids seem smart. Solid heads on solid shoulders and all." I hadn't talked at all, despite a few grumbles when we first got there, so not quite sure why the guy was dragging me into this. "I'll tell you what, how about I drop the price to four and we'll call it a day."

Adriel's eyes glanced down at the hand sweaty-bald guy held out to him. A look close to disgust crossed his handsome features. "We'll give you twenty-five hundred."

"Listen son—"

"Let's go, Lark." Like the badass I will—sometimes—admit he could be, Adriel turned around, tapped my elbow, and nodded for the car.

Yes, sir.

"Alright, wait. Wait!" We stopped walking, and Dri turned his head just enough to shoot me a wink. I rolled my eyes, like that would make ignoring how hot that looked easier. "I'll let it go for twenty-five hundred, but you should know I'm letting you get away with theft here!"

We turned back towards Rick, and that smug smile I was all-too familiar with pulled across the blue-eyed scoundrel's face. "Excellent, let's go sign the papers."

And that's how I ended up with a 2007 Volkswagen Beetle.

"I'm waiting." Adriel drawled when he finally left the little run-down car dealer's shack. It was a small building, not a shack, but there were a few shattered windows and an AC that refused to work. As far as I was concerned, the thing was an outhouse. I waited outside.

"For what?" I asked and caught the keys he tossed my way. Though I had a pretty good idea what he wanted.

"My 'thank you'." That arrogant smile pulled across his devilish lips, and I forced the flutters it sent to my stomach away.

"I didn't even want the car."

"But you got one anyway. I want my 'thank you'." He pressed his hand against the top of the driver's door, effectively blocking my way into the vehicle. I crossed my arms over my chest and glared at him.

"No, I'm mad at you."

His smile fell into a smirk that I was ashamed to say made my mouth water. "For buying you a car?"

"Yes." I hissed and reached over to tug at the door handle. Adriel refused to budge. "And for not listening to me."

"I listen to you all the time."

"You know what I meant."

"Come on, Lark. Three words and the car's all yours." He chuckled, which did nothing to help my sanity.

I raised an eyebrow at him. "'Thank you' is two words."

"I want you to say my name all happily at the end of it."

"You're a jerk." I emphasized the 'you're' and glared pointedly at him, but the dark twinkle shining in his eyes only mocked my words.

"True, but I'm still waiting."

I let out an irritated sigh. The heinous man wasn't going to move until I 'thanked' him, and I really wasn't in the mood to get into a physical altercation in the middle of a used-car lot. But I would make sure I enjoyed this too.

Adriel's blue eyes widened as I pressed close to his chest and stood on my tiptoes. He didn't move, not even when I pressed my lips harshly against his stubble covered cheek and used my hand to squish the side of his face forcefully against mine. I released the hold with a loud 'smack' of an overexaggerated kiss and shot him a wide, beaming, sarcastic smile. "Thank you, Adriel."

Those dark blue eyes I loved so much glared down at me as I pulled away, but my satisfied smirk didn't plan on leaving anytime soon. He had stepped away from the car during my attack, and I pulled the door open and slipped quickly inside. Take that, you freaking jerk. Dri stood in the same spot for a moment, his hands clenching and unclenching at his side before he let out an irritated sigh.

Awe. I missed the sexy jaw clenching thing he did whenever he was irritated. Shoot. But then he was leaning down through the open window, his dark eyes blazing as he reached over and—flicked my face.

"See you at home, brat."

"You have got to be freaking kidding me." I grumbled down at the stupid, useless map clenched viciously between my fingers five days later. Five peaceful, dreamless, restful days later might I add.

"Where the fuck is it?" I pulled the blurred black lines closer to my face like that would help clear the words that were squished together. Whoever printed these really needed to be fired. It was Monday, the first day of classes and I couldn't find anything. Though I tried to stay as far away from that mountain and its weird brain-numbing noises and man-eating cats as I could.

"Whoa, someone's got a potty mouth!" Laughter from directly behind me only caused irritation to swarm through my veins. I whirled around to glare daggers at the skinny kid chuckling a few feet away.

"Mind your own damn business." I snapped at the long-legged, pale-freckled, brunette carrying a thin black backpack—that looked like it was made for children—slung over his shoulders. Maybe I would have felt bad for snapping at the guy if I didn't have this overbearing distrust in strangers. Trust in others was something you lost quickly as a foster kid, especially one who grew up in California.

His bright hazel eyes widened as he held his hands up in surrender, a small amused smile pulling on pale lips. I was really getting sick and tired of how amusing everyone seemed to think I was. "Easy there, Slugger. I'm not trying to piss you off." He continued to laugh, even though his words did seem genuine enough. "Maybe I can help find what you're looking for?"

Okay, I did feel a little bad after that.

"You know where the Humanities building is?" I tried not to sound too hostile, even though I was still irritated at the stupid map.

The guy's smile widened, and those bright eyes flashed in the light of the sun. "Yeah, I actually have a class there in twenty minutes. I can show you, if you want?"

I eyed the skinny kid wearily, until Adriel's words about trying rang through my head. I promised him I would try. "Um, sure. That would be great, thanks." I gave him a small smile, like that alone would make up for my rude first impression.

He didn't seem bothered what's-so-ever though as he fell into step at my side. "I'm River by the way, and I like your aggression." River nudged my shoulder gently, even though he was nearly as tall as Dri if not taller.

"Right, I'm Larkin. Lead the way."

He raised a pale brown eyebrow at that, and turned in the direction of the Humanities building. "Larkin? That's a weird name."

I shot him a narrowed look. "Like River's any better?" His laughter suddenly filled the air around us and cascaded down the sidewalk. A few other students walking nearby turned to look.

"Good point. What class are you going to?" He asked once his chuckling had died away.

"Oh, um," I glanced down at the weekly class schedule I printed out that morning—with a printer Adriel insisted I needed. "It's called Deshua of the Ages. I'm not really sure about it, but it's a general education course so—"

"Oh cool!" River interrupted with glee. "I have that class too! You can sit next to me and my friend! You'll like her, she's violent like you."

"I'm not violent."

He shrugged his thin shoulders and shot me a beaming smile. "Violent, volatile, aggressive, same diff. You'll like her. Heads up though, she's goth and a freak." I resisted the urge to say 'and you're not?' but then I figured that wasn't very friendly.

The Humanities building ended being in the back corner of campus, right next to the very mountain I was trying to avoid. I held my breath as we passed its surrounding forest, and wanted to sigh in relief when no strange noise sounded in my ears. Think again lil' cougars. Go eat a squirrel, not me.

"You'll like Professor Shorzin. He's real chill, like one of those hippies from the seventies. He gets really into his lectures though, so try not to laugh."

I was actually beginning to enjoy River's company as we walked. He was a second semester freshmen who started school early and knew a lot about the campus. I told him about how I was really only interested in art courses, and he gushed about how great the art program was.

He was gay too, a fact he made pretty damn obvious when we both stopped to watch a group of guys playing tag-football shirtless. He whistled. I drooled. Which was quickly ruined when I started comparing them to a shirtless Adriel. None of them won.

"Siena! Siena!" River sang when we finally walked into the large seminar room side by side. He had his hand raised high in the air and was waving to one of the only people in the entire room, even though class started in ten minutes.

"Yes, River. I see you." A girl dressed head to toe in black and purple hissed from the middle of the raised seats. The seats all sat in rows, one step higher than the other, as they wrapped around the back of the room. The Sienna-chick was already camped out in the dead center.

"Just making sure!" He called happily to his friend, though his pale lips were pulled in a sneaky smile. "Come on." He glanced down at me then nodded towards the sneering goth. "She's grumpy, it's great." I wasn't as sure about that as I followed him up the carpeted steps and slid into the same row as her.

"Look what I found, Si!" He announced as he plowed through the ripped black skinny jeans and combat boot covered legs that were resting on top of the seat in front of her. "We made a new friend!" Her gaze flickered to mine, and I realized it wasn't just her outfit that gave off a creepy vibe. Siena's eyes were such a bright shimmering gray they looked almost silver in the dim light of the lecture hall, and thick, black, make-up only added to the effect.

"Larkin, this is Siena. Siena this is Larkin. She's violent, like you." He nudged his friend who turned that creepy stare on him.

"I'm not violent."

"That's what she said!" River cheered before plopping into the chair at her side. "See? You guys are friends already." Siena made a 'hmph' noise in the back of her throat before turning her attention to the laptop stretched out in front of her.

"Do you mind if I sit here?" I gestured at the seat beside her. I figured being polite was the best thing to do in that situation.

She glanced over then shrugged. "Go for it."

I sat down and pulled the wooden slab attached to the arm rest up and over until it was sitting in front of me at an angle. I guess that was their version of a desktop here. Siena and River were arguing—I think—but I tuned them out and reached into my bag for that damn laptop. It was nice of River to invite me to sit with them, but I wasn't going to force a friendship. Just because I promised Adriel I would try didn't mean that I was going to put that much effort into it.

A loud sigh drew my attention away from the overpriced computer. "So, River says you like art."

"Yeah, I like it enough."

Siena nodded, and the high ponytail she had her straight black hair pulled into bobbed as she did. "So do I."

"Cool." An awkward silence fell over us until the professor finally waltzed in. Though, waltz is definitely too sophisticated a term for the guy.

His long pale brown hair was pulled back in a low ponytail. He wore what must have been a twenty-year-old Hawaiian but-ton-down, khaki shorts, and open-toed sandals. River must have noticed my bewildered look, because he reached across Siena to poke my arm. "See?" He snickered. "I told you so."

"Good morning, everyone!" The professor's surprisingly deep voice boomed across the lecture hall. It wasn't until the loud murmurs surrounding us died away that I noticed nearly every seat had been filled. "For everyone returning, I hope you all had a great summer, and for our freshmen, welcome to college!" All eyes were glues to the teacher as he plugged his laptop into some big cord running into the wall and hit a button that dropped a massive screen from the ceiling.

"This class is lecture based, which means it consists of me talking and you taking a lot of notes." At his words, the sound of rustling paper and fingers tapping against keys surrounded the room. Professor Shorzin laughed. "You don't have to do anything yet. The first week is always syllabus week, which you can pull up in Blackboard."

"Alright, so over the course of the semester we will be discussing the folklore established around Oregon, and more specifically Deshua."

I wanted to scoff. Deshua? Folklore? Yeah, freaking right.

"Deshua's history holds a rich mythical aspect that you all will find more than fascinating. Throughout the semester we will be studying the town's legends from its creation to present day."

What a load of bogus.

A student in the front row raised their hand, and I rolled my eyes. First row kids already raising their hands. Tsk. Suck ups. "Yes?"

"I was just wondering if you could tell us what exactly the mythical origin of Deshua is?" The skepticism in the student's voice mirrored my own thoughts on the subject. I slouched back further in my seat. Guess I wasn't the only one thinking this was dumb.

"We will actually be going over that in two weeks. If you look at the schedule I have posted in the syllabus, you will see each week has been assigned a different topic. Though I will leave you with this." Shorzin paused to let his eyes roam over the crowded room, then his lips pulled up at the corners.

"There are a lot more angels on Earth, than in Heaven."

CHAPTER 7

I knew those five nights of dreamless sleep were too good to be true.

The nightmare tore through me like a hurricane wrecking the Gulf of Mexico. Much like the first night in that god forsaken town, I stood at the base of the beautiful cathedral. Unlike that night, dozens of people surrounded me. Their lips pulled into cruel smiles with pointed teeth. Deep, ruby, red eyes watched hungrily as I fled up the large marble steps.

Heat suddenly pressed against my back and licked at my sides. I turned, expecting to see those demons right on my heels, instead fire had engulfed the whole town. The bright red and oranges flames rolled over buildings charring their ancient bricks. I blinked, and the fire gave way to bodies coating the cobblestone streets.

I fell harshly against the rough marble, blood coating my skin and staining my white dress red. I looked desperately around for someone, anyone, but no one came. Not even the shadowed man with the pitch-black eyes. I was alone in a mass of fire and death.

"Larkin." A strong grip suddenly wrapped around my arm and yanked me from the darkness. My eyes shot open, and I choked down tears of desperation. I will never cry because of a nightmare again.

Adriel was sitting on the edge of the bed, the warm palm of his hand placed gently on my shoulder. I let out a shaky breath and closed my eyes against the worry in his. "I thought your nightmares were getting better." He spoke softly, and that low dark timber washed away the fear racing through my veins.

"So did I."

His thumb rubbed slow soothing circles into the skin of my shoulder. I had worn my usual tank-top to bed and the heat of his skin against mine made my heart race for a whole new reason. "Do you want to talk about it?" I shrugged my free shoulder. "Come on, Lark. It will help."

His grip coaxed me into a sitting position, even though I just wanted to curl up in the corner and wallow in self-pity. "It was just... really weird." I tried not to pay attention to the fact that he placed his hand on the bed beside my waist and all but caged me in his strong arms. I wonder what it would feel like to wrap my hands around that bicep and squeeze.

"What happened?"

I shrugged again, and my eyes dropped to my fingers as they played with the edge of my comforter. "There were these—I don't know what the hell to call them—people chasing me. They had fangs, and red-eyes. And then there was this fire and it burned the whole town, and then it disappeared, and everyone was just dead."

I stopped resisting the urge to touch him and lowered my forehead until it rested against his strong shoulder. "And there was blood everywhere, Dri." I let myself cuddle into him, my arms wrapping tightly around the one he had thrown across my torso. Fudge it. I just dreamt of blood and fire eating me alive. If I wanted to hold the damn man than I was going to.

"It's alright, Angel. It was just a dream." His lips pressed softly against the top of my head and those strong fingers eased through the loose curls of my hair. I relaxed into him. Adriel made everything better.

"I—I didn't tell you this earlier, because I thought I was just being ridiculous. Especially with the nightmares and the sleep-walking. But the other week, when you gave me the SUV for the day, I swear I saw a group of guys with red eyes."

Adriel was silent for a moment, but that hand continued to stroke through my hair and lull the terror away. "Really?" His voice was quiet in my ear, but not surprised. I guess the whole 'me screaming about a shadowed man in my room' was the cherry on top of my insanity, and nothing I said seemed surprising now. In all honesty, I judged him for not sending me away to a looney bin.

"Yeah, I'm convinced they were just contacts, though. But I think that's where the dreams are coming from."

Adriel shrugged and pulled gently on the ends of my hair. "Maybe, but don't be afraid to tell me something like that next time. I won't think you're crazy."

"Yeah right." I grumbled against his bare skin. He chuckled, and the sound shook through my entire body.

He never wore a shirt to bed, a fact I admired quite a lot whenever we ran into each other in the middle of the night. His body and muscles were nicely toned from his job, but not overly buff like those gym junkies. Still, I knew those fists could do some serious damage to anyone who tried him.

He also had this huge intricate knot tattoo running from the top of his left shoulder down to his elbow. One time I asked him what the design was supposed mean, but he had just glanced down at it before shrugging and said, "Not sure, I just liked it". I wasn't quite sure why I found that nonchalant response so attractive.

"We're all a little crazy. The world wouldn't be any fun if we weren't."

"Are you admitting to being crazy, Mr. Perfect Adriel Marko?" I teased and forced myself to pull away from him.

His lips pulled up at the corners. "Only a little." Then he leaned slightly forward and bumped his forehead against mine. "Can you go back to sleep, or do you want to watch a movie with me?"

"Movie, please." I answered without hesitation. It's not that I wouldn't have been able to fall back asleep, he had chased all the fear away, but I jumped at any chance to hang around him when he was shirtless and not being all arrogant.

"Alright, Chainsaw Massacre, or As Above so Below, you pick." His smile with teasing as I groaned.

"I just had a nightmare, Dri. Why can't we watch like Princess Diaries, or something?" I pushed against his shoulders in annoyance.

He 'hm-ed' curiously, his face pulling into a serious scowl like the decision took a lot of thought. "The first or the second?"

"Second, obviously."

"Deal."

"Larkin! Over here!" I glanced across the large studio styled room to see Siena, of all people, waving at me. I gave her a polite nod but kept my steps cautious as I walked towards her. Last I knew the pretty goth girl didn't give one flying bat wing about me. Hehe, get it?

"Hey Siena." I greeted and set my stuff down on the easel beside her.

"Hey, look, I wanted to apologize for yesterday. Despite what River says, I'm not usually like that. It just takes me a minute to warm up to people." I instantly relaxed at the apologetic smile pulling on her purple stained lips.

"No worries, I can be the same way."

We fell into an easy conversation after that. I found out she was a second semester freshmen like River and majoring in Art History and Conservation. Emphasis on the Gothic era—though she didn't say that. I did. In my head. She even invited me to get coffee with her and River after class.

"We get done with our classes today around two, if you want to come hang with us." River announced sometime later as we all sat around the small circular table in the café, drinking coffees filled with chocolate and caramel.

"Thanks, but I have to get home to pick my foster sister up from the bus stop." Even though Dri promised to get a babysitter A.S.A.P. I knew it was hard since we just moved in, but like, come on, that's why they have apps for this kind of thing.

"Oh, your family takes care of foster kids? That's awesome!" River exclaimed with those bright hazel eyes wide in astonishment. I tried to ignore the painful jab it sent to my heart.

"Um, kind of, but I'm the one they took in..." It was always weird talking about being the sad little orphan with no parents. It was even worse when I was reminded that I tore apart the one family that actually did want me. Rafael was too young to remember, but Adriel should have hated me. I had no idea why he didn't, why he cared so much. I judged him for that too.

"Ah, that makes sense. You give off 'parent-issue' vibes." River sat back in his chair with a dramatic sigh. Those creepy gray eyes of Siena's snapped over to the tall skinny kid with a scowl.

"Way to be considerate, moron." She muttered and reached over to punch him hard in the shoulder. He swayed out of his seat and fell theatrically to the ground.

"Siena! How you break my heart!" River cried but jumped quickly to his feet. I tried to shove down my amused smile. They were both weird, but definitely entertaining. "And I didn't hurt her feelings! Look, she's fine." He threw one long thin finger my way and gestured towards my homeless appearance.

After last night's latest nightmare episode, I stole one of Adriel's flannels—again—and wore it like battle armor. The yoga-pants and Converse were just added comfort. It's not like I was there to impress anyone. The only guy I cared about looking good for had seen me in every possible scenario except the one I desperately wanted us to be in. Even though I knew that could never happen. It would only destroy what little sanity I had left.

"You don't know that." Siena hissed, but kept her hands to herself as River sat back in his chair.

"No, it's okay. He's right." I shrugged and pushed the rest of my coffee away. I suddenly wasn't in the mood for caffeine anymore. "I have no idea who my parents are, but the family I live with now are better than anything I could have ever asked for." I didn't mention how they didn't have parents anymore either. I didn't feel like that was really a good 'bonding' topic.

Siena suddenly leaned over, those creepy gray eyes almost warm as her slender fingers and black painted nails squeezed my hand reassuringly. "They sound awesome." I gave her a smile and didn't rip my hand away like my first instinct told me to.

"Yeah, they are. Um, if you guys to want to come over and hang with me and my sister you can." I wasn't sure where the thought came from, but the words were passing my lips before I could stop them. "Her brother might not be back for a while, and she's only nine, but the kid is scary smart."

"Yeah! That sounds awesome!" River's smile was bright enough to outshine the sun, that hurt expression from before completely gone. "I love adventures!"

And that's how we ended up on the wooden floor of my foyer playing 'Monopoly' with a manipulative nine-year-old.

"Damn..." Siena said on a bewildered breath as Raffie wiped out the rest of her money. That bright gray gaze flickered to the kid, who was shining that sweet manipulative smile of hers over at the goth. "You're a little too good at this."

Raf shrugged her tiny shoulders and divided the money into their specific amounts. "I had to be to beat Adriel. He never lets me win, even though he lets Larkin." She pouted, and I narrowed my eyes at the little turd.

"He does not let me win."

"Yes, he does." She argued, and those big blue eyes glared at me. "He says he doesn't like seeing your sad face, so he always slips more money onto your pile when you're not looking."

My mouth dropped open. "He does not!"

"Yeah huh!"

"Nuh uh!"

"Ladies, ladies! I'm sure this 'Adriel' guy can resolve the issue when he gets home." River intervened at great personal risk. Both of our daggered gazes snapped to his, fists clenched and jaws tightly shut. He held his hands up in surrender.

"What am I resolving?" That familiar tingle bringing voice of the older Markos reached our ears. My head whipped over to see him stepping through the front door with a small scowl on his lips. "And who are you?"

"They're friends from school!" I answered quickly before he could go all macho 'get out of my house' caveman on them. One eyebrow raised as he locked that dark gaze on mine. I gulped. He really was good at making me want things I couldn't have.

"You made friends already?"

The hot electricity surging through my body disappeared as I crossed my arms over my chest. "You don't have to sound so damn surprised." I snapped as he closed the door.

"Adriel!" Raf suddenly exclaimed at my side. "Tell Larkin you let her win!" Adriel shot a narrowed glare at his sister as he dropped his toolbelt on the bureau by the door.

"You weren't supposed to tell her that."

"Ha!" Rafael cheered and pointed in my face at the same time I shouted, "Adriel!".

"Yeah, I don't want to be a part of this." The blue-eyed monster grumbled as he walked towards the stairs. "Hope you had a good day." He leaned down to kiss the top of his sister's hair before glancing over at me. "Did you take one of my flannels again?" Adriel sighed as I gave him a sheepish smile and pulled at the ends of the button down tightly.

"I promise I'll wash it."

He rolled his eyes before starting up the stairs. "Whatever, I stopped caring about that a while ago. Nice to meet you two." He nodded at Siena and River, even though they hadn't uttered a word since he got there.

I watched him walk away with a small pout. He seemed grumpier than usual, or just a lot more tired. I shouldn't have let him stay up with me the night before. He was the one that had to get up early all the time, and I'm sure dealing with me wasn't easy. I was being selfish.

"That is your foster brother?" River finally chirped at my side. I glanced over to see those bright hazel eyes following Adriel's beautiful body until he disappeared into his room.

I let out a small sigh and started gathering up the Monopoly pieces. "Yeah, that's Adriel."

River scoffed, and Siena's pale cheeks were tinted slightly pink. I guess I wasn't the only one who found that man beyond attractive. "Now I know why you don't live on campus."

"What does that mean?" Raffie asked with her own little pout as I swept away all her 'hard-earned' money and deposited it back into the box.

"He's just being funny, Raff." I answered quickly before River and Siena could start talking about how hot her brother was.

Though, maybe it was for my own benefit. I suddenly had the strangest urge to shield Adriel from anyone that wasn't us. He wasn't mine, he never would be, but that didn't mean I wanted someone else to have him. Switching the topic was the best course of action.

"Do you guys want to stay for dinner? I'm making chicken." I asked politely as I placed the game back on the shelf next to the stairs.

"Thanks, but I'm going to head back and start working on that art project. Better early than late." Siena answered with a long stretch as she stood to her feet.

"Yeah, I don't think I can be around that meat-stick for much longer without doing something I'll regret." Siena shoved River with a pointed look at the kid, who was watching them with wide and confused eyes. "Oh, uh, I meant the chicken! I'm a vegetarian." That was so not smooth, but he beamed at me and Siena like it was the best possible response he could have come up with.

"Thanks for coming over, guys." I said instead of prolonging that conversation and walked them to the door. "See you at school tomorrow!" I called as they walked down the stone steps and towards River's car. They waved at me in acknowledgment.

"What's a vegetarian?" Raffie asked from the bottom of the stairs as I turned to head into the kitchen.

"It's someone that doesn't eat meat." I answered as her little bare feet followed me.

She gasped. "Not even chicken nuggets?"

I couldn't help my smile as I grabbed a baking pan and took the defrosted chicken out of the sink. "Exactly, not even chicken nuggets."

"They must not be human."

Turns out, not a lot of people were.

CHAPTER 8

"Your foster brother is hot."

"Huh?" I mumbled around my coffee the next morning. River was sitting across the table at the college's cafe with those hazel eyes wide in exclamation.

"Adriel? The cranky guy from yesterday? He's smoking like a bon-fire."

I let my lips pull into a small smile. "Yeah, the guy's hot."

River raised a pale brown brow suggestively. "You two ever bump uglies?" Despite the completely disgusting way to ask if Dri and I ever had sex, I couldn't ignore the heat licking at the back of my neck. Thinking about Adriel and sex made my insides do funny things.

I forced the embarrassment down. "No."

"But you want to, right?" He wiggled his brow, which earned him a swift smack on the back of the head by the artsy goth at his side.

"Ow! Siena, you bitch!" He grumbled at his best friend.

"Stop asking questions that are none of your business." She snapped and set her heavy shoulder bag decorated in Dracula pins on the floor.

"She doesn't have to answer if she doesn't want to." River snapped back and ripped what looked like a blueberry muffin out of her hands.

"I licked it already."

"Ew!" The skinny kid shrieked and dropped the breakfast pastry back into her hand. "You're nasty!"

"No, you're just a germaphobe."

"Am not." He muttered and wiped both palms against his black skinny jeans. Siena rolled her eyes.

"He refuses to eat or drink after someone. If their saliva has touched it, he'll vomit."

"Don't be dramatic." River grumbled in distaste and eyed the muffin like it tried to kill his dog.

"Says the theatre major."

"Whatever. Unless its during sex, no one else's saliva needs to be in my mouth." That had a laugh bubbling pass my lips-a real one. Not my usual forced ones. "Speaking of sex..." Those hazel eyes were back to the wide suggestive look he had been giving me all morning.

"Look, it doesn't matter if I do, alright? He doesn't want to, and I'm not about jumping someone who doesn't want me." In any sense of the matter. I was just another person he felt responsible for. Had to take care of. That was Adriel. The ever observant, over-protective, caring golden boy. Whoever he ended up falling in love with better be worthy of him, and realize how special he was. Or I would make them.

"Honey," River paused and leaned over to rest a reassuring hand on my arm. "Listen and listen really good. You're gorgeous. The only reason a guy isn't going to want to fuck you is if he's gay--and that smokestack doesn't make my gay-dar go off at all. Which is very tragic, might I add, but I digress."

I smiled through the heart ache. "Thanks River, but it would ruin everything." Everything we were now, everything he did for me because he cared, that would all go away. I would lose him. I couldn't lose him. I refused to.

Ignoring Siena's scowl, River sat back in his seat with a small shrug, though the excitement had left his eyes. "Your call, but I'll bet my Apple Watch he wants to sleep with you." A part of me wanted to argue, but a larger stronger part had to let the conversation die. The less I thought about Adriel rejecting me, the better.

It was Wednesday, all my classes were done by noon and I went home shortly after our conversation. I used the excuse that I needed to find Raf a babysitter, and ignored the fact that I was running away from another feeling I didn't want to face. I did, however, spend the rest of the day combing through babysitter websites. Not that I didn't love the kid, but I wasn't going to be able to get her every day and her brother wasn't supposed to be home until six.

The house was creepy when I was alone. Its vacant hallways and dark corners reminded my over-active imagination far too much of the deadly nightmares that haunt my thoughts. I could have sworn I heard soft ghost-like whispers hiding before corners as I sat at the end of the dining room table with my face buried in that damn laptop. It sent a nasty shiver down my spine.

I had to play music on my phone to drown out the eerie creeks of the old manor.

"Ah!" I screeched as a loud 'bang!' suddenly sounded throughout the entire first floor. "Adriel, you moron!" I shouted at the beyond smug male standing beside me-an arrogant and satisfied grin pulling across his handsome face.

"Hi to you too."

"Not cool." I snapped and shoved at the large toolbox he had slammed onto the table. He laughed, and the sound did nothing to settle the nerves raging beneath my skin.

"Awe, don't be mad." Adriel cooed in fake sympathy as he reached over to tug on the end of my hair.

"Prick." I muttered loud enough for him to hear.

My racing heart sounded vicious in my ears. So not what I needed. He knew how creeped out I had been lately-if the motion detectors on the front and back door were anything to go by. Unless he was purposely trying to give me a heart attack that was so not cool.

Adriel's chuckle shook through me as he plopped his heavy body onto the chair at my side. "What are you even doing here?" I grumbled, and tried-emphasis on tried-to turn my attention back to the babysitter add I had been studying.

Dri shrugged, and his red flannel hugged those toned arms nicely as he did. "My lunch was at one. I figured we could eat together." His dark blue eyes were almost warm as I cast him a sideways glance. My anger dissipated as his smug look disappeared, but I kept my face hard. No matter how sweet he suddenly decided on being.

"Yeah, well, I don't want to eat with you." I closed the laptop and stood quickly to my feet.

"Oh, stop. Don't be like that. I was just having a little fun." Adriel groaned as I turned towards the kitchen. Arrogant, cocky, good-for-nothing, jerk. I kept my internal grumbling to myself, but it wasn't long before a loud sigh sounded from the overly obnoxious male and the scraping of his chair against the hard-wood floor reached my ears.

I was already making mac n' cheese when he entered the kitchen, but that smirk pulling on his lips made me want to stop. "I'm only making you food because you let me live with you." I narrowed my eyes and held the wooden spoon up threateningly.

"If you say so." I ignored the way those blue eyes made my chest clench, and turned back to the slowly boiling water. It was becoming more than a little hard to not stare at the straining muscles hidden beneath his clothes. And then he had to go and lean against the doorframe with his arms crossed-which only gave me the insane urge to kill him. Or jump him. I couldn't be held accountable for either.

"I'll make some sandwiches."

"Oh, is my mac 'n cheese not good enough for the oh-so-mighty Adriel Markos?" I grumbled but kept my back to the infuriating man as he went to the fridge.

"You know I can eat four of those little boxes by myself. I'm going to need more. You probably should too, and that is pure carbs, Lark. Aren't you the one always trying to get us to eat better?"

I bristled at the chuckle in his tone and my grip on the spoon tightened. "It's the middle of the day and you have to go back to work. You'll be able to work off the carbs before your body rests-"

"Alright, alright, relax. I'm just messing with you." His laughter filled the kitchen, and I had to suck in a deep breath before letting it out slowly. I had no idea what was wrong with me. Adriel's teasing usually didn't bother me his much. It had to be the lack of sleep.

We fell into a quiet lull where I finished the cheesy noodles and he made sandwiches. It wasn't until I was draining the water from the noodles that he spoke, and scared the shit out of me again in the process.

"Hey..." Strong arms were suddenly circling around my waist as I stood over the kitchen sink, pasta strainer in hand.

"Fuck... Can you stop doing that?!" I snapped as the noodles precariously sloshed in the strainer. "I almost dropped the pasta."

His low chuckle sounded directly in my ear and made every nerve ending beneath my skin strum to life-like they were guitar strings waiting eagerly for him to play. It took all I had in me not to panic as those strong hands circled my waist and pulled my back against his chest in a hug I was so not prepared for.

"I just want to say I'm sorry... for the other day." His handsome face was pressed against my neck and shoulder, and those strong arms were wrapped so tightly around my waist I couldn't move. Not that I particularly wanted to.

This was--new. Adriel and I didn't touch much, especially not like this. He saved hugs for important things, like nightmares and other terrifying matters. He didn't use them to say sorry, not that he often apologized, and he never hugged me like this before. I could feel my heart thudding like an anvil in my chest as his mouth brushed my skin so softly I wasn't sure even he realized what he was doing.

I just continued holding the strainer and pasta out awkwardly in front of us as he cocooned me into the warmth of his hard body. "I was only trying to tease you, and I took it too far." I had no idea what he was talking about, nor did I care. I would pretend to be completely torn apart inside forever if he kept holding me like that. "You are dedicated, and intelligent, and driven, and you don't just try, you do."

Oh... That's what this was about. I had almost forgot about that whole conversation, except for the slight twinge of pain in my chest that had formed because of it.

"I know you can have a job and do your school work perfectly at the same time. I just don't want you to have to do that."

"Dri..." I started on a soft sigh and finally set the strainer down in the sink. Those arms tightened around me as I rested my hands against the fabric of his flannel. "I can't express how grateful I am for you, for your family-but I can't let myself depend on you all the time. That's why I want a job."

He didn't say anything for a moment, but he didn't let go either, and as my hands gripped lightly at his forearms, he rubbed his face against the exposed skin of my neck. The guitar strings beneath my skin turned to butterflies shooting straight for my stomach.

"Is it that bad?" Adriel finally muttered, though his voice was much softer than before. "Depending on me?" I was surprised at the quiet sadness pulling in his voice, and even more surprised at my immediate need to make him feel better.

"What? No, of course not." I tried to turn to face him, but those arms were iron around my waist and wouldn't let me budge. "I didn't mean it like that, Dri. If I let myself always rely on you, then I'm not going to be prepared for the day I can't."

For the day he's gone. For when he finally gets fed up of taking care of me, of forcing himself to believe I'm a part of this family. Because no matter what he said, or maybe convinced himself to believe on the surface, how could he ever accept the person that got his parents killed? How could he ever love them? Love me?

His arms went stiff around my waist, and my breath caught in my throat as he pulled his face away only to press those mind-numbing lips against the shell of my ear. "Why are you always trying to leave me?" Something dark had crept into his voice, and his palms felt like fire through my shirt as he suddenly pressed them against my stomach. I wasn't sure what to do, or how to react as his strong arms shook slightly beneath my fingertips. "Stop trying to leave me."

Then he was gone, his touch disappearing like it was never there to begin with. I spun on my heel and stared at him with wide, bewildered eyes, as he picked up his plate of sandwiches and turned for the doorway. "Hurry up with that mac n' cheese. I'm starving." He shot me a wink before walking casually from the kitchen. Like the entire interaction hadn't just happened. Like that over-active imagination of mine was at play again. If it wasn't for the heat lingering on my neck and stomach, I probably would have believed it was all in my head.

I hesitated in the kitchen for a few moments. My hands were resting against the sink behind me, keeping my suddenly very heavy body standing as I forced my lungs through a couple of deep breaths. What in the hell just happened?

I stayed there a while longer, not really sure if I should play it off like nothing happened or go storming in there. But then a disgruntled, "Lark, hurry up I'm starving! And I got to be back in twenty minutes!" Sounded from the impatient male in the dining room. I let out a heavy sigh and turned backed for the noodles. Play it off like nothing happened for the win.

"I found Raffie a babysitter by the way." Adriel announced as I sat down beside him with the noodles. He was the picture of innocence, no indication of whatever just happened showing anywhere on his person.

"You could have told me that earlier. I've been looking for one all afternoon."

"I know, I saw your laptop. Honestly though," He continued at the narrowed look I shot him, "It just didn't cross my mind to tell you. I'm sorry." The tone in his voice was genuine enough, so I let my accusing stare fall away. Three apologies in one day? He must have put something in his coffee.

"Who's the sitter?" I mumbled around the bite of sandwich I shoved into my mouth. If he wanted to pretend nothing happened then fine. I'll show him what a great pretender I can be. Those blue eyes flickered to mine, and the smile pulling on his lips wasn't at all arrogant. I felt my heart clench.

"A high school junior who lives a few doors down. I ran into her this morning when I took Raf to school. She seemed nice enough." He shrugged and sat back once he had annihilated three-quarters of the food.

Oh, yeah, I'm sure. What high school teenage girl wouldn't be 'nice enough' to him? He was one of the most attractive men I had ever seen, the only one capable of making me blush. I've seen girls throw themselves at Adriel before. Girls my age, a few years younger than me, and more than a handful older, but he would always politely decline no matter how pretty they were. Then he would turn to us and roll his eyes before mumbling something about 'female hormones' under his breath so Rafael wouldn't hear. I would be infuriated at the disrespectful assumption if it wasn't true. He was hard to resist.

"She doesn't, like, worship Satan or anything, right?"

A slow amused smile tugged on the corners of his lips. "No."

"Well, that's good then." I nodded but kept my gaze glued to the now-empty paper plate. Our little embrace was still fresh on my mind, and River's words from earlier were pounding in my ears-putting very vivid, explicit, thoughts in my brain. I was terrified Adriel would be able to see every single one if I glanced at him for too long. I guess I wasn't that good at pretending.

"She starts tomorrow." He began a few quiet moments later. "But has to leave early for some band recital. So, I need you here by four."

"Yeah, I'll be here don't worry."

"Good." Then he sighed and stood slowly to his feet, completely ignoring the distasteful look I shot his way. "I need to get going."

I tried to shove down the panic that shot through my chest. I didn't want to be alone, no matter how irritating he could be. I didn't look at him as I grabbed the empty mac n' cheese pot and took it to the kitchen. Hanging out with River and Siena between classes helped a lot with being away from the siblings. It was times like this, when I would be alone until Raf came home, that the fear crept in.

"You alright?" I didn't realize he had followed me into the kitchen until his voice sounded from the doorway. There we were again, in that little space, almost the exact same position as before. I turned on the hot water and reached for the sponge to try and ignore the thousand different emotions swarming through me-and totally not an invitation for him to hold me like that again.

"Of course, why wouldn't I be? Is there anything specific you want for dinner?" I asked before he could answer my first question.

He was silent for long while, but I could feel those dark eyes staring like hot embers into the back of my head. It wasn't until he walked slowly over, leaned down and pressed a warm kiss to my cheek that the panic faded away. "Whatever you want is fine, Angel. I'll see you at six." Adriel spoke softly and turned for his forgotten toolbox.

"Yeah, have a good day." I mumbled after him, as that heat turned my cheeks into an inferno.

Chapter 9

The next morning was fairly... ordinary. River, Siena and I all got coffee at the café, discussed the latest gossip revolving around a rather scandalous party in the freshmen dorm the night before-even though it had been a Wednesday-and went home for lunch, where Adriel was waiting with some crummy take out. But I didn't complain. No matter how badly the guy could get under my skin, I would never scoff at spending time with him.

It wasn't until later that day when I went back for my afternoon classes, that things took a turn for the worst.

"Oh my God. Did you guys hear?" River exclaimed loudly, despite the quiet of our Deshua of the Ages classroom as he took a hurried seat at my side. My raised eyebrow matched that of Siena's pierced purple one. "That freshman party last night? A girl went missing!"

"And why exactly do you sound excited about that?" Siena drawled at my other side, but I didn't pay much attention. An icy chill went down my spine as a tight ball of anxiety settled heavily in my stomach.

"Because it's a mystery, Siena! Finally, something interesting happened in this God-forsaken town."

"She probably just got too drunk and wandered off. I'm sure the girl will show up soon." Siena's disinterest was the exact opposite of her best friend, who was so excited that he was practically bouncing out of his seat.

"We should go look for her after class."

That ball of anxiety grew, but I couldn't find the words to figure out why as Siena rolled her eerie gray eyes. "I'm sure the cops are doing a good enough job of it on their own."

"Really? I figured you would take up any excuse to go see Lady Jess." The goth perked up almost immediately at his words and the disinterest in her eyes faded to excitement.

"I have been wanting to buy a few new crystals."

"Lady Jess?" I said around the unease slithering through me. Whatever the reason, this whole situation didn't feel right.

"The town's psychic. Si is obsessed with her." Siena lifted her arm behind me to shove at River, but the ball in my stomach turned to lead.

"A psychic?" And her name was Jess?

"Oh yeah, you're going to love her."

I wasn't so sure about that.

"Come on," Siena laughed as her pierced tongue flicked out to lick that ruby red lollipop clenched between her slender fingers. The stark contrast of the candies color and her dark purple lips made her look even more edgy-not that the black charcoal eyeliner circling her bright gray eyes needed any help with that. "You can't tell me you've never been to a psychic before."

I shrugged my shoulders and glanced away from the cavity-wielding sugar. "Never really had a desire to." I didn't need some crook telling me my love life was shit, and that I suffered a hard past. I knew that well enough on my own, but the excited gleam in Siena's eyes made the disdain die on my tongue. Besides, if a girl really was missing and if this Jess character knew how to find her, it wouldn't be right to ignore it. Despite the unpleasantness swirling in my gut. Though I only had about an hour to play hero before I had to go relieve Raf's babysitter.

"Lady Jess is so fucking cool. She knew about the scar I have on my shoulder, even though I was wearing a jacket! And she knew exactly where it came from!"

"Everyone has a scar or two." River scoffed at his best friend. "And anyone can figure out you fell and scraped it on a rock." Even though he was the one who suggested going to see her River had been grumbling the whole way. Apparently, he didn't believe in the psychic mumbo-jumbo either, but suggested it to get Siena on board with the search. This was just a 'pit-stop' in his plans-as he called it.

"You weren't there, River." Siena snapped and shot icy gray daggers his way. "She knew right off the bat. The ladies legit!"

"I can't stay long guys." I reminded them as we turned towards the center of town, leaving my little yellow bug parked on the side of the road. "I have to get home for Raffie."

"Yeah, yeah, you already said that. It shouldn't take long though, she's really good. We'll even have a chance to get our own readings once she figures out where that girl is."

I really didn't want one of those readings, no matter how 'good' she was, but Siena was pointing towards a brightly decorative shop and the argument died from my lips. Crystals of various sizes hung inside the window, along with colorful charms and antique looking candles. It was just like any other psychic shop I had seen in California.

The only interesting thing this one had going for it was that it stood right across the street from the cathedral. My eyes glanced back nervously at my car as Si dragged us through the shop's door. There was a plain wooden sign hanging above the entrance reading: Embrace the cleansing aura of dreams.

Clearly, this woman has never been inside one of mine.

"Back so soon, Siena?" A light gentle voice greeted as a bell rang behind us. There was no one in sight, and suddenly the space around me was too small, too tight. We were caged into the place, surrounded by walls and walls of candles and crystals, and various plants. With no escape. I sucked down a shaky breath.

"Yeah, we were wondering if you could figure something out for us." Like she had been here a million times before, Siena pulled me through the multitude of shelves lining the store until we reached a counter at the far back-the only space not littered with merchandise. We had already lost River in the tightly compacted aisles, but from the soft snickering behind us I assumed he found something to amuse himself with.

There was a girl standing behind the counter, one who couldn't have been more than a few years older than us. She had long straight blonde hair cascading in a waterfall down her back, a thin heart-shaped face and pretty smile that shone brightly against her tan skin. She was wearing a pair of skinny jeans and large sweater, nothing like the long dresses and clanging jewelry I saw on the psychics in California. If it weren't for those unnaturally bright green eyes, she would have looked like any other girl walking down the street.

"This is Larkin." Siena announced as her grip on my wrist pulled me right smack into the counter. I shot her a narrowed look before glancing back at the girl.

A sense of warmth and calm washed through my veins as-who I'm assuming was-Jess turned that sweet smile on me. The feeling was so strange and foreign that it had the completely opposite effect. The anxiety in my stomach started to creep like ice through my veins "Larkin? That's a-"

"Weird name, I know."

The girl's smile widened, and those bright green eyes seemed to spark in amusement. No way was that color natural. "I was going to say unusual, but there is nothing wrong with weird either." She ran her hand through the top of her hair, brushing the long streaks back across her shoulders from where they had fallen. She moved so fluidly, with calm, soft motions that seemed to discourage any unnecessary adrenaline.

"If you say so." I muttered as I forced my gaze from those unnerving eyes. Siena was leaning against the counter beside me, her gaze wide in encouragement. I resisted the urge to reach down and check the time on my phone. This place was giving me the creeps, and if I didn't get home soon Adriel was going to be furious. "Look, I'm kind of on a time crunch, so if you could just help us out that would be great."

"Of course," Jess spoke softly, that easy calm smile still resting on her lips. "I'm free right now." Jess stepped towards a dark purple curtain at the back of the room that I hadn't noticed before and swept it out of the way. "Come right through here. I always ensure every customer's privacy."

Ugh customer. How much was this bogus shit going to cost?

"We're not here for ourselves." Though Siena's narrowed glance suggested otherwise. "A girl went missing from the freshman dorm last night. They were hoping you could help-"

"The girl is fine. Drank too much and stumbled home with some overzealous junior boy. I've already informed the police."

Well, that was quick and easy. Though I wasn't sure if anything she said was true. "Great, thanks. Let's go." I mumbled toward Siena who shot me a disapproving frown.

"Oh no, you still have time before you have to go back. It's not even three-thirty."

"Siena..."

"Just do one reading! Live a little Larkin. It's not going to hurt you." I groaned as she gripped onto my shoulders and spun me to face that dark purple curtain still held open by Jess. I ignored her warm inviting smile. I wasn't a fan of the dark, especially not in creepy shops with strange people I didn't know.

Siena gave me a little shove towards the curtain, and despite my grumbling I went without a fuss. The goth was weird, but if listening to some woman talking nonsense for a while was going to make her happy, then why the hell not? Trials of making friends, and I did promise Adriel I would try.

I walked slowly behind the counter and slipped by Jess's outstretched hand. The room was small, only two silver barrel chairs sat on either side of a square wooden table, with-what looked like--the galaxy painted on the far wall. A stack of tarot cards rested on the end of the table farthest from the door, and four large different colored candles sat directly in the middle. That uneasy chill from before ran down my spine as the 'psychic' closed the curtain. The room became shrouded in darkness.

"Sorry about the dark." That soft, gentle voice filled the air, and I followed its sound as she brushed by. "I prefer only candle-light when I read." The white candle in the middle of the table flared to life at her words. My eyes widened. "Have a seat, Larkin. I want to get you home in time for your sister. The babysitter leaves at four, right?"

"Uh, um, yeah." I stammered uncertainly before taking a seat on the chair closest to the entrance. The girl was already sitting in the other, her hands clasped loosely together on the tabletop. I know I sure as hell hadn't told her any of that.

"Professionally, I go by Lady Jess, but you can just call me Jess if you want." The smile was small, secretive, like she already knew things about me that I didn't even know. "Have you ever been through a reading before?" Her voice was casual enough though those bright green eyes studied me intently. The candle lit the table but cast shadows over her features and kept the rest of the room in darkness.

"No."

"You don't believe in them." It wasn't a question, and that smile of hers turned more sly than warm.

I nodded.

"It's alright to be skeptical, most people are. And it doesn't help that there are so many out there without gifts who only deceive."

"And you claim to be the real thing?" I didn't bother hiding the scoff in my tone, but she didn't seem offended.

"I'll let you decide that." For the first time since I sat in the barrel chair, those unnatural eyes turned away from mine to glance down at the candles. "There are many different readings I can do, though the two that most are familiar with are palm and tarot." She started softly, her voice smooth and light as it eased the anxious knots tearing at my shoulders.

"With palm readings I can see into your past, and your future. With tarot cards I can see the struggles you are or will be facing and how to overcome them. Since this is your first reading there will be no charge. The choice is yours."

No charge? "You'll do either one? For free?"

She nodded, her hands still resting patiently against the table-top. I bit my lip and shrugged. I didn't really care much about my future, and I already knew my past. But if her little cards wanted to somehow magically tell me how to get over my struggles, who was I to stop her? Maybe she'll tell me how to get over my lustful thoughts about a certain pig-headed, arrogant, blue-eyed male.

"I guess the tarot cards?"

She finally pulled her hands away, that smile pulling at pale pink lips. "Good choice. Palms can be tricky, and some people's spirits are a lot stronger than others. I can't read everyone." Jess spoke nonchalantly, like it was completely normal to discuss reading people's spirits. "I like cards, they can't hide anything. Though they often hold dozens of meanings."

Well, that didn't sound very reassuring.

"First thing to know before we get started, are the importance of the candles." She raised one, slim, delicate hand over the flame of the white candle, just high enough so it wouldn't burn her skin. "The white is for peace, and purity. It is used often with divination and the cleansing of bad spirits." Despite not believing in any of it, she had my complete attention as her palm moved over the next candle. "The black is for safety and protection. It is used to banish the negative and welcome the positive." The candle's wick lit as she spoke, and I had a hard time convincing myself it was just a parlor trick. Batteries or hidden wires or something.

"The purple is for spiritual power. It helps awaken the third eye in both myself and you." Like the black candle, the purple's wick flared to life. "And the blue is for protection, and focus. It helps me safely see into that which is hidden." Once all candles were lit, and a soft warm glow washed over the small room, Jess pulled her hand away. "Each one serves a specific purpose and will help us on this journey."

Just great. Now we were taking a journey together. I better get paid mileage.

"Now, it's very important you do as I say." Her tone was still light and gentle, but it sounded with an authority that I wasn't about to challenge. "Take the cards." I reached slowly across the small table and grabbed the deck. "Good, now shuffle them." I did as she said and used my really awful shuffling skills to mix the cards together. "Split the deck and put both halves on the middle of the table."

"Good job." She announced cheerfully once I did everything she had asked.

"Thanks, I put all my effort into it."

She laughed and shook that delicate head before reaching for the cards. "I see why Siena thinks so highly of you."

"When did she say that?"

"When she brought you over to the counter."

"But she didn't-"

"Sh, you need to be quiet now so I can see."

I sat back grumpily in my seat and crossed my arms over my chest. I was getting really sick and tired of people telling me what to do. She picked up the two halves, shuffled them together herself, then laid out three cards in a row. That's when the show began.

"The Lovers is a very common card and has many different meanings." Jess announced softly as she pointed at the first card with the image of two separate hands holding a stitched together heart high into the air. It was gruesome looking.

She placed the palm of her hand about an inch over the card and closed her eyes. "You are... struggling between what your heart wants and what your mind is claiming." I tried not to roll my eyes. How freaking basic was that? Almost everyone in existence struggles between what they want and what they think. Nothing spiritual or exciting there. "You battle over your lust for him and his for you."

"Um, no, no. No one's lusting after me." I interrupted halfway through her explanation, heat flaming the back of my neck. She might have gotten her guess right on my whole attraction for Adriel, but he sure as hell wasn't lusting after me. I paid so much attention to the guy it would be impossible not to see if he did.

That unnatural gaze of hers blinked slowly open, and her lips pulled at the corners. "If that is what you wish to believe. I just say what the cards read."

M'kay, sure. Right.

"And what about this one." I pointed towards the card clearly labeled Death at the bottom. As if the giant grim reaper looking creature pointing directly at me wasn't enough of a sign. "Let me guess, my love is doomed to fail?"

"No, on the contrary, you have nothing to worry about your love." What the hell was that supposed to mean? "The Death card is corresponding to this one." She gestured to the third card she had laid down. "Judgement usually follows Death in matters of reincarnation." The one she was referring to had a young blond boy hanging in clouds with purple wings sprouting out of his back and a long trombone looking instrument pressed to his lips on the top half. The bottom of the card had three very naked people standing out of rectangular dirt graves. Their pale, thin hands raised to the angel.

"Reincarnation?" I raised my brow in blatant disbelief. "Are you saying I'm reincarnated? Like The Mummy?" This girl was more bonkers than I thought.

"No, not like The Mummy." Jess let out a small laugh, not at all concerned with the graphic images before us. "It is not uncommon to see. Many souls are reincarnated throughout the years. They are known as 'Old Souls'. It's quite an honor to be one actually. Those picked by Azrael often serve high purposes than regular souls."

"Whose Azrael?"

"The Angel of Death." She pointed again at the Death card. "He is in charge of sending souls to Heaven, Hell, and back to Earth." She held her hand over the judgement card and let out a slow breath. "And he has apparently sent yours back quite a bit."

I let out a haggard breath and tapped anxiously on the edge of the table. This girl was freaking nuts. Heaven and Hell didn't exist. There was no such thing as angels or souls. There was only us. That's it. When you died, you died. There was no such thing as reincarnation. I had to get out of there. Raf and the babysitter were expecting me, and the longer I spent with this lunatic, the more my brain cells died.

"Listen, Jess, this has been fun and all, but I need to get going."

"Wait, there's one more card in the reading." She spoke softly, sounding not at all offended that I wanted to leave. She flipped the card as I stood to leave.

"I really need to go-"

"Wait." She suddenly sprang forward, her thin hand wrapping tightly around my wrist with more strength than I had expected her body could hold.

"What the actual fuck lady?" I snapped and tried to rip my wrist from her grasp, but those slender fingers were like iron around my skin.

"Does this card mean anything to you?" She pointed down at the card, but I didn't want to look. This whole thing was massively creeping me out, and I was going to give Siena hell for asking me to do this.

"I don't care-"

"Look." Her voice held a certain authoritative tone that was hard to ignore. I couldn't help it, my eyes snapped down to the card. The very air around us seemed to freeze, and my pulse pounded against my ears.

"Is this some kind of joke?" My voice was soft even to my own ears. My breath came out shaky as my eyes locked on the depictive image. Large black eyes stared from a blood red canvas. Raven wings coated the cards edges, their feathers circling that unwavering gaze in an iron cage. I knew those eyes. I had seen them often enough in my dreams.

"No, it's not. Do you have any idea what that is?"

"You tell me!" I snapped before finally ripping my wrist from her grasp. "They're your damn cards!" My breathing started to turn into hard, fast pants and I backed unsteadily away from the table.

"That's not my card. I don't have anything like that in any of my decks."

"You're lying." I stumbled back against the galaxy-painted wall. My eyes were wide in horror as they stayed locked on that black soul-shaking gaze. "How did you know?" I never told anyone about those dark body-binding dreams. Not even Adriel, though I wasn't necessarily sure I could tell him about my erotic visions of a man I could never see.

"Larkin-"

"How did you know?" I was seething now, my gaze finally tearing from those black eyes to lock on hers. Those unnaturally bright green irises were wide, her lips slightly parted in surprise as she stood slowly to her feet.

"Larkin, you have to listen to me." Jess began softly, her thin hands outstretched as she took a step forward. "There is a legend, an old one. You are in danger." I stepped hastily away from her hand. The wrist she had grabbed clutched tightly to my chest.

"Yeah, from crazy people like you!"

"No, not from me. From them."

"Y-You're insane. Stay away from me!" I burst through the dark purple curtain and raced for the shop's door without a second thought.

"Larkin? Wait, what's wrong?!" I ignored Siena as I ran past her and River, making a vicious beeline for the exit.

I was so close. So close to the freedom of outside and my little yellow bug, when Jess's retreating words sent a sucker punch straight to my stomach. "Stay out of the shadows, Larkin. They're looking for you."

CHAPTER 10

"Where have you been?" The eerie calm in Adriel's voice as I burst through the front door was nearly as terrifying as that freak knowing about the man in my dreams.

"I'm sorry." My breath was still coming out in short pants as the fear from before spread panic through my veins.

"You're sorry? Do you have any idea what time it is? You were supposed to be here an hour ago."

Adriel was pissed. I could see it in the way he stood at the bottom of the stairs, his body nonchalantly resting against the banister, strong arms crossed over his chest. It was the ice in his eyes that had me hesitate against the door. No matter how badly I annoyed him, he's never given me that look before.

"I got caught up at school. I'm sorry." I didn't want to lie, but I also didn't think telling him I went to see a 'psychic' was a good idea either.

"Your last class was at two, Larkin. I needed you to be here for Raffie." His words cut through me as I tossed my keys onto the bureau and kicked off my shoes. "How am I supposed to trust you when you can't do the one thing I ask?"

"One thing? Adriel, you ask me to do shit all the time, and I always do it!"

"Asking you to stop cussing around my sister and clean up after yourself is common sense. I needed you to be here today. I trusted the fact that you would be." He pushed away from the staircase, fury replacing that icy indifference as he stepped towards me. "So, what am I supposed to do when the sitter calls me, freaking out, because she has to be at her band concert, and you're not answering your phone?"

"I—I...." I was at a loss for words. I didn't realize what the time was when I left. I thought only minutes had passed, not an hour. But I knew he had every right to be mad, I let both him and Rafael down. That was the last thing I ever wanted to do.

"I had to leave work early so Angie could go. I'm the boss. I shouldn't be leaving early because you're an immature teenager who can't handle any fucking responsibility!" His words ripped through me like the jagged edge of a knife. I had to take a shaky step away. I've never seen him that mad before, at anything. A clenched jaw and a few had words were one thing, but yelling... I've never heard him yell before, especially not at me.

"I'm not immature—"

"Then stop acting like it."

I pressed my back flush against the front door in some kind of form of stability. I had no idea why he was this upset. He's never been this upset when I missed plans before. "I'm sorry—"

Adriel cut me off with a scoff and tore a hand aggressively through his dark hair. "Do you have any fucking idea how worried I was? You weren't answering your phone, I had no idea where the hell you were, and I thought— I thought...." His voice trailed off, but the tension in his shoulders didn't seem to subside.

"I never meant to worry you. I thought I had more time." Which was such a pathetic excuse, and I knew it was too, but there was nothing else I could offer him. I could see images flash through my mind at his words, images of a twisted bent over car and a decrepit bus stop. This went beyond my being late. He had been worried about me.

"I really don't want to hear it." Adriel let out a hard sigh as he turned to face the living room, those dark eyes focused pointedly on anything but mine. "I can't—I don't want to be near you right now." My heart seemed to drop to the pit of my stomach at those words.

"Adriel—"

"I couldn't find you!" All words died off my tongue as I watched the fire in his eyes turn molten, then slowly choke the light from them. "I'm serious. I need you to leave me alone for a while." Adriel turned with a shake of his head and stalked slowly back up the stairs. He didn't look back once.

I let my body slide down the cool glass of the front door, shaky breaths escaping my lungs as I forced down the knot in my throat. I wouldn't cry. Not over this. Adriel didn't make me leave when I killed his parents, he hadn't let me leave. He wouldn't push me away because of this. But that didn't stop the hollow ache in my chest.

This day really was turning to complete shit.

"Larkin..."

Wind brushed across my shoulders, tangled my dark curls, and kissed my cheeks. I tilted my heard curiously to the side. There was music in my ears—a soft dark lullaby gently carrying all thought away.

"Come to me..."

Something wrapped around my chest and pulled, urging my feet to follow the lyrical dark path. A twig snapped in the distance and the music died away until there was nothing but a soft lull urging my eyes closed—urging me to give in.

"Come to me."

When I opened my eyes again, he was there. The man from my dreams. He was still clouded in shadows, but I could just barely make out the rough outline of clothes, of dark jeans and a jacket, though that was as far as the details would go. Yet despite that, I knew he was smiling at me, his hand held outstretched in invitation.

"We have places to be..." The shadowed man said, but his voice seemed different. More disembodied than before with an urgency lacing his words. I didn't move closer. He never tried to urge me anywhere, and always seemed as curious as I was about what I was dreaming. This time was different. I shook my head and took a step away. That hidden smile fell.

"We must go."

No, no I didn't want to go.

The man stepped towards me, which I matched with a receding step of my own. "I don't want to." I said to the shadows as the forest thrummed to life. I liked it here. I didn't want to leave. So often I hated wherever my mind took me, but this place was nice. This place was soft, and warm and it sang. Sang to me. No one ever sang to me. Why would he want me to leave?

He took another step forward, his hand still outstretched. "We must go now—"

"Larkin." I turned at the voice, at the feeling of warmth and sunshine despite the darkness radiating from him. He was there, behind me, completely shrouded in shadows, no ounce of light or detail to be seen, but I felt an immediate sense of ease. Like a curtain had been lifted from my mind, I knew that the other one was a fake. A dark creature sent to fool me.

Those midnight black eyes washed curiously over me, slowly rolling over every inch of my body—as if he were checking for something the naked eye couldn't see. Then that gaze flickered to the other shadow being, and I watched fire burn to life in cracks between the darkness. Like burning coals in a fire.

"You are lucky she is not hurt."

"She's mine! They promised!" That disembodied whisper from before turned to oil, and I spun back around as the creature took a threatening step forward. The black of its eyes once used to fool me were now as red as rubies in the setting sun. I took hurried steps away from its outstretched hand as talons began to break through shadowy skin.

An arm wrapped around my waist, solid and strong, despite the iridescent shadow of its being, and pulled my back into his iron chest. "No..." The shadow man said as his other hand traced a tauntingly slow path along my bare arm and over the sleeve of my white dress. "She's mine." I didn't know whether to shudder or whimper as his tongue traced a slow sensual path along the side of my throat.

I couldn't move, couldn't speak, or even think as his free hand reached up to cover my eyes. "Close your eyes, beautiful." His voice was that usual low erotic lull in my ear, so much like the singing from the forest before. A dark song meant only for me. I did as he said, though I couldn't see anything besides the shadow of his hand.

I didn't want to know what happened next, especially when the screaming started.

It wasn't until his hand and the heat from a body that didn't exist disappeared that I bothered opening my eyes again. There was nothing left of the creature, nothing but black dust floating away on the breeze, and a scorch mark left on the Earth. I could smell the stench of burning fur and tried not to gag.

I turned away from the sight and could just barely make out hands shoved into pants pockets of the man before all detail disappeared. "I am sorry." He said a quiet moment later. "For that—thing ruining your dream. It was supposed to be a good one."

"It was."

"You like this place then?" Those pitch-black eyes, like a moonless night without an ounce of light, glanced around the sunset lit forest.

I nodded.

"Good." He seemed to nod, before turning without another word.

"Wait!" I called after him, though I wasn't exactly sure what I wanted to say. He paused, and the shadows surrounding him slid across strong shoulders and down his back. "Thank you." I wasn't positive but I could have sworn he smiled.

"It is never my intention for you to have nightmares, Larkin." Then he just disappeared, right into thin air, and I wasn't at all sure he was ever really there. Dreams with him usually ended much—differently.

I turned back towards the trees, waiting for screams and a burning fire to rip through the leaves, but none came. Even the burning mark on the earth slowly disappeared as that dark music started again. I sat down on the grass, my back and head resting against a rough tree. I closed my eyes and let the song wash over me.

Yes, I liked this place very much.

The next time I woke, I had no idea where I was.

It was cold, and dark, and something kept crumbling beneath my fingertips. Leaves. I was outside.

I jerked into a sitting position with a start. What the actual fuck—I must have slept walked again. Despite the bell on my door and the motion sensors, I had walked completely out of the house, down our street and to... well, I had no idea where the hell I was. I climbed hastily to my feet and spun around in a panic.

Trees. There were trees everywhere, from what I could make out through the soft light of the rising sun. "No... No, no, no, no." I could feel the panic rising in my chest, and my fingers pulled viciously at the curls in hair. I wanted to scream in frustration, to hit my hands against a tree or my own head as if that would somehow fix everything. What was wrong with me? Why did this keep happening?!

I glanced around for something, anything, that would help me figure out where I was, but came up with nothing. Only darkness and trees. I was still in my pajamas too, a tank-top and short-shorts that did little to nothing in stopping the frigid morning air. Despite a pair of, now dirty, fluffy socks I wasn't wearing any shoes, and there was no cellphone in sight.

I let out a ragged, lung shuddering breath, and wrapped my arms tightly around myself to keep in whatever body heat I could. A plan. I needed a plan. It was still too dark to maneuver through the trees, but the sun was slowly starting to rise. I would just have to wait to try and follow the path back from where I came, or—or something. God, this was awful. The dreams weren't ending, only getting worse, and the sleepwalking just got way too out of hand.

Why hadn't the chime woken me? Why hadn't the sensors gone off? Maybe they did but I was just too far gone to hear them. But then, why didn't Adriel hear them? There was no way he could be that mad at me, no way he would willing ignore the alarm going off. No matter how angry, he wouldn't just ignore everything and let me wander off.

Would he?

We hadn't spoken for the rest of that horrible evening. I stayed away like he wanted me to, even though doing so while he was so furious tore me up inside. He was the one person in this world I cared about disappointing. The only one whose opinion matter. And he wouldn't even look at me. I had stayed in my room for the rest of the night, even though when I opened the door to go to the bathroom, a sandwich and paper plate had been waiting outside my door. He had put food together. Even infuriated, Adriel still took care of me.

No, no he wouldn't ignore the sensors.

I was so lost in thought, trying to ignore the eerie sounds of the animals skirting around in the underbrush, that I hadn't noticed the sun light the trees until its warmth brushed against my skin. I blinked up at the pink and orange sky that was just barely visible through the treetops. There, barely visible through thick branches and leaves, was the college's clock tower. My heart stammered at the sight, and not because being here meant I had slept walked across the entirety of Deshua.

I didn't look behind me as I headed in the direction of the school. I wouldn't turn around and see it. The mountain I knew for a fact that was at my back. That would make it too real. If I could just pretend it was some random patch of forest that I had unconsciously stumbled into, I could deal. But that mountain—no I refused to believe it had anything to do with this.

Turns out I hadn't wandered too far into the trees, and I quickly cleared the forest. But my feet ached from the hidden rocks and branches I kept stepping on, and parts of my skin began turning blue from the cold. I didn't care though. All I wanted was to get to a phone and call Adriel. I paused at the thought.

He was already pissed at me for yesterday, did I really want to add onto it with this? It would just upset him more knowing the sensors hadn't gone off, or how far I had walked away from the house. It would just be extra stress he didn't need to deal with. Besides, despite being sore and cold—and insane—I was perfectly fine. There was nothing else to do about the sleepwalking, short of tying me to my bed that is. Which I was definitely not up for.

There had to be an Uber or something in this God forsaken town. I just needed to find someone with a cell phone—

"Larkin?" I never thought I would be thankful to hear that voice, but as a bright flash of blond caught my eye, I felt relief course through me. "Oh my God, Larkin. What happened to you?"

"Can you take me home?" My teeth chattered as I pulled to a stop in front of a bewildered looking Luke. Any hint of that golden boy smile was gone, and despite the dark glasses covering his brown eyes I could tell they were wide in shock.

"Take you home? Are you okay? What are you doing out here? Its freezing and you don't have any shoes—"

"I know." I muttered and squeezed my blue fingers into my bare arms. "Please just... take me home." I didn't care if he gave me the creeps, or if every hair on my body stood on end when I was close to the guy. He was the only thing that was familiar then, and I needed... to get... home.

"Whoa there." Pale slender hands reached up to grasp my upper arms in support as my body swayed. "You need to go to a hospital, not home. How did you even get out here?"

"N-no hospital." I was stammering now, I knew it too, but there was nothing I could do to stop it. I couldn't even pull away from his grip. I was so tired, and cold, and my head hurt. "Just home..." Everything was starting to spin.

"Easy." Luke grumbled as I sagged against him. I was falling to the ground, hard, and the heavy grunt he let out as his arms kept me from hitting solid rock wasn't at all reassuring.

"Okay... alright. I'll take you home." His voice was surprisingly soft, despite the hesitation ringing there. "But I still think I should take you to the hospital." I could only shake my head as he adjusted his grip and hauled me into the air.

"56 Haniel Drive." I mumbled pass raw lips and tried not to make it obvious I was clinging to the heat radiating off him. Later I would worry about giving a guy who gave me the creeps my address or letting him take me home—if that was what he was doing—but at that moment I didn't care.

I was so out of it that I could have sworn he held me against him with one hand and texted something into his phone with the other, but then I blinked and both arms were wrapped around me. Great, I could now add hallucinating to the catastrophe that was the pass few days.

I vaguely remember him putting me into a warm car, a smooth ride through the neighborhood streets of Deshua, then finally to a stop at the front of the Markos' house. The sense of relief that raced through my veins nearly chased away the horror from the night before. Nearly.

Movement caught my attention, and I lifted my head enough to see the black of Adriel's hair as he placed his work bag in the SUV. My heart fluttered. I didn't even care that he was still probably furious at me. Just the sight of one of those familiar flannels made warmth chase away the fear.

"Is that your—?"

"Adriel." I sighed and leaned my heavy head back against the window. "That's Adriel." Luke didn't say anything else but nodded as he stepped out of the car. Adriel turned at the sound of the door closing, and those blue eyes narrowed at the college kid walking around to the passenger side.

Luke opened the door I was hunched against as Adriel's voice brushed against my ears. "What are you—Larkin?" The shock resonating through his tone as Luke pulled me from the car did little to ease my headache. The sound of his toolbox slamming into the ground as it fell from his hand ricocheted like a gun shot. But then he was there, tearing me from Luke's arms, those dark blue eyes wide in worry.

"What happened? What's wrong? Are you okay?" I stood against him, his hands clutching tightly at my arms as that frantic gaze glanced over every inch of me. He must have noticed what I was wearing, and the blue tint of my skin, because he left me standing long enough to rip his flannel off, wrap it tightly around my shoulders, and pull me back into his chest.

Then those eyes turned to the blond who had taken me home and turned to ice. "What the fuck did you do to her?" A cursing Adriel was so not a good thing. Luke seemed to take a decent step away from the fuming man cradling me almost desperately to his chest, his hands held up in surrender.

"I found her like that, stumbling out of the woods by the university."

"You better pray that's what happened—"

"He brought me home, Dri." Those dangerously cold eyes snapped down to mine and his arms tightened. So much for not wanting to stress him out further. I sighed and pressed into him, my fingers curling into the soft fabric of his flannel and t-shirt. Home. It was good to be home.

A warm, calloused, hand urged my face up until that gaze was scouring every detail of my own. "You sleepwalked again..." It wasn't a question, but I nodded anyway. Adriel's jaw ticked shut, and his hand dropped back to my waist as he shot Luke one last look.

"My apologies. Thank you for bringing her home." It was the closest to an 'I'm sorry' that I ever heard him give anyone besides myself.

Luke lowered his hands before shoving them into his jacket pockets. He gave Dri a nod, before glancing down towards me. "Get better, Lark. I'll—see you around the school." I could only give him a polite smile in thanks before Adriel gathered me closer to his chest and turned for the manor. He didn't wait for Luke to get back in his car.

There was a stiffness in Adriel's movements as he rushed us through the front door, the solid wood banging shut heavily behind us. "I don't know how this happened." He mumbled more to himself than me, as he carried my still trembling body quickly to the second floor. "I checked everything before I went to bed. The sensors and locks were all fine..." I let him keep muttering to himself as he sat me down on the bed and bent to take off my now destroyed socks.

"I can do that..." I started softly, though one hard look from those blue eyes had my mouth zipping shut. Well, if he was that set on taking care of me, I wasn't going to be the one to stop him.

I sat huddled in on myself on the edge of my bed and watched as he turned for my dresser and pulled open my pajama drawer on the first try. He ignored my raised eyebrow and set a t-shirt that was two sizes too big for me, and had stolen from him a year ago, on the bed as well as a new pair of shorts.

"Put those on while I go call into work, okay?"

"No, you don't have to call into work. I'm fine. I just need to sleep for a little bit—" My words died at the look that took over his handsome face. His 'no nonsense I'm not budging on the matter' look. I sighed and reached for the clothes. I never won when he gave me that look.

Adriel left my door opened just a crack, and I stood slowly to my feet as he raised his cell to his ears. "Yeah, its me, I'm not coming in today—" I took the cold ruined pajamas off as quickly as my still chilled fingers would allow and pulled on the fresh ones. The urge to sigh as soft fabric brushed my raw skin was immense, and I pulled his flannel back on before slipping under my bed's blankets.

I must have dozed off at some point because I didn't hear Adriel come back in, and barely felt the gentle hand he brushed over my forehead then through my hair. "I'm going to take Raf to the bus stop... I'll only be a moment, okay?" I could hear the hesitation in his voice but managed to nod before falling back asleep. I was too exhausted to worry about sleepwalking again.

CHAPTER 11

I was in and out of sleep for most of the day. At some points I could have sworn Adriel was sitting on the bed beside me, his hand running gently through the loose curls in my hair. At other points he was sitting in a chair at my side, a book or phone in one hand, his head resting heavily in the other. Regardless, I had a feeling he didn't leave my side the entire time.

"Lark, wake up." I grumbled something unintelligible and turned away from the gentle hand trying to pull me from sleep. His low chuckle was enough to make my eyes blink open. "Come on, Angel. You've been sleeping all day. You need to eat."

"I don't want to." I mumbled and buried my face back into the pillow.

"You have to, and we need to talk." He spoke the last part much softer than the first, and it pulled at that thing beating slowly in my chest. I sighed and rolled over until I could blink up at those blue eyes.

"If I eat, will you let me sleep?"

I wasn't sure if his answering smile was confirmation or just wishful thinking on my part. I pushed my groggy body up into a sitting position and let Adriel place a bowl in my hands. I blinked down at the chicken and noodles. "You cooked?" I spooned the chicken and let it fall back into the bowl. That smile turned more into a smirk as he took a seat on the edge of the bed.

"Sure, if you count opening a can and heating it in a pot 'cooking'."

I smiled but didn't say anything as I sipped a noodle into my mouth. We were quiet for a long while as I ate my soup and Adriel played absentmindedly with the edge of the comforter. "Larkin..." He finally started sometime later. "I can't even begin to tell you how sorry I am."

I sighed against the back of the spoon I had just finished licking. "It's not your fault, Dri."

"The sensors didn't go off. I put those in. I checked the locks—and I didn't wake up when you needed me. It's completely my fault." The remorse in his voice tore at my heart and I set the half-eaten soup down on the nightstand before leaning closer.

"You can't blame yourself for technology not working, or for my subconscious going insane." I rested my hand against the intricate knot tattoo hidden beneath the sleeve of his t-shirt. Dark blue eyes glanced slowly over me, the look swimming behind them too hard to read.

"I promised you it wouldn't happen again. You could have gotten hurt. I didn't even... I thought you were just staying in your room because of—of the day before. I didn't know—I had no idea you weren't here." Adriel raised a heavy hand and ran it raggedly through his hair. "I should have known."

I had never seen him like this before. So unsure of, well, himself. Adriel was confident, so confident it turned arrogant on more than one occasion. It was one of the qualities I admired the most about him, though I would never admit that to the guy. Seeing him this upset was unsettling. I scooted closer to his large body, the one taking up more than its fair share on the edge of my bed. His lips pulled upwards at the action.

"I-I'm sorry, for yesterday." I said slowly, my fingers playing nervously with the bedsheet. "I really thought I had more time to get back home. I shouldn't have gone with them at all."

A warm palm pressed against my cheek and urged my gaze to his. "I'm the one who needs to apologize. I overacted and never should have yelled at you. I just..." Adriel paused, and my full attention went to the gentle touch of his thumb brushing along my jaw. "I didn't know where you were, and you weren't answering your phone. I just... panicked. It's no excuse though." His lips pulled into a sad smile. "I will never do that to you again."

I let my hand raise to his and pressed the warm palm into my cheek. His presence seemed to chase away the chaos of the last few days. "I'll fix it, Lark. The sensors, the locks, whatever. I'll do anything to make you feel safe."

Safe. It was something I had only let myself feel the past two years, with his family. With him. "It won't matter, not if I turn them off myself." Because that's the only way I could have left without the alarm going off. I must have deactivated them on my own. My subconscious desperately wanting out of that house.

"I'll take care of it."

I sighed and pulled away, pulled that warm hand from my cheek, and stared down at the callouses dusting his palm. "You were right. I am an immature teenager, and I need to grow up. You can't take care of everything."

"Watch me."

Those two words made my heart jump to my throat. I couldn't remember a time in my life where anyone wanted to take care of me, but I knew if I kept letting him, let him chase away all my demons, that I wouldn't be able to handle them when I was alone. "And I was wrong. You've been through more than half the people in this world could ever imagine. No immature teenager could handle that." Adriel leaned forward and nudged his forehead against mine with a small smile. "It's okay to let me take care of you. So, let me."

"I feel like I'm losing my mind." I admitted on a shaky breath, our foreheads still pressed together. "I'm too afraid to go to sleep anymore. Every time I close my eyes, I see horrible things. Now I'm terrified of waking up in the forest again, or drowning in a lake, or—or..." Adriel must have heard the hitch in my breath, or maybe noticed the words tightening in my throat, because his hand came up to cup the back of my neck and pulled me against his chest.

I wrapped my arms around his waist, buried my face into the crock of his shoulder and tried to force down the iron grip wrapped around my throat. "It'll be okay." He pressed a kiss against my hair and caged his arms tightly around me. "It will all be okay, I promise."

Maybe it was because that confidence of his was back, or the sure surety in his voice, but I believed him. I let myself believe.

Even if it had nothing to do with him. Even if I had to overcome my demons on my own, as I had for most of my life, everything would be okay.

I stayed pressed against him a while longer, my hands wrapped tightly around his waist. When Adriel was like this, sweet and caring and so unbelievably perfect, it made my head spin. Add that onto the fact that I could feel nearly every inch of his hard torso and I couldn't tell my left hand from my right. He made my thoughts turn to fog, my breathing to heavy pants, and sent this feeling I didn't quite understand coursing through me. As if, for once, I wasn't alone.

Memories of broken glass and an ear shattering scream ripped through my mind.

"How do you not hate me?" My words came out as a hoarse whisper when I finally pulled away from him. The hand he had cupped on the back of my neck allowed me to retreat only far enough to see the confused frown that pulled across his deadly beautiful face.

"What do you mean?"

"You're parents—"

"Stop."

"No, I can't. You should hate me, but all you do is worry and care."

"I said stop, Larkin."

"I killed your parents, Adriel!"

"Enough." The calm reassurance in his voice from before had turned dark, and those blue eyes blazed dangerously as the hand on the back of my neck tightened its hold. "We've discussed this already. You did not kill them. Do you understand?"

"If I hadn't called them, they never would have gone to get me, and—"

"A drunk fuck with busted headlights killed them—and almost killed you too." That hand tangled in my loose curls and pulled slightly until my head was arching up to his. And, despite the whole morbid conversation, I had to ignore the way the possessive action sent a bolt of electricity straight to the hot spot between my thighs. "Did you forget that?" Adriel's voice was quiet but his thumb was gentle as it rubbed against my hair and the side of my throat. "I almost lost you too."

"You didn't even know me."

The smile that pulled on his lips was sad. "I knew you enough to know that losing all three of you would have been my undoing."

I realized something then, as those eyes that were darker than the deepest sea gazed into mine, why he cared so much. Why, after all this time, he had ever bothered looking after me. I was replacing them in his life. Not as a parent or caregiver, but as someone who was in that car with them, and survived. To Adriel, I was the only thing left alive from that night where he lost the two people he had loved the most. That was why he cared.

I wasn't quite sure why that knowledge made me so—sad. I guess, for a while there, I had let myself believe he cared about me for me. Which was silly in retrospect. Nobody ever had before, why start now? That feeling from before, of not being so alone, it disappeared.

"Lark..." Adriel started softly, that darkness slowly draining from his eyes.

"I'm tired." I went to pull away from him, but the hand wrapped in my hair wouldn't let me get far. "Adriel, please." I was ashamed at the whisper that passed my lips, at the obvious beg for him to just—just leave. "I just want to sleep."

"I upset you." There was no question in his voice, and despite the grip he still had in my hair, I couldn't look into those soul shattering eyes. "I did not mean to." His fingers eased, if only to rub tenderly against my head through the curls.

"You are the only thing that matters to me." My gaze snapped to his at those words, and I suddenly forgot how to breathe. "You, and Raffie of course." Though that smirk suggested he was very aware his sister had been an afterthought. "The beautiful girl my parent's let into our home, sleeping in the room next to mine. So quiet, so—sad. How could I not care for you? How could I not want to do everything for you?"

Something was happening inside my chest, something with my heart. It was beating so fast I could hear it pounding in my ears, then dropping to my stomach and sending something far stronger than butterflies ricocheting throughout my body. This was so not like him. Not the stoic, over-confident, not-touchy, Adriel.

"You thought... I was beautiful?" Not quite sure why those were the words that finally slipped pass my lips, but he smiled all the same.

"Anyone with eyes can see that." He was close, and that hand of his was still wrapped in my hair, still angling my head towards his. It made very naughty, very inappropriate thoughts pop into my head. "But yes, I think you're beautiful, Angel."

I couldn't get air into my lungs. Adriel Markos calling me beautiful was one thing in its own entirety, but combined with that look in his eyes made my quickly crumbling sanity take a swan dive. I wouldn't take credit for what happened next. Oh no, mister 'you're the only thing that matters to me' with the 'come fuck me' eyes was totally one-hundred and fifty percent to blame.

I leaned forward at the same time he urged my head higher, and pressed my lips to his. Adriel's mouth took mine hungrily while his free hand circled my waist, pulling me tightly against him. His tongue brushed against my lips, once, twice, and when I was just about to open for it to slide against mine, he ripped away. Probably for the best too. There was a fire burning inside me that started in my chest and spread through every limb until it settled hot and heavy between legs.

Kissing him was dangerous.

We stared at each other, neither moving from the entanglement we had found ourselves in, though Adriel's breathing came out just as hard and fast as mine. There was something else though, something like surprise crossing those deadly beautiful features. "That wasn't supposed to happen." And like an anvil falling from the sky, my heart sank to the deepest pit in my stomach. I licked my bottom lip, and fought the sudden urge to book it for the front door.

"I-I'm sorry. I don't know what just happened." I went to pull away from him, complete and total embarrassment ripping through my chest. Fuck, this was not good. I was going to have to make a run for it. Go stay with River or Siena for a day or two until this whole fiasco died down. I can't believe I fucking kissed him—

"Hey, nuh uh." He pinned me in place with a hand wrapped around my arm, and the other tightening around my waist. "You're not running from me."

"I'm not running." I tried to sound firm, but the heat—and not the good kind—staining every part of my body was making that rather hard.

"And now you're lying too? I don't think so."

"Adriel—" His lips were suddenly pressing back against mine, that hand snaking into my hair where it had been for most of the night. I let him arch me against him, pull my chest to his as he stole all breath from my body. I was panting more than a little heavily when he pulled away again, though this time he took much, much longer to do so.

"I said that wasn't supposed to happen." His voice was a low groan against my lips, and that dark blue gaze flickered briefly to mine before glancing at my mouth again. "Not that I didn't want it to."

I sucked in a shaky breath and finally let my fingers curl into his black t-shirt like they had wanted to do all night. "You should have been more specific then." My words were breathless, though I don't think either one of us cared as I started leaning into him once again.

"I'll make sure to fix that from now." He barely finished speaking before his mouth was crushing against mine, his tongue brushing just barely at my lips before I let him in and he took over. Like in everything he does, Adriel had taken complete control.

Suddenly he was pulling us off the bed and into the air, his strong hands picking me up like I weighed close to nothing. A warning alarm was ringing in the back of my mind somewhere, screaming that this wasn't a good idea. That this was Adriel, and doing any of the things that were running rampant through my mind with him would so not end well.

But I was done with it. Done with behaving. I wanted him. I've always wanted him, and for whatever reason, in that moment, he wanted me to. A small part of me thought I deserved this though. Deserved to find a little bit of happiness and pleasure with him, even if it was just for a little while. We had both been through enough, both been alone for long enough. I would damn the consequences until the morning.

"Larkin..." I shuddered at the sound of my name passing his lips in a low sensual whisper as he caged me against the wall, then pressed his lips back to mine.

I curled my hands into the top of his jeans, my fingertips barely brushing the skin beneath his t-shirt. He didn't let me leave them there, or explore much before he was lifting me against the wall and wrapping my legs around his waist. We broke apart for a brief moment as he tore his shirt over his head, but then his lips were back on mine and my hands were tangling in his hair. He had let it grow from its short crop-cut, and I loved the feeling of the silky strands gripped between my fingers.

He pressed my back so hard against the wall, I hit it enough to leave a bruise. I didn't care. All I cared about was how his tongue kept rubbing against mine, and that fire he set racing through every inch of my being before pooling between my legs.

"Angel..." He murmured just barely against my lips before his tongue went back to mouth-fucking mine. The simple endearing nickname, that I never felt like I deserved, shook through whatever reservation I had left about what we were doing—not that I had many. I arched against him and all but moaned into his mouth as his hands slipped beneath my shirt and touched bare skin.

His hands were trailing the expanse of my sides, my back, the flat of my stomach, until just barely brushing the underside of my breasts. I let go of his hair to try and pull at my own shirt in clear indication of what I wanted him to do. Adriel didn't hesitate. His waist kept mine pinned to the wall, his lips leaving just long enough to pull the shirt over my head, before they were dominating mine once again. I gasped as his thumb brushed over the tip of my breasts, and the feeling went straight to that aching part of me.

My hands were back in his hair, my lips pressing against his desperately, pleading with him to do to my body what his tongue was doing to my mouth. His hands let me lower to the group, but stayed so close that every inch of my body rubbed against his as I did. A moan tore from my throat as that pulsing point between my thighs rubbed against him through the fabric of my pajama shorts. His hands tightened at the noise.

"Fuck, we need to stop." Adriel voice was gravel against my lips. Despite his words, his hands were tracing slow dangerous paths along my skin before dropping to the elastic on my shorts.

"I don't want to." I admitted on a breathless voice, my own fingers trailing softly from his hair to run along his strong neck before dropping to the the hard muscles in his shoulders.

He groaned, and his lips dropped to my jaw before tracing hot, wet, kisses down my throat. The soft sucking sent shivers down my spine and straight to the hottest my neediest part. I ached to rub against him, even if it was just against that hard knot in his jeans. I needed something to ease the tension.

Technically I had sex before, in my junior year of high school right before I moved in with the Markos. The boy had been cute enough, nothing like Adriel or even Tommy from tenth grade, but he was sweet and seemed to really care about me. I was eager to get the deed over with, which in retrospect should have been a clear sign that I wasn't ready. The boy, whose name was Cody, clearly had no idea what he was doing either because there was barely any foreplay and just some really bad kissing before we actually tried anything.

I definitely wasn't physically ready because it hurt so damn badly I made him stop. I was too afraid of the pain to try it again after that, even though my body didn't seem to get that memo with Adriel. Everything inside me begged to drag his jeans off and let that man do whatever he wanted. Pain and all.

"Lark..." He was back to murmuring, his calloused hands gentle as they slipped just barely under the waistband of my shorts. "You should tell me to stop."

"I don't want to." I heard myself say again as I let my fingers trail over the hard planes of his chest.

"How far are you wanting this to go?" Adriel's mouth was at my collarbone now, his tongue gently flicking out to lick my heated skin as his fingers slipped further beneath my shorts. The stayed just on my hips, but their soft touch sent the lightening inside of me into overdrive.

"As far as you can." I was panting now, my face pointed towards the ceiling as his kisses turned to gentle sucking the lower they went.

He paused at my words, his movements stilling as those dark eyes flickered to mine. "That's pretty damn far."

"Good."

His chuckle reverberated through his entire chest, and the muscles in his shoulders shook beneath my fingers as he placed another kiss just below my collarbone. "Are you saying you want to have sex with me, Larkin?" He raised his body until our faces were mere inches apart. That dark gaze stared curiously into mine, but not arrogantly or condescending, or winning in anyway. Just curious—with such a knee-rattling intention that it made me want to tear the rest of my clothes off for him.

"Yes."

Those blue eyes seemed to blaze, and his lips, that were so much softer than they looked, pulled into sly smirk that I was ashamed to admit was sexy. "Well, then," Adriel seemed to purr while his head lowered until his teeth nibbled softly on my bottom lip. "I do always hate denying you anything."

I watched his every move as the strong hands resting on my hips pressed into the skin connecting my legs and pelvis, and his fingertips pressed gently against the top of my ass. "You can't take this back when it's over." His lips brushed my ear as the sides of his large hands began easing my shorts down. Chills racked through my body.

"I know."

"You sure you want this?" He pressed again, though his hands didn't stop slowly guiding my shorts down my thighs. More than anything. Is what I really wanted to say, instead I just gave him a little nod. "I'm going to need you say it, Angel. Or I won't believe you."

"Yes, Adriel." I really hoped he didn't hear the plea in my voice. "Yes, I'm sure I want this." His chuckle was back, and it made his bare chest vibrate deliciously against my own.

"If you say so, beautiful."

Beautiful. I don't think I would ever get used to him calling me that.

It was barely two seconds later that he had my shorts on the ground and I was kicking the useless things away. Never in a million years did I ever see myself being that desperate for any man. Yet, there I was, standing naked in front of him, pressed against a wall, hot and needy and practically begging him to fuck me.

Adriel took a few steps away, and the look in his eyes as they took in every single exposed inch of my skin made heat pool between my legs. I wasn't ashamed of my body, but for once I found myself nervous of what someone else thought. Of what Adriel thought. But then that gaze was snapping to mine, and the smile pulling on his lips made every single care in the world disappear.

"You really are too damn gorgeous for your own good."

I could feel a blush stain my cheeks and flood the back of my neck. I hated that he held that power over me. A few assurances and praise from the man turned me into a nervous, giddy, middle schooler. My door was closed so the only light came from the moon shining in my windows, but it was just enough to turn the blue of his eyes into a burning ember. The way they glistened made my knees shake

"Come here." His voice had taken on that command he used whenever he wanted to be obeyed. And like always, I did.

I walked the few feet separating us and placed my hand in his outstretched one. "Adriel!" I snapped when he suddenly threw me down on the bed. He laughed, and the sent delicious shivers down my spine.

Adriel climbed over me then, his strong hands resting on either side of my head with that hard toned stomach just in reach. I raised my hand to trace the hard lines of his abs, goosebumps appearing on his skin as I did. I didn't bother hiding my own smirk as his body trembled the further down I let my touch go. He was still wearing his jeans, but the sudden urge to rip them open with my teeth was hard to resist.

"Behave." His voice was a dark growl in my ears as my fingers traced the edge of his pants. I smiled innocently.

"I'm not sure what you mean."

He rolled his eyes and leaned down to bite my bottom lip. "You really are going to be the death of me." He sighed before biting gently along my jaw. The sharp little stings sent bolts of lightning through my veins and straight to the part of me that needed him most.

I reached down for the button of his jeans but his grip caught mine before I could undo it. "Wait, Lark." He brought my hand back up until he had it pinned securely above my head. I pouted. "I'm not ready for you to do that just yet."

"But I'm ready." I whined and tried to reach for his jeans with my other hand. He grabbed that one and pinned it above my head with the other.

"No, you aren't." He chuckled again, and I was starting to get fed up with how funny he thought the situation was.

"Yes, I am—oohh..." His mouth dropped down to my left breast and sucked the pointed tip between those warm lips. My body arched against him, my hands trying to pull desperately from his hold as he licked my skin. The feeling shot electricity straight from his mouth to the wet heat pooling between my legs.

Then his teeth were suddenly sinking into the pink, hard tip, and pleasure shot through my being. "Adriel!" I gasped at the sharp sting which he quickly licked away.

"I like you gasping my name." He muttered against my skin as those soft lips trailed kisses from one breast to the other. "I can't wait to hear you scream it." Then his tongue was licking and sucking again as his free hand traveled slowly down my bare side to pause at my hip.

His teeth rolled the tip of my breast gently between them, sending little sharp tingles straight from the bud to every inch of my body. I was too focused on that to notice that his hand had trailed lower and lower until the intense feeling of his fingertips brushing over that bundle of nerves tore through me.

"Oh my God." I groaned as my back arched at that insane star-brining sensation washing over me. "A-Adriel..." I was unconsciously stammering as his fingers pushed softly between my lower lips and rubbed against the pressure that I so badly needed him to ease. My hips raised on their own, trying to rub harder against his hand.

"Stay down." He growled against my skin, his hand leaving my core to push my hips almost viciously back down to the bed.

"O-Okay, down. I promise." I would have told him anything to make him go back to rubbing the patch of nerves. The grip he had keeping my hands pinned above my head tightened, and my back arched at the pressure. Adriel didn't give me long to grumble about the hand situation before his free one was back to slipping between my wet folds and brushing lower.

I tried to keep my hips pressed down on the bed, but with the way his mouth felt against my breast, and the soft rubbing on my clit made any rational thought fly completely out the window. Then his fingers were rubbing lower until one started to push against that tight bubble of pressure practically begging him to pop it. I gasped as he started to slowly ease that finger inside me. The fire raging through my veins burned like the blue flames of his eyes as it shot straight to the apex of my thighs, where his hand was playing me like it was its job.

Cody never did anything like this when we tried to have sex, and I never let poor golden-boy Tommy even dream of getting down there. Though, God, if it felt like this all the time, I wish I had. It didn't hurt, there wasn't any pain like before, but there was a hard hot pressure that I really fucking enjoyed. Adriel's thumb rubbed softly against my throbbing bundle of nerves as that finger pushed further inside.

He paused then, a dark look taking over his gaze as he leaned away. I wanted to scream at him to go back, to keep moving that hand and just fucking kiss me, but words wouldn't come to my lips. "You're really fucking tight." His voice was dark, low, and so incredibly sexy that I let my hips raise to try and rub against his hand.

"Adriel..." I moaned into the suddenly stuffy air of the room.

"Larkin." The serious tone taking over his voice had my eyes locking with the intense blue of his. His hand was still pressed against me, his finger still halfway buried inside my body, and every ounce of my being was on fucking fire—but the made us stop anyways. "Are you a virgin?"

I felt the blood drain from my face, but it did little to staunch the fire in my veins. "Not technically." I grumbled and wiggled my body uncomfortably. Suddenly I realized how very open and exposed I was. My hands were pinned above my head, my breasts thrust into the air, cold and wet from how he left them, and a hand was practically buried in my vagina. Not necessarily the best position to have an embarrassing conversation.

"What does that mean?"

"Dri, please. Is that what you want? Do you want me to beg? Cause I'm hanging on by a thread here and I can't decide if I want to scream at you, cry, or flip us over and make you finish this."

One dark eyebrow raised, and that sly smirk pulling on his lips did little to help my sanity as his thumb went back to softly circling my clit. "I just don't want to hurt you." His voice was suddenly low and gentle as he leaned down to whisper in my ear, that finger resuming its slow path inside me.

"You won't." I reassured him and closed my eyes as my mind enveloped in that sensual fog once again. "You would never hurt me." Not intentionally, but I refused to admit that he was the one person that could hurt me, very badly in fact. The only one I ever truly cared about. I sighed in pure bliss as my legs shifted wider apart, as if that alone would ease him further inside.

"Oh, Lark." He sighed into my ear as that finger reached as far as it could go. I gasped when he pulled out and pushed slowly back in. "No, I'll never hurt you." He pressed a kiss to my lips, and then the talking was over and all those pleasure-sensations took front and center.

He kissed my cheek, my chin, and then trailed those lips along my jaw. He placed light kisses across every inch of my skin as he traveled lower and lower, pass my chest and over my stomach. I giggled as his tongue tickled the soft skin of my belly button. I felt him smile against me. "I'm going to let go of your hands. Do not move them." He ordered. I gave him an obedient nod and did as he said.

That strong hand went to my hip, though the other stayed slowly easing in and out of me. His lips kissed lower and lower, and I was suddenly more than thankful I had shaved everything that morning. I sucked in a shaky breath as his own blew against my most sensitive area. Then my world flipped completely upside down when those soft lips wrapped around that throbbing bundle of nerves and sucked

"Adriel!" I shouted into the dark room, not caring one bit there was a sleeping child barely two doors down. I went to wrap my fingers in his hair, but the second they touched the soft locks, those dark eyes snapped to mine and narrowed dangerously. I raised my hands reluctantly back over my head.

His eyes stayed locked on mine, even after I did what he wanted. That beautiful dark blue burned like lava against my skin. My breathing came out in hard pants as my hips rose to meet his finger and tongue. That strong hand of his gripped my waist and shoved me back down, his dark grumble reverberating against my core.

His tongue licked slowly between my folds, rubbing softly over those nerves before dipping just barely against the hole he was still sliding his finger into. I couldn't think straight, my lungs were at breathing compacity and my lips kept releasing foreign noises that were nowhere close to actual words.

His eyes closed then, and his mouth moaned against me. That spell his gaze had put my mind under broke and my back arched into the air. I wanted to shout in frustration when his finger slipped out of me, but only mewled in delight when his mouth quickly took over its job. "Oh my, oh my, oh my, oh my." I panted over and over as his hot tongue circled that sensitive hole before pushing slowly in.

His tongue thrust into me once, twice, and by the third time I was seeing stars, crying out his name, and begging him to never stop. Then he suddenly ripped away, and I was left cold and unsatisfied—until my eyes shot open and I saw his strong hands pushing those jeans down his corded thighs. "Adriel..."

"I'm sorry, Angel. I wanted to do this slowly and take my time, but I need to be inside of you. Now."

I couldn't find any words at that, so I stayed silent and watched with rapt fascination as his pants and boxers disappeared. For the first time since we started this, I felt a tinge of fear run down my spine. Cody was no Adriel, and he had hurt like fucking hell. He also didn't do any of what Dri just did.

"Now you look terrified." Adriel's voice was a dark lull as it caressed my skin, but he still climbed back over my body, my hands still held above my head.

"I just... I wasn't expecting..."

He chuckled and leaned down to press a gentle kiss against my lips. I didn't even care about where they had just been, or the strange taste. "I'll go slow, okay? If you want me to stop I will."

"O-okay..." And because I trusted him with every ounce of my being, I was willing to risk the pain.

His hands grabbed my waist, his own thighs pushing mine as far apart as they would go. "You're gorgeous, Larkin." He murmured against my skin, his lips brushing softly over my cheek and along my jaw. I let out a heavy breath and the tension that had built in my chest slowly faded away with it.

One hand kept a tight grip on my waist, the other went back to ensuring my hands stayed pinned down, and then he was easing slowly inside me. I sucked in a gasp as my entrance automatically had to expand far more than for his finger. "Breathe, baby." He murmured softly into my ear. "You have to keep breathing. I can't have you passing out on me." I let out the shaky breath I hadn't realized I was holding.

"T-There's so much..." I panted, my back arching up into him as he pushed a little further in.

"Do you want me to stop?"

"N-No, I just need a second." It didn't hurt like before, not really. With Dri it was just a lot of wet pressure, and I could feel my body stretching to try and fit him.

"Let me get in first, beautiful. Then I'll give you all the time you need, okay?" I could see the concern in those dark eyes, could see the hesitation as if he were ready to stop the minute I so much as winced. I nodded before I realized it.

"I want my hands." He immediately let go of his hold, and I lowered my palms until they could rest against his strong shoulders.

"Do as I say." Adriel ordered as his hand gripped tightly on my hip to keep my waist pinned to the bed. I nodded. "Wrap your arms around my neck." I did, and even let my fingers play with his soft, dark hair. "Take a deep breath in." I held the breath in my lungs even though I wasn't sure where he was going with this. "Let it all out." The second I started releasing the air he began pushing further in.

The stretching was uncomfortable, and slightly painful, but nowhere near as bad as the first time, and even though it felt like he was shoving my insides around to make room, it wasn't awful. "That's my good girl." Dri murmured into my ear, and the slight praise made pride swell inside my chest. "That's it, take all the time you need."

"No time, just move."

He pulled back enough so I could see that raised eyebrow, but I just shook my head and tried to move my hips against his. "You sure?"

"Uh huh." I nodded and gripped tightly onto his strong shoulders. There was a little pain, but not enough to override the pleasure of him being inside me.

Adriel did as I asked. He moved slowly at first, pulling barely out before pushing back in. He increased the amount with each push, until he was nearly leaving my body completely before easing back in. My back arched that time, my breath catching in my lungs as I tried not to shriek. "So beautiful." He groaned down at me as his movements picked up their pace.

I could feel that pressure from before building, could feel the pulsing fiery heat flooding my body with each thrust of his hips. He kept mine pinned down, no matter how badly I wanted to raise them. "Dri..." I panted as that pressure kept building and building. "Adriel, I feel—feel..." I moaned when one of his thumbs suddenly rubbed slow soft circles into my clit. "Don't stop." I groaned as his pace sped up, his thumb pressing harder against my pulsing bundle of nerves.

"Let go, Angel. It's okay." And with the endearment slipping pass his lips, he pinched my clit and thrust hard inside me.

"Adriel!" I screamed as fireworks erupted between my legs and behind my eyes. Stars clouded my vision, and my fingernails curled harshly into the strong skin of his shoulders.

"Fuck, Larkin!" He suddenly ripped out of me—not quickly enough though. He came all over my skin, sticky liquid covering my inner thighs and lower stomach. "Shit, fuck, I'm so sorry." I didn't understand the sudden shame in his tone as I glanced down at the mess he made.

I laughed. "You made a mess, Dri." Those blue eyes snapped to mine, and the worry there completely disappeared.

"You made me make a mess." He leaned down and pressed a lingering kiss to my lips before pulling away. I tried not to pout as he climbed off the bed and walked around to the corner of the room. I watched as he picked a towel out of my laundry basket before coming back over. I stayed where I was, completely satisfied and immobile as he started wiping the gooey mess off my skin.

Then dark thoughts filled my mind and that satisfied, pleased smile fell away. "Adriel?" His eyes flickered to mine, though his jaw tensed at the hesitation in my voice. He chucked the towel back in the hamper. "Did we just screw everything up?"

He didn't say anything for a moment, and the longer he was silent the worse that feeling in my stomach grew. Then he let out a soft sigh and climbed back over me, his fingers gently brushing along my skin. "No. No, we didn't." I wouldn't have believed him if it wasn't for that strong conviction in his tone. "Things are just going to be different now."

"Different how?" It was the 'different' part that I feared.

He shrugged but didn't seem all too concerned as his strong arm wrapped around my waist and lifted me until my head was against the bed's pillows. "Well, obviously I'm not going to go around pretending that I don't think about you like this—" He ran his hand over my bare side and down my thigh, "anymore. But it doesn't change who you are to me."

I let my fingers trace softly over the strong muscles of his shoulders, and down to his hard chest. "And who am I to you?" His eyes flashed brightly, and those lips pulled up into that smile that could make me do anything.

"The girl that makes everything better."

CHAPTER 12

A vidus

I watched the Immortal with narrowed eyes. Annoyance rippling through me. Not only was he failing at his task, he was becoming so lazy that he couldn't even sense my presence. This would not do. Too long had I been waiting for this. For her. I would not let his idleness ruin it.

Yet I sat in the pathetic excuse of an office chair quietly, watching him fold laundry, and waited. I kept track of how long it took for him to notice. Every minute would be a year he suffered in the cells beneath Accalia—the Cathedral at the center of town.

The last few days had put me in foul mood. I could feel her pain as if it were claws ripping through my chest. Could see the nightmares she suffered deep within my own mind. Every night. Every fucking night I was pulling her from demons and fire and blood. It was the nights I couldn't get into her mind fast enough that bothered me. The nightmares I couldn't quite save her from. It had to end. They had to end.

"My Lord!" The Immortal's sharp intake as he turned to put away his clothes pulled me from my thoughts. The fear slithering into his eyes appeased my mood slightly. "How long have you been there?"

"A while."

He gulped and the sound was palpable throughout the apartment's bedroom. I smiled. "You seem awfully... fearful today." I mused gently as my shadowed fingers brushed along the armrest of the office chair. Good. I wanted him afraid. He was failing in his tasks and my little human was suffering because of it.

"You look rather formidable today." He countered, though the usual casual banter I allowed between us was not there.

"Hm." I stood slowly on shadowed feet. It was not a form I enjoyed being in for long. It made me too detached from the world, from reality. The shadows sang to me, encouraged me to forget, to let go, to sleep. I was done sleeping. I was done waiting. Larkin was within my grasp for the first time in seven centuries. I would not let her be stolen again.

"Her nightmares are getting worse. They are getting real. I had to kill a daemon in them the other day, in a peaceful dream that I had given her. I worry they will send more."

"You were aware then? Of the sleepwalking?"

I paused, the darkness of my fingertips leaving shadowed mist on the glass frame dusting his desk. "I was not aware of the extent."

"Avidus—"

"You are failing at your job, half-breed." The Immortal bristled at the word, at the reminder that no matter how beautiful or dangerous his kind were, they were no match for mine.

"I'm trying. Larkin is hardheaded and she knows there is something... off about me. However," He added quickly at the sideways look I gave him, "I did save her the other day. She might like me more now."

"I saved her." I felt an anger rise within me that I had to shove down. He wasn't there, in her dream. He didn't burn the creature to ash that threatened to steal her from me. I did.

"Yes, my lord." He added quickly, as if he too could feel the caged fury within my chest. "But I did take her home. Perhaps now it will be easier."

I let out a strenuous sigh and stepped closer to the shadows of his room. I would have to go soon. I had been in this form for too long. It was becoming hard to differentiate time and darkness. "I do not want her to struggle here. I want her to feel at home." For this place was my home as well. "It's your job to protect her when I cannot."

I slipped into the darkened corner of his room, the fabric of reality already wrapping around my shoulders, curling down my arms and around my torso, ready to rip me back through realms.

"Continue disappointing me Lucious, and it will be the last thing you do."

Larkin

I blinked over at the man still asleep at my side, one of those beautifully defined arms wrapped around my waist. I couldn't remember how to breathe. I woke up only a few minutes ago, slightly groggy until my fingers curled around his soft dark hair that I had been playing with in my sleep. Last night rushed back like an avalanche and I laid frozen in Adriel's arms with wide eyes.

Oh God... What did we do? What did I do? Threw myself at him. That's what.

What was I supposed to say now? What was I supposed to do? We crossed a line I never thought in a million years we would, but now he was sound asleep, cradling me in his arms. I needed to get away. Needed space to think, to breathe. Adriel and I had slept together.

I let out a shaky breath, and tried to slowly slip out from beneath his arm. I froze when the man made a gruff noise in his sleep, but let out a relieved sigh when he simply rubbed his face against the pillow and stilled. I was a coward, and I knew it too, but I couldn't face him. I needed time to process. To figure out everything I might have just ruined.

Adriel didn't wake, didn't so much as budge again as I slipped slowly from beneath his arm and hastily threw on the pajamas from last night. Please, let there be clothes in the laundry room. I pleaded in my mind as I slipped quietly from the room. It was roughly around five in the morning, if the slowly rising light of the sun was anything to go by, and he and Raffie would have to wake up soon.

I took a quick shower and brushed my teeth before hurrying to the laundry room in a towel. I wanted to cry in relief when I saw a pair of leggings and overly large sweater—that had to be Adriel's—folded neatly on the cabinet. I threw the clothes on before locking myself in the hallway bathroom. I had to get out of the house before they woke up.

What was I supposed to say to him? "Good morning, thanks for fucking my brains out last night it was amazing."? I could just see him arching a dark eyebrow at that, see that stupid heart fluttering smirk pull on his lips. Heat suddenly stained the back of my cheeks, and I had to splash cold water on my face to force it away.

Damn, just thinking about that look had me all hot and bothered. This was so—so not good.

"Larkin?" I nearly jumped as Adriel's gruff sleep-stained voice spoke from the other side of the door. "Are you in there?"

"Y-yeah! I'm just getting ready." I let out a nervous laugh and splashed more water on my face.

He was silent for a moment before his voiced sounded again, though the gruff gravel of it did funny things to my insides. "It's five in the morning, Lark. You don't have to be at the school for a few more hours."

"Um, yeah, big project coming up. Told my group I would be there early today."

"You're lying." My heart skipped a beat at his words, and I tried not to let my breath sound shaky as it escaped my lungs. "You know how I feel about lying." But then he let out a rough sigh and pulled away from the door. "I'm going to make breakfast then wake Raffie up. I would love it if you joined us, but if your group needs you that badly I understand."

I wasn't sure how he was able to make me feel like a coward and remorseful all at once, but I hated it. Hated how easily he could see through me, read everything on my face, hear it all in my voice. Breakfast. Breakfast. I could sit through breakfast, especially since Raf is going to be there. He wouldn't try to talk about last night in front of her. I could handle that. Even if one look from those blue eyes would make my cheeks flame in embarrassment.

The thought made me pause. Did I regret last night? Is that what this feeling was? No, no, not regret but fear. The same fear I had ever since his parents died and we became close. The fear of losing him. What did he think of me now that we slept together? Was I just another one of those 'hormonal teenagers' he scoffed at? He had said I was the girl that made everything better, but that wasn't right. I made everything worse.

Thirty minutes later the three of us sat at the dining table, eating pancakes and bacon. I was too lost in my own head to care about the sugar and syrup they poured all over their food. Adriel noticed my lack of scolding though, he always noticed.

"Raf, why don't you go get your backpack?"

My eyes snapped over to the blue pair watching me with that stupid knowing look of his. I clenched my jaw and tore my gaze to the kid, silently begging her not to leave the table. She completely ignored my stare, and shot her brother a big smile before skipping off towards the stairs. "Well, I should really get to school—"

"Sit down." A tight grip on my wrist as I jumped to my feet forced my butt back into the chair. I let out a strangled sigh and slumped down low, like a scolded child.

"I don't want to talk about this." I grumbled and played absently with my fork. Adriel ignored me as he shoved more pancake into his mouth. I shifted uncomfortably in my seat. "Adriel—"

"No, Larkin. We're not going to start this." He set his fork down before leaning heavily against the back of his chair. His fingers drummed across the tabletop, those dark eyes staring holes into my own as his tongue flicked out to lick his bottom lip. My mouth went dry. "You do not get to pretend like nothing happened and ignore me for the rest of the day."

"I wasn't—"

"Do not lie to me." I crossed my arms defiantly over my chest and let out a 'huff'. He stared at me for a few long seconds, before that dark gaze seemed to soften and he leaned forward. "I was disappointed when I woke up and you weren't there, Angel." My gaze flickered to his, and something in my stomach seemed to flutter at the look in those blue eyes.

"I just... needed to think." I admitted softly as his hand reached forward and strong fingers brushed gently across my jaw. I leaned closer to him.

"About last night?"

"Yes."

His fingers stilled against my skin, but he didn't pull away. "Do you regret it?"

I paused, one second too long if the pained look flashing through those dark eyes was anything to go by. "No. No, Dri. I don't regret it." I reached up to cup that hand to my cheek when he started to pull away. He paused.

"Then what's wrong?"

"I—I don't know." I breathed softly and closed my eyes against the look in his. I clutched his palm to my cheek. "Last night was amazing, but I'm terrified of it. Of what it means. I don't want anything to change. I don't want to lose you."

"You are not going to lose me, Larkin." Adriel pulled his hand from mine to grip lightly on my chin and raise my gaze to his. My heart stopped at that blue, the blue of the darkest oceans I would gladly drown in. "I didn't let you run after the crash, and I'm not going to let you run now. If you would just realize that you mean more to me than I ever could to you, then you would never worry about losing me." I let out a shaky breath as he rested his forehead against mine, much like he had the night before.

I breathed him in, not caring one bit that he smelled like bacon and pancakes. That was probably the most endearing, heart wrenching thing he had ever told me. It only made my heart hurt more. We stayed like that for a few silent intense seconds before he pulled his forehead from mine.

"Last night doesn't have to change anything. We can pretend it never happened if that's what you want." Adriel's tone was soft and reassuring as it rolled softly over the goosebumps on my skin.

"No, that's not what I want." I admitted quietly as his fingertips once again brushed along my jaw.

"What do you want?"

"I don't want to forget."

He sighed and pulled completely away, leaving a cold sad path where his touch had once been. "Alright, we won't forget, but maybe that should be it." That dark gaze glanced towards the stairs, away from me, completely ignorant of my heart dropping to the floor at his words.

"Like a one-time thing?"

"Yeah, like a one-time thing."

I tore my gaze from him and gripped my hands tightly together in my lap. Is that what he wanted? A one-time thing? It wasn't what I wanted. I had just wanted time to think, to sort through all those raging emotions and feelings tearing through my mind and heart. I would never stop wanting Adriel. I doubt I would even know how too. But if he didn't want anymore then the line would be drawn. That would be it. A one-time thing.

And maybe—maybe that would be best if that's all we let it be. Our relationship was so complicated, getting involved with each other anymore than we already had couldn't be good. For either of us, or Raffie. I knew Adriel said I would never lose him, but that fear would always eat away at my heart. Sleeping with him just made it ten times worse.

"Okay, a one-time thing."

I was sitting in the college's café later that day, my laptop opened to some article I was supposed to be reading about the history of Realism, but my eyes were locked on my cellphone. Adriel had sent me a text ten minutes ago that I still hadn't opened. If he needed something he always called, never texted.

"Dude, what happened to you the pass few days?" River asked as he plopped down into the seat beside mine, a half-eaten granola bar in his hand.

"What?"

"The other day at Lady Jess's shop? You just took off! Without even saying bye and then you skipped school yesterday!" His hazel eyes blazed brightly as Siena took the other seat at my side.

"Yeah, what was that? You just beat feet for the hills."

I sighed and ran my hand raggedly through the loose curls of my hair. I almost completely forgot about the creepy psychic. "Sorry about that, she just freaked me out a little." I didn't want to go into details about my sexy-dream demon guy, or about how that crazy Lady Jess knew about him.

"See!" Siena suddenly chimed, her gray eyes brightening as she did. "I told you she's the real deal! But I didn't make a run for it when I found out." And just like that, I was forgiven and they both relaxed.

"Yeah, well, I'm over it now." Though I wasn't so sure. It had been a crazy few days, first with the psychic, then the sleepwalking, and then Adriel. I felt like my mind had been through more than a few spin cycles.

"Then why do you look like you ate too many bananas today?" River asked around a mouthful of granola.

"What?"

"Bananas? You've had that constipated look on your face since I showed up." Those hazel eyes flashed in amusement.

"Shove it." I grumbled and flipped my phone over, so the screen was pressed against the tabletop.

"Hey, I'm just worried about your colon—"

"Don't be disgusting, River." Siena snapped and those bright gray eyes narrowed dangerously.

"You guys have no sense of humor. Seriously though, Larkin. You okay?" The amused light in River's eyes faded some as he finished his snack and wiped the crumbs from his hand.

Siena glanced over at his question, and that creepy gaze scanned my face like she was seeing me for the first time. "Oh, you do look down. What's wrong?"

"Nothing's wrong." I grumbled and stabbed my fork down into the salad beside that damned laptop. Suffer my wrath, leafy greens.

"Right, okay." She dragged out sarcastically before taking out her own computer and placing it on the table beside mine.

"Oo, if it's not about the psychic, is it about that yummy foster brother of yours?" River glanced over my screen like I had a picture of Adriel taped there.

"They're not my foster family anymore." No, I just ate their food, lived in their house, slept with the oldest one, and mooched off them in every possible way. I pushed my salad away. I didn't have an appetite.

"So, it is about him!"

I sent the overly excited brunette a dark glare. "No, it's not."

"Then why did you get all upset when I brought him up?"

"Leave her alone, River. She's probably just not in the mood for your crazy psycho-analysis today." Siena sighed as she reached over for his unopened water bottle. Those gray eyes stared him down as she undid the cap, brought the bottle to her lips, and drank from it. He glared at his best friend in bewildered disgust, his mouth dropping open. I couldn't help the snicker that pass my lips. I really did like Siena. She was spunky.

"Bitch." The skinny boy hissed as he sat back and crossed his sweater-covered arms over his thin chest. "I was just trying to help. Obviously, something happened between them otherwise she wouldn't be sitting her all mopey."

"River—"

"No, it's okay, but really everything is fine. I'm just dreading all the projects we have coming up." Which wasn't a complete lie. I had two art pieces to create, a literature analysis to write, and I had to start preparing for the big essay we had in that Folklore class. Though, those all seemed more like a reprieve from what my life was quickly turning into. A giant fucking mess.

River didn't look like he believed me, but Siena's gray eyes were all understanding. "I'll see you guys later." I said with a small smile as I packed up my laptop and rose to my feet. "I have to get to class." I threw my bag over my shoulder and waved, though I didn't bother looking back.

It wasn't until I exited the little café with my phone clenched in a death grip in my hand that I glanced down at the screen. Adriel's name flashed against the little text icon. I let out a deep breath and clicked the message open. I'm getting pizza for dinner. I couldn't help the laugh that tore from my lips, and I shook my head as I put my phone in my pocket. I didn't know what I was expecting, but it definitely wasn't that.

Chapter 13

"You look exceptionally miserable today." River announced to the entire cafe as he plopped down in the seat beside mine. I shot him a dark glare. He really did have such a way with words. "Have a nice little chat with the yummy 'not-brother'?"

"If you could call it that." I grumbled and kicked my feet up on the empty chair across from me. It was early Thursday morning, and despite a tense "have a good day" before he left, Adriel and I were fine. We even spent the rest of Wednesday afternoon together and finished off the pizza.

"Spill that tea, my dear." River sighed dramatically and sipped on his frozen coffee.

"There is no 'tea'." I air quoted the word with my fingers like he usually did. "We both agreed it was best if what happened stayed a one-time thing."

"Oof. Well, that's no freaking fun. How am I supposed to live vicariously through you if you refuse to fuck the guy?"

I rolled my eyes but ate my bagel without snapping any rude comments. "It was his idea, and it's for the best. Things would just get too complicated if we kept sleeping together." No matter how badly I wanted to.

"Whatever, you two are going to bump uglies again, bet you all the money in my bank account."

"You two are still on this?" Siena sighed as she sat down at my other side. She wore her usual dark attire, except her usual purple lips were a deep, dark blue that reminded me a little too much of a certain person's eyes. River wore dark gray shorts, and a floral blue button down that didn't really go together but he somehow managed to make it work. I gave Siena a small smile as she slapped her microwave to-go breakfast down on the table.

"He is." I grumbled and nodded over to the skinny brunette as he slurped on his drink.

She rolled her eyes. "He's hornier than I am. And that's saying something." I let out a laugh, but River just shot her a look.

"Not all of us can walk up to random guys and get fucked—literally."

"Grow a vagina and it's easy."

"You make it sound like I haven't tried." That actually got a laugh out of Siena, which was apparently pretty rare. I smiled and relaxed back in my seat. I enjoyed how they nagged each other.

They tossed various insults back and forth for the next few minutes until River glanced down at his Apple Watch. Those hazel eyes suddenly became alive. "It's Thursday!" He sang happily.

"I know, that Folklore professor is already assigning papers next week." I groaned, and completely didn't understand the enthusiasm in his eyes. We had barely began discussing the 'mythical' beginnings of Deshua, and the teach' already wanted us to write a paper.

"Oh, no. That's not why I'm enthused at all." His large smile disappeared into a scowl as he brought his way too tiny backpack up on the table. "Ever heard of Thirsty Thursdays, Larkin?" River asked on a dramatic, elated sigh. Those bright hazel eyes of his staring off into some lust-filled distance.

"Uh, sure. A bunch of kids from high school used to throw parties on Thursdays."

I was never much of a partier—I was never much of anything really. Ever since I turned sixteen all my free time was spent working various part-time jobs so I could afford to live on my own when I became legal. That all changed when the Markos took me in. I still worked a part-time job on the weekends, but they insisted I should be a kid for my last two years of high school. I was worried about not making enough money, until then their parents admitted they were actually putting some away for me for college. No one ever cared liked that.

Then when they died and Adriel made me stay, my whole perspective changed. He didn't want me working while I was in school at all, which was why I didn't try to get one here. Dri was convinced he made enough to keep the three of us comfortable, and even if he couldn't, his parents left them with a shit ton of money.

"Have you ever been to a college Thursday party?" River's voice pulled me from my thoughts, and I flicked my gaze towards his.

"No."

"Honey, they are awesome. All the drinking, smoking, loose inhibitions. It's a great, great time." He sighed dreamily and Siena rolled her eyes.

"She might not like parties, skank." The goth spat at her best friend. That was something I noticed pretty quickly with these two. They might have been 'best friends' but they were the meanest people to each other. Even meaner than I was to Dri! And I call that man all kinds of things.

"Why are you calling me the skank?" He raised a pale brown and leaned forward against the table. "I'm not the one who fucked some rando' last night."

My eyes widened and I looked over at Siena whose cheeks had flushed a bright pink. "Well, look at you miss anti-social." I teased and nudged her softly in the shoulder, so she knew I was joking.

"He wasn't completely random." She spoke calmly enough, but her creepy, bright gray eyes sent River a narrowed glare. "We've been talking for a while. And don't act like you aren't king of one-night stands." She took her spoon out of her on-the-go oatmeal and jabbed it at her friend.

"Never said I wasn't." He stuck his tongue out before leaning back causally in his seat with a smug smile. Men. No matter their sexual orientation, they were all the same.

"Pig." Siena echoed my thoughts with a look of pure disgust.

"Anyway..." River rolled his hazel eyes before turning that bright smile back on me. "What do you say, Lark? It's the first real week of school, there's for sure going to be dozens of parties."

"In the dorms?"

"Only if you're a grungy-freshmen." He laughed, like that was the funniest joke in the world.

"We are freshmen, moron." Siena snapped and reached up to chuck her used napkin at River's face. He dodged it effortlessly.

"Yes, but we're not grungy, Si. That's the difference. I got the hook-up babe, don't you worry." He nodded excitedly, his eyes flashing like we shared some deep secret. "All the upper classmen party in the apartments off campus. That's where we're headed tonight!"

I let a laugh escape and shook my head as he passed his beaming smile between Siena and I. "Thanks for the offer, but I have to be home by four today to look after Raffie." Despite what happened between us, I wasn't going to risk Dri's wrath at being late again. No way.

"That's the great thing about college parties, Lark!" His words were loud enough that the students sitting a few tables over looked at us curiously. "They're at night! His 'hot-ness' will be home in time to watch her. Hell, invite him along! I'd love to get that man all drunk and loose, as much as you would. If you know what I mean." He wiggled his eyebrows suggestively.

I let out a small sigh. "Adriel never parties. I've never seen him drink either. Besides, even if he did want to go, we wouldn't have anyone to watch Raf. Sorry." I gave him a one-shoulder shrug, as a pout slowly fell over his pale lips.

"Fine, but you're still going to try to go, right?" The hopeful look that overtook his boyish, adorable features really did pull at my heart. I felt bad for saying no.

"River—"

"Awe, come on! You can get dressed up all cute, come over to mine and Si's apartment and we can all get drunk together, then head to the parties!"

I let my gaze fall away and ran my fingers through the long, loose curls tangling my hair. "I'll... talk to Adriel about it." I wasn't so sure he would be thrilled about me spending a night with a bunch of drunk college kids.

"Yay! Don't worry about bringing any alcohol, I have loads." He clapped once excitedly, and even Siena sent me a small smile.

I tried to shove down the unease in my chest as River kept rambling on. The last time I ever went to a party I ended up being so uncomfortable I called the Markos. No matter what Adriel said, they died because I did that. I might not have killed them, but I still was the reason it happened. I never wanted to go to a party again. But the campus was close enough to our house to walk, and I wouldn't call Adriel to come get me.

No matter what.

"A party..." Dri rolled the words around his tongue uncomfortably, like he was tasting them and decided he didn't like their flavor.

"Yeah, River—the guy that was here last week—invited me." More like persisted until I conceded, but I didn't think that would have sat well with Adriel.

"Hm." Was all the blue-eyed, insanely good in bed, man muttered as he turned his attention back to the dishes in the sink. I quietly wiped the clean ones dry and put them away. "And you want to go?" He asked a moment later, his gaze focused on the soapy water. I shrugged and wiped down another plate.

"It's part of the college experience, right? And I did tell you I would try."

He sighed and pulled the plug out of the drain when the last dish was washed. "I wanted you to try and enjoy the town. Not get fucking trashed around a bunch of people you don't know." There was a hard bite to his tone I hadn't quite heard before. The last thing I wanted to do was upset him, even if I loved the way his muscles tensed and strained against the fabric of his t-shirt. Muscles I had my fingers curled into two days before.

"Well, I know Siena and River. And I only have one class tomorrow at noon so it's not like I'll sleep through it..."

"Whatever, Lark." Even though he spoke low, that hard snap in his tone cut through my chest like ice. "Do whatever you want." I sighed and stepped forward to place a soft hand on his arm. I didn't want to make him upset, no matter how much his muscles bulged. If he didn't want me to go than I wouldn't.

"Dri—"

"It's not like you need my permission." He snapped and pulled away, those dark blue eyes blazing. "You're an adult, and I'm not in fucking charge of you." Adriel brushed past me with his jaw grit tightly shut and all-but stormed from the kitchen.

"Adriel!" I called after him, my mouth hanging open. He didn't stop, and I was too shocked to go after him. What the fuck was that? Guilt suddenly weighed heavily on my shoulders. All I did was tell him about some stupid party! He didn't have to get all pissed off! I wasn't even sure if I was going to go!

Was this a fucking jealousy thing?! He was the one that suggested the whole "one-time" thing anyway! And it's not like I was going out to fuck a bunch of random guys! That guilt quickly fell away to rage. Fine. If he wants to get pissy over something stupid like that than fuck him—metaphorically speaking. No, he wasn't in charge of me, and I sure as hell didn't need his fucking permission.

He wants to be angry? I'll give him a reason to be.

It was ten o'clock by the time River, Siena, and I were all walking sloppily to the upper classmen apartments behind campus. I didn't drink, like ever, so the two Vodka and Crans' I had at their apartment were making me feel more than a little good. I had sat giggling on the couch as they threw back four or five shots. I stopped counting after a while. For someone as skinny as River, he sure could hold his alcohol. Despite the fact we were all stumbling by party-time.

"And this is Luke Acton's place. He's a junior who is far too yummy for words." River announced as he swayed against me before that grip on my arm tightened and he pulled us towards the bustling front door. Luke? I knew that name. Creepy boy Luke?

"Creepy boy Luke?" I asked out loud, my feet stumbling slightly as River dragged us up the apartment's stone steps. College kids were streaming in and out of the door, all laughing and cheering and drinking deeply from plastic water bottles. Though the liquid inside them definitely was not water.

"What did you say?" Siena shouted over the pounding music when we were finally able to push our way into the way too crowded living room. The apartment was pretty big, with a living room and kitchen that took up the entire first floor.

"I said," I raised my voice, like that would help any. The music was too loud and there were way too many people. "Creep boy Luke?!"

Siena just scrunched her face up but just waved me off. My mind was too gone to really care, and I just turned my attention to the thin boy gripping my arm. "Stay close, Lark!" River shouted over the music as he pulled us further through the crowd. "These things can get crazy!" As if to prove his point, there was suddenly the loud sound of glass breaking as someone threw a heavy object at the living room window.

This was nothing like that cheerleader's party in high school, and I honestly wasn't too pleased. There was no room to dance, you couldn't hear anyone, and I swear to whatever the hell was out there, that if that guy behind me touched my ass one more time I was going to deck him in his ugly little nose. Not that I knew if his nose was ugly or not. I couldn't see anything, and my mind wasn't all that present. Though my complete discomfort was slowly sobering me up.

"Having fun?!" River shouted over the noise, a beaming smile pulling across his pale lips.

"Oh, so much!" I replied sarcastically, but I knew he was too drunk to notice.

A tug on the bag of my short skirt caught my attention, and I wheeled around ready to deck whoever had the audacity to tug on my clothes, when I came face to face with a sheepish Siena. "I really have to use the bathroom!" She shouted over the music, an apologetic smile on her face. "Come with me?!"

"Of course!" Anything to get out of that mess. We told River where we were going, and he just shot us a thumbs-up before getting back to gyrating on a random guy who had grabbed his hips. Siena grabbed a hold of my hand, tightly might I add, and started dragging us through the crowed until we reached the stairs for the second floor.

There actually weren't too many people up there, I guess all the fun was in the mash pit below. Siena must have been here before because she expertly weaved us down the hallway to the last door on the right and barged in. Thankfully there was no one in there. She turned to me again, that sheepish smile pulling on her lips, which were painted a bright neon green instead of their usual purple. I imagined it was to match the sudden green streak in her hair and the black and green maxi-dress clutched desperately tight to her body. She looked good. For a goth.

"Thanks for coming with me, but I get a little pee-shy. Do you mind waiting out here?" I could tell she was sorry by the look on her face, but I sure as hell didn't mind. Not like I wanted to watch the girl pee anyway.

"Sure, Si. No worries." I backed out into the hall and closed the door behind me. There was a windowsill to my right which I leaned heavily against and fanned my heated skin. I had worn a short skirt and crop top, thinking that would be appropriate for a party. I guess it didn't really matter what you wore to one of these things. You were going to sweat regardless.

The music and noises of the crowd weren't too loud up here, and I was able to hear a rustling at the end of the hall. Then a loud 'thump' reached my ears. I stood away from the windowsill as a different door opened. My back went ramrod straight as that familiar flash of blond hair crossed my vision. Luke turned towards the stairs as he closed the door behind him, his jacket-covered sleeve reaching up to wipe at his mouth. He had just reached the railing above the steps, when his gaze flickered to mine. My heart dropped to the ground at my feet.

His eyes were red.

CHAPTER 14

"Larkin?" Luke sounded surprised as I shook that disturbing image from my head.

"Luke..." I blinked as the red I thought I'd seen disappeared. The shocked look on his handsome face quickly fell away to that signature charming smile.

"I'm surprised to see you here, but I'm glad came!" He left the stairs to walk towards me, his now-brown eyes shining happily in the darkened hallway. I sucked in a shaky breath as the sound of a toilet flushing reached my ears. I just imagined the red eyes. I've been drinking, I'm not comfortable here, and I've been stressing about those freaks at that ice cream shop all week. Luke's eyes were normal—normal. But that didn't change the creep-a-zoid vibe I got from the guy.

"Uh-uh, yeah. My friends wanted to go partying since it's the first official week and yeah..." I let my voice trail off as I listened intently to Siena washing her hands. Let's go, girl. I got to get the hell out of here.

"Oh? You made friends already? That's great! See, this place isn't so bad!" Luke was beaming down at me, and I couldn't tell if he had been drinking or not. He seemed completely sober, not that I was one to really be judging or anything. "Hey, why don't you come hang out with me and some of my friends—"

Siena finally decided to open the door then, her dazed gray eyes widening as they landed on handsome, creepy guy. "Luke Acton..."

Those brown eyes snapped to her and he sent that pleasant, perfect-toothed, smile her way. "Yeah, but you can just call me Luke. What's your name?"

"Siena." I answered before she had the chance and wrapped my hand around her wrist in case we needed to make a hasty retreat. "Thank for the invite, Luke." I continued as I eased around his nicely toned body and pulled her carefully with me. "But we should really be getting back to our other friend downstairs."

His smile didn't falter as we headed for the steps, though his brown eyes watched my every move. "No worries, maybe some other time." Luke followed us to the stairs, and my dazed mind noticed half-way to the first floor how he purposely kept his body between that door he came out of and us.

He followed us all the way downstairs and half-way through the crowd. I was convinced Luke planned on being our night-long stalker, so I turned around to snap something rude, but he wasn't there. I blinked at the bodies surrounding Siena and myself. I could have sworn he had been right there.

"Where's River?" She shouted over the music.

"No idea! But, I'm ready to go home! Let's find him!"

She tugged on my hand as I turned to push through the crowd, her bright gray eyes widening. "Oh, he's not going to want to leave until the cops show! If you want to go, I'll stay with him and make sure he doesn't get into too much trouble!"

I didn't want to leave either of them, especially after witnessing all the alcohol they both drank. But I sure as hell didn't want to stay if cops were going to be showing up. I already completed my mission anyways—completely, and totally pissing Adriel off. He had been leaning against the entryway to the living room when I left, his blue eyes bright with fury, but the sardonic smile sitting on his lips was what scared me the most.

An angry, jaw clenched Adriel I was used to. Not one who was so beyond pissed that he was smiling. He had seen what I was wearing too, and that smile fell slightly—just slightly, before he rolled his eyes. "Nice look, Larkin. Have a good night." The icy edge to his tone made my back stiffen, but I kept my mouth shut as I walked out the door. I didn't turn back to look at him either.

Point 1 for Lark.

I had enough adventure for one night though. "Alright, Si. I'll help you find him first." We spent about ten minutes hunting through the massive, sweaty crowd.

I never saw Luke again, though I wasn't sure if that was a good thing. I almost wished we hadn't found River when we finally did. The guy was pressed against the back wall of the party and basically sucking the tongue out of that rando' from earlier. Well, at least one of us was getting some.

"Are you sure you're alright?" I asked Siena as she took up camp at the kitchen counter, right next to her best friend and the guy whose face he was practically eating. She nodded, those gray eyes focusing slightly more than before.

"Yeah, I'm good. You alright to walk home?"

"Always am." I shot her a thumbs-up, and a quick goodbye before heading back through the crowd. I would just text them in the morning to make sure they got home okay. And I'm sure the 'king of one-night-stands' is going to want to talk all about his little adventure.

I wasn't sure if it was the mistaken red-eyed scare, or maybe just the lack of alcohol for the past hour and the hot, sticky air, but my mind seemed to be sobering up. I shoved through the crowd, the front door my only objective in mind. I got outside easily enough, although someone did reach under my skirt and grabbed my ass. I spun around and sent my fist sailing through the air in the direction of the perv. I didn't notice who I hit, but the throbbing pain in my hand I tried to shake out as I walked down the street let me know I definitely nailed someone.

The upper classmen apartments were at the back of campus, with roads leading in every which direction. I focused on the familiar tall buildings of the school and headed in that direction. If I could get to the middle of campus, I could get home. I had my cellphone in the waist band of my skirt, but I absolutely refused to call Adriel.

First of all, I was still beyond pissed at him, and I didn't want to deal with that smug attitude when he found out I didn't have fun at all. And secondly—well, secondly, I was terrified of what could happen to him. Just because they were in college, didn't make them smart, and I knew a handful of those people back there would be driving. All it took was one drunk driver and busted headlights to change lives forever. Maybe it was just the party-setting tying the two events together for me, but I would never endanger him like that, or anyone. Never again.

I had been walking for a while when I realized something wasn't quite right. Those weren't the campus buildings surrounding me, it was the center of town. I paused on a dimly lit street, the only light coming from a few streetlamps hanging sparsely through the area. Town Square? I could have sworn this was campus.

Damn it. I groaned out loud as I dragged my heavy, achy feet towards the marble cathedral in the distance. Town center was twice as far from the house as campus. I had a lot more fucking walking ahead of me. Oh well, calf muscles for days, right? Besides, the cool night air and exercise would help clear my head more.

I had been walking the desolate sidewalk of the square, passing by closed, dark shops, when I felt an all too familiar feeling. Someone was watching me. I wrapped my arms tightly around myself, my hands gripping at my upper arms. It was the end of August, and I hadn't worn a jacket. Though, walking around in just a short skirt and crop-top didn't feel like the best idea anymore.

Just hurry up, stupid. I chided myself and quickened my pace. Besides, what real harm could come that I haven't faced before? It's Deshua freaking Oregon. A town in the middle of nowhere, with people who have lived here their whole lives and will probably never leave. I grew up in every area of California you could imagine. I could handle kicking a few pervs ass. I've done it plenty before. But I didn't hear any footsteps as I kept walking. No other sound of someone else's presence reached my ears as I made a beeline for the street that would lead me to our subdivision.

But I could still feel eyes watching every step I took.

The streetlight above me flickered, and then sputtered out. My breath hitched in my chest as darkness shrouded the sidewalk. My gruesome nightmare suddenly flashed across my mind. And I remembered the square filled with bloody thirsty, beautiful demons with red eyes chasing me up the cathedral's steps. Completely, totally, sober now I nearly started jogging through town. This was the absolute last place I wanted to be.

I knew this night was going to be shit. I knew the minute River asked me to go. But I just had to be a shit-eating brat and shove it up Adriel's ass. I didn't even know why the guy was so fucking irritated!

Turning my thoughts onto that infuriating man eased the fear raging through me, and I tried to keep the anger running hot as I hurried down the dark street. The fury didn't work. As I turned away from the town's center and onto the street that would lead ours, the streetlamps behind me started to flicker off. That's when I heard the footsteps, and the deep rolling male laughter following them. I was wrong, there wasn't just one person watching me. There were many.

Breaking off all false pretenses of walking I burst into a sprint, not giving one shit about the skirt riding up my legs or the Converses on my feet. The laughter increased as I ran, and I had a brief flashback of the group sitting in the ice cream shop. The group with the red eyes. That laugh sounded like theirs. It carried over the houses and sidewalk in an effortless, intoxicating allure. If I wasn't so scared, I would have been tempted to stop and listen for an eternity. I ran faster.

"Little girl!" A light, tumbling sound of a guy's voice reached my ears. "Don't run! I want to have some fun!" The voice sounded young, lacking years of rasp and gruff tones that came with age. It did absolutely nothing to slow me down. That laughter danced around my skull.

"She's fast!" Another voice hollered with laughter as I booked it down the street.

The fear raging through my veins only seemed to pump energy through my body and I didn't stop—until my street came into view. I stumbled. I was being followed, but a bunch of fucking creeps. Did I really want them to know where I lived? I slowed until my feet came to a complete stop just a few streets shy of Eyre Drive. No, I couldn't lead them right there. Right to Raffie, and Dri.

"Fuck!" I shouted into the air and ripped my hand almost viciously through my long curly hair. That laughter echoed around me. What the fuck was I going to do? A flash of silver caught my attention, and my gaze snapped done to a broken, jagged pipe hanging out of someone's trash can on the side of the street.

First things first. I ripped the pipe out of the trash can and held it tightly in my right hand. It was about two feet long and would sure hurt a fucking lot if you got hit by it. I didn't want to face those guys, but I wasn't quite sure what else to do. Even if I took the time to call Adriel, he wouldn't get there fast enough. And no matter how strong he was, there was no way he could stand up against three, if not four, guys.

"Awe, little girl!" That first voice sang as another streetlight flickered off. Alright, now I knew they were doing that somehow. No way in hell all of the town's lights were being janky when I needed them the most. My heart pounded viciously in my chest. "You did stop to play!" Their footsteps grew closer, but it was the sound about them that had anger slowly pushing the fear away.

They were walking. There was no sound of running, or even jogging, just simple walking. Like they had all the time in the world—like they could catch me no matter how fast I ran. Now that pissed me off.

"Listen, fellas." I snapped as the light to my left flickered and turned off. "I might be cute, and pretty, but I played softball in high school and I got one hell of a swing." I swung the pipe in emphasis and was pleased at the loud 'swoosh' sound it made as it sliced through the air.

Their laughter echoed around the empty street. "Fiery!" A completely new voice cheered as they grew closer. "I like the fiery ones." I couldn't see any of them, not in the utter darkness surrounding me, but I knew how many there were, and where every single one stood. Their presence was like four dark, pulsing, shadows that pushed against my vision.

The streetlights on the opposite end from where I was running started to sputter and die. One by one they flickered off until only one stayed alight—the one directly above me. I braced myself against a large, wooden, private fence, ready to use it as momentum if I had to. All I had to do was distract them long enough to run a few streets down then cut through a few yards until I reached ours. It wasn't a great plan, but it was the only one I had.

Then they were in front of me. Four, dark shadows standing directly beneath the only lit streetlamp. I forced down a terrified gulp of fear. "What the fuck do you want?" It was a stupid question. What else would four, creepy as fuck, people with the ability to control the town's lights want?

One of them laughed, and the sound was so pleasant it almost cocooned around me, urging to put down the pipe clutched in a death grip in my hands. "We just want to play a bit, that's all."

"Easy Adam." Another guy chimed in, his voice was deeper than the others. "You know he doesn't like us playing with the food."

I so did not hear that right.

"Oh, lay off, Pete." Adam sighed and stepped closer. "What 'boss-man' doesn't know won't hurt him." The way he said boss came out way too sarcastically to be genuine.

The four of them spread out in a slow, large arc, and stepped carefully closer. I realized a little too late that they were caging me against the fence. Even if I was able to hit the one closet to me and take off running, the others would cover the distance in no time. I could try to hop the fence behind me, but I was starting to have a sick feeling I really wasn't going to get out of this.

They stepped closer until the light of the lamp was no longer covering them in shadows and I could see their faces. Ice ran through my veins like a deadly avalanche. It was the group from the ice cream shop, all four of them. And just like then, their eyes were glowing a bright, ruby red.

"Y-You're the freaks with the contacts..." The words slipped past my lips on their own accord, and my grip loosened on the pipe in surprise.

"Oh? You remember us? How perfect." One of them purred, like straight up purred, the word perfect.

What the actual fuck?

"Though 'freaks' is a little harsh, and they're not contacts." The one on my right spoke, his eyes flashing in response. "They're all-natural." I was starting to believe him.

God, maybe I was a lot more drunk than I thought and had passed out at the party. This could all be a delirious, alcohol in-duced dream. I had thought I'd seen Luke's eyes red too, before the liquor started to wear off. It was a weak hope, especially when that encompassing arc of theirs closed slowly in around me.

"I will beat the fuck out of you with this." I tightened my fingers around the heavy metal once again and raised it in emphasis.

Red eyes flashed in amusement. "I don't doubt that, but I'm sure we can all play nice. There's no need for violence. We just want to have some fun."

"I really don't think I'm going to enjoy your 'fun'." I dealt with enough perverts in California to know that you never crack under pressure. No matter how much fear and anxiety were running through you. Never let them know your completely shit-eating terrified.

They laughed again, and I had to physically shake off the temptation to drop the pipe and just listen. "You never know, you might actually enjoy it." Adam spoke again and his pale hand reached out for my pipe. "Why don't you hand that over to me, and we can show you how much fun you can have." His voice had turned soft like silk and as sweet as candy. The sound of it seemed to pass through my ears and wrap around my mind in a tempting commanding way.

I shook it viciously away and raised the pipe in the air. The look that passed his red eyes could have been disbelief, but when he glanced over at his friends it was more confused than anything. "You try." I didn't know what that meant, but then another one was trying to reach for my pipe. I swung it as his hands.

"Whoa, she's got a bite too." He laughed, though the look in that blood-colored gaze was not amused.

"Leave me alone."

"The compulsion's not working, just taking the fucking thing and get this over with." That Pete guy snapped, and his red eyes flashed in the sole light of the one streetlamp. "We've been at this for too long already."

Adam sighed and adjusted the open lapels of his suit jacket. Yeah, the fuck was wearing a suit. "Alright, fine. You're right. I'm getting fucking hungry anyway—" He had taken a step forward as he spoke, his hand outstretched for the pipe when he stopped dead in his tracks. Ruby red eyes widening as they locked on something behind me. But there was only wood fence pressed against my back.

"No." His mouth dropped open, mimicking the other three's perfectly. "No, it can't be..." The Adam guy hissed, like straight up cat hissed and stepped unsteadily away. I blinked, and they were gone. All four of them.

Just like that.

I clenched the pipe as possibly tight as I could and forced my-self to step away from the fence and look behind me. Whatever they had seen there had made them so terrified their already pale faces had turned ghostly white. I wasn't sure what I was expecting to see, but I was ready to take off running as fast as I could when I did. My gaze landed on simple wooden fence slats. I frowned. The only other thing there was my shadow, and that sure as hell wouldn't scare anyone.

The streetlight slowly flickered back on as I stood there dumbfounded. Then realization dawned on me and I took off down the street as fast as I could. Home. That's the only place I wanted to be. And I doubted I would ever leave again.

CHAPTER 15

I still ran a street pass mine and cut through some random people's backyards just in case those red-eyed freaks were still lurking around. I burst through the back door of the manor and slammed the wood shut so loudly I was sure I woke even the ghosts in the attic. The ghosts I didn't believe in. I didn't know what I believed anymore. I made sure the deadbolt was locked before running to the front door and testing that one.

"Larkin?"

I whirled around to see a half-asleep Adriel standing in the entry way of the living room. He was yawning and rubbing at one of his dark blue eyes, still wearing the same clothes as when I left. It had to be two in the morning, easily, and the thought that he must have tried to stay awake for me flashed through my mind. I would feel guilty about that later, but right then I was so happy to see him I nearly cried.

I raced across the space between us and threw my arms tightly around his neck. "Whoa..." He rasped sleepily as my weight crashed into him and forced that toned body to stumble back. "Lark, what's wrong?" I couldn't answer him. I was terrified that if I tried to speak the barriers I had built in my eyes would break and I would start balling like a baby. So, I just squeezed my arms tighter around him and tried not to shake.

"Hey. Hey, it's okay." I didn't realize I was trembling until his strong hands were running gently over my back and cradling me against him. "I'm right here, Angel." That officially broke the dam, and I couldn't force down the sob that racked through my body. But he didn't pull away and force me to tell him what happened. He just held my body tightly against his and rubbed those strong hands down my hair and over my back, whispering sweet words and reassurances the entire time.

I nearly protested when he eventually started to pull away, but I had been attached to him like a parasite longer than I realized. "Come on." He took my hand and led me through the dining room and into the kitchen. I let him pull out a bar stool and gestured to sit. "Did someone hurt you?" Dri asked softly a moment later as he wet a washcloth and walked back over.

I tried to sniff the rest of the tears away and shook my head. Still too afraid to talk. "You know you just have to tell me who they are, and I'll take care of it." My eyes flickered to his, and the complete seriousness there tore at my heart.

"No, Dri. No one hurt me." Not for lack of trying though. His stony expression didn't ease, but his touch was gentle as I let him wipe the tears and ruined make-up from my cheeks.

"Tell me later?" He asked softly, and I nodded even though I felt like such a complete and total dick. I knew he was going to be worried and concerned until I told him what happened, but how could I explain something that I didn't even know?

"Were you waiting up for me?" I asked softly, my voice raspy from crying, as he went back to the sink to rinse the cloth out.

"Of course." Those two simple words made my chest clench and had the guilt weighing on my shoulders feel like icy boulders.

"You have to go to work in a few hours."

He shrugged and came back over to keep wiping gently at my face. "I wanted to apologize for being such a fucking ass earlier." My eyes widened at his words, and the small smile pulling on his lips eased the guilt raging through me. "I shouldn't have gotten so upset, I'm sorry."

"Why did you?"

Those dark blue eyes flickered away as he tossed the wet, make-up stained cloth into the sink. "I just... I know what college parties are like. I was worried about you." He was standing in front of me, his strong body tense as I reached for his strong hand. That gaze snapped back to mine as I thread my fingers comfortingly through his.

"Thank you." He smiled and squeezed my hand. "Dri...?" I started softly as he went to pull his hand away. He paused, one dark eyebrow raising in question as a small hint of red began to stain my cheeks. "Does that one-time thing count for kissing too?" I don't know what made me ask that, especially after the complete mind-fuck I went through the past two days over what we did. But sitting in that kitchen with his strong hands holding and taking care of me, made my lips crave his more than anything.

His mouth pulled up at the corner, and those dark blue eyes flashed against the ceiling light hanging above. "Not if you don't want it to." I didn't say anything as he leaned down, his entrapping gaze focused on mine. My bodies reaction when his lips pressed against my own was automatic. My fingers curled into the front of his shirt, my eyes closed, and I arched up into his strong chest like a freaking cat.

It wasn't a sensual kiss. Well, it didn't start off as one at least. But then his tongue was gently pressing between my lips and I was opening them without hesitation. I didn't want sex right then, especially with all that fear and terror running through me, but his kiss was so intoxicating it turned everything else numb. His tongue rubbed against mine, his fingers wrapping softly in the curly mess of my hair as I moaned into him.

Adriel pulled away all too soon. Though, in retrospect, it was probably for the best. I wasn't in the right state of mind, and it would only fuck with my head even more the next day. "It's really late." He breathed against my lips, his dark eyes flickering from my mouth to my gaze. "We should get you to bed." I chocked down a sound of protest as he pulled away, his fingers slipping from my hair to wrap back around my hand.

He pulled me gingerly to my feet, with a small smoldering smile on his lips as he nudged us towards the dining room. I followed closely behind him as he led me from the kitchen and up the stairs, my hand still wrapped tightly around his. I was too afraid of what would happen if I let him get too far away.

Even though he's already seen, and explored pretty thoroughly, every inch of my body, he waited politely in the hallway as I changed into a pair of shorts and a large t-shirt—that I stole from his room the other day. It was a sweet thought, but I didn't care if he wanted to watch me strip down for the rest of my life.

I glanced over at my alarm clock when he opened the door and walked into my room. It was two-thirty in the morning, and I felt like complete, guilty shit for keeping him awake all night. Dri didn't complain, he didn't even complain when I asked him to keep my door open and the hallway light on.

I was surprised when he climbed onto the other side of my bed—over the covers—and let out a soft sigh. I was expecting him to go to his room and try to sleep for an hour or two, but this was so much better. He must have changed when I did since he was shirtless and in a pair of basketball shorts.

I held the blankets clutched tightly to my chest with my body turned towards his. I inhaled the scent of his body wash. I could almost forget there were monsters with glowing red eyes when Adriel was this close and laying in my bed. That endearing, dark blue gaze washing protectively over me. Almost forget.

"Why aren't you dressed?" I heard Raffie ask her brother through the crack in my door.

"I'm going to stay home with Larkin today after I take you to the bus." I could just barely see Adriel helping Raf pull her backup onto her tiny shoulders.

"What's wrong with, Lark?"

I was losing my freaking mind, kid. That's what. I was buried beneath the covers of my bed, the dark green sheets clenched tightly in my hands as I pressed them to my chest. It was five-thirty in the morning, barely two hours after I finally went to bed, but I hadn't slept a wink. Every time I closed my eyes all I could see were four pairs of glowing red ones and that one, lone streetlamp.

"She's just not feeling well, and I don't want to leave her alone." Which he hasn't since I threw myself at him the night before. We didn't talk about the kiss in the kitchen, nor did we share another one. Which I knew was for the best, especially right then, but that didn't change the fact that I so badly wanted to.

"Oh... Can I stay home too?" Raffie asked eagerly, and I could practically see her beaming smile in my mind.

Adriel laughed, and the sound was far warmer than the blankets wrapped around me. "Nice try, kid." Then the floorboards creaked as a heavy body walked towards my room. My door opened a little further. "I'm taking Raffie to the bus. I'll be back in a minute, okay?" Those blue eyes were dark with concern as he gazed over my all-but cowering form.

"Y-Yeah, okay." I really didn't want him to leave. I didn't want either of them to leave, especially with those things lurking out there in the dark.

Adriel didn't look so certain. He was gripping the edge of the door and standing half in my room half in the hallway, his gaze never leaving mine. "I'll only be a few minutes." It sounded like he was trying to reassure himself more than me. I forced a smile on my lips so those tense shoulders of his would relax.

"I'll be okay, Dri. Tell Raf 'bye' for me."

"Bye Larkin! I hope you feel better." Those big, blue, doe eyes of the nine-year-old's suddenly peeked around her brother.

"Thanks, Raffie. Have a good day." She shot me a large grin and little wave. Little jerk was so darn cute.

"Ten minutes, tops." Dri spoke up as he shooed his sister away from the door and towards the stairs. "Try to sleep, Lark." He called softly over his shoulder as he turned to follow Rafael down the stairs. Even though the morning sun was starting to rise and shine through my windows, he kept all the lights on. I don't think he realized how endearing that was.

I closed my eyes as the sound of their retreating steps and the front door opening then closing reached my ears. But as that eerie silence of the empty manor filled my ears, I knew I wasn't going to be getting much sleep for a while. My mind had been racing the entire time I laid in that bed, my eyes wide open.

I had been drinking, and even though I could have sworn I was sober by the time that thing happened—was I really? How real was it? Maybe someone had slipped me something at the party, even though I didn't drink anything there. There was a lot of touching and brushing past people though! Maybe they were like poking people with drugs or something. But even if that was the case, I wouldn't have been anywhere near coherent to make it to the center of town.

No matter how many different theories or scenarios I ran through my head, I couldn't shake the fact that it had been real. That there really were four, red-eyed monsters that can control the cities lights and want to play. Which I'm pretty sure was just another word for 'eat', if their constant comments about being hungry were anything to go by.

I was going down another rabbit hole of theories when my door creaked open once again. I sucked in a sharp, icy breath and jumped straight up at the noise. "It's just me." Adriel stood in the open doorway, a small, apologetic smile on his lips even though those blue eyes shown in worry. My heart was racing furiously in my chest, and I had to gulp down a shaky breath before laying back against the pillows.

I really needed to chill the fuck out.

"You really need to get some sleep, Angel." He spoke softly as he stepped towards the bed, his hand outstretched to brush the hair off my forehead.

"I'm not sleepy."

"Liar." But he laughed softly as the word left his lips. Then he walked around to the other side of the bed and laid down on top of the covers. He had stayed like that all night until he got up to get Raf ready. I don't think he slept either.

I turned around under the covers until his strong arm was in my line of sight. I closed my eyes and let out a shaky breath, the tension in my shoulders leaving with his close proximity. "I wish you would tell me what happened." Dri murmured softly and turned on his side until I was facing his strong chest. My eyes closed as his hand reach up and rubbed soothingly down my messy hair.

"You wouldn't believe me if I told you." I sighed into his touch and tried to fight off the exhaustion that was suddenly weighing down my eyes. Strong fingers ran gently through the ends of my hair, the only part that wasn't in a curly, tangled mess.

"Try me."

I placed my fingers against his stony chest and tapped lightly on his tan skin. Could I tell him the truth? How would he take it? Fuck, he'd probably lock me up in an insane asylum. "I wasn't feeling the party we were at, so I left to come home." I started softly with my eyes locked on the fingers I had pressed against him. "I thought I was heading back to campus, but I guess I got the buildings confused and ended up walking into town."

"Wait, you were by yourself?" I tore my gaze from his chest to glance over at those dark blues. They weren't happy.

I chewed anxiously on the inside of my cheek. "Um, yeah. River found a—a date, and Siena didn't want to leave him alone—"

"So, they left you alone." That strong jaw of his clenched shut and the muscles beneath my fingertips tensed. "I don't like these friends of yours." He rolled the word 'friends' off his tongue with distaste.

"Don't get mad at them. We had all been drinking, and it's not like we're that close or anything." I muttered quietly, which did nothing to ease that angry haze in his eyes.

"That doesn't matter, Larkin. I didn't want you walking around by yourself during the day, much less at night." Adriel let out a long sigh, his chest rising and falling deeply as he did. "Did someone follow you after the party? Did they hurt you?"

I couldn't stare into those demanding blue eyes for much longer, and I dropped my gaze back to his hard chest as I forced the words from my lips. "I don't... I don't know who they were. I don't know if they were from the party or just happened to see me in town."

"They?"

"Yeah, Adriel. They. Are you going to let me tell you what happened or not?" His hand had left my hair to grip tightly at my upper arm and I dared a glance at that glaring blue gaze. His face was set in stone, that jaw line impressively chiseled as his teeth clenched shut.

"Larkin, I swear to God if someone hurt you—"

"No, no one hurt me." I reassured him again with an exaggerated sigh and resisted the urge to roll my eyes. At least when he was being aggravating, I wasn't worried about red-eyed demons. "Now shut up, or I'm not telling you anything else."

"Yeah, fine, whatever." And that grumbled response sounded so much like something I would say, it made me laugh.

"Like I said, I thought I was heading towards campus, but turns out it was town square. I thought I felt someone watching me but there was no one else around so I just tried to hurry up. And then things got... weird." His hand squeezed my arm reassuringly as my voice trailed off. How the hell could I explain this to him? Any sane person would just laugh and tell me I was seeing things. I almost wished he would be one of those people.

"Weird how, Angel?" The anger had slowly fled from those dark eyes, and even though his face was still stony, the look he gave me made my heart ache.

"Well, weird stuff started happening." A dark eyebrow raised at my statement, but he didn't say anything. "Like the street-lamps started turning off, and then there was this creepy laughter when I got into the neighborhood, and then these guys suddenly appeared out of nowhere, and they had red eyes!" Once it started, it wouldn't stop, and I was spewing out everything that happened like a dam had exploded in my mind.

"I didn't want to lead them to the house, so I stopped and grabbed this pipe, and then they cornered me against this fence, and were talking about like eating me and stuff! And then they saw something behind me, freaked out and took off even though there wasn't anything there! I ran a few streets back and cut through people's backyards just in case. And then you were there and yeah."

I blinked up at a wide-eyed Adriel, my blankets clutched to my chest as he stared at me in silence. He took in a deep breath and let it slowly out before speaking. "So, you're saying that a group of red-eyed people, were chasing you to try and eat you..." I suddenly felt like a complete and total idiot when the disbelief in his tone registered in my brain. I dropped my eyes and took my hand back from his chest.

"You don't believe me."

"I believe something terrified the ever-loving shit out of you, but red-eyed people trying to eat you? That sounds like one of your dreams, Lark."

Actually, now that he mentioned it, it did sound like one of my dreams. But that didn't change the fact that it really happened. Or, something happened at least! "I'm not lying, Adriel."

"I don't think you are." That warm hand rubbed gently over my arm before traveling up to rest against the side of my face. "You're gorgeous and there probably were some fucks going after you. It's one of the reasons why I don't like you wandering around by yourself." Despite his words there was still that doubt in his dark eyes, but his touch was gently as that thumb brushed lightly over my cheek bone. "But you were drinking, Angel. Maybe your drunk mind just added all the weird stuff because that's what's been going on in that subconscious of yours lately." He nudged his forehead against mine, his oh-so-yummy lips pulling softly into a warm smile.

"Yeah... maybe."

Adriel just gave my mind the out I had been looking for all night. I had been drinking, and I had been dreaming of those red eyes and the whole 'eating me' thing recently. I wanted nothing more than to agree that they were just a group of disgusting, horny college guys trying to get their kicks in with a girl walking around by herself in the middle of the night. No red eyes, no ability to control streetlights, just my drunk mind and their unwanted advances.

Then why did I keep repeating over and over in my head 'but I was sober then'?

"Hey." Dri's voice pulled me away from those thoughts, and that soft touch of his traveled to my jaw. "That doesn't mean what happened wasn't serious. Please don't ever go off by yourself like that again." His dark blue eyes were narrowed in worry, and I had to force myself to ignore the straining muscles in his arm. "Call me next time okay? No matter if were arguing or if you're mad at me, or whatever, I don't care. Just call me."

I nodded, even though I didn't plan on going to another party any freaking time soon—much less ever drink again. The last thing I needed was my mind turning those dreams into a reality. "Say it, Larkin. Say you'll call me next time, or I won't believe you." I rolled my eyes at that controlling tone taking over his voice. It might have been hot while we were having sex, but it was just plain annoying any other time.

"Yeah, Adriel. I'll call you."

That hard look slowly slipped from his handsome face and he leaned forward to press a kiss against my forehead. "Thank you, sweet girl."

I tried not to let him see how giddy that little praise made me, and I forced down my smile. One-time thing. We both agreed to keep what happened between us a one-time thing. But that didn't stop this unbearable need to tear those short away and climb on top of him. And that kiss the night before. I wasn't in the right state of mine, but it still made my head spin.

Then there was the way he was looking at me now, his eyes all dark and smoldering, and how close we were laying. I wanted to change that one-time thing to a two and more-time thing. His face leaned closer to mine until those mind-numbingly soft lips just barely brushed against my own. "You should really get some sleep." He murmured into the quiet of my room, his lips pulling away as a cold, loneliness washed over me.

I let out an internal sigh and tried not to latch onto him as he put space between us. He was right, though. I should get some sleep and continuing down that path we had just been on wouldn't do either of us any good. Yeah, sure, he promised I would be 'one of his girls' forever, but that didn't change the fact that guys get bored.

I was more at risk of falling in love with the man than he was with me. And hell, the guy was drop dead fuck worthy. I literally saw three girls line up in a row to give him their number once. He could have anyone he wanted. It wouldn't be long before he figured out that wasn't me.

"Don't leave." I mumbled on a yawn as I curled up against his side, my forehead resting against the hard muscle of his bicep as I clenched the blankets to my chest.

"You know I never will."

CHAPTER 16

I so did not want to go back to school on Monday. Honestly, I didn't want Raffie or Adriel leaving the house either. I was used to guys making unwanted advances in California. I could handle that. But despite a weekend long spree of convincing myself that Dri had been right about what happened, I still wasn't so sure I imagined what I saw. What else was lurking in the dark, waiting for me and my family to walk into it ignorantly?

I had to shake my head and unclench my fingers from Rafael's. She stared up at me with her big, blue, doe eyes, and one eyebrow raised. The sight reminded me a little too much of a certain arrogant male for my taste. "So, why are you taking me to school again?" The nine-year-old asked as I drove my little yellow bug over the smooth streets of Deshua.

"I just want to make sure you get there on time." I lied and slowed the car down as we approached the school's speed bumps. Adriel was going to take her to the bus stop that morning on his way to work, but I insisted on driving her instead. I couldn't control what happened between the bus stop to the school, couldn't protect her from any red-eyed demons lurking in the shadows.

"The bus gets me to school on time every day, Lark."

"Whatever, kid." I grumbled as we pulled to a stop in the long line of cars dropping their children off.

"Are you going to creepy-drive me home from school, too?" Both of her eyebrows raised that time, even though that sneaky smile pulled at her little lips. I rolled my eyes.

"No, the bus can take you home." It would be the middle of the day then, with the sun shining brightly over everything. "Not get out of my car. I'm done looking at you."

"Love you too, Lark!" She sang happily as she hopped out of the bug with her bag clutched tightly around her little shoulders. Little turd.

"Love you too, Raf."

She shot me a beaming smile before slamming the door shut and skipping off for the school's entrance. I let out a groan as that whole side of the car shuttered. Did she really have to slam it so fucking hard?

I had another hour before my first class started at eight, but I didn't want to go back to the empty silent manor. Adriel had thought that going back to school after our long weekend of me cowering in my room and him and Raffie trying to coax me out, was a good idea. But I could also tell he didn't want to leave. Those dark blue eyes had hesitated before he left for work, his strong hand staying an extra minute on the front doorknob as I made sure Raffie had everything. He made me promise to call him if I needed anything.

I didn't want to keep worrying him. Adriel hadn't left my side all weekend, and despite how close our bodies were that entire time, he never pushed limits like most guys would. That dark, encompassing concern shining brightly through his eyes squashed all thoughts of even daring trying to make a move on him. I so wasn't in the right state of mind anyways. Besides, it was only a one-time thing, including that kiss in the kitchen. That was all I could ever allow it to be.

I went home long enough to grab my backpack and laptop, then locked the doors and hightailed it to school. The psychic's words had started ringing in my ears Friday afternoon when I turned the lights in my closet on before cowering back under my covers. "Stay out of the shadows." I still thought the lady was crazy, but after recent developments, I started taking her words to heart. I avoided all dark corners and spaces, even in the safety of the manor. I kept all the lights in my room on, even begged Adriel to keep the hallway lit. He had raised one, dark, suspicious brow, but didn't argue when I jumped for the light switch.

Thankfully it was a bright sunny day and there weren't a lot of spots on campus for creepy red eyed monsters to be lurking. You imagined it, Lark. I had to keep repeating those words in my head, no matter if I wasn't sure that I believed them. I was tapping my pen nervously against the little fold-away table in my usual seat when Siena and River walked into the lecture hall. They were both smiling and talking like the world wasn't fall apart.

"That was some crazy party, right!" River all but cheered when he plopped down in the seat beside mine, his hazel eyes bright with glee.

"Yeah. Crazy." I muttered under my breath. "It seemed like you got lucky though." I tried to keep my voice calm and casual, and so totally not terrified. The room was pretty big, and the only light came from the large windows on the far wall near the roof. There were more than a few dark spots and corners.

"More like the other guy did." River rolled his eyes as both he and Siena took their laptops out. "I've had better."

Si rolled those creepy gray eyes and let out a sigh. "At least you go some. I was busy making sure you didn't get lost all night."

And I was busy running for my life.

"You could have got laid too! There were a handful of creep-a-zoids making eyes at you!"

That blush crept into her pale cheeks, which I actually found endearing. For someone who sure hated most of the world, she did blush a lot when it came to sex. "I wasn't going to leave you alone, moron." She reached over and smacked his arm. I didn't know what it was like to have a best friend. The closest I ever had was in middle school when some random girl shared her lunch with me. And well, now I have Adriel, but I don't think he counted as a friend. I'm not really sure what he counted as, but I knew I couldn't live without him.

"Alright class!" Dr. Shorzin announced to the relatively packed lecture hall a few moments later. He was wearing his usual khaki shorts and floral button down with sandals. Shorzin looked more like he belonged on a beach than in a college. "I hope everyone has something to write with, it's a note-taking day!" I rolled my eyes and pulled up Microsoft Word as he turned the projector on. Every day was a note-taking day in his class. It was a freaking lecture seminar.

"If anyone paid attention to the syllabus, and from our lovely little discussion on the first day, you would have seen that this week we start on the supernatural origins of Deshua." Shorzin started in that energetic, attention captivating way of his—which was really just his loud voice booming across the entire arena-styled room. "And today..." He drawled dramatically as the first image in his PowerPoint appeared on the large drop-down screen. "Is fallen angels!"

My breath turned to ice in my lungs. A dark image appeared on the screen, one that was suddenly tearing shreds into my mind. It was of an angel, or what once was an angel. It laid sad and broken on the floor of a blood-covered Earth. Its' beautiful face crying as it held an outstretched hand pleadingly towards the sky.

But it wasn't the sad beauty that caused panic to fill my chest. It was the wings. Pitch black wings that were larger than the actual angel cascaded from the crying creature's back. I had seen wings like that before, felt them wrap around my body and brush sensually against my skin as their owner murmured dark promises against my skin.

"That's a cool pic, huh?" River's voice snapped my mind out of the insane spiral it had started down.

"S-Sure." He didn't comment on the stammer in my voice, his gaze was too focused on the crying angel.

This was so not what I needed right now.

"There are many stories, legends, prophecies, whatever you prefer to call them, about fallen angels throughout the ages." My back stiffened when the word 'legend' left Shorzin's mouth. It was the same term crazy Jess had used when she went psycho. "Technically speaking, in Abrahamic religions, fallen angels are those who were expelled and cast out of Heaven. Usually because of defiance and sin."

The professor clicked to the next slide, and my stomach fell when it was just another picture. I had a bad feeling that whole PowerPoint was full of them. This image showed an angel falling from the sky, its' white wings burning in the heated rays of the sun.

"From studying all kinds of literature pieces around the globe, historians have concluded that there are, supposedly, hundreds of fallen angels littering the Earth. Some far more powerful than others." He clicked to another slide that had a slowly spinning scorched globe rotating around its axis. Bright, golden dots decorated the continents. "And legend says that Deshua was founded by one such angel." The little video suddenly zoomed in on one of the glowing dots until Oregon came into view, and then Deshua itself.

I wasn't even sure what the hell I was supposed to be taking notes on.

"Now, you all must remember, that this is the folklore of the town, and that your history class will teach you something completely different. But if you ask me, this way is far more interesting." A few snickers sounded around the room as Shorzin's beaming smile washed over us. He clicked to another slide and an image of an angel with black wings standing proudly against a dark cliff shined back us. My heart hammered viciously in my chest. These pictures were becoming a little too much for me.

"Avidus, the Latin term for eager, desirous, or greed was given this angel by the archangel Michael as he cast him from heaven." The sounds of fingers hitting keys filled my ears, and I forced my attention away from the PowerPoint to type a few quick notes. A part of my brain kept repeating what a load of shit this all was, while another kept making snarky comments about psychics and red eyed monsters.

"Angry at Heaven and the angels that shunned him, Avidus created the town as a way to scorn them all."

In my notes I wrote 'Greed guy got pissed at the white-wingies and built Deshua as a giant fuck you.' It didn't really save space note-wise, but it made me feel better.

"This was long before Europeans inhabited the content, and Native Americans were far too wise to trust the fallen. Legend has it that Avidus coaxed mortals away from Europe, Africa, and Asia to join him. While their will was their own, and their souls could not be controlled, fallen angels and demons can be very manipulative."

Shorzin walked away from his computer as he spoke, his hand flowing smoothly with his words as his loud voice boomed across the lecture hall. He held my complete attention with rapt fascination. This might have all been a load of bogus, but at least it was interesting.

"Avidus in particular swayed mortals with promises of immortality, and eternal beauty for the simple price of following him. What they didn't know was that the price of following him was a lot steeper than it seemed. They had to surrender their souls to the dark and become creatures far less than human. Beings that required the blood of others to live—a sick joke of Avidus', I imagine."

A student in the second row raised their hand, and Shorzin paused to nod at him. "Are you saying that this Avidus guy turned them into vampires?"

'You know he doesn't like us playing with the food.' One of those red eyed freaks' words suddenly shot through my mind and got stuck on repeat. Drunk or not, why would I imagine that?

Quiet snickers sounded around the room at the guy's question, but Shorzin didn't seem offended as he gave him a large smile. "That is one term for what they became, yes. However, many literature pieces found in the cities cathedral and ancient manors refer to them as Immortals." The laughter died away at his words, and a dark tension filled the air. Fear was shooting down my spine. Things were becoming a little too freaky to be coincidences. I wanted to be there even less than before.

"I can see all of your minds spinning but bear with me a while longer." The professor addressed as amusement flashed through his dark, crinkled eyes. My fingers tapped anxiously against the fold-away table. I wasn't so sure I wanted to hear any more. "Not all who came to the town agreed to become Immortals, and the population quickly tore in half." Shorzin continued his lecture, against my internal pleas for him to dismiss class.

"Those who had surrendered their souls and drank the blood of others followed Avidus faithfully. They worshiped his every move and followed every order. Those who chose not to, quickly grew to scorn the angel's existence. Avidus was greedy and dark, true to the name Michael had bestowed upon him, and he wanted what all powerful beings did—more power."

Another picture appeared on the large drop-down screen as he clicked to a new slide, one that was far gruesome than any yet. A large, dark creature sat on stone throne held into the air by dozens of shadowed creatures. You couldn't see any of their features, only black, hazy outlines, with glowing red eyes. I gulped as unease started churning my gut. My leg began bouncing quickly against the floor, as if it wanted to run away as fast as my mind wanted them to.

Red eyes. Red eyes. Red. Eyes. Why the fuck was that characteristic haunting every aspect of my life?

"Avidus' reign grew quickly pass the town and across the seas. The mortals of the area knew they had to stop him, if they hoped to save the world from his desires. So, they pleaded and prayed until Michael heeded their call and gifted them with the one prison that would hold the fallen angel for an eternity. Yes, a prison." The professor added with a small chuckle, even though no one had said anything.

"Angels cannot die, forsaken or not. The only way to stop his terror was by imprisonment. But not one made from steel or stone. A man-made creation could never hold a fallen. It had to be a prison of flesh and blood. Heaven gave the mortals a soul specifically designed to entice and trap him." A couple of students scoffed, and even Shorzin let out another chuckle as murmurs started around the lecture hall.

I guess I was the only one terrified to shit.

"Yes, laugh if you must, but Michael gave the mortals a girl completely and totally created to trick the fallen. A trick he fell for. Tempted by his own primal desire and need, Avidus craved the one thing just out of his reach. He followed the girl to his own demise, and with her blood they bound him to an eternal slumber. Many believe he still sleeps to this very day, buried and chained beneath the stone streets of Deshua, waiting for that soul to return. The lock is the key."

Yeah, freaking right. This professor, who had a doctorate, was going to stand there and tell a huge class full of college students, that Deshua existed because an angel got pissed at a bunch of other angels? And that a girl was the reason he stopped making all his little monsters? What the hell was this? Romeo and Juliet Demon-Edition? Yup, okay. I'm in crazy town. It's official. First the psychic, then the party, and now this. How much more of this bull shit was there?

"Your first papers are due in two weeks. You can pick any piece of lore we have discussed so far, as long as you delve into a specific aspect of it. I want detail and I want to see effort."

I suddenly wanted to drop that class. I didn't even care if it was a required general education course. These people were crazy, and I was getting closer and closer to begging Dri to move again. I tried, that's all he asked me to do.

Why does my trying always have to come back and bite me in the ass?

CHAPTER 17

I just got home for the day and was about to make lunch for Adriel and me, when my phone lit up with a message. I frowned down at his bold name flashing across my screen. This man never texted me before in his life, now I get two in a two week-period? Can't come home for lunch. Stuck at the site.

Well that's just great.

My mind had been reeling all day from Professor Shorzin's lecture, and I was really hoping to see Dri for a while. This week was starting to suck just as much as the last one. I didn't want to be alone in that house either, not with all it's dark corners and shadows. Then a thought flashed through my mind, and a wide smile pulled at my lips. Adriel still got a lunch, he just couldn't leave the site. I knew he didn't pack any food that morning since he was supposed to come back here, and the crazy man would be starving by now.

I put together a few hastily made sandwiches, with five different kinds of cold cuts that insane male always ate and threw a few bags of chips into his lunch box. I tried to ignore the eerie silence of the house as best as I could, but I couldn't help feeling like the monsters under beds and hiding in closets were real now. But they weren't. No matter what my dreams thought, they were just dreams. I believed in what I could see. Except, my mind was now playing tricks on my eyes.

I didn't know what I could believe anymore.

I hurried to my car with a smile pulling on my lips. It was the first time that entire day I felt anything close to happy. Not that it had anything to do with that arrogant, pig-headed, insanely fuckable blue eyed idiot I was bringing food to. I assumed the 'site' was that big construction dig in the center of town he said he would be working at occasionally. I pulled into the once-upon-a-time park's parking lot a few minutes later.

The sun was still high in the sky, and there were no dark spots slinking around the area. I frowned at all the workers and their hard hats crowding around the overturned piles of dirt and construction equipment. They all looked exactly the same. Everyone was wearing flannels or black t-shirts, with dark boot-cut jeans, construction boots, and tool belts. They all had hard hats on too, so I couldn't clearly make out anyone's face.

Where the hell was he?

I glanced over at a hillier area of the site where two more men were standing on top of a tightly compacted dirt pile, one of them holding a large clipboard and radio. Well, that looked like a boss, and Dri did say he was in charge of people. I'm taking that as my best bet, or they could tell me where he was at least.

I maneuvered easily around the large work-trucks but trudging around piles of dirt and workers was another matter. There were a few wolf calls, and whistles, while others yelled that I wasn't supposed to be there and to get out. I ignored them and made a bee line for the two guys at the top of the hill.

I had just started up the little hill the two were on when voices reached my ears, and sure enough, one of them was Adriel's. "We had a deal." Dri's voice was a hard sigh as the guy at his side gave a beaming smile to the blue-eyed idiot.

The closer I got, the more I could see of his 'friend', and let me say, the man was gorgeous. He was tall, like Adriel, with tan skin, golden-blond hair, and eyes such a sparkling gold they could put the sun to shame. "And I haven't broken that deal." The guy spoke, that bright, beaming smile still on his lips.

Adriel stepped closer to the guy, his grip tightening on the clipboard as that hard jaw clenched tightly. "Listen—"

"Oh, hello there." Those insanely bright gold eyes were suddenly locked on mine, and that smile was directed at me. "How can we help you?" I felt my heart stop. It wasn't possible for someone to be that unearthly handsome. There was something else that made me pause though, something that stirred deep in my stomach. It was a weird Déjà vu feeling, like I had met the guy before. Like I knew him.

Adriel whipped around faster than I expected, those dark eyes blazing angrily at being interrupted, until they landed on me. The fury quickly left his expression, and that gaze widened. "Oh, um, I—I..." I was stammering like an idiot. Never before had I actually got flustered around anyone except Adriel. Now there was two insanely attractive men staring over at me expectantly, and heat suddenly flamed the back of my neck. "I'm just here for Adriel." It was harder that I would have liked forcing those words out steadily.

Dri blinked, and then that stupid smirk was pulling across his insanely kissable lips. "Awe, I see." The golden man said as I came to a stop at their side. I couldn't hold his gaze for long and I found myself staring at his dark green t-shirt rather than at his beautiful face. He was practically glowing. "Adriel, you didn't tell me you had a lunch date. I wouldn't have held you so long." Gold-guy's smile turned sly and those bright eyes flickered to Dri.

"I didn't know either." But Adriel's voice didn't sound upset, and when I glanced up at him there was only light shining from his dark gaze. Don't fucking blush, Larkin.

This was ridiculous. I didn't get flustered over men, no matter how ridiculously attractive they were. I forced my gaze to the gold-guy and put a smile on my lips. "I'm Larkin, nice to meet you..." I let my voice trail off as those ridiculously gold eyes flickered back to my gaze. I had to literally repeat over and over again in my head not to look away. The feeling that washed over me whenever our gazes locked was one of complete and total unworthiness. Like I wasn't worthy enough to be near him. It was a very unnerving feeling.

But then the guy's smile turned genuine and ease washed over me. "Micah, and it's very nice to meet you, Larkin." Then he did something I was so not used to that my mouth actually dropped open. Micah lifted my free hand, the one that wasn't holding Adriel's lunch, and kissed the back of it. Those shimmering eyes flickered to mine as he did, and it was like the ground beneath my feet disappeared.

"Alright, that's enough." Then Adriel was suddenly taking my hand from golden-guy and puling me against his side. I would have shot him a narrowed look if my mind wasn't spinning. Dri wasn't the jealous type, but I could have sworn that was what was flashing through that dark gaze.

Micah stepped away with a small laugh, those bright eyes seeming to glisten in the sun. "Yes, I believe it is. I should be off, anyway. Too much to do in too little time I'm afraid. I'll leave you to your lunch, Adriel." That gaze flickered from mine to Dri before he stepped away.

"I'm sorry," I stopped him as he started to turn away, and my heart gave a little flutter when that gaze locked back with mine. "But have we met before? You seem really familiar."

Micah's lips pulled up at the corner, his gaze never leaving mine as his head tilted curiously to the side. "I would never forget such a pretty face." And then he turned and walked down the hill without a backward glance. My eyes stayed trained on his back until he disappeared into one of the work trucks. Despite his words, I could not shake that familiar feeling.

"You done staring?" Dri's tone had taken on a hard edge, and the fingers that were wrapped around my hand tightened.

"Done being jealous?"

"I'm not jealous."

"You're glaring at me like I just kicked your puppy."

"Whatever." He rolled those dark blues and tugged on my hand. "Is that food for me?" He pulled me closer to peak at the lunch box clenched in my free hand.

I shot him a narrowed look. "Only if you start being nice to me."

He sighed, but it was one of aggravation more than anything else. "You want me to kiss the back of your hand too?" Heat flamed my cheeks and I instantly looked away so he couldn't see.

"No, don't be ridiculous."

"Or maybe you want me to kiss something lower—"

"Adriel!" I snapped and ripped my hand away from his with wide, bewildered eyes. He did not just say that! "Yeah, go ahead and kiss my ass!"

"I'm kidding! No, wait, Lark, I'm just joking!" He called after me as I started an angry stomp back down the hill. His booming laughter caused more than a few workers to glance our way. I had just reached the bottom of the dirt pile, ready to jump straight back into my car and deal with the creepy silence at the house, when he was suddenly at my side. "I'm sorry." His voice was a little breathless, but there was laughter dancing in his eyes as his strong grip wrapped around my upper arm.

"You're an ass hole, Adriel."

That was a joke I was so not okay with. He didn't get it, and I shouldn't have expected him to. How could he possibly understand this insane need I have for him? Or how my body was constantly fighting against my heart? I wanted him so badly that it literally made my chest ache, and it was to save whatever the fuck relationship we had that I pushed the urge away. He was a guy they had a crazy sex drive already, and it was just a one-time thing to him. He would never understand.

"Larkin, hey..." His hand let go of my arm to nudge at my chin, the clipboard still clenched in his other. I didn't want to look at him. I wasn't in the mood to be buddy-buddy right then, or to be around him at all. I just wanted to go home. "I really am sorry."

I glanced up at those blue eyes, saw the genuine apology there as they washed over my face. I looked away again.

"It's fine. Here's your lunch." I pulled away from him and raised the lunch box up for him to take. His gaze dropped down to the food, then flickered back to mine.

"You're not going to stay?" I had to ignore the sudden remorse in his tone, and the way those blue eyes darkened.

"No, I have a paper I need to get started on." I didn't want to be around him right then, or those blue eyes. I didn't want to admit how much his little 'joke' bothered me, but god he could be such an ass hole! And after everything that happened in the past week, inconsiderate jokes from the one person I put above everyone else was definitely not what I needed.

He took the lunch from my hand, all traces of amusement vanishing from those handsome features. "I shouldn't have said that. I'm really sorry."

"Yeah, you've said that. I'll see you at home." I turned around and headed straight for my little yellow bug, the one he bought me. I could feel that gaze staring into my back as I crossed the parking lot and unlocked my car. Maybe I was acting a little childish, and I knew he really was sorry, but that didn't change the fact that he said it. That he actually thought it was okay to. He would never understand the turmoil constantly tearing apart my heart.

I frowned at the brown teddy bear half my size sitting on my bed when I got out of the shower. I clutched the towel tighter around me and reached down for the card clenched in its paws. "What the hell?" I grumbled as I flipped open the card covered in little hearts. 'I'm sorry for being a dick.' Was scrawled in Adriel's neat cursive against the plain white background. I couldn't stop the laugh that past my lips.

Yeah, I overreacted earlier, but I also didn't really blame myself. After the shit show that happened last week my mind had been completely and totally fried. Plus, I knew Dri had the potential to be the biggest dick of the century, just as much as he could be the sweetest, most endearing person ever.

"Hi..."

I whirled around to face the uncertain voice coming from my doorway. I clutched the towel tighter around my naked body when my gaze landed on the sheepish blue pair.

"Hey."

It was six-thirty in the afternoon, and he had showered and changed out of his work clothes already. The black t-shirt hugging his toned torso and the low hanging plaid pajama pants didn't do anything to keep my gaze from washing hungrily over him. I watched as he reached up to run a hand through his quickly growing hair, an ashamed smile pulling at his lips.

"I got you a bear."

"Yeah, I see that."

"I'm really sorry, Angel."

I sighed and turned around to place the card back in the bear's lap. "I know, Dri. It's okay. I shouldn't have made a big deal about it." I walked away from him, and the bear, to step inside my walk-in closet.

"No, it was really insensitive of me." His low voice caressed my ears as he stepped further into my room. I tried to ignore him as I eased the closet door closed a few inches so he wouldn't see me change. I had just pulled on the rest of my pajamas when the door opened and Dri stood there in all his sheepish glory.

"I was changing." I scolded and crossed my arms grumpily over my chest.

That amused smirk pulled on his lips. "I waited until you were done."

"You were watching me?" My mouth dropped slightly open, and my gaze narrowed at him dangerously. He chuckled.

"No, just your shadow."

"Pig."

He rolled those eyes before stepping further into the walk-in area. "I wanted you to know that you were right, Larkin." Heat suddenly raced through my veins as he grew closer, that smoldering look I was becoming quickly familiar with crossing his gaze. Oh God, what was he doing? "I was jealous." There were gentle fingertips suddenly brushing over my cheeks, and my legs became a little wobbly.

"Adriel..." I spoke softly, my eyes wide as his flickered briefly to mine before narrowing on my lips.

"We decided kissing wasn't part of the one-time thing, right?" His voice was low, tempting as it washed across my skin and teased my heart. His words made my chest flutter, and my thighs clench.

"Dri—"

"Because I really want to kiss you." That fluttery feeling washed over every part of me, and electricity shot from his fingertips through my skin. I really wanted to kiss him too.

"I-I can't." It took all I had not to make my words sound like a plea. I couldn't do this, to either of us. With the way he was looking at me, and with the way my body was reacting to those gentle touches, that kiss would turn to something else very fast.

Adriel pulled away, that smoldering gaze slowly fading to one of concern. "You know you'll never lose me, sweet girl."

I closed my eyes and leaned away from his touch. "I hate when you do that." Like he can read my fucking mind. Its infuriating.

He gave me a small, genuine smile, one that lacked the sly amusement he usual wore. "You wear your emotions on your sleeve." His hand brought mine to his lips and he kissed the underside of my wrist for emphasis. My other hand was resting against his hard chest and I relished in the strong planes beneath the soft texture of his shirt.

"Who was that guy anyway?" I asked instead of falling back into that lustful trap his eyes were eagerly ready to cage me in.

Something dark flashed across his gaze, and that stony jaw clenched shut. Oof, I did love when he did that. "A business partner of 'Avid' that has recently found a love in fucking with my work." Then his lips pulled up in that smirk that made me want to roll my eyes. "And I'm not going to let him fuck with you." I did actually roll my eyes at that, even as he leaned down to nudge his forehead against mine.

"Alright, so if you're not going to let me kiss you, can I at least make dinner?"

I pulled away with a raised eyebrow. "You actually want to make dinner?"

He shrugged those strong shoulder, a snarky humor flashing in his dark gaze as he stepped back into my room. "Make dinner, get take-out, same difference."

I groaned and followed sluggishly after him as he headed for the hallway. "You're going to kill your arteries one day, Markos." I grumbled as he leaned down to turn my side lamp on. Ease washed over me as light filled the room, chasing away the dark shadows creeping in the corner.

He laughed as we stepped out into the hall and walked to the stairs. "I'm not too worried about that, and foods food, Lark. You in the mood for burgers? I want some burgers." I stopped at Raffie's door as he sauntered down the stairs, his quiet laughter following behind him. I shook my head.

That man would be the death of me.

CHAPTER 18

"Larkin! Hey, Larkin!"

The groan that escaped my lips when that familiar voice reached my ears was so loud a passing male student stopped to glance at me. He raised a suggestive eyebrow. I shot him a nasty look. The guy scurried off. I would have ignored that voice and made a bee line for the nearest academic building, regardless of which one it was, if he didn't sound so damn close already.

"Hey, Luke." I greeted reluctantly and turned around to face the blond creep-a-zoid heading my way. Maybe I was a little too harsh with the guy. He hasn't done anything bad, and he was always very nice and charming. But that gut-wrenching twist in my stomach every time he got near didn't seem to agree.

Dark sunglasses were covering his deep brown eyes and that usual charming smile was resting perfectly on his lips. "Hey, I was hoping to catch up with you again at the party, but I didn't see you." Despite jogging from wherever the hell he had spotted me he wasn't out of breath. It had to be eighty degrees, and he was wearing a dark black jacket, without an ounce of sweat on him. Some people really were born gifted.

"Yeah, I wasn't feeling good and decided to go home early." He didn't need to know the details of that night, no one did.

It was Wednesday afternoon, two days after that lunch fiasco with Dri and nearly a whole week since the 'party'. I didn't want to remember it. Ever. I spent more than enough time convincing myself that what happened didn't. Vampires did not exist, not matter what that crack Shorzin said.

"Oh damn, that sucks I'm sorry." Luke's smile actually did fall, like he really cared about my health or whatever. I couldn't stop my eyes from narrowing suspiciously at him. Freak. "I'm glad I ran into you now though!" The momentary lapse forgot his face lit up as he gestured towards the park besides us. "I wanted to introduce you to my friends and try to convince you to hang out more."

No. Thank. You.

"Thanks for the thought, but I actually have a class I need to get to."

Which was a lie. It was twelve-ten in the afternoon, and I was done with all of my classes for the day. Not that he needed to know that. I did want to get home in time to make lunch for Dri and I though. Something I had gotten far too excited for every week—even with what happened Monday. That blue eyed idiot knew better than to make those comments now. And I knew how badly I actually wanted them to happen. We were walking on very thin ice, and I wasn't sure it would hold much longer.

"Awe, come on. It will only take a minute, then I'll let you go." His smile was still charming, his voice soft and sweet as he pointed towards a crowded sitting area in the middle of the campus's park. "My friends are right over there. Let me introduce you, then you can run off." That smile fell into a small smirk that didn't bother hiding the humor in his voice when he said 'run off'. Like he knew how badly I wanted to.

Ugh, I really didn't want to. But I also didn't want to be a massive bitch either, not when he's only been nice. A quick 'hey, I'm Larkin. Yeah, I know it's a weird name' wouldn't kill me. "Yeah, alright." I nodded, and the bright smile that took over his lips was almost attractive. Hell, it was very attractive, but that didn't kill the nausea in my stomach.

"Awesome! They're really chill, you'll love them."

Yeah, well, I wasn't so sure about that, but I kept my disgruntled thoughts to myself. Luke led the short distance between where he found me to the sitting area his friends were at. Despite the short walk he somehow managed to squeeze in a full-blown conversation, asking about my classes and how I was fitting in. I kept my answers shot and polite, but all I really wanted to do was go home and see Dri.

"Hey guys!" Luke called to the back of his friend's head as we approached the wooden lawn chairs they were sprawled out against. The area was seated perfectly under this large tree that provided a perfect amount of shade. "This is Larkin, the girl I keep telling you about."

He actually tells people about me?

When the hell did we become friends?

That thought didn't last long as four heads turned our way. My heart fell to my stomach, then sky dived straight for the ground. No... You have got to be fucking kidding me! I couldn't speak,

my breath was ice in my chest, and it didn't help that they looked
just as surprised as I was. Even Adam's eyes widened.

It was them. The four that cornered me, the four in the ice
cream shop. Luke's friends. I knew there was something fucked
with that guy!

I took an immediate, shaky step back, my eyes as wide as
saucers as they flickered between the four boys nervously.
"Larkin, you alright? What's wrong?" I ripped away from Luke's
outstretched hand, concern falling over his once charming face.

"Stay the fuck away from me!" I snapped and that concerned
expression became more confused.

"I don't know what's going on—"

I turned towards his friends, raised a shaky hand and jabbed it
in their bewildered direction. Their eyes weren't red then, just
various shades of brown, blue, and green. But red eyes or no,
they still tried to corner me, and have 'fun'. I hadn't imagined
that. None of them said a word, though what little color their
faces had drained away when they looked at me. They actually
looked scared. I guess those fucks were still afraid of my shadow.
Pussies.

"Stay the fuck away from me." I didn't bother waiting for a
reply as I turned on my heel and took off running in the opposite
direction. Luke called after me, but I didn't stop. I refused to. I
didn't know what sick game they were playing, or trying to drag
me into, but I refused to be a part of it.

I tried to shove down the fear swamping through my stomach.
I hated being afraid. I hated feeling like someone held power
over me that I couldn't overcome. When Adriel was there he
usually chased that feeling away, but I knew he couldn't all the

time. I kept running, with no idea where I was headed, not even sure if they were following me or not.

I didn't stop until I turned a corner at the end of the brick building and ended up running smack into a dead-end alcove. It was just a little weird opening in the back of the building. A stone bench sat pressed back against the far wall, leaves and vines completely littering every ounce of brick. There were small purple flowers growing out of the vines on the walls and covering the stony floor. I glared at the dead-end in aggravation, my hand reaching up to run viciously through my dark curls. I had no idea if they tried to follow me, but I definitely didn't want to be stuck if they had.

"Larkin!" Dread filled my chest when Luke's voice reached my ears. The universe really hated the thought of giving me a freaking break.

I spun around to face him with my bag's straps clutched tightly in my hands. "Get away from me." I snapped as my eyes landed on his. He had been running after me, but just like before he wasn't out of breath or sweating—which I definitely was. I hadn't exercised since high school, but I knew I was a hell of a runner. The guy should at least be fucking winded!

Luke stopped at the entrance of the alcove. His sunglasses were pushed to the top of his blond head so I could see the complete confusion in his brown eyes. "I just wanted to make sure you were okay. I don't know what happened back there—"

"Your friends happened!" I snapped and took another step back into the vine covered area. It probably wasn't a good idea cornering myself, but he wasn't making a move to enter.

"I don't know what you mean." He shook his head, that charming smile nowhere in sight.

"I mean," I sneered as those brown eyes flickered up to the vines surrounding the alcove. "That your fucking freak-a-zoid friends cornered me after that party and tried to—tried to..." Hell! I didn't even know what they were trying to do! I shook my head and turned hard eyes back on the bewildered blond. "They're no good, need-to-be-locked-up, perverts!"

He blinked those brown eyes, and his mouth hung slightly open before it snapped shut. "They tried to what?" But there was more aggression in his tone than a question. I didn't answer him, but I didn't think he really wanted me to. "All four of them?" He plowed on, those warm eyes now blazing in fury. I nodded and he placed his hands on his waist with a large, disgruntled sigh. "They're so fucking dead." He hissed under his breath. I didn't bother commenting. I just wanted him to move the fuck out of the way so I could hightail it home.

Another tense angry moment passed before Luke let out a heavy breath and scrubbed his hand down his face. "Look, I'm sorry about them. That never should have happened." He went to take a step into the alcove, his foot just steeping on the vines of the floor before he winced and took a step back.

"What the fuck was that?" I didn't care about being nice anymore. After today I planned on never talking to this fuck or his friends again.

Those brown eyes glanced almost anxiously over to the flowers streaming the walls before back to me. "I'm just allergic to the plants in here."

"Whatever, just leave me alone."

That smile was nowhere in sight, and the blatant look of anger, unease, worry, and just altogether stress flashing in his eyes made me nervous. "I'll leave you alone, but I really am sorry, Larkin. I'll make sure this doesn't happen again."

"Just keep them the fuck away from me."

"I will, I promise." Luke tried to give me a small smile, that charm from before barely tilting his lips, but I made sure not to drop my bitch-face. He let out a small sigh and shook his blond head. "This really isn't how anything was supposed to happen." No shit Sherlock. "I'm sorry. I'll see you around."

Not likely, but I didn't say anything as he turned and walked away, being careful to avoid stepping into the alcove.

What a fucking shit show.

I pulled my cellphone out of my backpack's cup-holder and groaned when I saw the time. It was twelve fifty. I didn't have time to make Dri and I the lunch I wanted to. Looks like its mac n' cheese and sandwiches again. I was just about to leave the alcove and make a beeline for my car, wherever the hell I parked it, when my eyes landed on those purple flowers.

Eh, what the hell. Better safe than sorry.

I picked a handful—or two—off the nearest vine and shoved them in the front pocket of my backpack. Maybe if Luke was allergic to them than those over fucks would be too.

Don't do it. Don't do it. Be strong, Larkin. Don't do it. But then he was standing there, looking all big and strong and secure and I really, really wanted to.

Those dark blue eyes locked on mine and Adriel smiled. "Hey, Lark."

I did it. Or, at least a part of it. I raced over to him, not carrying one bit that he had his toolbox and belt in both hands and threw my arms around his toned waist. I was still shook-up over the little run-in with Luke's friends, and despite his promise that he would keep them away from me, I didn't trust any of them one bit. I squeezed the ever loving shit out of Dri.

He laughed, oblivious to the knot I kept forcing down my throat. Just hearing his voice made everything better, but that didn't mean I was going to let the poor guy go anytime soon. "I missed you too." Adriel chuckled and dropped the box and belt to the ground to wrap those strong arms around me. He got the picture when I didn't let go after a while.

"Hey, you alright?" His warm hands ran soothingly over my back, his cheek pressed against the top of my hair. I shook my head, even though I spent the pass twenty minutes convincing myself that telling him what happened wouldn't be a good idea. I pressed further into him. "What happened, Angel?" He gripped lightly on my shoulders and tried to ease me away from his strong chest. I frowned but let him pull me off him.

I bit my lip and gazed over to the living room. I didn't trust myself when those blue eyes were staring down at me. He could play me like a fiddle if he wanted to, and I could never hide anything from him. It really didn't help when he reached up to pull my bottom lip away from my teeth, and the rough pad gently traced over the pink skin. My eyes snapped to his, and my heart pounded a thousand miles a minute in my chest. God, that fuck really knew how to drive me insane.

"I'll you have to do is tell me what happened, and I'll take care of it." His thumb left my lip as I let out a sigh and pulled away. I closed my eyes like that could block out all the naughty images suddenly racing through my mind. At least I wasn't scared anymore.

"You can't take care of everything, Dri." I wouldn't want him to, not when there was a risk he could get hurt. There were four of them, five now including Luke. Adriel was just one guy. One insanely hot, fuck-worth, panty dropping, mouth-watering guy. But still just one. I mean, I guess I could call the police, but I didn't know all of their names. I couldn't even describe them, despite seeing their faces today.

"The hell I can't." His strong hand wrapped around my wrist and pulled me back to face him. "I take care of what's mine, Larkin. I always have and I always will." That dark gaze was hot and smoldering as it glared down at me. His strong jaw clenched together and the muscles in his arms even strained in that way I loved so much. Mine. There was something funny that always happened to my insides whenever he referred to me as 'his'. I knew he didn't mean it in the way I wanted it to, but that didn't keep me from imagining.

"Just tell me what happened, please. I don't like seeing you upset." That dark look slowly faded as he spoke, and the hand that wasn't wrapped around my wrist reached up to brush my tangled curls away from my face. I resisted the urge to close my eyes and fall into him—resisted the need to press my lips against his and see if he still tasted as good as I remembered.

"I..." I closed my eyes and let out a shaky breath. Was I really going to tell him this? It would just worry him even more. "I saw those guys today."

Guess I was.

"Guys?"

My eyes flickered open to glance at his. "Yeah, Dri. Those guys from Thursday." It took a moment for realization to dawn on him, but when it did—oh boy he wasn't happy. The grip around my wrist tightened.

"Where were they?"

"The park on campus, they're friends with his guy I met the first week we were here." I don't think I told him about that actually.

"Who are they?"

I shrugged. Even though I didn't honestly know I wasn't so sure I wanted to tell him. Adriel looked like he was about to go all Taken on their ass and that worried me. "No idea, but they're those freaks I told you about with the contacts! One of their names is Adam and another is Pete." I didn't catch the other two, but they were probably just as basic as the first.

"And you know this 'friend' of theirs?"

I shrugged again. "Well, not really. We've met a few times but that's about it."

"I don't want you hanging around him." He grumbled as the grip on my wrist eased some.

I rolled my eyes. "Trust me, I won't be. I don't even like the guy. I was just being polite."

"Well, don't."

I pulled away as he stood simpering in the foyer. "Don't be crabby, I made you two boxes of mac n' cheese." That stern look in his gaze faded some as I turned for the dining room. He followed closely behind me.

"I'm just worried about you." Adriel sighed and plopped that large, beautiful, toned body down in front of the plate I had set up on the table.

"Yeah, well, you're the one that wanted me to go to college anyway—"

"Don't start that." One sharp narrowed look from those blue eyes had me snapping my mouth shut grumpily. Fucking jerk. Bossing me around like he's the... well, the boss! He's not! But I still do every fucking thing he says.

"Just eat your stupid noodles." I grumbled and spun the handle of the pot I had put in the middle of the table on an oven-mitt towards him. That sly smirk pulled at his lips, but he kept his mouth shut as he reached for the wooden spoon.

"Where's your plate?" He asked with a raised eyebrow as I sat back in my seat beside him, noodle-less.

"I ate before you got here." I didn't actually, but I knew if I told him I wasn't hungry he would force feed me. I couldn't eat right then, not after that little adventure at school. My stomach wouldn't settle down and I kept glancing around the windows nervously, looking for any sign that those freaks followed me home.

"You're lying."

My gaze snapped over at his accusing tone and I crossed my arms grumpily over my chest. "Am not."

"I know when you're lying, Larkin. You suck at it."

"No, I'm amazing at it. You suck." He rolled those blue eyes but did the great service of keeping his big fat mouth shut. A mouth that looked a little too good for my sanity. Fucking jerk.

We sat quietly after that as he ate. I played with the edge of the dark wooden table as Adriel stuffed his fat, gorgeous face with cheesy noodles. I made him a few sandwiches too which were sitting on the kitchen counter, but he could get those himself.

My gaze flickered over to him as he ate. He had one strong arm resting against the table beside his plate, the sleeves of his flannel were rolled up to his elbows and I could see the oh-so-yummy muscles straining in his forearm. I had a problem, a serious one. Even his freaking forearms were turning me on. He shifted and I could just barely make out the black V-neck he wore beneath the flannel, one that hugged his chest a little too nicely. I let out an internal sigh. That man was too damn sexy for his own good.

Why did I agree to that one-time thing again? Because I fuck everything up. But that didn't mean I had to stop looking at him or thinking about him doing naughty things to my body.

"Larkin."

"Hmm?" I hummed and tore my eyes away from the biceps straining beneath the fabric of his flannel. A dark eyebrow was raised at me, and those stupidly delicious lips were curled up at the corner.

"That was the third time I called your name."

"Oh..." Don't you dare blush. I would not get flustered. I refused to. I don't even care if he caught me mind-fucking him. But it wasn't like I could really control the heat staining the back of my neck. "Sorry, my mind's somewhere else."

"Oh, I'm sure."

I narrowed my gaze dangerously at him, which he just ignored as he pushed his empty plate away. Ass hole. "You know all you have to do is say so, Lark." He sighed a moment later, those blue eyes trained towards the kitchen as he reached up to run his hand through that dark hair. He was letting it get long, or as long as I've ever seen it. It didn't touch the collar of his shirt or his ears or anything, but it was a nice change from his usual crop cut style.

"Say what?"

That gaze flickered to mine, and the hot, entrapping look there made my heart flutter. "That you want to sleep with me."

I gulped as that heat flaming the back of my neck grew. I really hate how he had the ability to do that to me. I tore my eyes from his and forced my gaze down to my clenched hands. "We can't." No matter how ridiculously bad I wanted to.

Adriel's hand was suddenly prying mine apart so his strong fingers could slip between mine. I watched as he raised my hand to his lips and pressed a soft kiss against its back. "I know." He murmured softly against my skin, even though those blue eyes were sending electricity straight to every part of my being. "Just know I'll be there when you change your mind." His mouth pulled up into that smirk, his lips brushing softly against my hand before pulling away.

I rolled my eyes and grumbled something about him being an idiot, even though that was only to cover up the heat coursing through me. I knew I couldn't 'change my mind', not if I wanted us to stay as we were. Though I had a sick feeling that resolve wasn't going to last long.

Not when he kept looking at me like that.

CHAPTER 19

The nightmare was back. I couldn't escape them, no matter how badly I wanted to. There was fire everywhere, hot flames scourging my skin as I ran for my life. Large, strong wings flapped in the distance. There was screaming, and only too late did I realize that it was my own. I could feel the heat folding around me, could feel the fire burn into my flesh. And those eyes were everywhere.

I woke screaming, my head splitting open in pain as I tried to slap the fire away.

"Hey! Hey, it's okay." Dri's voice cut through the vicious pounding in my skull, and those warm hands were suddenly pulling mine from their brutal grip in my hair.

"It hurts!" I gasped. My skin felt like I stepped into a furnace, and it was nearly impossible trying to suck in a deep breath.

It was Wednesday night, barely a few hours after my little run in with Luke's friends. I should have known I couldn't escape my subconscious for long. I had been doing so well too. No dreams, not even those erotically charged ones.

"You need to relax." Adriel's low voice ordered, but it didn't help the tremors racking through my body. "It's okay." His hands were cupping my face, his strong thumbs brushing the panic away as I tried to calm down. "Just work through it, Lark. That's it." My breath was stuttering as I forced air down my throat. I could barely make out his dark blue, concerned gaze as I blinked viciously.

"That's my girl." He soothed softly as those strong hands coaxed the pain away. It was working, he was working, and the fire burning my lungs slowly faded. The pounding in my head took a little longer to follow.

"Dri..." I rasped as I fell into his strong bare chest. His arms immediately went around my waist and scooped me close, and one of his hands reached up to hold my head against him.

"It's alright, I got you. I always got you." He murmured into the quiet room, his warm touch chasing away the horrors of that nightmare. The bedroom door was closed, and the only light came from the one in my closet and the moon through my windows.

"Do you want to talk about it?" He asked softly a moment later as his hand brushed down my hair. I shook my head and pressed further into him. I didn't want to talk about it. I just wanted him to hold me and erase those awful images from my head.

We sat like that for a moment longer before I decided that wasn't enough. I pulled away only to wrap my arms tightly around his neck. He chuckled quietly into my ear, his strong embrace wrapping firmly around my torso as I super-glued myself to him. Nothing could get me when he was there. Or, at least, I could pretend nothing ever could.

He dropped a soft kiss onto the bare skin of my shoulder, then another on my spaghetti strap. "It will be okay, sweet girl." Adriel's voice was a soft whisper as his warm lips pressed against my skin. Electric tingles shot straight through my body at the action.

I tried not to shutter as his warm hands traveled slow paths up and down my back. I only had the thin material of my tank-top on, and I could feel the heat of his touch against my skin. It made those hot lonely parts of my body, that desperately wanted him, quake. My arms loosened their tight grip around his neck so my hands could run slowly over his strong shoulders. I traced the intricate design of his tattoo, my fingers so small in comparison to his large arm.

I really should not have been doing that, especially with how intensely I reacted whenever we got too 'touchy' with each other. But I was upset, he wasn't wearing a shirt and his muscles were practically begging to be explored. He wasn't being any better either. Those soft, warm lips of his were tracing a path of slow kisses across my shoulder and up my neck. My breath caught in my throat as those touches sent bolts of lightening straight through me. I wasn't planning on stopping him though. I doubt my body would have let me even if I tried.

One of his hands was curling into my long dark hair, the other slowly traveling down the length of my back. "Larkin..." He murmured when those kisses reached my ear. There wasn't a question in his voice, just my name slipping endearingly from his lips as my fingers trailed softly over the lines of his muscles.

"Hm...?" I asked in a daze. All the pain from the dream had faded away but was being quickly replaced by a different kind. It was the same as the first time. I wanted him. More than I wanted anything. It was practically wavering on need at this point.

"I'm not so sure this is a good idea." Adriel's voice was low and dark in my ear, and it did absolutely nothing to help the little situation I was having in my underwear. It also didn't help that his strong hand had slipped underneath the bottom of my tank top and was slowly rubbing along my bare skin. "You didn't want us to do this." My breath caught in my throat as his thumb brushed the side of my breast, and then trailed slowly away again.

"I know." But that didn't stop my hands from trailing over his oh-so-yummy arms. And then I felt it. That hard member beneath his boxers that hit between my legs in just the right way. I couldn't hide the moan that tore from my lips as I pressed my body down onto his. All false pretenses that we weren't going to do this went straight out the window.

The hand he had in my hair was suddenly ripping me away from our 'hug' and his mouth crashed against my own. My hands instantly went to his hair, and my fingers curled into those dark locks as his lips ravished mine. His free hand moved until it could grip tightly on the back of my knee and pulled me so roughly down against him that the impact forced out a gasp. Dri didn't waste any time. His tongue slipped easily past my lips and he was pushing me back against the bed before I had a chance to think.

I didn't want to think though. I didn't want to stop this. I needed this. Needed him. He always made the nightmares go away. Always made the bad disappear. And always made me crave him. "Fuck, you're so damn beautiful, Lark." He took his lips back long enough to say before his tongue was back to conquering mine. Yeah, definitely conquering. His mouth moved like I wanted his body to.

I pushed off the bed to try and kiss him harder, but he only let out a disapproving noise and shoved me back down. One of his hands was on the back of my knee, holding my leg up against his waist as his other tugged almost viciously at the end of my tank top. "Off." He broke away to growl and started dragging the tank up my body. I raised my arms without a fight—like I was going to stop this—and let him drag the fabric over my head.

Those bright blue eyes raked hungrily down my body, stopping briefly on my breasts before traveling down my stomach to gaze at the purple bikini underwear I wore to bed. "These are cute. I hate them." He snapped the elastic on the undies, leaving a sharp sting against my skin. I wasn't going to argue with him, not if that meant he would take them off soon. I rested my hands against his strong biceps as that gaze traveled slowly back up my torso.

Adriel made a low, rough sound in the back of his throat before dropping his head slowly down to my chest. "Oh Angel, you shouldn't let me do this." He murmured against my skin, that dark tone gone for a moment as he kissed the valley between my breasts. And then his hot mouth was wrapping around one hard point and I lost it.

"Dri..." I moaned into the silence of the room as the sensation of him lightly sucking went straight through me. His dark chuckle against my skin sent shock waves through my system and left me cold when he pulled away.

"I love your little moans." Dri muttered against my skin as he traced gentle kisses up my neck.

Then his lips were back on mine and all I could focus on was how his tongue started mouth-fucking mine. Until that grip on the back of my knee tightened and he rocked against the center between my thighs. I gasped as he rubbed against me through the fabric of our underwear. He did it again, and again, until I was on the verge of begging him just to rip the fucking clothes off and get inside me. He knew I wanted him too, if that dark smile pulling on his lips against my own was anything to go by.

"You're not supposed to do this to me you know." He murmured against my lips as that hand of his left the back of my knee to travel a slow aching path up my thigh. "I'm supposed to take care you." His strong fingers curled into the edges of my purple underwear, both thumbs brushing softly against the skin beneath.

"You are." I pushed through gritted teeth. If he didn't fucking do something about the mess between my legs in the next ten seconds, I was going to lose my ever-loving mind. His dark laugh did naughty things to my insides. Then those hands started slowly guiding the thin material over and down my thighs, until it was just a piece of useless cloth hanging from his fingertips. He tossed it to the floor, those blue eyes glittering with something dark.

"Hm..." Adriel hummed to himself, his gaze washing over my naked skin as his hands slowly followed their ravishing path. "I'm never going to get used to this." His mouth dropped to my belly button, then the spot between my breasts, then finally pressed against my lips. "You sure you want this, Lark?" He asked softly, his hard thumbs rolling over each of my nipples until I arched my back in ecstasy.

"I hate when you ask me that." I gasped breathlessly against his lips, which only pulled into that stupid smirk.

"That's only the second time I've asked you that." His fingers were still playing with my breasts, but those strong legs of his were prying mine open until I was completely at his disposal.

"Well, stop." I panted and let my own fingers curl into the waist band of his boxers as his fell to my waist. He raised a dark eyebrow as I started pushing them over and down his hips.

"Eager much?"

"You ripped my clothes off first."

He laughed, and the sound did nothing to cool the heat raging through my veins. "That was not ripping." Then his mouth lowered to mine and his teeth bit sharply into my lower lip. The small sting went straight between my legs. "I can show you ripped, Lark." I didn't doubt it, but I also didn't care. Not right then at least. I just kept easing his boxers down until that part of him I desperately wanted was freed.

He finished taking the useless material off as my eyes zeroed in on him. There was that tinge of fear, like before, but it quickly disappeared. Adriel wouldn't hurt me, he didn't last time, and I doubted it would now. My eyes closed in pure pleasure when those strong fingers brushed lightly over my clit. "Oh my God..." I moaned as his fingers slipped even lower, every single sensation shooting through my body all at once. His dark chuckle followed.

And then one of those strong fingers was pushing inside me and I about lost it. "Adriel!" He was smiling, his usual dark eyes bright as the started pumping slowly into me.

"Mm, you're wet, Lark."

"I know, you dick." I panted breathlessly as that finger kept its slow torturous pace.

"That's not very nice." He teased, but I didn't care. My legs were trying to push my hips up against his hand, but his free one held my waist firmly against the bed.

"Dri!"

"Yes?"

"Stop messing around." I was close to sobbing—to begging him to just take me. He knew it too.

"Is there something you want, Larkin?"

"Yes!'

"You have to use your words, beautiful. I can't give you what you want if you don't tell me." His words were teasing, but that voice only added to the pressure building between my legs, one that steady pumping finger was doing nothing to ease. My fingers grasped tightly at his strong shoulders, my nails sinking into the hard muscle.

"I want... I want..." I gasped as his thumb suddenly brushed over that bundle of nerves and sent electricity shooting through my entire body.

"What do you want?" His voice was in my ear, his lips pressing soft kisses against my jaw.

"You. Inside me. Please."

"See? I told you that you only had to say so."

I wanted to snap at that cocky arrogance in his tone, but then his finger was slipping easily away, and those strong hands were pulling my thighs further apart before I could. "I'm not planning on going easy on you this time, Lark."

"I don't want you to."

Those blue eyes flashed, and a dark smirk pulled slowly on his lips. "Mm, you're going to regret saying that."

I would have thought of something witty to say, except those strong hands pushed my thighs as far apart as they could go, and he was slowly sinking into me before I could. All rational thought flew from my mind and I gasped as that length of his stretched me more than I thought possible. His large hands kept my waist pinned to the bed until he had sunk in as far as he could.

"Hands up." He ordered on a low growl and I automatically reached my hands above my head. "Good girl." My thighs clenched at the little bit of praise. I might have fought him in all aspects of daily life, but I thrived on the complete control he demanded during sex.

He made sure my legs were how he wanted them wrapped around his waist before reaching up with one hand to grip tightly at both of my wrists—keeping them pinned above my head. Then he was moving, and the sensation made my body shake. He rocked inside me, his pace slowly increasing with each thrust. I wanted to rip my hands away from his and wrap them tightly around his shoulders or thread my fingers into his hair and ride out the pleasurable waves, but he refused to let go.

His free hand was gripping tightly at my waist, his fingers sinking into my skin as his tempo increased. "Dri..." I groaned into the musky air as he started retreating all the way, then shoving completely back in.

"Yeah, Lark. Moan my name." He leaned down against me, his hand still wrapped tightly around mine as his mouth pressed against my lips. I moaned against his tongue as his body did to mine what I had been begging it to all night. I could feel the pressure build with each thrust, and that hand on my waist was slowly slipping between our two bodies until his thumb could rub against my clit.

And then he thrust in at the same time his fingers pinched my clit and his teeth bit my lip and the world behind my eyelids exploded. Heat and electricity raced through my veins as I rode out the orgasm against his pulsing length. I hadn't realized he had stopped moving and raised off me until I came down from the high and could finally blink my eyes open. He was gazing down at me, those blue eyes warm as his lips pulled into a small smile. Then I had to ruin the moment.

"I thought you said you weren't going to go easy?"

That gaze flashed and his smile turned into a deadly smirk. "Oh, sweet girl. You're cute." Then both of his hands were on my waist and he was pulling out long enough to roughly flip me over.

"Oof, Adriel!" I shrieked at the aggressive maneuver, but he was gripping onto my thighs and pulling me flush against him before I had time to register. He pressed my torso down onto the bed but pulled my waist up until he could slip easily back inside.

"Hold on to the blankets, Angel. You're going to need it."

"So much for a one-time thing." I grumbled a while later as we lay exhausted on my bed. My body was thrown lazily across his, my right leg cradled between the two stone ones of his while my head rested against his hard chest. My hand gently traced the intricate design of his tattoo.

He grunted as one strong hand ran gently over my bare back and down my side. Goosebumps followed his touch. "I never liked that idea anyway." Dri grumbled before tilting his head to press a kiss against the top of my hair.

"You suggested it."

"Because you didn't know how to handle it." He pinched my ass in emphasis. I slapped his chest.

"That hurt." I groaned and reached behind me to rub the sore butt cheek. His chest shook beneath me with quiet laughter.

"Good."

"Ass hole."

"I can fuck that too if you want."

"Adriel!" I gasped and slapped his chest again, this time harder. His laughter echoed around the room.

"I'm joking, Larkin." His voice was dark as he chuckled, and his arms wrapped tighter around my waist when I tried to pull away. I settled back against him reluctantly as he pinned me against him. Well, not really reluctantly but he was still a vulgar piece of shit. "I mean, I will if you want me to—"

"Oof." I tried to jerk away, but he just held on tighter and kept laughing.

"Kidding, kidding. Sorry, you're just so easy."

"You're a jerk."

"True, but I'm a jerk you want to sleep with." I would have argued with him if he wasn't so damn right. I grumbled when he rolled us over until my back was pressed against the mattress, and those dark eyes could gaze down at me. That amused laughter slowly faded away.

"I don't want this to be another one-time thing." Adriel admitted softly, as one of those strong hands reached up to gently trace my bottom lip.

"Well, it's not like the first time worked out so well." I mumbled and gestured towards our naked bodies. Those insanely soft, smexy lips pulled up slightly at the corners and his fingers trailed gently over my jaw. "What do you want?" I asked as those blue eyes just continued to gaze down at me.

"I want..." He paused and glanced away, that admittedly skillful tongue flicking out to lick his kiss-swollen lips. "To do this whenever we want." I reached up to gently trace the strong outline of his stomach as he spoke.

"I do too. I'm just worried that—"

"That it will change everything, yeah, I know. But I already told you I won't let that happen." He gripped onto my chin and pulled my face up to his. "Has anything changed since the first time?" I nodded even though I knew he wanted me to say 'no'. He raised a dark eyebrow, his fingers still gripping my chin. "What?"

I shrugged and gestured between us, even though there wasn't much space. "I want to do this all the time now." That smirk took over his features once again and he leaned down to nip at my bottom lip.

"Don't act like you didn't want to do that before."

I frowned and went to cross my arms defiantly over my bare chest, but his strong hand stopped me. "You're one to talk." I grumbled as he leaned down again and started nipping gently along my jaw. Those godawful tingles were starting in my stomach, and I had to physically force my hands from reaching up and pulling his hips down against mine.

"I never said I was." His voice was a dark murmur in my ear, but his hands were gentle as they left hot trails across my skin. I couldn't keep my back from arching as they rubbed slowly down my sides. "The only thing that is going to change," Dri started softly as that mouth left warm, wet kiss down my neck. "Is how good you're going to feel every morning."

"Every morning?" He raised his head at the question in my voice, but that smirk didn't waiver.

He shrugged. "Or whenever you want. Doesn't matter the least bit to me." He leaned down and pressed a short soft kiss to my lips before pulling away. "Or we could not have sex again. Totally your choice." He leaned away with that, like he was actually going to leave.

I made a noise of disapproval in the back of my throat and wrapped my legs around his waist, keeping him right where I wanted him. He raised that eyebrow again, his blue eyes dark as he leaned back down to me. "Do you know how gorgeous you are?" Dri suddenly murmured as my arms reached up to wrap tightly around his neck.

"Mhm." I teased as his lips went back to kissing my jaw, even though my heart fluttered at his words. He let out a dark chuckle.

"What do you want, Lark?" He asked quietly a moment later, all humor and sarcasm drained from his tone. I wanted what I always wanted. Him.

"I want you." He smiled at my words, and those teasing hands traced slowly over my thighs that I still had wrapped around his naked waist. "And I don't want to lose you."

His brow furrowed, but he didn't pull away. "I already told you that you never will."

"Yeah, that's all fine and dandy now, but what about when you get bored of having sex with me and then everything really does change?"

His blue eyes widened, and he pulled slightly away. "Bored? You think I'm going to get bored of sleeping with you?"

I rolled my eyes at his incredulous tone. "Yeah, people get bored of sleeping with others all the time."

"I'm never going to get 'bored' of sleeping with you."

"Easy to say now." I grumbled as I dropped my gaze to the dark tattoo covering his entire arm.

"No, nuh uh, don't do that." That bossy tone was back, and his strong fingers grabbed ahold of my chin once again. "Is that what you've been so worried about? Me getting 'bored' of you?" It made me sound so clingy when he said it like that, but that didn't make it any less true. I shrugged and that blue gaze narrowed. "You're ridiculous." Adriel grumbled, but his lips were warm and gentle as they pressed against mine.

"That doesn't answer anything." I muttered when he pulled away. He rolled his eyes.

"I'm not going to get bored of you, ever. You're stuck with me, Angel."

CHAPTER 20

Adriel and I decided to disband that whole one-time-thing. Even though it's been nearly five days and we haven't slept together since that night. I'm not sure who was waiting on who, but I was too prideful to walk up to him and just be all like 'I want sex', and I'm sure he just wanted the satisfaction of having me make the first move.

Though, in retrospect, I was the one that started all of this.

Despite the whole no-sex-again thingy, we didn't go back to being completely platonic. Every once and while, when Raf wasn't looking, Adriel would squeeze my ass when he walked by, or trace that hand slowly around my waist. I would shoot him angry glares and tell him to stop every time, even though something in my stomach fluttered whenever he did. He would just chuckle, then slap my ass for emphasis. Freaking jerk.

One time, over the weekend, when I was in the kitchen doing the dishes, he even attacked me. Well, not really, but it makes me feel better saying that.

I had been scrubbing a plate clean when those strong sneaky hands suddenly circled around my waist and slipped under my shirt. Then he licked my neck. Like straight up licked my neck and nipped at my jaw. I was so surprised that I dropped the plate and it shattered in the sink. He only pulled away when Raf came in at the noise.

I watched my back after that. I couldn't allow anymore sneak attacks when his sister was in the next room. Even though I think Dri only did all of that because he loved the reaction it got out of me. Ass hole.

There were a couple of cute moments too. Like a few hidden kisses, or little neck massages when we were all sitting on the couch watching TV. I wasn't sure if Raf would even care that her brother and I were 'touchy' now, but I wasn't going to risk ruining her little nine-year-old mind.

It was Monday when it finally sank in that Dri and I were... Well, that there really was a 'Dri and I'. We weren't like a couple, or dating, or anything. At least, we didn't talk about that, but I knew he was the only man that I wanted. I couldn't even swoon over the shirtless guys playing flag football in the campus park anymore without comparing them to him—and how much better he would look out there instead.

I had no idea what he thought about me, just that he liked us sleeping together and liked squeezing my ass. He did promise he would never leave though, so I guess that was a good sign.

"You look good!" River announced when I finally walked into Shorzin's class and sat beside him.

I raised an eyebrow at the look in those wide hazel eyes. "Why do you sound so surprised?"

"You just seem so down in the dumps lately, but now you're like glowing."

I tore my gaze to my laptop I set up on the foldaway desktop. "I just had a good weekend." A great weekend actually. I always felt better after spending time with Raf and Adriel.

"Good morning class!" Shorzin announced as he walked into the room, decked out in his usual khaki shorts and floral button down. "No lecture today! You're going to be picking the topics for you papers and can use the rest of class time to start creating your outlines." The happy murmurs that filled the room when the professor announced we wouldn't have to take notes died away at the mention of the paper.

Ugh, the last thing I needed was a stupid paper to write.

Shorzin put a list of topics we could choose from up on the board if someone couldn't think of any themselves, and I picked the easiest one I saw. 'How does the environmental setting of Deshua effect the 'mystical atmosphere' according to legend?' At least I could just Google a bunch of shit for that. And it was the closest topic away from that god-awful fallen angel bull shit that I could find.

River didn't share my disdain. He decided to dive headfirst into all that unnerving nonsense. "I'm going to find that girl." He whispered excitedly as the sound of fingers typing and quiet muttering filled the lecture hall. I slanted my eyes towards his, not agreeing with the bright light shining there.

"If there even was a girl, she's dead."

"Oh, I know that." He chided before typing his topic on an open Word Document. "I'm going to figure out who she was. Maybe write about the clothing style back then. I mean, come on, there's no way 'no visible-ankle McGee' is going to turn some powerful immortal guy's attention." River rolled his eyes heavenward like that was the most normal thing anyone has ever said.

"None of this exists, River. Shorzin even said it's all a legend." At least trying to convince him helped try to convince me.

"Well, it's a legend a bunch of people believed. I'll probably go to the town's archives later this week to pull up all the info I can, if you two want to join." His voice was far too excited for his own good. No one should have that much fun writing a research paper.

"Yeah, sure. Sounds good." I mumbled as I opened my own Word Document. I really didn't want anything to do with those archives, or that legend, or stupid angel bullshit, but I figured going with them would be better than doing it by myself. "What are you going to do, Siena?" I called to the brooding goth. She was wearing her usual black-gear get up, her lips painted that dark purple that matched her claw-like nails. Those creepy bright gray eyes flickered over to my gaze.

"Probably research that Avidus guy. He seems hot." She shrugged her shoulders, and the thin chain that connected the fabric of her shirt to her belt lope shimmered in the light. Figures the goth would find a greedy evil angel hot.

I didn't bother thinking about that stupid paper for the rest of the day. Honestly, I kept debating on whether or not I should just drop the class. It was still relatively early in the semester and they were allowing drops. I would have to take it again eventually, but at least all this crazy stuff with those red-eyed monsters and psychotic psychics would die down by then. I really didn't want to have to deal with that class while my mind kept tearing itself apart.

And the nightmares were getting worse.

I woke up in the middle of the night, panting and gasping for breath. There was always more blood with each dream, and the fire always seemed to burn hotter. I blinked around my dimly lit room. I kept the closet's light on when I slept now, with the door slightly opened. Call it childish or whatever, but it made me feel better. My bedroom door was closed, and I had to shove down the disappointment. I really shouldn't expect Dri to save me every time.

My hands shook as I gripped the comforter, and my heart beat a thousand miles a minute. I didn't want to go back to sleep. I couldn't pretend like I wasn't terrified of the dark corners of my room, or under my bed.

God, way to be a fucking child, Larkin.

I lived in some of the shittiest places in California that anyone could have imagined. I had to learn how to be tough and fearless quickly when I was younger. Or, at least I learned not to let anyone know I was afraid. But four boys with 'seemingly' red eyes turned me into a frightened squirreled instantly.

I wanted Adriel.

I carefully eased out of the warm safety of my covers and pulled on the pair of pajama shorts I threw off before going to sleep. Last thing I needed was Raffie catching me walking around in my underwear. The kid would never let me live it down.

I cracked open my bedroom door and peaked into the hallway. It was dark, except for the bathroom light shining into the hall that I asked Adriel to leave on. I stepped quietly onto the carpet and tried not to make too much noise as I passed Raf's open door. She didn't like sleeping with it closed.

I didn't know if I should knock on Dri's door or not. I didn't want to wake him, especially when he had to get up so early for work, but I also knew I wouldn't be able to calm down unless he was near. I didn't bother knocking, and slowly eased the door open just a tiny bit. I couldn't see anything. His room was pitch black and that made nerves shoot down my spine.

He shouldn't be sleeping in the dark, too many things held power in the dark.

I eased the door open further until the dim light in the hallway could shine on his bed. I frowned. Adriel wasn't there, but the sheets were rumpled, and the pillows were tossed around like he had been. The light in his bathroom wasn't on so I knew he wasn't in there either. Where the hell was he? I closed his door again and headed for the stairs. If he was in the kitchen, he better be making me a snack too.

I was halfway down the steps when I heard the soft sounds of voices on the TV drift into the foyer. A small smile pulled on my lips. At least I wouldn't be waking him up.

Adriel was sitting shirtless on the living room couch, watching an overly large, black and white, fake dinosaur crunch a bunch of obviously Lego sized buildings. I forced my eyes to his face when I walked into the room, the last thing I needed was for him to catch me checking those muscles out again. Dark blue eyes flickered in my direction as I stopped beside the couch.

"It's a little late, Lark."

"Look who's talking."

He let out a small chuckle, then raised that stony arm up into the air in invitation. He didn't have to tell me twice. I crawled under that arm until my butt was pressed against his thigh and my arms could wrap tightly around his neck. "Another bad dream?" He murmured into my ear as those strong arms cradled my body against his chest. I was wearing a large t-shirt, his to be exact, and the bare skin of my arm heated against his. I shrugged and held on tighter.

Dri sighed and his warm hands ran soothingly over my side. "I wish I knew how to make them stop." His voice was a low whisper, but the soft, sweet tone of it wrapped around my ears and spread warmth through my veins.

"Yeah, me too." My face was buried in the crook of his neck, my arms wrapped tightly around him like that would chase away all the bad images swarming through my mind. We were quiet for a while, with just the sound of the TV playing softly in the background. His strong fingers slipped under the bottom of my shirt to trail lightly across my back. I tried not to let the tremor at the feeling.

"You smell good." Adriel mumbled a moment later and bent his head down to sniff my hair.

"If you like the smell of sweat and fear." I grumbled against him, but he just let out a small laugh.

"You always smell good, Lark. Sweat, fear, and all." He pressed a kiss to my shoulder as that dangerous hand traveled further up my bare back. I pulled slightly away from him to glance at that naughty smirk pulling on his lips.

"I don't want sex." The words blurted past my lips before I could stop them, and the dark eyebrow he raised in response nearly made me blush. Nearly.

"Who said anything about sex?"

I forced my gaze to the wall of the living room and shrugged. "You're giving me that look." I grumbled as his hand trailed slowly from my back and to my side.

"What look?"

I sighed in exasperation and rolled my eyes. "That look. The one right before you always do something naughty."

"Oh..." That low voice drawled softly, and I knew I should have been worried when dark amusement flashed in those blue eyes. "You mean like this?" And then the asshole pinched my nipple! Like straight up just gave the poor thing a sharp pinch.

"OW! Adriel, you ass!" I shrieked and tried to jump away from him, my hand swatting at his ridiculously hard arm. His laughter echoed around us, and I only hoped Raf's room was too far away to hear. His arms circled tightly around my waist, stopping any hope of escape, and pinned me back down against his chest.

"I hate you." I grumbled against his heated skin as the fucking idiot cocooned me against him.

"No, you don't." He chuckled despite my complete and total seriousness.

"Yes, I do. I came looking for you because I was sad and scared and then you go and pinch my boob." I slapped his arm in emphasis which he completely ignored.

"Are you still sad and scared?"

"No, but that's not the point—"

"Yes, it is." He leaned down once again and pressed those stupid lips against the top of my head. "You're not thinking about it anymore, and we didn't have sex. So, you're welcome."

Idiot. Jerk. Moron.

Why the fuck isn't he kissing me?

"I still hate you." I muttered, but he just shot me that stupid smirk.

"Mhm, I'm sure."

I didn't bother saying anything else, but I did eventually relax and let him cradle me against his chest. I did feel better, even if my boob didn't. I let my fingers trace softly over the planes of his hard skin, then over his strong shoulder and down to his stomach. Adriel let me until I reached his taut belly button, then he let out a loud sigh.

"You can't keep touching me like that if you don't want to have sex, Lark." His low voice grumbled into my ear, and I pulled my fingers away with a reluctant frown.

"I'm sorry, I didn't realize it was bothering you."

"It's not." But the grunt in his voice suggested otherwise.

"Do you want me to move?"

"No, you're fine." He pressed another kiss to my hair. "You're just getting me a little too worked up." And like his words alone could summon the thing, I felt the hard poke against my ass. I couldn't help the laugh that escaped my lips. "Yeah, yeah, laugh at my misery." He grumbled and used those strong arms to shift my butt away from his dick. "Who's the jerk now?"

"Sorry." Which I wasn't really, but if it made him feel better, I guess I could say it.

"Hey," Dri started a moment later, his voice a good degree softer than before. "Look at me." I let out a quiet sigh but lifted my eyes to his anyways. Idiot. "You know I would never pressure you into anything, right?" The concern in his gaze tore at my heart, and my lips gave him a small smile all on their own.

"Yeah, I know." I leaned forward and pressed a kiss to his cheek. His dark blues were still on me when I pulled away, and the look shining through them made my thighs clench. Dri leaned forward until his lips could press against the corner of my mouth, then nipped at my chin, before hovering just barely over my lips.

"Kissing isn't sex." He murmured against my mouth, the soft feeling of his mouth brushing against my own sent electricity surging through me.

"No, it isn't." Which was all the permission he needed. I closed my eyes as his mouth pressed against mine, his tongue slipping easily between my lips. My arms curled around his neck again, and I let my fingers threaded through that soft, dark hair.

I sighed into him, all thoughts of nightmares and boob-pinching faded away as he took completely over. I was never going to get used to this. Adriel didn't try to grope me or anything the entire time, which I was honestly a little thankful for. The next time we slept together it had to be under good circumstances, not because a nightmare made me need him. I knew he understood that too.

One hand wrapped gently in my loose curls as the other stayed securely around my waist. He had to adjust me a couple of times on his lap, but other than that it was completely enjoyable. I wasn't sure how long we sat like that, making out like horny teenagers—which, I guess, I technically was—but I still felt like it was too soon when he pulled away. Even though my lips were starting to get raw.

"Do you want to sleep with me tonight?" Yes please. "In my room? It might help with the dreams." His low voice murmured against my skin, those dark blue eyes flickering from my mouth to my gaze.

"Will you keep kissing me if I do?"

The corner of his mouth twitched up in that sly smirk I found a little too damn attractive, and his hand ran slowly over my side. "If you want me too."

I always wanted him to.

CHAPTER 21

"I'm not going to be able to come home for lunch today." I said over my laptop screen as Adriel sat across from me, stuffing his fat face with syrup-covered waffles. He really didn't give one damn about his arteries.

"Why not?" Dri's voice sounded muffled around his food, though the disappointment there wasn't hard to miss. I tried not to let that get to my head—but I didn't try that hard.

"I have to work on this stupid paper with River and Siena for a class."

"Papers don't sound fun..." Raffie pipped up from her brother's side, stuffing her own face with waffles. Ugh I don't know why I bother buying healthy food. They never ate it.

"Trust me, they're not." I grumbled down at the keys of my stupid new—not new now—computer. I had hoped I could start some bullshit introduction about the geography of Oregon and then Deshua, but it was way too early for that nonsense.

"River and Siena?" Adriel's voice took on a sour tone, and the words 'show no fear' kept repeating over in my head as I forced my gaze to his. "The two that left you at that party?" His brow furrowed in a scowl, and that strong fist tightened around his fork.

"Technically, I left them—"

"No, not going to happen."

I let out a disgruntled sigh and raised my eyes to the ceiling in annoyance. "It's not like we're going to another party, Dri. It's the town's library. Literally nothing happens in libraries."

"I don't want you hanging around them."

"Trust me. The last thing I want to do is hang around a library, but I have to for this stupid paper—"

"Larkin." He said my name on that long drawn out sigh he always did whenever he thought I was being ridiculous. "Just be careful."

Huh... Adriel never let me win one of those. I tried to keep my pleased smile to myself as I tapped on the side of my keyboard.

"Is that the paper?" His voice was soft as he nodded towards my computer, even though that hard look in his eyes didn't fade.

"No, just the topic and my notes."

"Greedy guy got pissed at the white-wingies and built Deshua as a giant eff you?" Adriel leaned across the table to peer down at my laptop, one dark eyebrow raised in question.

"Yeah," I quickly reached up and shut the screen. "This crazy professor is trying to convince everyone that Deshua was founded by some stupid angel/demon thing who made a bunch of vampires."

That raised eyebrow was quickly joined by the other as he sat back heavily in his seat. "No fucking wonder you've been having those dreams. This moron's been feeding you shit for weeks."

That angry grumble was back in his tone and those blue eyes turned darker than ever.

"Adriel... bad words." Raf's doe eyes widened and her mouth opened in surprise as she turned towards the overly large jerk. I was pretty shocked too in all honesty. Adriel was always so careful what he said around her, and even got pissed at me when I swore.

He let out a heavy breath and the tension in his shoulders slowly eased. "Sorry, kiddo." Then he turned those deadly blues on me, and I nearly threw my hands up in surrender. Which I didn't, but still. What the hell was that look for? I didn't do anything!

"I don't want you taking that class anymore."

I snapped the computer up from the table and shoved it into my backpack to avoid rolling my eyes again. "It's a general education course. I have to take it."

"It's filling your head with shi—crap." Adriel's eyes slanted briefly towards his sister's. "Raf, stay here and finish eating. I'm going to talk with Lark alone for a minute."

Ugh, great.

I hate feeling like a scolded child. I didn't even do anything! But I let the overgrown asshat pull me to my feet and drag me into that all-too-familiar half-bathroom. "Dri," I started gently as he pressed my back up against the closed door. "Even if I drop the class now, I'm still going to have to take it eventually. It's required."

That strong, sharp jaw clenched, and those dark eyes blazed in the dim light shining above the mirror. "Your nightmares have only been worse since we moved here, you're actually seeing people with red eyes, and now I find out some freak is telling a bunch of college kids that this shit is real."

"Well, I mean, he's not actually saying its 'real'. He just says it's like Deshua's legend or whatever." I shrugged, but that didn't necessarily dull the angry look in his eyes. "And I saw people with red eyes before I even started school there."

Which I really shouldn't have said, but I felt bad for Shorzin. I had no doubt that Adriel would stomp all angrily down to the guy's office if he was pissed enough. He did towards the end of my senior year when the softball coach nearly kicked me off the team. It had only been a couple of weeks after his parent's death, and I guess the coach didn't care about 'grief absences'. He sure as hell did after that meeting.

"Right, the freaks with the 'contacts'." The obvious sarcasm in his tone made me feel foolish.

"You don't have to say it like that." I grumbled and dropped my gaze to our feet. "You're making it sound like I'm an idiot or something."

He was quiet for a moment, that hard gaze glaring into my own, before he let out a short 'huff'. "You're not an idiot, and I'm not trying to make you feel that way." Adriel's hands reached up until they were resting softly on my hips, and the rough pads of his thumbs slipped just barely beneath my shirt. "This class just seems to be a part of the problem, and I don't like seeing you so stressed and unhappy."

I closed my eyes and swayed into him as those lips pressed against my forehead. "This place is just so—so freaking weird." Was all I could think to say. Not a great argument for my 'I'm not an idiot' stance.

Dri only chuckled and let his hands travel slowly from my waist to my lower back. "It's just new, and a lot smaller than Sacramento. Once everything settles down it'll be better."

"Promise?" It was a stupid request to ask. Adriel couldn't control the town, or the freaks in it. I didn't expect him to either, but just hearing that strong confident voice say he would take care of everything made me feel better.

"I promise."

His lips pressed against the tip of my nose, then down to the corner of my mouth. "I'll miss you during lunch today." My eyes were still closed as I leaned into him, and the soft feel of his fingertips against my skin made my head all foggy. "Any chance you'll reconsider?" Dri's mouth moved just barely against mine as he spoke, almost like each word was a little kiss. It did funny things to my insides.

"Mmm." I couldn't think straight, and as those rough fingertips just barely brushed along the underside of my breast, I didn't care.

Adriel smiled against my lips. "Is that a yes?"

"No." I didn't hesitate as I blinked my eyes open, a smirk of my own pulling at the corner of my mouth as his disappeared.

Adriel rolled those dark eyes but didn't pull away. "You owe me then." His lips were soft as they pressed against my own, but his hands were hot, and they left scorching trails over my skin.

I leaned further into him, my fingers curling around the hard muscles in his arms as he gently urged my lips open. My mind spun when his tongue touched mine, and I had to admit that I didn't hate the faint hint of syrup lingering there.

The pig-headed asshat let out a quiet groan when I went to pull away, and his hands tightened around me in protest. "You have to take Raf to the bus stop." I mumbled against the mouth he was refusing to move from my own.

"Alright, but you still owe me."

"This is boring." Siena groaned later that afternoon as we sat in the basement of the beautiful, creepy ass cathedral, surrounded by dozens of old, dusty books. Turns out the town's library was in the basement of the ancient church. Which did totally nothing to help my mental issues. My forehead was pressed against one of those many ancient crinkled pages of a book older than the freaking country.

It was boring.

"Naw, this is awesome!" River cheered at our side. He had been shoveling through books like nothing I had ever seen before. He even had on these huge reading glasses that made his boyish face even that much more adorable. "I'm finding so much junk on this mystical crap that my paper is going to write itself!"

"I thought you were writing it on that girl or whatever." I mumbled and had to physically detach the page from my skin so I could lean off the book.

For being in the back corner of a basement it sure was fucking hot. It also didn't help that all my senses were on high alert. There were way too many dark corners and aisles in the ancient place. The only light came from the dim lamps hanging around the stone walls. There was no electricity.

It was an old area, almost as old as the books we were going through and it was pretty damn obvious the town liked it that way. I wasn't sure if it was the eerie atmosphere of the place or what, but I couldn't shake that horrible feeling that something was watching us—watching me.

"Oh, I am, but it's called background and fluff, honey. And quotes, lots of quotes."

"I've never met anyone as excited about writing as you." Siena grumbled as she used her boot-cladded foot to kick over a pile of books.

"Siena!" River snapped as the books all toppled over in a pile of dust. "Do you know how old those are?! Be careful!" The goth just scoffed and rolled those creepy gray eyes. I didn't say anything, but I didn't really like the action either. I might not be a huge fan of reading, or this stupid class, but those books were still history—old history, one of a kind. I could appreciate the art in them and didn't want to see them ruined.

"Can't find anything on evil demon guy?" I asked to try and change the subject, and kill that fury raging behind River's bright hazel eyes.

"It's not that. I found a bunch." She let out an exasperated sigh and tapped her giant pen with a bat glued ontop of the clicker against her notebook. "But it's all stupid stuff about like how he 'reigned' or whatever. Nothing hot or exciting. There's not even a picture of him!"

"Well, it is just a legend. He doesn't exist, so there's probably not going to be any pictures of him besides drawings of basic wings or something." I tapped absently on the empty space below my laptop keys. I had the intro paragraph done at least, some bull shit blurb about how ideal the geography of Deshua was. It wasn't ideal, like at all, but I figured sucking up to the professor would at least get me a 'B'.

"I've found loads of pictures." River interjected and held up the book he was currently speeding through. "Well, drawings really, and photos of drawings in the newer versions." The image he pointed to was one much like the professor showed us, a dark throne carried by a swarm of black shadows with red eyes. Except this one had crying villagers kneeling at their feet.

A dark shiver ran down my spine. Anyone that found that empowering needed to get their head checked. "This book has a ton of them, even a few depictions of the Avidus guy if you want to take a look after me, Si." He paused and shot her narrowed look. "As long as you don't throw it."

She rolled those bright gray eyes and threw a wadded-up piece of paper at his head. "I won't throw it. Just give it to me when you're done. Mama needs some hot demon in her life."

"He's not a demon—at least according to all of these and Shorzin." River waved at the stack of books surrounding the table. I glared at them disdainfully. I only bothered looking through a couple and pushed them away whenever they started talking about greedy guy and his creations.

"Anything that can create blood drinking monsters has to be a demon." I grumbled under my breath and tried not to stare at the creepy image.

"Right!" Siena pipped up at my side, her voice sounding a lot more cheerful than before. "Isn't it hot?" She glanced dreamily at the creepy book clutched in her best friend's hands.

"We have very different tastes."

"Agreed." River even narrowed his eyes suspiciously at the doey-eyed goth.

We fell into a calm quiet after that. River was still rifling through that book, Siena had reluctantly grabbed another one and was paging through it, while I was able to get into the Cathedral's weak internet and pull up Google.

I was trying to avoid going through those books as much as possible, even though I knew at one point I would have to. Shorzin made it part of our grade. Fucking prick.

"Ooo! I found it!" River announced excitedly sometime later. "There's a whole section on that girl!" He placed the book down flat against the table. I didn't move, but I did glance over my laptop as Siena jumped to her feet.

"It talks about exactly what Shorzin mentioned and even goes into some details about the mortals plans and their pleas to Michael." He pointed to the words as those hazel eyes scanned quickly over the page. "I wonder if there's a picture of her. She has to be hot to make an angel that infatuated with her."

"Um, did you forget you're gay, or something?" Siena flicked him in his boyish cheek which earned a swift glare in her direction.

"That doesn't mean I don't appreciate good looks when I see them. Besides," He chided and nudged her away from his side. "Larkin's probably right and none of this stuff exists. But I'm curious to see what they thought was hot back then."

"You rate people on scales, don't you?" I eyed him curiously as he started rifling quickly through the pages.

"Of course. What kind of question is that? You can't go for anyone below a six. It gets dangerous the lower they get."

I said it before, and I'll say it again. It didn't matter what their sexual preference was, a guy was still a guy. Pigs.

An image of dark blue eyes, intricate tattoos and a sly smile popped into my head and I had to drop my gaze. Well, maybe not all of them were pigs—even if Adriel liked making nasty jokes. He would never put me on a scale. I highly doubted he would ever put anyone on one.

He was caring, and usually kind, and put the ones he loved above everything. I'm not sure what would have happened if the Markos didn't come into my life, but I knew I would never be able to let them go now that they were.

"I found a picture!" River's excited squeal pierced through my skull. "Okay, caption says Emira, Deshua, 1532. Damn, that's old." River mumbled as those hazel eyes went to scan the image. "It's just a drawing, and kind of a poor one." The frown in his voice was obvious. "Clothes suck, so much for fashion back then, but the detail is pretty—oh... That's weird."

"What's weird?" That eerie chill from before crept down my spine as his tone turned confused.

"Well, it's just—weird I guess." He lifted the book, like that would make whatever he was seeing less weird. "Are you seeing this, Si?" He asked his best friend who stood glancing over his shoulder at the picture.

"Seeing what?" I tried to keep the snap out of my tone, but it was getting really hard trying to stay calm with those curious looks on their face.

"She kind of looks like you, Larkin." Siena spoke up as River's gaze flickered from mine to the drawing.

"What?" I wasn't sure what I was expecting to hear, but it definitely wasn't that.

"Yeah, kind of. It's hard to see with how faded and old it is, but I definitely see the similarities." He finally turned the book towards me and pointed at the picture of a rather thin person dressed in a plain white gown against a creamy backdrop. You couldn't see the face well, but her hair was long with dark loose curls like mine, and the angle of her features were similar. The picture was too old and distorted to tell for sure.

I was happy about that.

"Try to pull up the picture on Google, Lark!" Siena suggested excitedly, those creepy gray eyes bright with eagerness. I really didn't want to. The same hair and rough resemblance was enough to add onto that eerie feeling seeping through my veins.

"Oh, yeah! Good idea." River only added fuel to the fire.

I was outnumbered.

I tried to hide my disdain as I tore my gaze from the image to look at the Google browser in front of me. "Trying typing in the caption." I shot Siena a glare as she came to stand behind me, quickly followed by River, but her eyes were on the computer and didn't notice. I had to swallow my reluctance as I reached over and typed into Google.

I was relieved when an image of the book popped up instead of the girl, until River pointed out it was an online copy and would probably have a pretty good picture inside. I had to swallow down nervous saliva as I clicked the book open and typed in the page number the image was on.

The image was, in fact, much clearer, and the face staring back at the three of us was one I was way too familiar with. The very one I faced every time I looked in a mirror.

"Holy shit..." One of them gasped beside me, though my mind had taken too far of a swan dive to care who.

The universe really loved fucking with my head.

Chapter 22

"There you are." The sound of Adriel's voice drifting through the stale air of the kitchen was enough to make tension slightly leave my shoulders. Strong arms wrapped around my waist, and warm lips pressed gently against the side of my neck. I let out a deep sigh and tried not to make it obvious I was practically falling back into him.

"But Raffie—"

"Is upstairs taking a shower."

I didn't say anything else after that and let my head rest back against his shoulder. I could almost forget about the craziness of the afternoon, or how I looked exactly like some ancient mythical chick when we were like this.

"What's wrong?" Adriel asked a quiet moment later, his insanely addicting lips still brushing softly against my skin.

My shoulders grew tense again. I wasn't sure what to tell him. He wasn't exactly thrilled about any of this shit to begin with. Hell, he threw a little girl fit when I wouldn't drop that class. I didn't want to imagine how he would react to an ancient photo claiming I was some prison/not prison for a fallen angel that might exist.

"It's just been a long day."

"Awe, miss having lunch with me that much, huh?" His snicker quickly turned into a pained grunt as I shoved my elbow into his stomach. "Oof, rude." Adriel grumbled and unwrapped those strong arms from around my waist.

"Your dinners in the microwave." I said with an aggravated wave and turned my attention back to the dirty dishes in the sink.

"You hit me. Why are you being all grumpy?" He tugged gently on my ponytail, but I just reached up and swatted him away with a soapy hand.

"I didn't hit you. I jabbed you. There's a difference."

"It's the same difference." That stupid chuckle was back as he turned to heat his barely cold chicken and veggies. I was going to make those siblings eat healthy if it was the last thing I do. And with the way my life was going, it probably would be.

"Really though, Lark. What's wrong?" Dri's voice was casual enough as he leaned against the counter beside me, a quarter of his dinner already shoved in his mouth.

"I told you, it's just been a long day—"

"And you're lying, which I hate. You know that."

I let out a deep, dramatic sigh and tried to resist the urge to slap my hands against the soapy water and spray it all over the jerk. "This paper is just turning out to be a lot more difficult than I thought it would."

"Do you want help with it?"

"No! I-I mean, no thanks I have it handled." I didn't miss the sharp look he sent my way at the little fumble, but I plowed right on through like that would make everything better.

"It's just difficult trying to find primary sources that tie the landscape of Deshua and Oregon into like the mystical background. And Siena and River were far to focused on their own papers to help, and I'm just starting to regret my topic choice. But it's cool, I'm cool. I got it."

I wiped my hands dry on a kitchen towel and turned to make a bee line for the stairs. Like escaping from that awkward blunder would solve all my problems. Adriel was faster.

"Hey! No manhandling!" I scolded as one of those strong arms wrapped back around my waist and curled me between his chest and the kitchen counter, his dinner sat forgotten next to the sink.

"You like it when I manhandle you." That dark voice was teasing as it washed over me, and his blue eyes kept glancing naughtily down at my chest.

"No, I don't." I grumbled even though I was quickly falling weak at the way his hands slipped easily beneath the edge of my shirt.

"You and the lying today. I don't like it." Though there was no anger or scolding in his tone. If anything, he sounded like he was enjoying my 'lying' way too much. Those lips were back to leaving soft sensual kisses along my neck and I had to grip tightly on the openings of his flannel to keep from swooning into him.

Fucking ass hole.

"Adriel—"

"You owe me remember?" He traced those kisses from my neck to my jaw and then at the corner of my lips.

"Lunch. I owe you lunch." Even though it was a weak attempt at resisting him. Not that I would ever want to resist him but watching those blue eyes flare made my stomach feel all fluttery inside.

"Exactly."

"You're a pig."

"So you keep telling me." But we were both smiling and for the first time in nearly a week I felt myself completely ease. Nothing was wrong in the world when we were like this. I would have given anything to make sure that never changed, but we all know how much the universe loved fucking with me.

My eyes closed and I leaned further into him as those lips pressed against mine. It wasn't meant to be a sexual kiss. Just a soft touch of his lips against mine, but even that sensation was enough to make heat flare through my body and had my thighs clenching.

He broke away barely a few seconds later, and it was harder than it should have been letting him. "I'm going to go take a shower." Adriel murmured against my lips. I blinked my eyes open to find his blazing heat into mine. "It you want to join me."

I had to purse my lips to keep them from smirking. "You said Raf was taking a shower.""

"In the hallway bathroom, mine is wide open." One of those strong, calloused hands slipped teasingly along the bare skin of my back underneath my t-shirt—daring me to say yes and go with him.

"She can't be alone for too long—"

Adriel rolled his eyes and pulled slightly away. "She's nine, not four, Lark. She can handle being alone for half an hour, more probably if you gave her the chance."

I raised my eyebrow as he stepped away and grabbed his dinner plate once again. "A thirty-minute shower?"

He raised that gaze to mine and winked. "Or longer if you want." I blew air into my cheeks to keep from laughing like an idiot. I could deal with pruning skin for thirty minutes of wet alone time with Adriel. Pun intended.

"Tell you what," Dri started as he finished off his food and put his plate in the once-empty sink. I was so not cleaning that one. That's all on him. "I'll wait an extra ten minutes, and if you decide to join by then you're definitely more than welcomed to." He leaned over, pressed a kiss to the top of my head and then turned for the dining room. "Your choice, Angel. Always your choice." He called over his shoulder before disappearing around the corner.

I stared almost longingly after him. There was nothing more in the world that I wanted right then than to join him. But a part of me just felt like complete shit for leaving Raffie alone in the middle of the afternoon to go have sex with her brother. The dead of night was one thing, but when she was wide awake and probably going to end up wondering where we were? That I wasn't so 'okay' with.

I still hadn't decided if I would go or not when I walked up the stairs a few minutes later and paused at the second-floor landing. Rafael's door was wide open, and she was dressed in her cute little Eeyore onesie I bought for her birthday with her dark hair drying in a pinned-up towel. Those big, blue, doe eyes were staring wide-eyed at her TV as she played a game on her Xbox.

"You alright, Raf?" I knocked softly on her opened door, and she barely spared me a look before looking back at the creepy ass gory game. It was like a warped, beyond morbid version of Alice in Wonderland. For loving pink, princesses and My Little Pony, this kid was into to some dark ass entertainment.

"Yeah, uh huh. I'm fine."

"Do you need anything?"

"No, I'm busy. Can you close my door please?"

I rolled my eyes and reached over for the door handle. "You going to be playing that for a while?" I asked before I closed the door on her little morbid game-fest.

"Yup. Gotta' beat the next five levels before Adriel makes me shut it off. Love ya, bye!" Then she waved at me like I was a fly buzzing annoyingly around her head. I laughed and shut the door with a shake of my head.

Well, if she was going to have her fun, then so was I. After all, how hard could shower sex really be?

"Don't give me that look." Adriel laughed some time later as I sat grumpily on the edge of his bed, wrapped in a fluffy white towel, and rubbing the back of my head.

Turns out shower sex was very hard, and not the good kind either. The water didn't help with anything, like at all, and even though he had a nice master-size shower it was still awkward trying to maneuver in the thing.

"This is your fault." I pouted and tried to ease the knot on my head away. He rolled his dark eyes and wrapped a washcloth around the icepack he had went downstairs to get.

"I wasn't expecting you to slam your head against the wall. That's all you."

I just glared at him as he sat beside me and eased the icepack over the bump on my skull. His lower half was wrapped in a towel and that oh-so-nice chest was out for all to see. All being just me, but same diff.

"Alright, so maybe we just won't try that again." His dark laugh did nothing to ease the embarrassed frustration ringing through me and I glared at him as readjusted the cold compress.

"Whatever, jerk."

He laughed again and leaned down to press a kiss against my bare shoulder. "Easy beautiful, or I might start thinking you actually like me." I stuck my tongue out at him which he took as an invitation to actually lick it.

"Weirdo." I grumbled and turned away from him, even though all that anger completely came from my own embarrassment.

We barely started anything fun when I hit my head and had to stop. He was his perfect Adriel self about the whole thing. He didn't get upset about stopping, and didn't make in fun of me, he even went to get an ice pack right away. I kind of wanted him to get a little upset actually. It would give me a good enough reason to get pissed and storm off instead of pouting like an mortified child.

He smirked before pulling away with orders to 'hold that there and don't move'. I rolled my eyes but did as he said anyway. "I'm going to go check on Raffie and make sure she's getting ready for bed. Hang out in here, yeah?" It wasn't a command or even a strong suggestion. He was genuinely asking me to stay and that made my chest squeeze all giddily.

"Yeah, okay."

Adriel smiled before turning to pull on a pair of basketball shorts and slipped into the hall. I was thinking about going to my room to put some pajamas on when a pleased thought hit me. His clothes. I let the ice pack fall to the bed as I hopped up, ignoring the pain in my skull and hurried to his dresser. I dropped the towel to the floor and pulled one of his black t-shirts that was two sizes bigger than me over my head.

Adriel wasn't gargantuanly tall, or big in any way, but his shirt still fell to my upper thighs and just barely covered my naked butt. Though I had a strong feeling I wouldn't be needing underwear that night.

I flopped back down on his squishy bed and placed the icepack on my head. He didn't think I hit it too bad, and my memory was still good, so we ruled out a concussion. I really didn't want to go to the doctor, especially not in this town where they probably chant spells to heal people and drink the blood of infants to turn immortal.

I shivered at the thought and climbed over his silky bed-sheets. I breathed in deeply and sighed as the familiar smell of his body wash and fabric softener reached my nose. Though I smelled the exact same way now. He used his body wash and the excuse that he needed to 'double check my cleaning abilities' to run his hands over every single inch of my skin.

I hadn't realized I started to fall asleep until the bed dipped, and strong arms were wrapping around my waist. My eyes blinked open and I let out a yawn as that familiar dark gaze shined down at me. "You know," Adriel started softly and leaned down to nip at my chin. "If you have a concussion you can't fall asleep."

"I thought I didn't have one." I grumbled sleepily and reached up to rub my eyes.

He shrugged those strong shoulders, the intricate design of his tattoo moving as he did, and that smile turned sneaky. "Even so, we should find ways to keep you awake just in case." I laughed and shoved against his chest as he tried to press his heavy body against mine. "Where's your ice pack? Do you want another?" His tone had taken on a serious note and I shrugged.

"No, I'm fine. It doesn't really hurt now. And I think I tossed it." Sleepy me likes to throw things.

He just rolled those eyes and leaned back down against me. "Raf's down for the night. If she's not sleeping now, she will be soon."

I let a relieved breath escape my lungs and felt my muscles relax back against the bed. I had a feeling Dri and I were going to be awake for a while, and the last thing I needed was her walking in on us. Talk about traumatic.

"Mm, you smell good." Adriel murmured against my neck and brushed his lips against my skin.

"It's your body wash. Me smelling like a guy turns you on?" I raised an eyebrow which he choose to ignore.

"No, but you smelling like me sure as hell does." He took a giant wiff of my neck to prove his point and I laughed as it tickled my skin.

"That's very caveman-ish of you, sir."

I could practically feel that arrogant smirk against my skin. "We already established how you like that about me."

"Did not."

"Keep telling yourself that, Lark."

"I will, 'cause it's true—Ah!" I gasped when he suddenly pulled away enough to flip me completely over and push the t-shirt up. "Adriel you fucking ass!" I all-but shrieked, and my voice echoed around his room. He only laughed as those hands rubbed slowly over the back of my thighs then kneaded into my bare bottom.

"I hate you." I snapped and tried to wiggle out from under him, which he was not letting happen.

"No, you don't." Which he was completely right about, but I wasn't going to let him know that. He was also right about the whole manhandling thing too. Well, at least when it came to sex. In any other situation, the man knew I was going to slap him upside the head if he tried to do that shit.

His strong, slightly rough hands from working in construction, left their massaging position on my ass to trace over my lower back and then along the curves of my side. I felt those familiar, sensually shivers start to race through my body. I didn't fight him as his hands roamed over my skin, completely oblivious to the fact that the shirt I was wearing was pushed all the way up to my shoulders and he had a clear few of everything.

My hands were curled into the extra bit of pillowcase that my forehead was pressing firmly against. Adriel's lips dropped down to my skin and started pressing hot, open kissing along my spine. My back arched as his touch sent electricity surging through every part off me. One of his hands went back to gently kneading my ass while the other slipped sneakily beneath my chest and started playing with my boob.

"You're mean." I grumbled down to the bed as those strong legs of his slipped between mine and gently pried them open.

"How so?" He asked on a laugh and pressed a kiss to my shoulder blade.

"You know how." Yet, despite my grumbling, I so did not want him to stop. For the first time in a long time I felt somewhat okay. There was no nightmare filling my mind, no thoughts of red-eyes, or creepy photos, or demon/angel things. Just Adriel and how those stupid hands put me on Cloud 9.

"I'm not sure I know what you mean." But his voice was teasing like he knew exactly what I meant. I squeaked when he suddenly pinched my poor nibble then squeezed the whole boob.

"Ow! That hurt jerk!"

"Sorry, beautiful." Though his voice suggested he was anything but 'sorry'.

I was about to turn and send colorful words flying his way, including how he could forget about anything sex related, when one of those strong fingers slipped between my legs and all rational thought flew from my brain. I gasped and pressed my face firmly into the pillow as he moved slowly inside me, the pad of his finger touching every single nerve along the way. My back arched down on its own accord, shoving my butt and lower region further against him in open invitation.

What a traitorous fucking body. I couldn't even trust myself. Typical.

Adriel leaned away from me and let out a low whistle, his finger moving steadily as he did. "Now that's a sight I'm never going to get used to." His voice was low as it wrapped around us, almost like he hadn't meant for me to hear—or cared that I did. I tried to scoot back further into him, like I could egg that finger to go faster if I tried hard enough.

Dri just chuckled and pressed his free hand against my lower back. "Easy."

"No." I grumbled defiantly and pushed back again, which only earned a swift slap on my ass. I squeaked again and moved to shoot away from him, he didn't let me do that either.

"You know," He started softly, and I just knew whatever he was about to say was going to be a ringer by the smirk in his voice. "For someone who doesn't like to be manhandled, you sure are wet, Lark."

I felt heat flame my face, whether that was from his words or the way his finger curled inside me I'll never know. Or let onto knowing. "Left over from the shower." I mumbled down into the bed, which he didn't believe for one minute.

"Mhm, right."

I wanted to groan in disappointment when his finger slipped slowly out of me, but I knew from past experience he only did that when something far better was about to happen. Dri must have taken his shorts off before he got onto the bed because there was no moment of hesitation where he would have re-moved them. Instead the second he removed his finger I felt that familiar pressure of something far bigger pushing at my entrance.

"You sure you want—"

"I swear to god if you ask me if I'm sure about this again I will give you a black eye."

It was taking all I had in me not to just shove back on my own and impale myself on the stupid thing. Not that it was stupid, not at all. Actually, it was quickly becoming my favorite part of his body. Figures the one thing I liked most on the walking, talking, dick was his actual dick. Just kidding, I liked all of him. Well, I actually kind of love the asshole, but that's not important at the moment.

He let out a quiet laugh and rotated his hips in a way that made the hot pressure of his head rub teasingly against me. That feeling alone sent mind numbing sparks straight to my brain. I moaned and had to bite down on the pillow to keep from begging him.

"I just want to make you're okay."

"I'm fine, just fucking fuck me."

I had a feeling sex might always be like this between us. We weren't cute romantic people that talked about feelings and love all the time. We weren't even before the whole 'sleeping together' thing. I highly doubted that would change now that we were.

"Alright, horny girl." I didn't even care that he laughed when he said it, or that he called me 'horny' instead of 'sweet', because then he started easing inside of me and all rational thought flew away.

Dri liked to go hard, and I sure as hell did too, but for the first thrust or two he always went slow, like he had to actually get me to loosen up and accept him. Which it probably was a fucking process for him. It didn't hurt anymore, but I still sure fucking felt a big ball of pressure every time he pushed in. Then he just kind of filled me and it was serene pleasure.

"You know what the great thing about my bed is?" He asked only a few beats in, he hadn't even started picking up pace yet which I was one millisecond away from begging him to do.

"What?" I croaked against the bed, all my concentration going into not moaning like a hungry whale. My grip disappeared on the pillow as he reached over to fling it off the bed.

"Those." He paused all movement until I glance up at what he was gesturing to. A smile pulled against my lips. Bars. The bottom of his headboard was made up of bars. "Grab on, baby, and hold tight."

CHAPTER 23

I tried to ignore it as best as I could. That completely insane, unfounded, stupid urge to ask about that picture to her. Yet, there I stood the next day, staring at that crystal covered window and the bizarre entry sign. 'Embrace the cleansing aurora of dreams.'

Yeah right.

If someone asked me why I thought this was a good idea, I would have laughed and said, 'it's fucking not'. But I never did have many good ideas.

I tried to avoid Siena and River all day. I wasn't sure I could face them again after my hasty getaway at the library. I could have played off finding the image as a coincidence, but when they both started exclaiming 'holy shit, maybe the legend is real', I had to bail. Spending time with Dri only worked at pushing the insanity away when he was there. Last night had been perfect, but as soon as he got up for work reality crashed back down on my shoulders like an eighteen smashing into a cement wall.

And I was getting a sick feeling it was a reality I wasn't going to end up surviving.

I can't believe I was starting to believe in this shit.

I sucked in a shaky breath, and another, then another until I could control my breathing enough to face the crazy psychic. I really wasn't sure why I was doing this, but I couldn't think of anything else that would help. I skipped the second have of classes for the day just to avoid an awkward conversation with Adriel about why I wasn't home. He made it pretty clear he wasn't happy about any of this stuff. I had a feeling he would just make my life harder if I told him everything.

I pushed through the door, the entry bells jingling as I did. I couldn't see her or the counter around the many aisles and shelves of witchy crap, but I could practically feel her in the back. Waiting for me.

Our eyes locked as I rounded the corner, and she made no move in surprise. That look in her gaze was anything but shocked. She had been expecting me. "This is a dreary time for you, dear." Was her greeting as I stopped a few feet away from the counter. Those bright green eyes were drawn in concern, and her long dirty-blonde hair was tied in an elegant braid down her back.

I bit the inside of my cheek anxiously. "Yeah, you can say that."

"Come with me, we can talk." She turned and walked out from behind the counter. I had a fearful moment where I thought she would take me back into that freaky dark room, but she flipped the 'open' sign to 'closed' and walked towards a door on the other side of the store instead. I hesitated only a moment before following her. I was bound to die eventually, at least if she tried to kill me I had a fair chance of defending myself. She was pretty small.

"I live in the apartment above the shop." Jess explained as we walked through the door and up a row of stairs. She took out a set of keys from the back pocket of her skinny jeans and unlocked her apartment door.

I walked into the small living room hesitantly, but it wasn't as creepy as I thought it would be. There was a wall of windows pressed against the back of the room, with plants hanging from various hooks and on the window bench. A comfortable looking couch, coffee table, and recliner sat facing a flat screen TV, and a small bar on the other side of the room lead to her kitchen.

I stood awkwardly in the middle of everything, unsure of what to do with myself. Jess smiled as she walked in behind me and closed the door. "Please, have a seat. Make yourself at home." She nodded towards the dark purple couch covered by a thick hippie-esk blanket. "Would you like a coffee?" Jess asked as I sat gingerly down on the blanket and dropped my backpack to the ground.

"Um, sure." Although I'm not sure caffeine was a good idea at the moment. My nerves were making me jittery enough.

"Milk, no sugar, right?"

"Yeah." I didn't bother being surprised that she knew exactly how I liked my coffee.

She gave me an endearing smile before disappearing behind the bar to make the coffee. "I had a feeling you would be back soon." She announced a minute later as she came back around the corner with two small cups in her hands. I took one from her outstretched hand uneasily and kept my eyes glued to the 'psychic' as she sat on the floor across from me. The coffee table resting between us.

"Had a feeling, or just knew?" I grumbled down into the cup before taking a careful sip. The coffee was good, light with a touch of cinnamon. I drank it greedily.

Would it be too much to ask for a shot of vodka?

Ugh. Probably.

Jess shrugged her shoulders, that small smile still pulling on her lips as she sipped her own coffee. "Neither makes a difference. The only thing that matters is why you're here."

"And do you know? Why I'm here, I mean."

"I can only imagine the questions you must have. With our first and last meeting I believe you have experienced events none would willingly dare undergo." The way she talked was so weird. Like she spent her free time taking vocal grammar lessons. Jess set the little coffee cup down on the table, and the rings covering her slender fingers glistened as she did.

"You could say that."

She sighed softly, though the action sounded more sad and tired than exasperated. "I'm afraid your challenges are not yet over."

"Yeah, I'm starting to see that." I threw back the rest of the coffee and set the cup down on the table. "Look, I'm not really sure why I'm here, or how the hell I expect you to help me, but things are becoming a little too freaky to just be coincidences. It's starting to really freak me out."

Jess threaded her fingers together and those bright green eyes stared curiously into mine. "There is no such thing as coincidences. Everything happens for a reason. Even if you do not believe in the paranormal, or spiritual, you understand the abnormalities of what is happening around you. Do not take your instincts for granted. Listen to what they have to say."

"It's not like they talk to me." I scoffed and scrubbed a shaky hand through my long curls. "Usually I just feel sick or like someone punched me in the stomach."

She shrugged again, though the action was more like a ballerina dancing then anything else. The girl looked way to graceful in everything she did. It was beautiful. And annoying. "There is more than one way to listen. What do you want to do most right now?"

"Get the fuck out of this town and go as far away as possible." I leaned back heavily against the couch and continuously clenched and unclenched my fist. I was literally one thread away from telling Adriel that I was done and begging him to pack us up and get the hell out there.

I tried. I was still trying. That's all I promised. I did my part, now I just want it to be done.

"You've seen something that's made you feel this way, yes? That is the only reason why you would come to."

"Yeah."

"Alright, what have you seen?" There was no condescension in her tone, or arrogant amusement shining back at me in those bright eyes. I appreciated that, almost as much as I was creeped out that she seemed to freaking know everything.

"There's a picture of a girl that looks a shit-ton like me from five hundred years ago. The book we found it in said that she was the 'prison' or whatever the hell it's called for that demon-angel dude that founded the town." I paused and waited for Jess to interject but she just kept that silent, steady gaze.

"And you were the first person that ever talked to me about crazy shit, so I guess coming to you about it was my only opti on..." I wasn't sure what she was expecting me to say. I sure as hell didn't know, but she should, being an all-powerful psychic witch thing or whatever the fuck she was.

"You seem surprised." She spoke a moment later, her delicate head tilting to the side as if she were studying me. "I've already told you that you have an old soul. That you've spent more than one life in this world. It was only a matter of time before you stumbled across the proof of that."

"Okay, but I thought that was crazy, psycho stuff. I didn't believe you."

"And you do now?"

"Now I—I don't know what I believe anymore."

The curious look pulling on her face faded away to a soft, endearing smile. Her hands relaxed on the table and she even kicked her feet out beneath it. She no longer looked like the eerie witch-thing who knew about the black eyes and dark feathers of my dreams and warning me to stay out of the shadows, but a girl my age who was just trying to live as best as she could too.

"Don't force yourself to believe in anything. I like to go with the flow. Sometimes things happen, sometimes they don't."

"That's easy for you to say." I grumbled and let my hands fidget with the straps of my backpack. "So, you think that picture is a past me or whatever?"

"Yes." There was no hesitation in her voice or questioning light in her eyes. Just solid, unwavering conviction.

I let out a large, exasperated sigh and scrubbed my hand down my face. "Alright, well how does this reincarnation thing work?" I didn't know if I believed it, but knowledge is power, I guess.

Jess's face pulled into a warm smile that did little to ease the anxious nerves rushing through me. "Old souls are ordained by Michael, God's right-hand angel and leader of his army." That smile of hers turned sly for a brief moment. "If you believe in all of that."

I ignored that little remark and nodded my head. "Yeah, one of my professors talked about him when we learned about the demon dude."

"Avidus is not a demon, though there are many who will refer to him as such." Those creepy ass pictures would suggest otherwise, but whatever. "Usually old souls have significant preordained plans on Earth that they have not yet accomplished, or act as the bridge between this world and Heaven." She gave another slender shrug of her shoulders, and I was starting to wonder is she was trying to seem—relatable? I'm not sure, but the girl was freaking weird.

"Once Michael picks the soul, Azrael, whom we've talked about before, sends them back every time their past life dies until their mission has been completed. Sometimes they may never reach that goal and are constantly recycled into a new generation."

"Like me." It wasn't a question. I remember her comment about how that death-angel dude Azrie, or whatever the fuck his name was, has sent my soul back quite a bit.

"Yes, and I have a feeling your reasoning for being in this world will be accomplished very soon."

"Why's that?"

Jess gave me one, slow, unnerving blink that made those bright green eyes shine eerily. "I have it on good authority this has been the only time you have returned to Deshua since your soul's origins. Fate would not have brought you here otherwise."

God, this place really fucking sucked.

"Then what the hell is my 'purpose'?"

"You're in that class, yes? You've heard the legend. You know what it is."

"What? You're seriously telling me that my preordained mission in this world is to wake greedy guy up? The girl was created to put him in prison! Why they hell would they want me to let him go?!"

That bright gaze flickered away as my tone rose, but I didn't care enough to feel bad. I mean, come on, seriously? What a load of shit this was. I wasn't even sure I believed in any of it!

"It is not our job to question Fate's design."

"Yeah, well, Fate can suck my design. I don't want anything to do with it."

Jess let out a small sigh, and all pretenses of her smile disappeared. "Whether you do or don't doesn't matter. There are people in this town who are looking for you. Dangerous people. You must be careful, Larkin."

"Trust me, I'm trying." I sat back heavily on the couch with a scoff. "But as you mentioned, I can't escape Fate, and it really likes fucking with me."

"There's more you can be doing, precautions you should be taking."

"Like what?"

"Like plants to use to ward off evil, metals that will hold them off."

My head felt like it was going to explode. Begging Adriel to leave sounded more and more like the best option. Especially if people are looking for me to wake up some demon/angel greedy guy that probably doesn't even exist!

"Who even are them?"

Her face grew pale and those bright eyes slowly turned dull. "They are not... normal by any means. They are dangerous and hold far more power than you could ever imagine."

"You're not talking about those creature things demon/not-demon dude created, are you?"

"Yes, I am."

I didn't want to believe her. It was easier to laugh and scoff and tell her she's crazy and full of shit. I should have walked out of there and put all of this crap behind me. It was ridiculous. But then the image of those red eyed kept flashing through my mind. Red eyes and those guys talking about eating me. No matter what Adriel said, or how much I tried to convince myself, I knew what I saw.

"Alright, what do I do?"

"Get Yarrow, lots of it. The plant wards off evil and acts as a repellent against the Immortals."

Immortals. That was the same term Shorzin used to name the creatures. I cannot believe I was entertaining this.

"What does it look like?"

"Little flowers in clusters, they come in many different colors, but I know there is quite a few purple vines growing around the campus."

"Purple flowers? You mean, like these?" I reached down for my backpack and pulled the nearly dead flowers I had stuffed in the front pocket a few days ago out for her to see.

Her green eyes and whole facial expression brightened immediately. "Yes! Exactly, how long have you been carrying those around?"

It was my turn to shrug as I shoved the plant back in my bag. "A few days. This creep-a-zoid trying to talk to me said he was allergic to them, so I stuffed a few in my backpack."

Jess laughed, and I was surprised at how warm and light it sounded. "Excellent, great thinking. Be wary of anyone saying the same thing."

Already ahead of you lady.

"Hopefully you won't be put into another situation where you will need to defend yourself against them," I didn't bother acting surprise that she knew I had before, "but there is very little that can hurt them. Steel can penetrate their skin, and iron can burn their blood. Try to carry around both."

Okay, because carrying around sticks of steel and iron were oh-so easy.

"Alright," I sighed and resisted the urge to rub my fists into my eyes. "Is there anything else?"

"Stay out of the shadows. The sun doesn't hurt them, but they are stronger in the dark."

"Duly noted."

"Larkin..." My gaze snapped to hers when Jess suddenly reached over and placed her tiny hand on top of mine. "You will have to make a decision in the very near future, one that will decide the fate of yourself and the entire time. You cannot run away from it." Which is exactly what I had planned on doing.

"It is your choice. If you wake him, you're risking the lives of not only Deshua, but anyone he will come across." Her hand tightened around mine, and those bright eyes grew hard. "Make sure you choose wisely."

If, by some insane anomaly all of this was freaking real, couldn't I just not choose at all?

Looks like running far away was sounding like by best option.

Not that I was every any good at that.

-&-

I almost didn't notice the gentle fingers sweeping my hair over my shoulder as I sat huddled against the armrest of the couch. But then they were tugging at my ear and I had to tear my gaze from the TV to blink over at him. "I'm worried about you." Jumping straight to the point, such an Adriel thing.

We haven't talked much in the past few days, or I haven't at least. After my meeting with Jess I needed some alone time to sort out my thoughts. And as much as I loved spending time with Dri and Raffie, I couldn't really think with them around. They made me forget everything, at least for a little while, and even though I craved that distraction it wasn't going to help anything at the moment.

I tried to make my eyes all big and wide and confused as I blinked up at that concerned blue gaze. "Why? I'm fine." His hard look didn't waiver.

"I hate it when you lie to me."

I shook my head and wrapped my arms tightly around my knees. "I'm just stressed with school and the dreams. I'm sorry."

Which wasn't a complete lie, but I knew I couldn't tell him what was really going on inside my head. He wouldn't believe me, just like with those red-eyed freaks after that party. Dri would just write it off as my imagination, or the 'bull shit' drilled into my skull by Shorzin. He wouldn't understand.

I was surprised when his heavy body plopped down on the couch beside me and pushed my legs down to the ground so he could rest his stupid, big, pretty darn attractive head in my lap. I smiled down at those dark eyes reluctantly and let my fingers play with his hair.

"How was your day?" I asked absently as the TV drawled softly in the background.

"Long, boring, worried about you."

I rolled my eyes and tugged a little harder on his hair. He didn't even flinch. Hardheaded jerk. "I told you I'm fine."

"And I told you I don't like it when you lie to me."

I sighed softly and poked repeatedly at his stubbly cheek. "This place is just so freaking weird." He lifted one arm to rest under his head and against my lap as I spoke, those blue eyes turning all concerned as he listened. Worry wart. "I feel like..." I started softly but couldn't find the words to finish.

"Like what?"

I let the hand that wasn't playing in his hair trace his strong neck. I didn't know how to explain any of this to him. I could barely explain it to myself. "Like everyone here is wanting me to go crazy and is living off the fact that I am."

His oh-so-yummy lips pulled into a small frown and the hand that wasn't propping his head up reached over tug endearingly on my sleeve. "I don't want you to go crazy." I laughed at the pout in his tone, and that simple action made me feel a whole lot better.

"Yes, you do. You just want me to go crazy in a completely different way."

He smiled, but the look didn't reach his eyes. "Come here." He switched our spots on the couch almost effortlessly, and I let those strong arms cradle me against his chest without a struggle. "I never wanted to make you feel like this." He murmured against the top of my head as I gripped onto the open lapels of his flannel.

"It's not you, Dri."

"I'm the one that brought us here." His arms squeezed tighter around me, and I could feel his chest rise and fall with the heavy breath he let out. "I never would have moved us if I knew how unhappy and stressed it would make you." The complete and total remorse in his tone tore at my heart, and I felt that boulder of guilt weigh heavily down on my shoulders.

"There's no way you could have known. Besides, even if I was a brat during the whole move, I didn't want you to miss out on the job." I shrugged, which was hard to do being so squished against him but whatever.

My forehead was pressed against his jaw, and he pulled away enough to press a kiss there. "There's always another job, another town. I don't care about staying anymore if it's only making you depressed."

"I'm not depressed—"

"Still," That bossy tone was back in full force as he interrupted, and he pulled away enough for those dark blues to stare down at my gaze. "We can leave if this place becomes too much for you."

I dropped my gaze down to a loose button on his flannel that my fingers had started fidgeting with. I didn't want to be that person. The one that begged to move just because I couldn't handle something. I knew running away wasn't very integral of me, but I didn't pick this fucked up life. Why should I have to suffer through it?

"Promise?" My voice was barely more than a whisper, but I wasn't brave enough to raise it any higher.

"Of course. Hey..." Adriel's fingers pinched my chin and angled my face up to his. My stomach clenched at the look in those dark eyes. He could make me do anything when he gave me that look. "You are the most important person to me. Besides Raffie." His lips pulled up at the corners in that smirk that made me both want to roll my eyes and attach my mouth to his at the same time. "I'd do anything for you. Getting a new job in some other town is nothing."

I tried to keep my smile from my lips as those fingers traced along my jaw. His words were making my heart a little too fluttery. "You're okay sometimes, you know?" I teased even though my voice sounded more like a mumble than anything.

Dri chuckled and the sound made ease sway the tension from my shoulders. "Yeah, I know." My heart jumped nervously when he leaned down to press his lips against mine, and I pushed my hand against his chest to stop him. The frown that pulled at the corners of his mouth was admittedly adorable.

"Where's Raffie?"

He rolled those blue eyes and readjusted his hold around my waist. "In her room playing on her Xbox."

"She can come down any second."

"Then I'll stop kissing you."

"But what if she sees?"

Dri let out an overly dramatic sigh and leaned back heavily. "Who cares if she sees?"

"Um, I do. And so should you."

"Why?"

"Because she's nine? And for all intents and purposes, she sees me as a sister for both of you." For someone who always seemed to know everything and how to handle every situation he sure wasn't comprehending this.

"Raf watches TV, she knows what kissing is, and she knows you're not blood related. I highly doubt she'll care if we kiss."

I frowned and leaned further away from him. This man cannot be that horny that he can't deal with not kissing me while his sister was around. "Please, Dri? I just don't want us to be like that around her."

His narrowed eyes washed over my face, before he let out a heavy sigh. "Alright, I'm sorry. It's always your choice, Lark."

I had a feeling I was going to get real sick and tired of people telling me that.

CHAPTER 24

After a lot of careful consideration and back and forth genuine mind-fucking, I decided not to ask Adriel to leave Deshua.

The man did almost everything for me, and despite what he said, I knew this was the one job offer he had been really excited about. Not to mention that he loved this house. When the Markos found out their great aunt had willed it to them, his face had lit up in genuine excitement. I couldn't ask him to leave just because I was losing my shit.

But that didn't mean I was going to let us live there all willy-nilly.

I pulled myself out of that depressed little state and spent the rest of week completely decking out the manor in Yarrow. I went to every single store in Deshua that sells the stuff and bought out all of their supplies—which might sound like a lot but really wasn't.

There were only four stores in the entire area that carried the plant, and just packaged seeds of the stuff too. I had to go back to that alcove at school and cut a bunch of the weed-like-flower from the walls for the actual thing.

I hung the plant all over the house. I pinned them above the doorways, wrapped them around the railing of the stairs and even entwined them through window curtains. I spent nearly two days digging out the overgrown weeds from the flowerbeds surrounding the house and replaced them with Yarrow. By the time I was done with the manor, it looked like a living flower advertisement.

After a whole week of just watching me throw the weedy flower around, Adriel finally said something when I was elbow deep in dirty outside. "Lark... what exactly are you doing?" He was standing halfway down the stone steps that lead to the front door, his strong arms crossed over his flannel and black t-shirt covered chest.

"What does it look like?" I snapped and stuck the little tiny gardening shoveling into the soil to make a hole for the seeds. "I'm gardening." My nose was so itchy! But my hands were covered in dirt and I couldn't scratch it. Ugh.

"Okay, but why? You don't like dirt."

"I like flowers."

"Yeah, I've seen the weeds all over the house."

I narrowed my eyes at the infuriating man. "They're not weeds."

He raised one dark eyebrow and leaned heavily against the stone wall surrounding the steps. "They look like weeds."

"Yeah, well, you just don't know anything about plants."

"And you do?"

"As a matter of fact, yes. I love them." I yapped with fake glee as I plopped the seeds in the hole and started piling soil on top of them.

"Right. Since when?"

"Since when do I need to have a 'when'? I like flowers, these to be specific. Why are you being an ass about it?" I knew I was being way too defensive, and a little harsh, but he wouldn't drop the damn subject. Why the fuck was he turning it into an investigation anyway? Just let me plant the damn things!

He raised both eyebrows at my tone and held his hands up in surrender. "Sheesh, sorry." He drawled sarcastically and stepped away. "I'll just leave you alone then."

I felt bad when he turned and walked back into the house. I didn't mean to be such a bitch, especially to him, but I didn't need him snooping around the Yarrow. And it's not like I could tell him they were going to keep us, and the house, safe from red-eyed freaks who wanted to eat them and force me to wake up demon greedy guy. He would send me to the loony bin.

"Hey, Larkin?" Raffie's questioning voice pipped up from the same spot her brother had fled a few minutes later.

"What's up, kid? I'm a little busy right now." I only had half of the front facing flowerbeds planted. I needed to get the whole side and back of the house done too.

"I really want to go to town square today. Can you take me?"

"Ask your brother, I have to get this done."

I looked over when she stomped her foot, huffed dramatically and crossed her little arms over her chest. "He says he has to go into work in a little bit and I want to goooo!" I raised my eyebrow as she stomped her foot again.

"You know I do not do temper tantrums, Rafael."

"Then take me to the square."

"First of all," I started pointedly while wiping the dirt from my hands on my pants. "That is so not how you ask." Her little angry face fell away as I stood to my feet and tossed the tiny shovel into the ground. "And secondly, it's Saturday. Why is Adriel going into work?"

Raf shrugged and started playing oh-so-innocently with the hem of her skirt. Sneaky, manipulative little child. God, I loved that kid. "I don't know, he didn't say. But will you pretty, please take me to town square?" She blinked those big, blue, doe eyes up at me as I walked over, like she wasn't just a little turd barely five seconds before.

I sighed and glared down at the soil stuck underneath my nails. Ugh, that was going to take a lot of scrubbing to get out. "I really need to finish planting—"

"Please, Larkin? You've been doing that all morning, and I want to go have some fun!"

"What possible fun is there in town square?" I groaned and rolled my eyes skyward. My last big experience in the square was nowhere near 'fun'. Unless you called being chased by four freaks with red eyes 'fun'.

"There's shops, and toys, and ice cream! And pigeons!"

"Pigeons carry diseases."

"They're cute!"

"You're not touching one."

For a minute I thought she was going to stomp her foot again and start screaming, but she just clasped her hands in front of her face and pouted at me. "Please, please, please Larkin? I haven't done anything fun in, like, two weeks. And I'm tired of being stuck in the house."

"You go to school." At this point I was just having fun messing with the kid.

"That's not the same, and you know it! School sucks, let's go buy stuff and ice cream!"

Sugar, sugar, sugar. That's all the kid cares about.

I looked wearily back at the flowerbeds. I really didn't want to leave until I was finished Yarrow-fying the manor, but I had been going out at all week. A break for an hour or two wouldn't hurt anyone.

"Alright kid." I finally relented after those puppy dog eyes started tearing up. "Just give me a little bit to wash up and change—"

"Yay! Great! I'll go tell Adriel!" Raf turned on her heels excitedly and took off for the entrance of the manor.

"And tell him I want to talk to him!" I called after her, even though I wasn't sure if she heard. The girl was fast.

He didn't mention anything about having to work today, even though looking back at it I never really gave him a chance. I've been so busy with the flowers and stressing out about protecting us that I haven't really had a legit conversation with either of them in days. And I snapped at him earlier. He probably wasn't happy about that.

I followed slowly after Raf with my gardening tools forgotten in the soil. I would just finish when we got back. I seriously wasn't planning on being gone for too long. Somehow, I was going to have to shove Yarrow in Raf's pockets without her knowing. I'll make her wear a hoodie and shove them in the hood or something.

I wasn't sure where they disappeared to, but I took their absence as free reign to take as long as I wanted in the shower. I made sure to scrub the dirt out from my nails and off my skin. I was so off in my own little world that I hadn't even notice the bathroom door open.

"You wanted to talk to me?"

"Eek!" I practically squeaked and whipped around so fast in surprise that I almost slipped on the wet floor of the shower. "Adriel! You scared the shit out of me!"

"Sorry." I couldn't see him through the purple shower curtain, but his dark chuckle let me know he wasn't sorry at all.

I rubbed the spot over my heart that was beating a little too fast to be normal. "Ever heard of knocking?"

"Didn't think I needed to."

"You always need to!"

He laughed again, but this time it sounded much more genuine and Adriel-like. "Okay, I promise to always knock from now on."

"Whatever." I grumbled and leaned my head back to rinse the conditioner from my hair. "Raf says you have to work today?"

He let out a long, drawn out sigh and I watched his shadow move behind the shower curtain. "Yeah." He grumbled before sitting down on the closed toilet seat. "Some paperwork got fucked up and they need me to go in and fix it."

"Sucks being the boss."

I tried to keep my tone light and worry free, but I honestly didn't want him out of my sight anymore. Not until all this crazy stuff was over. It's not like I could actually protect him from red-eyed monsters who liked to eat people, but at least I could shove a bunch of Yarrow in the side pockets of his lunch and toolbox. Maybe I could even find a way of shoving it in his boots somehow.

"Mhm. Definitely not how I wanted to spend my Saturday."

"How long will you be gone?"

"I don't know, maybe three or four hours?" He didn't sound so sure and I couldn't shake the uneasy feeling settling in my stomach.

"Oh, okay..."

There was a rather awkward moment of silence between us before he spoke again. "This whole 'plant' business isn't about what's going on lately, is it?" He said the word 'plant' as sarcastically as I say the phrase 'my life is completely normal'.

I sighed and let the hot water wash over my face. "Who cares if it is, Dri? It makes me feel better. What's wrong with that?"

"Nothing. Nothing's wrong with that, and I'm sorry I made it seem that way. I'm just..." He paused, and I could tell he wasn't thrilled with what he was going to say next. "I'm just not so convinced staying here is best for us anymore."

I didn't say anything as I reached over and turned the water off. I knew he was willing to leave if that was what I wanted, but I never thought that he would be the one that was starting to doubt the place.

"What do you mean?" I asked quietly as he stood to hand me a fluffy towel through the edge of the shower curtain. I wrapped it tightly around my body and pushed the curtain open. Dri was leaning almost lazily against the wall in front of me, the steam from the shower still filling the small hallway bathroom.

He shrugged, and that dark gaze flickered away. "You're not okay here, and the last thing I ever wanted to do was upset you."

"Dri, I'm fine, I promise." Or at least, I would make myself be if only to erase the guilty sad expression from his handsome face. "We don't have to move just because I'm having issues. It'll be okay—" He cut me off by scooping his strong arms around my waist and lifting me easily out of the shower.

I didn't fight him as he hugged me against his chest, those blue eyes finally locking onto mine. "It's not just for you, Lark. This move just isn't turning out like I hoped it would. The job's not what I thought it was, Raff's not really making any friends, and I'm starting to feel like Deshua is not for us."

Despite what he said, I had a sickening feeling he was just thinking of moving for me.

"We can go back to the city or try somewhere new. Whatever you want."

There he was, giving me everything I wanted since the second week we moved here. An out. An opportunity to leave this place and never look back. Never have to worry about red eyes again, or greedy demon guys, or reincarnation. Just him, me, and Raffie, moving somewhere new, where no one knew us. Starting over, being a normal family. It was everything I wanted.

So, why was I hesitating?

"Can I think about it?" I asked softly as he leaned his forehead against mine in that simple but endearing way he always did.

"Of course." He pressed his lips against my forehead, and then the tip of my nose. "I meant what I said, Angel. You mean everything to me. You and Raffie. I'll do anything to make sure you're okay."

I let out a small sigh before standing on my tip toes to press a soft, lingering kiss against his lips. "I know, Dri." That was the first time I had to physically stop myself from saying 'I love you'. I mean, I've said it before in a family context. Like, I love them because they're everything I have in this world, but that was the first time it would mean something else.

Because I did love him. In all his crazy, pig-headed, jerkish, sweet, caring way, I loved him. More than anything.

CHAPTER 25

I was actually having a pleasant time sitting in the stone courtyard outside that Cathedral. It was chilly rest against the marble bench, though licking an ice cream cone while I watched Raf didn't help either. Then, like usual, my enjoyment went to shit.

A heavy body sat down on the other side of the bench my butt was occupying. I glanced briefly over to glare at the intruder, but dread filled my stomach instead. Luke was sitting casually beside me, his usual dark sunglasses covering those brown eyes, as a black leather jacket sat perfectly over his square shoulders.

He would have made the perfect hot 'bad boy next door' that I would have typically gone for in Sacramento, if it wasn't for the all-consuming hatred I had for him and his 'friends'. And I was infatuated with Adriel.

"Get. Lost." I spoke each word between separate licks of my ice cream. I was honestly proud of how strong my voice sounded. No wavering whatsoever, even though my insides were consumed with anxious nerves.

"Well, that's not very nice." Luke spoke casually, with no malice in his tone at all. His lips even pulled up slightly at the corner in an amused smile. One I wanted to smack off his stupid face.

"I don't care. Leave."

"I just want to talk. I promise. Nothing else. We can even sit right here, in the middle of the day, surrounded by people if that makes you feel better." The way he spoke only strengthened that fear in my stomach. Like he knew that I knew. That he was one of them.

"You're one of them, aren't you? One of those freaks with the red eyes." Admitting out loud that I was actually starting to believe in this stuff was far from reassuring. I kept my eyes glued to Rafael, who was chasing pigeons a few feet away. Even though I didn't want her anywhere near the birds, it was a lot better than being on this bench right now.

"'Freak' is a little harsh, don't you think?" He stretched one long arm out across the top of the bench, his fingers barely an inch from my shoulder. I shifted uneasily away. I didn't like how at ease he was making himself, like he couldn't tell I had Yarrow shoved into every single one of my pockets.

Maybe that was why he was trying extra hard to appear comfortable, because he wasn't.

"No, I actually think it's pretty nice for what I really want to call you." I finished off the ice cream and tossed the cone into the trashcan beside the bench. "Now, I'm going to get my sister, and we're going to leave. Do not follow me, or I swear I will stab you with this iron knife I ordered on Amazon. Goodbye."

I went to stand up and walk away like a badass, but his hand reached out and grabbed onto my wrist before I could.

"I wasn't kidding about that knife. I swear I'll shank you in front of all these people."

He laughed, and I wasn't all too pleased at that. "Oh, trust me. I believe you. I promise, but I really just want to talk. I'm not here to hurt you. I'll even hold onto some of those weeds in your pocket if you want."

Ha! I knew he knew I had them!

Then a sickening thought hit me. "Wait, so they won't hurt you?"

What the actual fuck?! The whole purpose of the stupid plant was to keep him and his freaks away from us!

"Steel and Iron hurt, Yarrow just—slows us down, I guess you can say."

Jess told me about the steel and iron, hence the big ass knife I bought. One side was steel, the other iron. I felt like a badass when I bought it, and just as surprised that Amazon actually sold something like that. But why the hell was he admitting that? Telling someone that obviously hated him how to hurt his kind didn't necessarily seem like a great plan.

"Why are you telling me this?" I asked as I sat reluctantly back down. Raf was still chasing pigeons, and I prayed she didn't decide to come over anytime soon. The farther away she was from the guy, the better.

"Because I want you to trust me. I told you the truth before when I said it was never supposed to happen this way. I wanted us to be friends."

"Right, so you can convince it's a good idea to wake up your demon dude? No thanks, I barely even believe in this crap." I huffed and crossed my arms over my chest, even though it was just an excuse to check that my fancy knife was still there.

"He's not a demon."

I was getting really sick and tired of people telling me that.

"Okay, whatever, but like I said, this stuff is all a little too crazy to be completely real-"

Luke's long irritated sigh interrupted my tirade and he shifted in his seat to grab a little knife out of his pocket. "Alright, look." And before I could make a move, he stabbed himself in the leg.

Or, tried to at least. The blade bent the second it hit his jean-covered thigh and slipped harmlessly away.

I had to viciously gulp down the saliva building in my mouth. There was no way I could convince myself that didn't just happen.

"Give me your knife." He tossed his now useless pocketknife in the trash and stuck his hand out towards me.

"Fuck that." If anything, I was less inclined to let him see it now than before.

I could practically feel his eyes roll behind those sunglasses. "I just want to show you it will work. Here," He turned his palm up so it was facing me in invitation. "Cut my hand. I won't try to take it."

I didn't believe him, like at all. But he was giving me a free invite to test out my fancy knife, and after that whole pocketknife display, I really needed to see if it would work. Completely ignoring the fact that we were surrounded by people, I took the knife out and quickly sliced a little nick in his palm. I've had to defend myself before, the trials of growing up alone in California, so the action didn't really bother me.

Luke flinched and as blood swelled onto his palm, relief flooded my chest. Until that blood started burning, like smoke was literally coming off his hand. He grabbed the bottle of water from beside him that I hadn't noticed before, and quickly poured the whole thing onto this hand. The smoke died away.

I sat back against the bench completed flabbergasted, my eyes shifting between the blade and his hand. Okay... So, maybe, I really did believe in this shit. Or I had officially lost it.

"There, happy now?" Though his voice was a little shaky and when I finally tore my eyes from his hand, I saw how his face had gone white as a ghost. Damn, I guess the thing really does work.

"Uh, um, I-I'll listen to what you have to say now, I guess." I didn't think he was going to hurt me, and even if he tried my fancy little knife will def stop him.

"You want me to hold that little plant of yours?" Luke tried to sound casual as he sat back against the bench, but he still looked three seconds away from throwing up everywhere.

"No, no I trust you... for now at least."

He nodded and ran his hand through that blond hair but didn't hide the relieved look crossing his face well. "Okay, thanks, but do me a favor and put that thing away." He gestured towards the knife and then looked out at the crowd. I followed his gaze only to see more than a few people eyeing the knife, and me warily. But the scary part were the red eyes flashing back at us.

Fear raked down my spine and I quickly shoved the knife into the inside pocket of my jacket. The red eyes disappeared to normal colors and they meandered on their merry way. Now it was my face that was stark white. Those were a lot of red-eyed freaks. I couldn't take all of them, I doubted in a real fight I could actually take Luke.

"You look surprised." He chuckled softly a moment later when it was just us talking and Raffie chasing pigeons once again. "You're in Shorzin's class, you heard the legend. This town was founded by Immortals. There's a shit ton of us and we don't die, hence the name."

Okay, my mind was officially made up. That night, when Adriel came home, we were packing the cars up and getting the hell out of this place.

"It's just... a lot to take in."

"Yes, I'm sure." Though his tone was reassuring and not at all scornful. "You're important, Larkin. More so than you could ever imagine. No Immortal will hurt you."

Yeah fucking right.

"Right, because that little run in with your friends was just casual conversation."

A small, apologetic, smile pulled at Luke's lips and his expression turned almost sheepish. "I truly am sorry about that, and I took care of them. They will never bother you again, and the rest of us have been informed of who you are. No one will hurt you."

"Alright, and what about my family? This doesn't mean anything if they're in danger." I still didn't trust the guy, but I did know he was telling the truth about not hurting me. Apparently, I was his, and every other Immortals, key to freeing the demon dude.

"They're safe too, I promise. Well, from us at least."

"What the hell does that mean? Aren't you guys like the big baddies or whatever?"

That sheepish look turned concerned and he shifted uncomfortably beside me. "Yes, technically, but you see, there are two very different groups in Deshua. Mine, the Immortals, and the others."

"What, and let me guess the 'others' are your dinner, right? The humans." I scoffed and was a little weirded out that this conversation didn't necessarily seem so weird.

He shrugged one shoulder but glanced away uneasily. "Yes, they're part of it, but then there's the true others. The ones that still hold onto the old ways and beliefs. The witches that locked up Avidus all those centuries ago."

"I though Michael gave the mortals the girl for that, not witches."

"How do you think their words reached him to begin with?" Luke scoffed, and slumped further down in his seat.

"Just because he's a 'good' angel, doesn't mean he listens to humans. Prayer, after prayer, and soul after soul, tries to reach his ears. After the first billion or so, I'm sure he got irritated and turned off the radar. Only those with genuine power can penetrate an angel's mind—much less Michael's. And believe me, it's no easy feat, nor would anyone dare to do so again. Just because he is God's right-hand man, doesn't mean he isn't spiteful."

The fact that he was talking so causally about the actual existence of an archangel threw me for a loop. I wanted to scream that I was just a regular girl with a regular family that didn't sign up for any of this shit. But I knew that was never going to happen. I would never be 'normal' again. This was life now.

"Alright..." I started slowly, like my brain needed time to absorb all this chaos. "So, the mortals that got Michael's attention were actually witches, that still live here and—what? Want my family dead?"

"Well, they definitely don't want you to wake up Avidus, and I know they're willing to do whatever it takes to make sure that doesn't happen." Luke didn't outright say they would kill me and the Markos, but the implication as there.

"They spent all that time and power trying to get rid of him. There was a balance for a while after Avidus—'went away'—that they thrived on. We weren't strong enough to fight their power without him, and had to let go of our reign. Over the centuries we came to an agreement, never take more than we need, and they'll lay off any mass amounts of power. And it was working, until..." Luke's words trailed away, but I had a feeling I knew what he was going to say.

"Until I showed up."

That small smile was back, and he gazed over at me sheepishly. "When news that Key had returned, like legend said, that balance started to break. Everyone knows that things are about to change. Change how, is what remains uncertain." He nodded his blond head towards the dig site just barely in view behind the Cathedral. "They're not looking for a busted pipe. They're looking for him. A scroll was found in the catacombs a few years ago claiming the tomb he was entrapped in was buried there. They've been searching ever since."

Fear skyrocketed down my spine. That was the dig Adriel's construction site put him on. He was helping them look for greedy-demon guy. Bile started to build in my stomach. I definitely needed to get them away from this place. Even if the Immortals weren't 'supposedly' going to hurt us, I wasn't willing to risk those witch people.

Then a sickening realization hit me.

"Avid." I said out loud with a disbelieving scoff. "The construction company digging is named Avid." Like in Avidus. That knowledge felt like a slap in the face.

Luke let out a small, uncertain, chuckle. "Yes, he thought it would be funny to have me name the company that. Since they are 'avidly' looking for him and, well, his name is Avidus."

"You... you talk to him?"

Luke's face, which had started to look much better, paled again and he shifted uneasily. Like he wasn't supposed to have admitted that. "Um, sometimes. I was his—assistant when he still walked the Earth. He still has me do things for him now and then."

I already had a feeling Luke was 'in charge' of those freaks after the whole second run in with his friends. It wasn't hard to guess he was the 'boss man' they were talking about. But it never occurred to me that he was actually communicating with the locked-up greedy dude.

"How? Isn't he supposed to be trapped and asleep?"

"His body is, his mind travels in and out. Michael only gave the witches the girl, the power that binds Avidus was created by the mortals and has holes that he can slip through. Usually it's just his voice in my head telling me what to do. On rare occasions there's images, but those are few and far in between."

Horrible, gut wrenching dots suddenly connected in my head, and all breath escaped my lungs. My dreams. The ones with the dark wings and black eyes. With the soft, tender, intoxicating touches. Fuck. What if those had all been him? Had all been real? "You said it wasn't supposed to happen like this— He wanted you to find me, didn't he?" Then another sickening thought entered my mind and all I wanted to do was throw up. "You said you named the construction company. You created it?"

His sheepish expression was out for all to see and I nearly had to bend over to force the nausea away. "Oh my God. You found me in Sacramento. You sent Adriel that job offer to get us here. Holy shit! Did you kill his great aunt for the house?! Fuck, I'm going to be sick." I leaned over the side of the bench, ready to spew the contents of my stomach, when relief suddenly washed over me like a warm, soothing wave.

I sat back against the bench, the spinning in my head slowly fading away when I realized why. Luke had somehow managed to wrap his hand around the skin of my wrist, having had to push my sleeve up to do so, and the calm feeling was surging through the touch. I glanced over at him, and his smile was warm and understanding.

"It's an Immortal trick. I didn't want you to get sick." He let go and raised his hands in surrender at the narrowed look I shot him.

"No, you just want to fuck my life up."

He sighed and leaned away to run his hand through that blond hair once again. "Look, my job was to get you here, become your friend, and slowly introduce you to all of this. I wasn't expecting those four fucking idiots to ruin everything, but it was my fault. They knew the Key was here, but I didn't show them who. That's on me. I also wasn't expecting you to be so—aware."

"Aware? What the hell does that mean?"

"Aware. Like, you knew there was something off with me from the beginning. I could tell by the way you acted. You didn't trust me, which is fine. Some people have that ability to sense the paranormal. I just wasn't expecting you to have such an adverse reaction."

"I tend to get like that around people that want to eat me."

Luke shoved his sunglasses up enough to rub his fists into his eyes before letting the dark lenses cover them once again. "I don't want to eat you. I don't want to hurt you at all. Like I said, it's not the Immortals you need to worry about. We want you to wake him, I was just supposed to be the person to help you decide if you want to."

"You mean force me to."

"No, Larkin. Not force. You can't be forced to do anything." The complete seriousness that took over his tone zapped that sarcastic tone from me. I knew there was a dark, ancient secret hiding behind his words.

"You have a soul, which means you are in charge of your own will. You have the ability to your own mind, your own decisions. No one, not even true demons, can change that. It's the gift of having a soul." Luke's tone turned remorseful, so much it almost made me feel bad for the guy. Almost.

"When we choose to become Immortals, we sacrifice that gift. We willingly send away our souls. We are the only beings Avidus can truly control how he wishes. He will only wake if you genuinely choose to do so. It has to be your choice."

Your choice. See, I knew I was going to get sick and tired of that eventually.

"Let's say I do decide to wake him, which I really don't see myself doing, what happens to me then?" I had a sick feeling demon dude would kill me to ensure no one can trap him again. It's what I would do if I was in his place.

Luke tilted his head curiously to the side, like he really hadn't thought of that before. Great, well that was reassuring. "I'm not really sure, actually. Though, I assume he'll let you do whatever you want."

"You assume?" That was so not reassuring.

He shrugged again and glanced over at Raffie who had sat down to throw the breadcrumbs I gave her before we left the house at the pigeons. "More like I know. Your original life was able to trap him for a reason, and I highly doubt that reason has changed."

"Right, because trapping him inside his own body for centuries really makes the heart grow fonder."

Luke laughed for the first time since sitting down, and I hated to admit that the sound was somewhat relieving. "All I can promise is that he has never spoke an ill word about you. Usually he just demands that I figure my shit out and get you here. That's about it."

That wasn't reassuring either.

"Look, Luke, even if I believed the fact that he wouldn't hurt me, or my family, there is literally no incentive to wake his ass up. He created a bunch of vampires, enslaved mortals and wanted to take over the world. Why the fuck would I wake him so he can finish all of that? Hm?" I leaned my elbows against my knees in emphasis and 'harrumphed' at him.

"It's not what he wants anymore."

"Ha! Yeah, right, okay. And what exactly does he want now? World peace?"

Luke was silent as I scoffed and rolled my eyes, but I could feel his gaze penetrating the side of my face. He actually sat like that for so long it was starting to freak me out, more than I already was.

"I can't tell you what to do, nor is that my intention. All I can do is tell you the truth, and I have. But I also want to tell you a secret." He leaned closer and I resisted the urge to jump away as his lips stopped just a few inches from my ear. His words were so low I knew he did so for no other Immortal nearby could hear.

"They're digging in the wrong place. Please keep that little tidbit of information to yourself." My heart jumped as his words, and I stared at him with wide eyes as he pulled away and stood to his feet.

"The choice is yours, Larkin." Luke announced as he stretched his long limbs and glanced around the stone courtyard. "But if you ever need help making that choice, there were never cougars in the forest that day we met." With one last beaming signature Luke smile, he turned and began to walk away.

"I do hope you will see me as a friend one day." He called over his shoulder before disappearing into the crowd.

CHAPTER 26

I stood outside Adriel's office door in the Avid building, anger sparking deep behind my eyes. The only reason my hands weren't balling into fists was because of the nine-year-old holding tightly onto one of them.

Even though my conversation with Luke replayed over in my head like a morbid soundtrack stuck on repeat, and all I wanted to do was grab both of the Markos siblings and run from this place as fast as we could, those feelings were quickly pushed aside. Because there was Adriel, standing in his office, with a way too pretty blonde female standing far too close to him.

I liked to say in my previous boy experiences that I wasn't a jealous person, but none of those boys were Adriel, and she was being very flirty. I knew what that looked like-the hair flipping, the batting of the eyelashes, the gentle arm touches-I've done enough flirting in my life to know when it was being laid on thick.

"Lark? Are you okay?" Raf asked beside me and tugged gently on my hand.

"Yeah, I'm fine. Why?" But I couldn't unglue my eyes from the sight of the supermodel-pretty girl and Dri. It was such a stupid thing to be angry over too, not after that shit eating afternoon with Luke. I had way too much to worry about, but that lovely little sight sure as hell didn't make anything easier.

"Because you're squeezing my hand really hard and it hurts." Raf tugged down on my hand again and I immediately let go.

"Shit, I'm sorry kid. I wasn't paying attention."

"Obviously." She mumbled and flexed her little hand before slipping it back into mine. "Don't let go, just don't squeeze so hard." I could only nod. I had so much more to be concerned over instead of some girl getting too close to Adriel, but for some reason, it was the only thing my mind focused on.

She was wearing a business, knee-length, black skirt and white button-down blouse, that hugged her chest a little too nicely. Her nails were bright red and long, like claws, and her feet were strapped in a pair of delicate matching red heels. That long blonde hair was straight and pinned back behind her ears so it cascaded down her slender back like a waterfall.

Ugh. Blondes. Always showing up the brunettes. I found myself self-consciously tucking a stray dark curl behind my ear.

She was holding a clipboard in one hand while the other rested suggestively on his arm-his bicep to be exact with her pretty blonde head thrown back in laughter. He was smiling at whatever she had said, though his eyes were glancing down at the clipboard. He wasn't moving away.

Oof. Well, okay then.

I felt heat lick the back of neck, and a strange buzzing sounded in my ears. I regretted bringing us there now. After I grabbed

Raf away from the pigeons and all-but threw her in my yellow Bug, I hightailed it to Dri's office where he said he would be all day. I had every intention of just barging into his office to say we needed to get the hell out of this town, until that lovely little spectacle hit me.

I probably looked like an insane asylum escapee, standing there in front of his office window, glaring at the people inside while holding a nine-year-old's hand. What the hell do I do now? We could just turn around and go home and he would get a lovely little talk later that night, or I could barge in like I first intended and see what they did.

God, I really didn't like this jealousy thing. We weren't in a legit relationship. We weren't even dating. All Adriel and I had agreed to was sex. I knew that. He could flirt, date, fuck whoever he wanted.

Just as I was about to make the decision to take us home and ignoring Raf's demands about telling her what was going on, those dark blue eyes flickered up to the window. Fuck. Well, that's what you get for standing there a solid two-minutes staring like a freak. I forced my gaze from his and glanced down at Raffie.

"What are the chances your brother likes blondes?"

She tiled her head to the side in that adorable little confused way of hers and batted those big blues. "Um, blonde what's?"

"Ugh, never mind." I shook my head and turned to face the cause of my irritation as the door to our right swung open.

"Lark? Raf? What are you guys doing here?" The cheerful tone that filled Adriel's voice as he stepped into the hallway, with that stupid smile I thought was just for us, surprised me.

Oh, so he was happy to see us after his little canoodling with the pretty blonde? Right.

"Hey Adriel!" Raf cheered excitedly and let go of my hand to wrap her arms tightly around her brother's waist.

"Hey kiddo. What are you guys doing here?" He asked again, though his smile didn't fall from his stupid perfect lips. I would be smiling too if I had my own personal hot blonde to flirt with every day.

I knew I was being over dramatic, but I honestly didn't care. It's not like I walked in on them having sex or anything, but he had been smiling at her-and Dri only ever smiled around Raf and I. Which was a shit thought, in retrospect. I was glad he was able to be happy outside of us, not that I was exactly thrilled at the reason, but still.

I was a big girl, and I've handled things far worse than pretty girls flirting with the guy I was sleeping with. Compared to everything else going on in our lives, this should have been nothing. I sucked in a deep breath, made sure my big girl pants were on tight, and brought my gaze to his.

"I don't know. Larkin said she had to talk to you, but we've just been standing here for, like, ever." Raf groaned in that dramatic way she always did, and I rolled my eyes. She was too much sometimes.

Adriel raised his eyebrow at me but didn't comment about the 'standing there forever' part. "You wanted to talk to me?"

"Yeah, but it can wait. You and blondie are obviously pretty busy right now."

Both eyebrows raised at that, and those stupid dark eyes, that could make me do almost anything, flickered back into the office where the blonde was waiting, clipboard still in hand. When that gaze flickered back to mine, I wanted to punch him. The ass hole had the audacity to smirk at me. Straight up smirk!

Like he thought I was being funny!

Oh. I'll show him funny.

"Charlotte was just going over some data for the site with me."

"Well I hope you and Charlotte have a good fucking time. We're going." I grabbed back onto Raffie's hand, pulled her away from her pig of brother, and turned to stomp all haughtily away. We didn't get far before that stupid strong hand of his was wrapping around my wrist and pulling me to a stop.

"Look whose being jealous now." My head whipped around at the snicker in his voice, fire blazing angrily behind my eyes. It didn't help that he wasn't even trying to hide that stupid pleased smirk pulling on the corner of his lips.

"I'm not jealous."

He laughed and the sound did little to ease the anger strumming through me. "Right, because you're normally this mad at me."

"I'm not mad." I let out a shaky breath to try and control the pounding in my ears. Rafael was standing awkwardly in front of us, her hand still gripped in mine as those big eyes flickered between the two of us. "It's been a long day. I want to go home."

"I want to get lunch."

"Get lunch with blondie. I'm sure that'll thrill the skirt right off her."

"Larkin." I didn't miss the warning in his tone, and when his eyes glanced pointedly towards his sister then back to me, I knew I had to cool it.

I let out a long heavy sigh and pulled my wrist from his grasp. "Look, we're going home. I don't care what you do, just be home for dinner."

That amused expression fell from his face as I turned once again and began walking away. "We'll talk later." He called after me as Raf's confused frown disappeared and she turned to wave goodbye at the idiot.

"Whatever."

"I don't understand why you're mad at me." The casual, nonchalant tone of his voice sounded like nails digging into my skull.

I had almost completely forgotten about my conversation with Luke, or that there was a whole section of the town that wanted us dead, and the other wanted me. The only thing on my mind for the rest of the afternoon was that ass hole and 'Charlotte'. What a fucking joke.

"I'm not fucking mad."

"Says the girl wiping holes into a glass plate."

I slapped the beyond dry glass down firmly on the counter. "I'm not mad, it's just been a long day."

"Yeah, you've set that already, but for some reason I don't believe you."

My shoulders tensed, but I refused to turn and look at him as I grabbed another dish. Just because I was some demon's Key, or whatever, didn't mean I wasn't still a teenager. Hormones sucked ass, and when I was pissed, I was pissed.

"Well, you should, I'm fine."

The chuckle that filled the air only made my rage boil. "So, this is a jealous Lark? It's interesting."

Don't look at him. Don't. He would get way too much satisfaction at seeing the fire burning behind my eyes.

"No. There's absolutely nothing to be jealous of. We're not a thing. You're allowed to screw whoever you want to." I didn't bother keeping the venom from my words. I knew the whole 'screwing part' was farfetched, but I also didn't care. We weren't a thing. He could do whatever the hell he wanted, to whoever he wanted.

"What if I only want to screw you?" His voice was suddenly a dark, low, murmur in my ear. I hadn't even realized he walked up behind me until then.

My back straightened as the feeling of his breath sent shivers down my spine. Sex right then was the last fucking thing I needed, but my body didn't seem to get that message. Adriel's strong hands were suddenly caging me between his chest and the counter, with no escape in sight.

"Don't, Adriel." I tried to keep my voice steady and cold, but it was surprisingly a lot harder than a minute ago. Pun intended.

"Hm." He hummed against my skin, his lips gently trailing from behind my ear and down the side of my neck. "Don't what?"

"You know what." I hissed, even though he didn't seem to hear a word I said. His body pushed mine gently against the counter, and one of his hands slipped beneath my shirt to slowly brush along my stomach.

"Raf's down for the night."

"That's not why I said don't." I grumbled, even though it was a weak attempt at resistance.

"Do you want me to stop?" He asked teasingly as his mouth left a hot trail along my skin.

No. No, I didn't want him to stop-and the fucker knew it. My anger from before still simmered beneath the surface and only added onto the aroused fire coursing through my veins. His fingers teased the skin just above to edge of my leggings, and as his touch gently slipped beneath the fabric, my legs trembled.

"I'm fucking pissed at you."

"I know."

I couldn't stop the electricity thrumming through me, and I had to squeeze my legs together to ease the pulsing between them. "Tell me to stop and I will." Dri's voice was back in my ear, his teeth gently nipping at the lobe as his hand slipped further down my leggings. I had to force a ragged breath from my lungs as his body pressed against mine, until I could feel everything.

I had such a death grip on the dish towel that I was surprised my short, trimmed nails weren't cutting through the fabric. My other hand was holding a poor, defenseless plate viciously to the counter like it would jump up and run away if I didn't.

"I don't really think you want me to." His words were a dark caress on my skin that urged me to just let go, to give in as his strong fingers reached the edge of my underwear and slipped slowly beneath the elastic.

Fuck it. I was a goner. If he wanted to do this right now, then fine.

After all, we were just sex anyways.

I gasped and rocked back into him, as he reached the bundle of nerves begging for his attention. I let my ass rub over that hard knot in his jeans, and my legs seemed to part invitingly on their own. Then that chuckle was back in my ear, his lips sending sparks through my body as they trailed over my skin. His fingers slipped easily over me.

"There's my good girl." That little amount of praise he murmured into my ear made me feel all fluttery inside. Though I didn't have long to think about it since most of my concentration went into not gasping like a fish out of water when then that too-familiar feeling of his finger slipping inside me took over.

"Adriel...." I groaned into the stale kitchen air as he started that mind-numbing in and out motion.

My back arched over the counter, my palms had long let go of the towel and plate and were bracing the rest of my body against the cold marble. His other hand let go of the counter to reach under my shirt, slide quickly up my stomach and started playing with my nipples. I gasped as he squeezed the hard point through my bra.

I rocked against his hand, trying to ride it into the pleasure I so desperately wanted. He didn't let me for long though, and that finger was pulling away so he could flip my body easily around before I realized it. Neither of us bothered with sweet words or reassurances as our lips locked together, his tongue plunging against mine as those hands gripped like iron around my hips and lifted me onto the countertop.

My fingers automatically dropped to the button of his jeans as he began pulling my leggings and underwear down. We were both in such a hurry that we didn't care what was happening or who was ready. I wanted him fucking in me, and I knew he wanted that just as badly. I had just got his pants and boxers down far enough to be out of the way when he suddenly shoved up between my legs.

"Dri!" I did shout that time as he held my body pinned to the counter and didn't bother trying to go slow. One of my hands gripped tightly into his shirt as the other braced myself against the countertop. There was no mercy in his movements, or hesitation as he took my body as badly as I needed him to.

"Fuck, you drive me insane." Adriel growled as he gripped tightly onto my waist with one hand so the other could wrap in my hair. I let out a ragged gasp as he jerked my head back, never stopping the entire time. I blinked up at those blue eyes, and the dark, dangerous glint flashing through them only turned me on more. "This is what you do to me, Larkin." His words were like a hot, sensual caress rolling against my already heated skin.

I couldn't say anything, the pleasure coursing through my body was too much to control. I honestly had no idea how he was able to speak, but he was always good at multi-tasking, and his words sent shivers down my spine.

Dri's hand slipped from my hair and I let my head roll back to stare in bliss at the ceiling as his touch brushed down my neck and over my shirt. He squeezed my breast, and I let out a low moan as he pinched both of my hard nipples, before trailing slowly down my stomach.

He was taking me so aggressively I could almost feel my in-sides expand and contract each time he pulled away then shoved back in. I felt that fire building in the pit of my stomach, felt the arousal causing my inner muscles to clench. "Dri... Dri, God, I'm close." Some part of me gasped out as his fingers finally reached their destination.

"Are you looking for permission?" His voice was slightly breathless, but it didn't take away that insane pleasure.

"Nooooo." I groaned as he suddenly pulled all the way out and shoved back in. No, I didn't need his permission. But I sure as hell still wanted it. His dark laugh was back, and it reverberated throughout the kitchen.

"Go ahead, baby. Come for me." The words had barely passed his lips when those fingers pinched my clit and the world officially exploded.

"Adriel!" I screamed as pleasure washed over every part of my being.

I was on such an endorphin filled high I almost missed his grip tighten around my waist and his mouth sinking harshly down onto my shoulder. I wasn't sure if he meant it, but I could feel the bite through my shirt. Dri's hips jerked harshly against mine and then he was coating my insides as I fell slowly back to Earth.

We stayed pressed together, panting, against the counter. The dishes long forgotten. I felt him slowly soften, but he didn't pull out as we both tried to control our breathing. His lips pressed against mine, and I let my arms wrap loosely around his neck as his tongue licked my mouth.

"Still mad at me?" He asked teasingly when he finally pulled away. I narrowed my eyes and tried to scowl, but I was far too exhausted and satisfied to really care.

"Fuck off."

"Can't do that when I'm too busy fucking you."

"Jerk." I grumbled, and let out an odd, displeased noise when he lifted my body enough to slip easily out. He chuckled softly, his lips pressing against my forehead as those arms wrapped tightly around my waist.

"Sleeping with me tonight?" Adriel asked casually, that cocky, arrogant tone glistening through his voice as he held me easily in the air.

"No. You can fuck yourself." Yet despite my words, my arms squeezed tighter around his neck and I let him pull me away from the counter. His fingers were splayed out across my bare hips. Somewhere in the middle of all that, he had managed to finish taking my leggings and underwear off and they laid uselessly on the floor.

"Then who's going to fuck you?" He teased and bent effortlessly down, my body still wrapped tightly around his, and picked my bottoms off the floor.

"You just did."

He laughed and wrapped both arms under my bare ass to hoist my body further into the air. I was prepared for another witty retort and was gearing up with one of my own when those dark blues locked onto my gaze. My breath caught in my throat. He could be such an arrogant, pig-headed, ass of a man-but then there were the times when he gave me that look, and I felt like the only person in the world that mattered.

"You never need to be jealous, Lark. You're it for me."

CHAPTER 27

"So, there's nothing there?" I asked all nonchalant-like as my fingers traced the intricate design of his tattoo.

Adriel sighed for what seemed like the hundredth time and adjusted his other arm around my waist. "No, for the tenth time, nothing is there. She just works for the company and was going over the statistical analysis of the week with me."

I bit the inside of my cheek and tapped against the firm muscles in his upper arm. "You two seemed pretty touchy for analyzing statistics." I grumbled against his chest. I could almost feel him roll his eyes.

"Larkin, you know me. I don't make it a habit of being 'touchy' with anyone—except you." And then the sound of his hand slapping my ass echoed throughout his room.

"Ow!" I screeched and tried to rip away from the fuck-face, but he just wrapped those stupid arms tighter around me and rolled us over. "You're a fucking pain in my ass! Literally!" I snapped as he pinned my body between his and the bed. The jerk only laughed.

"As much as I love this whole jealous side of you," He chuckled and bent down to bite the tip of my nose, "you don't need to be. I've already made it very clear to Charlotte I'm not interested."

"Oh! So, she has tried to sleep with you. Funny you mention that now."

Dri dropped his face into my neck and groaned. The sound was so deep and annoyed it shook through my entire body. "You're impossible." He grumbled against my skin but didn't pull away. "She asked me out when we first moved here, and I said no. Then there was you, and she tried to ask me out again, and I said—very clearly—that I wasn't interested, at all. Happy?"

Not really, but it wasn't very fair to keep bothering him with my jealous little fit. "I didn't like see her touch you." I pouted like a child, but instead of another annoyed groaned he leaned up and smiled down at me. Though it was more of that smirky smile than anything else.

"I can tell."

I slapped him lightly on the arm, which was a little awkward to do since he still had me caged against him and the bed.

His chuckle washed over me, before that smirk slowly fell away. "It's just you, Lark. I swear. There's no one else in the world that I want. I love you, stupid." He pressed his lips to mine, like he was sealing his words inside my mouth so they couldn't escape. The stupid comment and all.

My heart thundered like a jackhammer. I stared at him wide-eyed as he pulled away, that smirk shining all smugly on his idiot handsome face. "Why do you look so surprised?" Dri laughed and did that silly forehead nudging thing to mine. "I've been making it pretty obvious for a while now."

"Yeah, well, I'm pretty awesome so I just figured it was a natural response."

Another eye roll and nose bite later, he finally unwrapped those iron bars away from me and rolled onto his side. I turned to face him and let my hand rest against his bare chest. I hadn't forgotten about my conversation with Luke, even though my crazy, jealous teenage hormones put it on hold for a while.

It was early in the morning, the sun wasn't even up yet, but I didn't think I would be getting any sleep at all. The little bit of sleep Adriel got that night, I spent staring at the ceiling, replaying the entire talk over and over again

"What's wrong—"

"Let's leave." I interrupted his question and splayed my fingers out against his skin.

He raised his eyebrow and glanced over at the alarm clock on his nightstand. "You want to get up? Alright, but it's only five in the morning."

"No, you ass." I rolled my eyes. "I want to leave Deshua. Today."

Adriel pulled slightly away, a confused frown pulling on his lips, and ran his hand through his short dark hair. "We can, but—"

"You don't want to anymore." Fear gripped my chest and I had to force my eyes away. We couldn't stay here, not anymore. It wasn't safe, from anyone.

Pretty blonde lady probably changed his mind.

Fucking drop it, Larkin.

"No! No, that's not it. I still think leaving is a good idea, I just don't have another job lined up yet, and we don't have anywhere to go." Dri quickly wrapped one of those arms back around my waist and pulled me into the warmth of his chest.

"Anywhere is better than here. I don't even care if we go back to California. I just need us out of this place." I snuggled into him and pressed my face against his heated skin.

The only thing holding me back from officially leaving before, was him. He had been so excited for the job and the move I couldn't ask him to leave that behind. But now that I knew his job was just some sick joke from demon greedy guy and his spawns of Satan, I didn't give one flying fuck.

"Please, Dri. I just want us out today."

"Alright Angel, if that's what you want." He sighed but squeezed his arm tighter around me and pressed his lips against the top of my head. "We can pack up the SUV and head out. I can probably tow your car behind us, unless you want to drive it. I'll explain the situation with Raf's school and work Monday, and you should probably call yours too."

I nodded as he started trailing off about everything we needed to get done. It was honestly kind of hot watching him organize and plan everything out in his head. He was just about finished listing off everything essential that we needed to pack and what we could leave behind when I realized he was asking me a question.

"What?"

Those oh-so-kissable lips of his pulled up at the corner in that smirk that made me feel all fluttery inside, or maybe that was how his hand had started tracing slowly across my skin. "I asked if you really want to go back to California, or try somewhere new?"

I didn't care where we went as long as he never stopped touching me like that. "Had somewhere else in mind?" I mumbled as my eyes dropped to the hard planes of his chest.

He smiled and leaned down to nip at my cheek, like the freaking weirdo he was. "I always wanted to see New York."

"Hm," I murmured and watched my hand as I let it rub slowly along his skin and then up and over his shoulder. "Then let's head there." Dri's smile turned naughty and I didn't pull away as his lips brushed against my own.

"Let's." He agreed with a little lick to my bottom lip. He had a thing with biting and licking me. I liked it.

"We have a lot of packing to do." I teased as his kisses started traveling down my chin and across my jaw.

"Mm, it can wait."

I laughed as he easily flipped us back over until I was under him once again. "And you called me the horny one." I flicked his ear since my arms were wrapped around his neck and it was the only part of him that I could reach.

Adriel's smile was wide and devious. "I never said I wasn't." His hands reached up gently, unhooked mine from around his neck and then pinned them down to the bed.

I raised an eyebrow at him. "You know I don't like that."

He tilted his head curiously to the side and blinked those blues innocently. That is where that little shit learned it from! Not me! Her stupid, jerk brother!

"You sure about that?"

"Yes." I grumbled and wiggled unhappily in his firm grip.

"You know," He started teasingly though I could see the serious light in his dark eyes. "You didn't say it back."

"I didn't say what back?" I muttered and gave up struggling against him with a 'huff'.

"That you love me."

I stilled completely under him, though my breathing made my chest rise and fall heavily. "You know I do."

I could tell he was fighting off a smile. "Do I?"

"Yes." I grumbled but couldn't find it in me to meet his eyes. I did love him, more than anything, and knowing that he loved me too made everything feel all fluttery and tingly inside. But I was afraid of admitting it out loud.

Every time something good happened in my life, the universe loved to fuck it up and take it away from me. I couldn't lose him. He was the only thing that mattered.

"I don't believe you." But his voice was teasing as his face bent closer to mine, and brushed his lips just barely against my own. "Be vulnerable for once in your life, Lark. It's just you and me. It's okay to let go."

I accepted the kiss he pressed lingeringly against my lips and didn't fight against him as his strong legs slowly pushed mine apart. He did everything for me, he was moving for me. The least I could do was admit out loud the one thing he asked to hear. Even if it would just add fuel to the fire.

"I love you, Adriel." It came out as a soft whisper, but it was enough to make him smile against me like he just won the lottery. Jerk.

"There, now that wasn't so hard." He teased and bit down on my bottom lip.

"Yeah, yeah, whatever." I grumbled but didn't move even when he let go of my wrists and propped his hands on either side of my head.

"We still have an hour before the sun comes up." His head dipped down so his mouth could trace softly down my neck as he spoke.

I didn't bother hiding the laugh that bubbled past my lips. "Sex?"

"Yes, please."

"But if you ever need help making that choice, there were never cougars in the forest the day we met."

I didn't need help making that choice. I knew waking demon dude up was a bad idea.

So, someone, please tell me why I was doing this?

Why the hell was I actually about to listen to Luke, of all people?

But there I was, five hours later, staring at the 'Deshua State University' sign the same way I had on my very first day.

I wish I could have ignored that nagging in my head ever since Luke 'hinted' at where the demon dude really was, but I couldn't. He almost gave me a literal invite to go check it out for myself, and greedy guy was trapped, right? Or asleep, or whatever the fuck. There were two things that always got me in trouble growing up, wherever that was: my mouth, and my curiosity. I knew one or the other would eventually get me killed.

It was now October, we have been in this hell hole of a town for nearly two months, and summer had died quickly away. It was cold. I had on Converse, dark jeans, a long sleeve t-shirt and a jacket that was two sizes too big for me—because I stole it from Adriel's closet, but that's not important.

What was important was the six-inch knife/dagger thing I bought off Amazon hiding in the jacket's inside pocket, and the industrial flashlight hiding in the other. I had a pretty bad feeling I was going to need both.

Eh, I was still going to send it.

After Adriel and I finally got up that morning, we explained the situation to Raf—who actually didn't care at all that we were moving again—and spent the next few hours packing. We were nearly done loading up the SUV with everything we needed, when I couldn't ignore that nagging in my head any longer.

I told Adriel I had to grab something from campus before we left, hopped into my little yellow Bug and drove straight there. I always kept the knife on me ever since I bought it, and the flashlight was part of that emergency kit Dri made me keep in my car. It was perfect for a quick little exploration of the woods, and then 'bye-bye' Deshua. See you never.

My motivation died when I reached the entrance of the woods. I hadn't heard that insane compelling sound again, not since my very first day. I completely forgot about it with everything else that had been going on, but now as I stood like an ant beneath the size of those trees, I felt fear creep down my spine.

Was demon dude really in there?

Come on, Lark. You probably won't even find him. Just look, and then leave. Adriel only gave me till noon to get back to the manor so he could hook the Bug up to trail behind it, and the time was quickly passing. Then we would be out of there.

"Hey, Larkin!" I turned at the familiar sound of River's cheerful voice. He was jogging up to me from the main walkway of campus, his hand waving enthusiastically in the air. "Where have you been? You skipped classes all week!"

I wanted to flinch at the worry in his voice. I hadn't bothered going back to campus ever since that talk with Jess, something Adriel had no idea about. I had been so worried about protecting us and dealing with all the crazy, I didn't give one flying flip about school. I even started ignoring his and Siena's texts and phone calls after that little debacle in the Cathedral's library. I didn't want to face their questions and exclamations. I was having a hard-enough time facing it myself.

"Hey, River. Y-Yeah, I haven't been feeling too good lately."

He pulled to a stop in front of me, a wide smile on his face despite the concerned look in those hazel eyes. He had that too-small-for-anyone backpack slung over his shoulders, even though it was Sunday. "Hey, that's okay, as long as you're doing better now." I suddenly felt guilty about not answering any of his messages, and not telling him I was leaving. They would find out sooner or later, but that didn't necessarily make me friend of the year.

"Yeah, I am, thanks." I gave him a reassuring smile, even though I wasn't feeling very assured of anything right then.

"Well, what are you up to? Why are you staring at the trees like a crazy person?" He laughed, but I didn't miss how those hazel eyes flickered uneasily to the forest pressed against my back.

"I was just about to go on a hike, what are you up to?" I was never really good with 'casual conversation', and I never had to be with him before, but that worried expression wasn't leaving his gaze and it was starting to unnerve me. I couldn't do this with him breathing down my back. Home boy had to go.

"A hike? In there?" River didn't bother hiding how stupid of a decision he thought that was, but I only shrugged.

"Yeah, why not? Seems like fun."

"Um, because there's cougars, and they like to take pretty good nibbles of humans."

I shrugged again but felt myself reach uneasily to make sure the knife was still there. "I have pepper spray. I'm not really bothered." I didn't have any spray, to be exact, but Luke had made it seem like the whole 'man eating cat thing' was just a ploy. Not that I was openly trusting him or anything, but still.

"Well, I'm on my way to meet Siena for lunch, why don't you join us? I'm sure she would be happy to see you, and it's a better option than getting ate." He let out another nervous laugh but kept his gaze pinned to mine, almost as if looking at the trees would conjure the very cats he was so afraid of.

"Thanks, but I really want to go for a hike. I won't be long though, I'll even text you when I'm done so you know I'm good." Even though that text will come from inside Adriel's SUV as we drove very far away.

"Alright... Just be careful, yeah?"

"For sure, thanks River." I gave him a warm, reassuring smile, if only to ease that concern shining in his hazel eyes. I never really seen that look from him before, and it made me uneasy. I mean, if River thought something was a bad idea, that said something.

Then why was it the push I needed?

I summoned up as much courage as I could, checked that my phone was in my jeans pocket, and turned on my heel. I didn't even care if River stood watching me hike through the thicket of trees blocking the entrance of the forest. I was thankful for my long warm clothes as I pushed through the thorn bushes and grasping tree limbs.

I don't know why I was expecting a regularly used, dirt, hiking path that would take me straight to demon dude, but I was surely disappointed when my eyes fell on more and more dark trees.

I sighed and took out the flashlight from my jacket. I could only pray that Luke had been telling the truth when he said no Immortal would hurt me, and that my knife would do enough damage to those witchy freaks that did. So much for staying out of the shadows.

The flashlight was enough to illuminate a good junk of the surrounding area, which was good since the deeper I trudged into the woods, the less natural light there was. I was half expecting that sound to appear again, like a dark, seductive caress in my ears lulling me to go find its source. But there was nothing, only the occasional bird chirping in the distance. It was fucking creepy.

The ground beneath my feet started to angle as I reached the base of that large mountain-like structure that the college backed up against. I paused and tried to calm down my winded breathing. Damn, I was less in shape than I thought. Wasn't sex supposed to count as exercising?!

There had been no sign of demon dude, or anything that was big enough to hide his body in, the entire way there. I even checked a few of the trees that looked suspiciously door-ish.

Luke was either lying through his teeth, or I had to go up the fucking mountain—and I so did not want to do that.

You know, in retrospect, the whole hiking-there experience was a clear warning sign from nature that I should not have gone any further. My dumb ass pushed ahead anyway, and I circled the base of the mountain/bolder thing for any sign of a pathway up. It wasn't too big, and I was able to reach the other side without much of a hassle, if you didn't count a shit ton of thorns and bugs as a hassle.

Each step I took as I reached the other side angled steeply up until I was stepping onto a raised grassy hill, leading straight to the top of the mountain. There was even a little dirt path. Bingo! I hiked quickly up the hill, on the lookout for any sign of demon dude, when I came face to face with a cave.

"You've got to be fucking kidding me." I groaned and resisted the urge to just plop my ass down on the grass and take a nap.

Was I really about to risk my neck in a creepy ass cave for something that might not even be there? Why did I even care if greedy guy was in there! For fucks sake!

I let out a tired sigh, gripped tighter on my flashlight and double checked for my knife. "Let's fucking do this then."

The cave seemed to suck out all-natural light the minute I stepped foot inside. An eerie chill ran down my spine, one that circled in my stomach and dropped to my toes. This wasn't a good place. I stood at the entrance of a rocky damp tunnel, my flashlight the only source of life in the entire place. My breathing sounded like a freight train against the dead silence of the cavern.

I sucked in a shaky breath and took another step forward. Maybe this wasn't where demon dude was. Maybe it was a cougar's den, or a bear! The last thing I wanted to do was stumble on one of those, but the light of my flashlight met no resisting enclosure as I walked slowly down the tunnel.

It grew colder with each step, and an unsettling feeling started in my chest. One of lost, longingly, death. It was like a part of me knew this place and held memories so dark and cold they still hurt five hundred years later.

My breath came out as fog in the dim light.

Just a little further...

The thought hit me out of nowhere, and I stumbled against a large rock I hadn't seen. I knew it was only a little further, knew that demon dude wasn't far away. I couldn't sense him or anything, I just knew. Like I knew the sky was blue and grass was green. It was there, imprinted in my head.

The second I stepped out of the tunnel and into an open space, light flared in my eyes. I gasped and ripped backwards. The light went out instantly.

"What the actual fuck?"

I stepped forward again but was ready to brace myself when the lights flared. Torches, there were real-life, hundreds of years old, torches hanging around the expanse of a wide circular space. Every time I stepped into the carved-out cavern, the torches would light on their own, and every time I stepped back into the tunnel they went out. I probably would have freaked out way more than I was if I hadn't seen Luke's blood literally burn the day before.

I always told myself I didn't believe in what I couldn't see, but I sure as hell saw that.

There were two other things I noticed once the awe from the magic demon torches died away, two things that chilled me to the very bone. The first, and admittedly the most terrifying, was a giant stone slab centered in the middle of the room. I couldn't see well from my trembling position at the entrance of the tunnel, but there was definitely a body resting on top. Chains held the persons legs and arms pinned to the surface, as strong stone pillars raised the slab off the ground.

The second thing was the pile of bones resting on the floor just beneath where the chained persons head was. I could clearly make out a small human skull, browning from age and decay. I gulped, and felt ice enter my lungs.

Fuck me. It was real.

He was real.

I had no doubt the person chained to the slab was demon greedy dude, but it had been almost easy to find him. I was expecting three magical trials to pass like in Harry Potter or some other magical book. But there I was, standing a few yards away from the being that created those red eyed freaks, and who has half the town after my head.

I couldn't really see any details on him, but there was this—air that radiating off the body. I could feel it pulse from the slab, charge the room with electricity, and wrap tightly around my lungs. It made me light-headed and want to run screaming for the hills just as much as it beckoned me closer. Urging me to embrace it, like it would solve every problem I ever hard, answer every question, and promised power.

I had to shake myself from that pull, though when I looked around again I had somehow managed to walk half-way to the slab.

What was I doing here again? What was the point? Prove to myself what I had feared all along that this was real?

Well, good job, Lark. It's real, not get the fuck out of there. I didn't.

I stepped closer to the slab, careful not to get anywhere near the bones resting against the floor and used my flashlight as a shield.

I stopped and stared in disbelief at the unmoving lifeless body chained to stone barely a foot away. He was huge, and not necessarily in the good way—though I wasn't going to check. A part of me tried to convince myself it was just a human that met and unfortunate end and I should call the cops, but there was no mistaking the fact that he was twice the size of any man, and the black wings tucked safely underneath him.

The dim light from the torches hanging on the wall and my flashlight shined just brightly enough to make out the worn, old, tattered, black pants covering the lower half of his body. His tan and toned torso was bare and that so-dark hair it was nearly black matched the long eyelashes resting against his soft cheeks.

He looked so quiet, so peaceful that if it weren't for the pitch-black feather wings coiling around his strong shoulders, I would have sworn he was human. Now I knew why everyone tried to convince me he was an angel, and not the demon I was dead set on him being. The fallen was unearthly, deadly beautiful.

But despite all those images Shorzin showed us on his PowerPoint, and the drawing River found that day in the Cathedral, there was absolutely no mistaking the beautiful face sleeping just mere inches from mine.

The one that belonged to the only person who ever mattered to me.

Adriel.

CHAPTER 28

I was going to throw up.

I shot away from the stone slab like it was electric wire, my flashlight flinging out of my hand as I did. The light flickered as it crashed against the wall and sputtered out. The soft warm glow of the torches was the only thing lighting the cavern now. I pressed my back against the far wall, my hands gripping at my chest as my breathing turned into hyperventilating.

No.

No, no, no, no! This wasn't happening! It wasn't real!

There—There's no way. This wasn't real.

There was no way.

It was just a dream, a nightmare! I would wake up any minute, in his bed, in his arms.

This wasn't real.

My back slid down the rocky surface of the cave as I pulled viciously at my hair, my stomach twisting in nausea. I officially lost it. I was crazy, insane. The town succeeded in screwing holes the size of walnuts into my brain. And now everything was shit.

"Larkin."

I was still hyperventilating when the sound of his voice reached my ears. Adriel stood at the entrance of the cavern, my Adriel. The human one I left back at the manor to pack up our cars so we could get the fuck out of that town. Not the one that was half dead and sleeping on that slab. Those dark blue eyes flickered between the demon's body and mine before he took an unsteady step forward. Air wouldn't enter my lungs, and I couldn't speak as I watched him.

"I know..." He paused and wrung his hands together nervously as that gaze scanned my face. "I know how you must be feeling."

I rolled over and threw up everything in my stomach.

He was there in an instant, one hand pulling my hair out of my face while the other was rubbing soothingly down my back. I wanted to shove him away, but I was dry heaving too hard to do any of that.

"It's okay, just let it out—"

"Get off me!" I was able to stop heaving enough to gasp out. I shoved him away and crawled like a literal toddler to the far corner of the cave, making sure to steer clear of him and those bones. Not the best idea, backing myself into a corner, but I wasn't exactly thinking very clearly right then.

"Lark, I can explain—"

"No! Stop! I don't want to hear it!" I curled my knees into my chest in the tightest ball my body would form and shoved the palms of my hands into my ears. "This isn't real. This isn't real.

This isn't real." I repeated out loud over and over again, until it would become true.

I was pressing my hands so hard into my ears it felt like I was trying to squeeze my brain out through my nose, but I didn't care. I could feel Adriel walking in front of me, but I refused to look. Because this wasn't real. None of it was.

"It's just a dream. It's just a dream. It's just a dream."

He didn't touch me, but I knew he was close. I could practically feel him sliding down the slab's raised legs until he was sitting directly across from my ball-like form. Waiting for me to stop chanting and look at him. Well, he would be waiting for a fucking while because I was doing this until I woke up.

A soft touch on my shin made me jerk tighter into myself and start chanting louder. I didn't realize I had let go of my ears to wrap my arms tightly around my knees until he spoke again. "Larkin..." There was no denying the concern in his voice, or the plead to get me to look at him, but it just made the insanity that much worse. I wasn't sure if I was hyperventilating anymore, but I was for sure sobbing and air just wouldn't enter my lungs. "Angel, you need to calm down—"

"Don't fucking call me that! Do you know how fucked that is!" I tore my gaze away from my knees to snap at him, though I wish I hadn't. The look on his beyond handsome face was so heartbreaking it only made the madness worse. He was leaning back against the base of the slab, his long legs sprawled out before us. A blatant gesture that I couldn't run, even if I tried.

Even now, when I was officially losing my shit, and the world was falling apart, I couldn't help but notice how beautiful he looked. Deadly beautiful.

"You're him, Adriel! T-That's not even your fucking name! Oh my God." I had to let go of my knees to press my hands against my stomach.

"That is my name—"

"I'm going to be fucking sick again." He started to spring forward, like he was ready to get my hair out of the way again if he had to, but I just held my hand up and pushed myself further away.

"You lied to me. It's all a lie. Everything is a lie." I tried to suck in some much-needed air, but the damn thing was dead set on evading me.

"No, not everything." He tried to reach for me again, but one sharp look had him pulling reluctantly away. "I never lied about loving you."

"Don't. Oh my god, don't." There were tears on my cheeks now, hot wet tears falling to match the sobs they created. "You used me!"

"I have never used you, nor will I ever."

I wrapped my fingers into the top of my hair and shook my head so viciously I could almost feel my brain rattle. "None of this is real." I choked out, though my voice sounded more like a strangled whisper than the strong steady tone I was going for.

"You don't know how badly I wish that was true." His tone didn't waiver from that soft, concerned, Adriel-like tone that he used to calm me down so many times before. Now it was just a vicious knife stab to the chest.

"You're lying." I shook my head again and closed my eyes. "What the fuck is happening?"

I wanted to believe that complete remorse in his voice, and the worried, heartbroken look in his eyes, but I couldn't. He was a lie. One big, fat, massive fucking lie. It all was. All his sweet words and gentle touches. All those nights he pulled me from nightmares, that I was now pretty sure he created, and all those lazy weekends spent together. It was all a lie.

"No, I'm not. I didn't want you to find this place. I want to leave just as badly as you do."

"Yeah right." I scoffed which was pretty hard to do around the hiccupping that had replaced the sobs. "You're him. The only thing you ever wanted was to get me here and wake you up. That's all this ever was." Every quiet promise, every night we spent together, all that fucking touching. It was all for this. To get me here. The one person I loved more than anything in this world wasn't real.

"Larkin, I was literally packing up the SUV so we can leave when I found out you were here. I was going to leave all of this behind for you. It was always more than getting you here. Always." I could feel those eyes staring holes into the top of my head, but I refused to glance his way.

I didn't know what to say to that. He had been packing and telling me to make sure I was back by noon when I left. Or was it all just a trick to manipulate me into staying? I didn't know what to think anymore. The world was no longer round—It was square, and Adriel was a lie. My entire life just got tossed down the drain and shredded by the garbage disposal.

"You tricked me." The tears had stopped falling, but now my throat felt like I swallowed one of those torches hanging on the wall.

I leaned my head back heavily against the damp rock and glared holes of my own into those sad blue eyes. Though it was a lot harder than I was making it seem. All I really wanted to do was crawl in those inviting arms, close my eyes and wait for this awful nightmare to be over.

Adriel/not-Adriel shook his head and flicked away a pebble that had been resting beside his leg. "No, I would never trick you, especially not into doing any of this. It had to be your choice, and I thought..." He paused and glanced away, his breath leaving on a heavy sigh before he continued. "I thought the only way we could be together was with my real body. That's why I had to get you here."

"I don't want to hear it." My heart felt like it had been torn to shreds, ripped out and pulled apart. I don't know what the hell he was going for but that sure as fuck did not make me feel any better.

"I need you to understand. Please let me explain." I could tell he wanted to reach out for me again but thought better of it. I stayed quiet as those dark eyes searched my face.

"I thought it was the only option, Larkin. It's the only reason why I would ever bring you back here. By the time I found out there was another way, that I could be with you like this." He gestured down to his body and pulled at his clothes. "Like regular humans, it was too late." I sucked in a sharp breath at the resilience shining in his gaze. "I never wanted to hurt you, I only wanted to be with you."

Tears swelled in my eyes again, but I shook my head and tried to force them away. This was too much. I didn't believe it. I couldn't. There was no way the one person I had in this world was an entire lie.

"I'm not a lie, Lark."

"Oh, great!" I let out such a harsh laugh that it hurt my throat as it passed my lips and sounded more like a bark. "You really can read my fucking mind."

The sad expression that had been plastered on his face the entire time fell slightly away to a sheepish smile. "Not really, only sometimes... When you're screaming at me."

"I'm thinking, not screaming, and that is such a massive invasion of privacy I could throttle you." Well, that and about five hundred billion other reasons.

"It's not like I purposely tried to." He defended weakly, though the guilty expression crossing his face proved he wasn't that great at lying. "Sometimes you get so loud it just get through. I'm sorry."

"That's honestly the least of my problems right now. You're a demon." I tried not to 'hiccup' out loud, since that would only keep proving how upset I was. "Your kind tricks humans all the time. I know the stories. How can I every believe a word you say?"

"I'm not a demon, and you have a soul. Even if I wanted to trick you, which I don't, I can't. Your will is your own. The choice is always yours."

"Your choice, Lark. Always your choice."

Oh God, how long had he been telling me that very same thing?

"Then why didn't you tell me from the beginning?"

He scoffed which was quickly followed by a dark, unamused chuckle. "Right, because telling you I'm actually an angel you put to sleep over five hundred years ago, and am still infatuated with you, would have gone over so well."

"You could have said something when I started freaking out about red eyes and all that other shit!" I felt rage start to boil inside my chest and I grabbed onto it like a lifeline as it pushed away that all-consuming despair. At least if I was angry, I wasn't crying. "How many times did I tell you about what I was seeing? Or dreaming? And you just pushed it away like I was making it up!"

"I told you, I thought the only way we could be together was in my real body. I wasn't planning on you falling in love with this me." He pulled at his flannel, his eyes blazing desperately as my breathing rose. "I was only going to help you—to keep you safe while Luke was supposed to do his fucking job. Be your friend, introduce you to everything slowly, and see what your decision would be. How fucking hard is that?"

Something dark flashed across his gaze, something I had only seen a few times before. Like the day he went down to my old softball coach's office or threatened to hunt down anyone that had ever hurt me. But he knew Luke... of course he did! They were probably best buds with bets over who could fuck with my mind the fastest!

"We weren't supposed to get close." Adriel/not-Adriel continued like he couldn't tell how badly I wanted to beat his face in and pound against his stupid chest. "We were never supposed to... I hadn't planned on us sleeping together. I didn't know that we could."

"I-I can't. I'm sorry, I can't do this." His words from that first night we spent together raced through my mind. Maybe he thought he really couldn't.

Fuck-face let out a disgruntled sigh. "That night, when you kissed me, I felt it. I can't feel things well like this, my mind goes in and out and sometimes it's hard to control. But I felt you, and I thought everything was fucked." His expression grew close to longing, and those blue eyes looked so remorseful that if my heart was still working it would have broken.

I felt my anger slowly die away, which was so not good. I shouldn't have listened to any of this. How could I ever believe a word he said?

"Then there you were, all sad and packing like you were going to try and leave me again, and I just—I couldn't stay away from you." He shook his head, those dark eyes glancing off into the other corner of the damp cave as if he couldn't meet mine. "It changed everything. I didn't need my body anymore, and by the time I realized how the town was affecting you, it was too far in to tell you the truth. I thought I was doing the right thing."

"The right thing..." I spoke those words on a low sarcastic laugh that hurt my chest, and let my knees fall to the floor. I leaned against them heavily. "Half the time we were here I spent losing my mind thinking that I had gone insane, while the other half I was worried sick that something might happen to you and Raffie because of who I was. And there you were getting off on the fact—oh my god, Raffie!" The thought hit me like a sucker punch to the stomach, and I suddenly went dizzy.

"Oh God, did you steal her from her real family or something? What about her parents? Did you kill them—"

"Larkin." The way he said my name made my voice die on my tongue, or maybe it was the sudden look of guilt swarming in his gaze. "She isn't real."

"What?"

Adriel/not-fucking-Adriel let out a long sigh and scrubbed a heavy hand down his stupid handsome face. "The power they used to trap me isn't the best, it has holes. I can get through if I try hard enough. It's how I'm able to be like this." He gestured down to himself once again. "It's how I created Shelby, Dave and Rafael."

She wasn't... real?

That little nine-year-old who gave me more hell than anyone I had ever met, which only made me love her that much more, wasn't real? Her big, blue, doe eyes that looked so much like Adriel's flashed in my mind, and I felt what little heartstrings I had left snap. I fell back against my heels, pressure building behind my eyes once again.

Was anything real?

"I didn't want you to find out—"

"Did you cause the accident?" My voice came out as whisper, because there was no physical way I could make it any louder.

"What?"

"The accident that killed them, Adriel—or Avidus—or what- ever the fuck your name is. Did you cause it?"

"No! I would never do something like that to you! It wasn't supposed to happen—"

"No, you just brought me to the town that wanted to kill or use me." I tried to scoff, but all my energy had been drained away. "I think they're skipping you for boyfriend of the year. Sorry."

What little relief came at the knowledge that he didn't cause the crash that killed his 'parents', was short lived. I was still nauseous, my head was spinning, and my heart felt like he ripped it out of my chest, stuck it in a paper shredder and tried to give it back. "You were my everything." I felt like I was falling. Falling through a dark, cold, endless abyss with no escape.

"Don't say it like that." His voice was suddenly a beg as he drew his knees underneath him so he was sitting like I was. "Like I'm not anymore." I didn't jerk away as he placed his hands on my upper arms, but my whole body felt like Jell-O. I wasn't sure I could move if I tried.

"Larkin, I love you. You are the only thing that matters to me." Those hands shook me once as I lifted my eyes to his. "I don't care about this place, I don't care about the Immortals, I don't even care about my fucking body, okay? I only need you."

"You put those dreams in my head." It felt like we were having two different conversations, one where my mind was trying to process every single thing that has happened since he came into my life, and another where he was trying to convince me he wasn't a sack of lying demon shit.

He let out a heavy breath and loosened his grip on my arms, though he didn't let go. "Only the good ones, never the nightmares. I tried to be there to wake you from every single one those."

That was true at least. He was there nearly every time I woke screaming and crying, or just in a state of pure panic. He always chased those dreams away. "The other ones..." I left the sentence hanging, just daring him to finish it for me.

"I told you I didn't think we could be like this. The other ones were me wanting you more than you could possibly imagine. When I found out we could be together without my body, I didn't need to send them to you anymore. I didn't need my body anymore."

That was true too, I guess. I hadn't had one of those erotic dreams since the first night we slept together, but I had just chalked it up to being sexually satisfied and not needing to think of some sexy dark stranger. Just another fucking thing I was so completely wrong about.

"So, what?" I asked sarcastically and tried not to sway limply back against the wall, though I don't think his hands would have let me get very far. "You figured out you can still get hard and you no longer want the demon body?"

"I'm not a demon."

"So, everyone keeps telling me, but you sure as hell aren't a fucking angel."

"Larkin, I..." He sighed, shook his head and glanced away. "I want my body. I want a lot of things, but I only need you."

"Because you love me."

"I do love you." He laughed then, and the sound was so strange in our current situation it made my shoulders tense. "Of course I love you. How the hell do you think those fucks were able to get me down here in the first place?"

I reached under his arms to rub my palms against my heavy eyelids as I let out a long, tired sigh. "Because you're the greedy guy that got pissed at the white-wingies and fell for always wanting what you can't have. You wanted to fuck me, but

couldn't, so you chased my ass here, and boom sleeping angel."
My interpretation of Shorzin's lesson didn't seem so bogus now.

"You always have such a way with words." This time his
chuckle was light and eased some of the tension strumming
between us. "And that's not exactly what happened."

I threw my hands up in the air in exasperation, not caring that
he was still holding onto me, and made a 'hrmph' noise. "Well
then please do tell me what really happened. Because that's so
fucking important five hundred years later!"

"It is important. You weren't just a prison a bunch of old
human fucks prayed for. You were created for me." The dark
look shining in his eyes pulled at my heart. "They had planned
on tricking me into a tomb, miles beneath the surface, but they
knew they needed more than their silly little spells for it to work.
They needed a soul." He finally let go of my arms to sit on the
dirt floor directly in front of me. Now unsupported, I found my
limp body leaning heavily back against the damp cavern wall.

"They used their stupid little chants and spells to call up my
big bad brother, sitting all high and mighty on his throne of bull
shit in Heaven, and begged for help." Adriel, because I refused
to call him anything else, mocked sardonically, and rolled those
blue eyes. "But Michael isn't an idiot, and he knew no man-made
prison could hold an angel, fallen or not. So, he gave them the
one thing that could trap me forever—you."

His gaze flickered to mine as the words slipped past his lips,
but I couldn't find it in myself to look at him. "The mortals
thought my lust would get the better of me, and I would chase
you here as you've been told. Michael knew better, he always had
a knack for being one step ahead of me. It's fucking annoying."

Yeah, I knew how that felt.

The tone that filled his voice was one of such annoyance and disdain that he could only be talking about an older sibling. And that broke my heart, because it wasn't Raffie speaking about him.

She didn't exist.

"He knew the only way to really get my attention was for a soul to call to every part of my own—the dark and all. Then you were there, watching me curiously across the stone courtyard of the town, and everything changed." Adriel's voice took on a faraway note, and his eyes grew distant like he was thinking of that time all those centuries ago. Where he fell for a girl that no longer exists.

"That was Michael's prison for me, the true reason he decided to help. I no longer cared about power, or that fucked up line I kept crossing. He knew I would stop it all and go away willingly, if you asked me to."

"So, you didn't chase the girl down here?"

His head tilted curiously to the side at my question, like he wasn't sure why I phrased it that way. "I would have chased you anywhere. I still would, but no, I didn't. I knew what they were planning, you didn't bother trying to hide it from me for long. I went because I wanted to."

My brow furrowed at that and I rubbed my hand across my forehead like that would dull the ache there. "Why?"

"You asked me to." I lowered my hand and blinked. He was staring at me with such a vulnerable, sad, loneliness that it only made everything inside me hurt more. "Like I said, Larkin. It's your choice. It always has been, and always will be."

I wanted to believe him. I wanted to believe him more than anything, but how could I ever trust him again? Everything he said from day one was a lie, from the moment the Markos took me in, to fifteen minutes ago. That was two years of deception and betrayal. I revolved my entire world around them. Every plan I had for the future I changed for the Markos—for him.

Not that I had a lot of plans, but still.

"So, if I wanted to leave right now, get in my car and drive as far from this town as I could and never look back, you would let me?"

"If that was what you wanted." But I could see the hesitation flashing behind his eyes, like he was desperately hoping I didn't pick that option. "Is that what you want?"

I sighed and dropped my gaze to my hands that were resting limply in my lap. "I don't know. This morning the only thing I wanted was for us to leave this place. I wanted you and Raf. Now I don't have either."

"Yes, you do." He reached forward again, and I didn't pull away as his hands wrapped securely around my wrists. "Raf is still there, at the house waiting for us. We can still leave, still pile into the SUV and get as far away from here as you want. None of that has changed."

"You're name's not even Adriel."

Another sigh passed his lips and I watched with tired eyes as he lifted my hands to press a soft kiss against my palms. "It is. Michael loves stripping our true names when we fall and give us new ones that represent the sin we committed. Adriel is my real name, Avidus is the shit one he deemed me worthy of. I couldn't stand the thought of you calling me something besides Adriel, especially not anything related to that fucking insult."

I think this was the most I ever heard him swear in one conversation, and I was somewhat relieved by that. If he had been all proper and arrogant, like he usually was, I would probably be throwing up again.

I sucked in a shaky breath and tried to force down the complete mind-fuck my poor brain was going through. "So, what do we do now?" I asked heavily and pulled my hands from his so I could scrub them down my face.

"What we were going to do this morning." Adriel stood slowly to his feet, his eyes never leaving me as he did, like he was afraid I would freak out again at any moment. I didn't flinch away as he reached down, hooked his hands under my arms, and pulled me easily to my feet. "We leave. We get in the SUV and we can drive as far away from Deshua as you want."

I studied his pleading gaze carefully, almost expecting to see a flicker of that black that had haunted my dreams, or for a dark demonic air to stream off him now that I knew. But there was nothing. Just my normal, everyday Adriel—pleading with me to believe in him. I wasn't sure how I felt about that anymore.

Everything was fucked.

"You really don't want the demon body?" My voice came out far weaker than I wanted it to, but he didn't appear to notice, or care.

"You are the only thing I need." He said with a soft smile, even though his eyes flickered briefly to the stone slab and the body chained to it before looking back again. "I'll live the rest of eternity like this if that's what you want." He shrugged, like it was no big deal that he was giving up his own body.

"I don't... I don't know."

I felt completely and totally drained. I couldn't even cry anymore. Every emotion from hell to high water just raged through my entire being in a twenty-minute time span. This was all too much, it had been too much for so long. Everything was a lie, he was a lie. How could I just overlook that and move on?

"You don't have to decide anything right now. There's no deadline, it's not like this place will disappear anytime soon. I made sure of that." Adriel's smile was small, and reassuring, but it did nothing to ease the nausea still swirling around my stomach. Hearing Dri, my Dri, talk so causally about building the town bothered me.

"What do you want, Larkin?"

There was that question again. I closed my eyes and sucked in a shaky breath, too afraid if I stepped out of his grip that I would fall to the floor in a heap. "I want—to forget everything. I don't want this to be real. I want it to be a dream." My voice sounded breathless as it passed my lips, but that didn't change the words.

I wished this never happened. I wished the day would start all over again, and I would help him pack up the car, we would grab Raf, and be halfway out of the state by now. I wish I never found out about any of this. Better yet, I didn't want any of it to be real. Just an insane, very bad, nightmare.

I didn't pull away as he brought me into his chest and wrapped those oh-so-familiar arms tightly around my torso. He squeezed me to him and sighed heavily in my ear. "I can't give you that, no matter how badly I want to. Please believe that I would give anything to take this away."

I had a hard time doubting the sincerity in his tone. I had gotten so well at telling the difference in his voice and feelings that I thought I knew exactly when he was lying and when he wasn't. Turns out that was just a sick joke too.

"Let's just go, okay? We'll leave Deshua, and never look back." His hands curled into my hair to press me as close to his chest as was physically possible. "I only care about you." I felt that pressure start to build behind my eyes again, like the tears didn't get the notice about how emotionally exhausted I was. But despite all the turmoil raging through my head and chest I nodded against him. Adriel visibly relaxed against me.

I had no idea how the hell I would process all of this in the next few days, hell, I doubt I would be sane in the next few hours, but I knew staying here wasn't going to fix anything. I didn't think staying with him was the best decision anymore either, but it wasn't like I had many options.

I knew he wouldn't hurt me, but I had no idea if I could trust him. Never in my life did I think I would be saying that about Adriel, the only person who had ever made my life bearable. And he was one big fat lie. But if this was just one giant mind trick to get me to wake him, why was he so set on leaving? Actually, he was set on doing whatever I wanted.

I needed to think.

"I can't—I can't handle this, Adriel." I whispered as he eased me away from his chest.

Those dark eyes washed slowly over my face, and his hands left my hair to press against my shoulders and rub down my arms. "Yes, you can. You're the strongest person I know. You can handle anything."

I scoffed and actually rolled my eyes. Surprisingly the action made me feel better. "You need a dictionary if you think this is 'handling' it."

The corner of his mouth twitched up in that amused smirk I both loved and hated. It was such an Adriel reaction that I felt another punch sent straight to my stomach. He promised not everything was a lie. He loved me. Could I really believe that?

I watched silently as he grabbed onto my hands and raised them until his lips could press firmly against the back of both. "I love you. I know you don't believe me anymore, but I swear I will do everything in my power to prove it to you. Let's just get out of here first, okay?"

I nodded before I could think of a better response.

I let him hold tightly onto one of my hands as he turned to pull us away from the tomb, and the body waiting patiently to be awakened. He didn't glance back as we exited the dark, damp crypt, but I did. The torches flickered out as we walked away, but I caught one last glimpse of the fallen angel.

Would Adriel really turn his back on himself, for me?

CHAPTER 29

The tunnel was just as dark and creepy leaving the cavern as it was when I entered, if not more My mind was still a complete and total mess, and it would be for a very long time, but I knew the only way to sort through everything was to get as far away from Deshua as I could.

"Awe, yes, Larkin. You were right River."

We had just exited the mouth of the cave when that voice reached our ears. Adriel pulled us to an immediate stop as I frowned and looked over his shoulder. "Professor Shorzin? What are you doing here?" I went to step in front of Dri, but his hand tightened on mine and he shifted until I was completely behind him.

"See? I told you they knew where he really was!"

"River? What are you guys doing here?" A whole crowd of fifteen or twenty people stood surrounding the entrance of the cave, and four of them I knew very well.

Shorzin, River, and Siena stood at the very front of the crowd. My folklore professor had an elated smile on his face, though River kept glancing at us nervously—well, he kept glancing at

Adriel nervously—and Siena just stood stalk silent beside them. Jess was there too, but she didn't look nearly as comfortable as everyone else. If anything, she looked worried.

"What the hell is going on?" I went to step around Adriel again, but he made a weird sound and pushed me back.

"Well, you see, when young River here saw you disappear into the very place we purposely made sure no one can go, we make it a point to follow. Especially after your little talk with our Jess here." Shorzin took a step forward, his beaming eyes, with the laugh lines at the corner, gleamed in the dim light of the forest. His usual ponytail was nowhere in sight, and his long hair framed like a curtain around his thin face. He still wore his khaki shorts, Hawaiian shirt and sandals which made the whole sinister air he was portraying all that weirder.

"Leave me out of this, Jemison. I told you I want nothing to do with it."

Shorzin just waved off the small woman's words and took another step towards us. Adriel's arm reached around until his hand could grab protectively at the sleeve of my jacket. "I'm sure you could imagine my surprise when pretty boy there followed after you too. Turns out we're not the only ones good at hiding." He let a chuckle follow his words, and I could practically feel Dri tense in front of me.

What in the actual fuck was happening? And why was Shorzin acting like a massive creep? Like he knew.

"Fuck off, piss ant."

"You always did have such a way with words, Avidus."

Oof. Okay, I guess he did know.

Adriel stepped completely in front of me at that, blocking every ounce of my view. His hold body tensed liked he was ready for a fight. I knew he could do some damage, but there were at least fifteen people surrounding us. I highly doubted he could take them all, even if I helped. He might have been the demon/not demon thingy, but this was still just a human body. I think.

I glanced over at River and Siena, who no longer held those inviting smiles. Were they apart of this too? Was anything in this fucking town real?! Siena was in her typical goth attire, but there was a dark fire in her eyes as she looked at Adriel that concerned me. River was standing between her and Shorzin with that nervous glint dancing across his bright eyes.

They weren't Immortals, I knew that much. They never flashed those signature red eyes and I never had that weird stomach-turning unease around them. Yet, they knew who we were and there were two different kinds of people in Deshua. If they weren't part of the group that worshiped Adriel, than they were part of the one that wanted to kill us. Or, kill me to be more specific.

"I had a feeling you were poking holes in the spell, but I never would have realized how much. Good job. Creating that whole little human life you got there must have taken a lot power. I'm envious." Shorzin applauded mockingly, though no one else joined him. It wasn't hard to figure out he was apparently the ringleader of the group.

Which was honestly pretty fucked if you asked me. I mean, seriously? The guy taught us all about Avidus and the Key!

He even seemed to idealize the guy! So did River and Siena! Everything in this town really was one, big, fucked up lie.

"Stay behind me." Adriel spoke softly over his shoulder, but never took his eyes off Shorzin and the others.

Fine by me. It's not like I planned on running through them.

"You always did crave more power than you could handle." Dri spoke louder then, his own tone of mocking slipping into the air.

That's when I realized how they were talking. Like the knew each other personally, from a long time ago, but Shorzin wasn't an Immortal. Not one of Avidus's at least, which didn't make any sense. I thought only the Immortals could be, well, immortal. But I couldn't shove down that sickening feeling that Shorzin was one of the witches that called up Michael. That stuck Adriel in that cavern. Which so did not bode well for us.

"Ha! Look who's talking! You weren't thrown from Heaven for giving away power." The professor-turned creepy weirdo-dude laughed viciously. Okay, I definitely had enough for one day. Scratch that, I had enough for a whole lifetime.

"True, but I knew how to handle it. You killed half the town."

"And you turned the other half into soulless man-eaters." His laughter died completely away and eyes so dark they could have been black locked onto Dri's.

Adriel shrugged, not at all concerned with the sudden change in Shorzin. "It was their choice. They knew what they were getting into."

"Even so," Shorzin paused to run a hand through his scraggily, greasy, brown hair, "We will not allow you to do so again. The prison was set in place for a reason. It cannot be broken."

I wasn't sure what Adriel was planning, but from how tense his back was, I knew it would involve fighting. Even though I knew there was no way we were going to get out of there by fighting, I reached for the knife hidden in my jacket. It was meant to fight the Immortals, but I hoped it would work just as well against Shorzin's group. There were humans, right? Well, at least compared to Luke and those red eyed freaks.

"We're leaving!" I tried to make my voice as steady as possible as I spoke up behind Adriel's back, though I'm sure I only sounded like a frightened child. Adriel's head whipped around to glare at me as I stuck my head around his shoulder, but I ignored him.

"I'm not waking him up, we're leaving Deshua and never coming back, I swear." I gripped tightly onto the sleeve of Adriel's flannel as all eyes turned to me. "Seriously! You can check our SUV if you don't believe me. We're leaving town and never coming back."

"I do not doubt you, child." Shorzin's voice was sickly sweet, like he was addressing a four-year-old who couldn't understand why they were in trouble. "But we do not like to take any chances. I'm afraid you must be handled."

I needed no clarification on how they planned on 'handling' me. I gulped and Adriel shoved me effortlessly behind him once again.

"Don't do this, Jemison." Dri tried to reason, though his voice was hard and his body unmoving. "You will not like what happens if you do."

Jemison waved his hand dismissively, like nothing in the world worried him. "As far as I'm concerned you are dead and hold no true power. And once your little girlfriend is out of the way, there will be peace again."

"Adriel..." My fingers curled tightly into the back of his flannel as my eyes darted around the crowd that had spread out around us. There was no easy escape in sight, and I had a bad feeling I wouldn't be leaving this alive.

"It'll be okay, Lark." But he didn't promise like he usually would, and his voice didn't sound so sure.

My eyes landed on River and Siena, and in a last-ditch effort I tried to plead with them. "Come on, guys. Are you really going to kill me? I thought we were friends."

They exchanged glances with each other and shrugged simultaneously. "It's nothing personal, Larkin. We really did like you." River started with a half-smile. "Peace and balance just come's first, you know?" Siena finished, but the way her lips curved didn't seem so remorseful. I had a sickening flashback of the first time we met, where she didn't care whether I was the new girl in town or a bug beneath her shoe.

God. I was so done with fucking crazy ass psychos.

"Larkin."

My name whispered into my mind like a cool breeze against heated skin. I whipped my head around and locked eyes with the bright green gaze of Jess. She was the only one of the group that didn't seem eager to kill me.

"You are going to have to run."

There it was again, her voice inside my head. It almost felt like a fly buzzing next to my ear. I instinctively reached my hand up to swat the bug away but met nothing.

Yeah. I was already planning on that, thanks.

"They will take him first. When that happens run back into the cave."

Yeah right. There was no way in hell I was going back in there. Cornering myself in a tomb with Adriel's real body didn't seem like the best idea.

"You must. It's the only way you will survive." She persisted like she could hear exactly what I was thing, which she probably could. She was in my head after all.

"Grab Avidus, he's only human now. He can't hurt you. Then take the girl." The minute the words left Shorzin's lips, the crowd around us began to descend like irritating mosquitoes.

Adriel pushed me away and was able to throw a few out of the crowd away, before their numbers overpowered him and they grabbed onto his arms. I ribbed my knife out of the jacket's inside pocket and raised it protectively in front of me. The two unknown men who had started on me paused at the sight of the sharp weapon.

Yet panic flared through my body as I saw Adriel get dragged down the hill, and despite what Jess said, I hesitated. I couldn't leave him, not when he was trying to save me, and even though he ripped my entire world apart, I still loved him.

"Larkin run!" He shouted as they dragged him further away, but I couldn't. I sucked in a shaky breath, raised my knife higher and then chased after his captors. "Larkin stop, go!" Adriel's voice was filled with rage as he tried to shove the men off him, but Shorzin had made sure to bring men far larger than him.

I raised my hand, ready to stab it into the nearest creep, when hands suddenly ripped me away. "Let him go!" I shouted as my knife went flying into the air, then lost in the mass of trees and brush. Those hands hoisted me effortlessly away. "Stop! Let him go!" I was screaming, though my throat was already raw from earlier.

I reached for Adriel, begging him to just take my hand so we could figure out how to get the fuck out of there, but another pair joined the ones holding me back and ripped us apart. He didn't stop fighting, but those dark eyes locked on mine, and the look there tore my heart from my chest. We really weren't getting out of this.

"Snap it." Shorzin ordered casually a few feet away, as those unfamiliar hands pulled me further from Adriel.

Then the most horrific sight I would ever witness played out before my eyes. The two guys holding Adriel stopped their retreat while a third walked towards them. I realized too late what was about to happen and could only watch in horror as the man placed his hands on either side of Adriel's face, and twisted viciously. The 'crack' sound was nearly as loud as the one in my chest.

"No!!" I screamed so loudly my throat felt like I swallowed fire. I kicked and thrashed my body viciously as the men tossed Adriel's limp body to the ground, but there was no leeway in their hold. "What have you done?!" I shouted in pure agony as those hands ripped me further away. If I thought my world had fallen apart before, it was nothing compared to the sight of the person, who was supposed to be your everything, get their neck snapped.

There was a sick smile pulling on Shorzin's lips as he turned to me. "Oh, relax. He's not dead. Well, at least not the 'real' him." He snickered, and there was nothing more in the world that I wanted than to take a very dull stick and shove it repeatedly into his brain. "I'm sure once he regains himself, he'll be able to build a whole new human body, maybe even reanimate that one if I don't decide to burn it. Sadly, I can't say the same for you."

I knew his words were supposed to terrify me, but I actually found them relieving. He wasn't dead.

"Take her to town square, we'll have a ceremony and-" Shorzin's face went slack, his dark eyes growing distant for the briefest of moments before he shook his head. "Actually, no. Take her into the tomb, let's have some fun."

I didn't notice or care about the hands holding me hostage and dragging me back into the cave. My brain was still replaying that horrific sight over and over. The only hope I had was knowing he wasn't really dead. That he couldn't die. I prayed to whatever god there was that that was true.

I caught the briefest glimpse of Jess before I was dragged back into the cave. There was sweat on her brow and those green eyes were glued to Shorzin, her slender mouth mumbling silent words no one heard. I had a feeling the sudden change of plans was her doing. But that didn't mean I wasn't going to give them hell.

"Let me fucking go!" I shouted as they dragged me back down that tunnel I was becoming way too familiar with. "You no good, peace of shit, fuck-tard!" My screaming fell on deaf ears, except for Shorzin who only laughed.

"You know, your first life was nowhere near this feisty. It makes things interesting."

"Suck ass, you fuck."

A sharp slap rang throughout the tunnel as the back of his hand connected with my face. The hit was so hard, I went dizzy, and fell limp in my captor's hold. "Now see, that wasn't so hard. I would say to learn some manners, but you won't be around long enough to do so." I could only groan in response as ringing sounded throughout my entire skull.

The torches flickered to life as soon as they dragged me into the crypt and threw my body against the stone base of that slab. My back connected sharply with its base and I let out a gasp as pain shot down my spine. I blinked dazedly up at the two who threw, only to not recognize the large men walking away.

Shorzin hovered only a few feet away, Siena and River still lingering at his side. God, this was really fucked.

"Are you sure leaving her is a good idea? She might try to wake him." Siena spoke up at his side, though Professor Fuck-Tard just scoffed and rolled his eyes.

"The girl is clueless. She didn't even know she was living with him. I doubt he told her what to do. You two may leave."

They nodded briefly at Shorzin, before turning and walking away without a glance back. I take back what I said earlier, they were the ones not winning the Friend of the Year award. It was all mine. Yay.

Then it was just Shorzin facing me, a wicked gleam in his dark eyes. "Does this seem familiar to you yet, Larkin?" He glanced almost nostalgically around the tomb, his eyes lingering on the skull resting at the base of the stone slab before dropping back down to where I was huddled on the floor. "Do you not remember the last time we were in here together?"

I didn't say anything as he walked forward, only used my elbow to scoot away from him. My head was throbbing, whether from his hit or just the whole fucking day I wasn't sure, and my back was screaming in pain. I could make a run if I really tried, but I had no doubt he had fuckheads stationed throughout the tunnel and its entrance. I wouldn't get very far.

I closed my eyes and sucked in a shaky breath. "Jess...?" I tried to ask as loudly in my head as I could, though I doubted I did it right. I wanted to cry when she didn't respond.

"I don't blame you if you don't. You never were too bright." He stopped at the base of the stone slab, right next to that skull. Then the psycho stepped on it.

What the fuck was wrong with him?

But the minute the old bone cracked and crumbled beneath his sandal the images hit me. I was no longer lying on the floor in fear, but standing next to the stone slab, holding the hand of the demon/angel thing to my face. He was still awake and smiling sadly up at me as I cradled his palm to my tear stained cheek.

"I'm so sorry."

"I know."

The words rushed through my ears as if they were spoken right next to me, whispering like soft lullaby's.

"Please do not hate me."

"I could never hate you."

I cried over him with my heart torn into a thousand pieces at the act I must commit. Then the images disappeared on black smoke, until new ones flashed through my mind. He was sleeping now, with those thick black chains binding him firmly in place. I hovered over his peaceful face, still crying while my tears seemed to leave permanent imprints against his cheeks.

"You have done well." I didn't need to glance over to know Jemison was behind me.

"It is not permanent." That was the only hope I could hold onto as I watched the man I loved fall into an eternal cage.

"Indeed, it is not... Which is why I am sure you can understand what I am about to do." I didn't have a chance to question him, or even turn around.

Just like my modern Adriel, hands wrapped around my head and snapped my neck swiftly to the side. Pain ricocheted down my back, but then I was no longer the girl who put the fallen angel to sleep but lying on the floor and watching her dead body fall beside me.

I gasped and the image disappeared completely. "You killed her—me. Right here."

"Hm, yes. As I must do again, I'm afraid. I can't risk you waking him, just like I couldn't risk it then." He traced his fingers leisurely over Adriel's stone slab, and I had the sudden urge to stand up and shove him away. "Rather ironic, don't you think? I killed your first life here, and now your bones will join hers. It gives me chills."

"You're fucking insane."

He paused and glanced down at me curiously before shrugging. "Probably, it's bound to happen when you live as long as I have. Avidus might have the power to turn humans Immortals, but I know the secret of long life. Dying is easy, living is much harder—but so worth it.

"Look," I tried in another last-ditch effort as he circled back to the entrance of the tunnel. I didn't really care how he was able to live so long, I only cared about surviving. "Even if you kill me, I'll just be reincarnated. You can't keep me dead. That Azzie-guy will always send me back until Adriel does wake."

Shorzin shrugged again, like he didn't have any care in the world. "Then I will kill your next life, and the next, and the next. I do not care. Killing doesn't bother me, actually I rather enjoy it."

What in the actual fuck was Adriel thinking bringing me here? Everyone here was fucking insane!

"Though, I think I'm going to enjoy putting you through a slow death." He traced his hand almost lovingly down the stone side of the tomb's entrance, his dark eyes flickering up to the roof. "Yes, trapping you in here with your lost love as you starve or suffocate. Now that is poetry."

"Larkin..." Jess's voice sounded in my head once again, though it sounded distant and jumbled. My heart raced in my chest as I tried to desperately cling onto her. "Blood... key..." Were the only words I could understand before she disappeared.

Shorzin stepped back into the tunnel, his hand still on the side of the entrance, his sickening smile shining brightly down at me. "Do enjoy your time with him while you can." Then, with a flick of his hand, the stones and dirt above the entrance shrieked and rumbled before caving in.

Sealing me forever in Adriel's tomb.

Chapter 30

I was having a panic attack. I laid flat on the dirt ground, next to the crushed bones of my first life and Avidus's trapped body, and hyperventilated. It started as soon as the entrance caved in and everything went silent. The only reason I hadn't completely lost my shit was because the torches still cast dim light around the cavern.

I wasn't sure how long I laid on the floor, gasping for air that I wasn't sure I would have for long, and praying to whatever the hell was up there that I would get out of this. That Adriel was still alive, and that Rafael was real.

I closed my eyes and sucked in air greedily. Just a dream. This was all just one really bad dream. I would wake up in my bed, sweaty and confused. Then Adriel would come in, tell me everything was okay, and hold me until I fell back asleep. Yes, that is what will happen. I was able to calm myself down enough to stop hyperventilating, but when I opened my eyes, I was still in that damn tomb.

I rolled over and forced my shaky body onto my hands and knees. I knew what I had to do, or at least half of it. The only way I, and Adriel, would get out of this, was by waking him. My choice had been officially taken from me, but I didn't care. I would wake him a thousand times if it meant keeping him alive.

I used the edge of the slab to help pull me to my feet and steadied myself against its side. I gazed down at the fallen angel chained to stone. He looked some much like Adriel it stole my breath away. My head and back were throbbing, and my body felt too sluggish to do anything, but I forced my hand to move until my fingertips could brush just barely against his cheek.

His skin was warm, and soft, and made my heart ache. Adriel, not Avidus.

Or, at least, I kept telling myself that.

I had to free him. I had to wake him, but Shorzin was right. In all the stories and conversations with Jess and Luke, no one told me how the fuck I was supposed to do that.

"Um, hey, Adriel. I-I'm not really sure what I'm supposed to be doing here." I poked the side of his cheek, like I could annoy him into waking up. "Look, we're kind of trapped, and I would really appreciate it if you wake up and kicked some ass." I lightly slapped his cheek like that would work where the poking hadn't

Then a bad idea struck me. Oh god, was I really going to do this?

Yup.

I let out a heavy sigh before heaving my body over the edge of the slab and onto the sleeping angel. I tried to place my knees on either side of his giant chest, but those black wings were everywhere, so I had to go down to his stomach. "Adriel!" I leaned over and shouted in his face, but he didn't move. He didn't even blink. I tapped his cheek again, and then slapped both.

"Fucking wake up!"

Nothing.

"What good is being the fucking key if I don't know how to pick a lock!" My voice echoed loudly around the cavern and shook something inside my head.

Blood... key...

Blood was the key. My blood.

Fuck.

What is with this town and blood?!

I sat back heavily on my heels and looked around for anything sharp enough that would pierce skin. I lost my fancy knife in all the commotion outside, and I was getting a really bad idea about the stone corner of the slab. It was the only idea I had. I sighed as I took my jacket off and rolled up my shirt's sleeve.

I really fucking hoped this worked.

I leaned far enough over the side of the stone so my forearm could touch the sharp corner. I pressed down as hard as I could and then ripped my skin down the edge. Pain shot through my veins and raced up my arm. "Ow!" I groaned and ripped my hand back to look at the damage. A breath of relief escaped my chest when I saw the thick line of blood start to pool out of the cut.

Thank god. I did not want to have to do that again.

I let the blood slip onto his bare chest, then his forehead and cheeks. I even placed a little on his lips—as gross as that was. I had no idea what the hell I was supposed to do, but I decided I bled enough on him and wrapped my jacket tightly around the cut like a bandage.

"Alright, so blood is the key. I'm supposed to be the key, so there. I bled on you. Wake up now, please."

Nothing.

I gazed down at the red staining his tan skin and dripping onto his dark feathers. Nothing was happening.

I tried to force back the aggravated tears that threatened to fall. Crying wouldn't help anything right now. I held my arm tightly to my chest and laid my head down against his chest, not even carrying about the blood my cheek was resting against.

"I don't know what to do." I mumbled against him. "Please wake up. You can't be dead. I need you." I sniffled and pressed my face further into him. "I wish you would just tell me what to do." But he didn't, and I was out of ideas.

I closed my eyes and didn't care about the tears wanting to fall anymore. I hated crying, it was weak, but I had a feeling for a while now that I wouldn't be leaving Deshua alive. I deserved to cry. That morning had just been a sick joke from fate. My last little glimpse of an escape, one where everything was still intact. Adriel was alive, Raf was real, and we were sailing free to somewhere new and safe. I should have just ignored the nagging.

Now he's dead, Rafael doesn't exist, and I was going to die inside an ancient tomb—again.

'Crack!' My eyes snapped open as the sound of rock splitting reverberated in my ears.

What was that?

There was nothing for a moment, until another 'crack' sounded throughout the crypt, and a bit of rock and dirt fell on my shoulder. I glanced up and could just make out a slit in the ceiling, a crack that was quickly growing. My heart hammered in my chest and I sat up as more cracks started to appear around the room.

Fuck this wasn't good. Shorzin must have triggered something when he magic-collapsed the entrance. Now the whole fucking tomb was going to cave in and smother us to death. A large chunk of rock fell from the roof and crashed to the ground. Then another, and another, until I was afraid we would be squished next.

I lurched forward and used my body as a shield to cover as much of demon Dri as I could. I knew he was immortal or whatever, but my first instinct was to protect the closest thing I had to Adriel. Besides, it's not like I was getting out of that alive.

I wasn't sure how long I laid stretched over him, cowering underneath the collapsing mountain, waiting to be crushed. I just kept whispering over and over, "make it quick, make it quick, make it quick", and listening to the sound of breaking rock. Until there was silence.

I didn't realize it was over until the feel of the soft, cold, October breeze rolled over my shoulders and filled my lungs. I stopped chanting and blinked my eyes open to the sight of chaos. The entire mountain had fallen around us. Boulders, rocks, dirt, and trees crashed down a large encompassing circle. Everything was destroyed. The forest surrounding the mountain, a few buildings that had been backed up against it, and even the stone courtyard of the college campus, all destroyed.

The only thing that had been untouched was the stone slab—and us.

"What...?"

I hadn't noticed I was already in a sitting position until I tried to pull away from demon Dri's chest, and strong arms stopped me. My gaze snapped over and locked on a pair of black eyes so dark I could see my own reflection. My heart stopped in my chest, and the air froze in my lungs.

"H-Hey..."

His head was tilted curiously to the side as those dark eyes studied me, but then he smiled and the sight sent warmth through my veins. "Hi." His voice was raspy and hoarse, like he hadn't used it in hundreds of years—because he hadn't. There was always a strange way to it, like he was used to speaking a thousand different languages, none of which were English.

He didn't sound anything like my Adriel.

He blinked those black eyes but otherwise stayed motionless. "I am your Adriel."

"Don't do that."

His smile turned more into that smirk I was so familiar with, and ease slightly chased away the tension in my shoulders. "It's hard to ignore when you're screaming at me."

"I wasn't screaming at you. I was thinking. In my head. Quietly. Where you shouldn't be."

Even though the entirety of his eyes were black, like, with no white at all, I could have sworn he rolled them at me. And just like that, I knew he was the Adriel I had been living with for so long. There was only one person in the world that I argued with over stupid shit that easily.

Then his smirky smile disappeared, and his head tilted curiously once again. "You have blood on your cheek." He unwrapped one of his arms from where they had been securely

                    EVIE CRAIGIE

around me to wipe the blood from my face. That's when I realized the chains that had pinned him down were completely gone, blown to smithereens.

"You have more on you." I mumbled as my eyes flickered embarrassingly to the red spots smeared all over his face and chest.

His shoulder shrugged, like he didn't give one fudge that I bled all over him. "You cut yourself?" Demon Adriel asked slowly, as if he had a hard time getting his tongue to work.

"Um, yeah." I held my jacket covered arm up awkwardly as those black eyes scanned my face. "Blood is the key, right?"

He gave me one short nod, before his gaze dropped to my arm. I didn't pull away as one of his hands unwrapped from around me to pull the jacket off. The cut had been bad. I was low key proud of myself really, but it was still bleeding, and I had a bad feeling it wasn't going to stop anytime soon.

I watched with wide, horrified eyes, as he raised my arm to his lips and then licked the entire length of the cut. I suddenly felt nauseous again. That was so not something I wanted to see. Yet when he pulled away, the cut had completely sealed and faded away to a thin white line against my skin.

"That was gross."

Those black eyes rose from my arm to glance at me, and he smiled. As if I were amusing. Oof.

That's when I realized how big he really was. My Adriel had only been a few inches taller than me, and as buff as any construction worker. This Adriel was twice his size. His torso alone stood a full foot and a half taller than mine, and you could probably shove two of me into its width. And his wings were massive. Each one seemed to span seven feet stretched out and were covered in the silky black feathers that had once haunted my dreams.

He seemed to glow too, like he had when I first entered the cavern. The air around him just pulsed with energy and power, and it was so dazzling I immediately felt inferior in every form of the word. It was the strangest feeling in the world, one of complete awe, adoration, and fear. I felt it once before, what seemed like a million years ago, though it had only been a few short weeks.

But, despite the massive size difference, and the wings, and the black eyes, he still looked like my Dri.

"I am your Dri."

"Stop. That."

His chuckle rolled over my shoulders and seemed to dance in the now open area surrounding us. I forced my gaze from his to glance around the chaos. "Did you... do all this?"

His eyes followed my own, and his arms seemed to tighten around me. "I could not stand when you started crying. I had to get you out of there, yes?"

I gulped down the knot that formed in my throat. That... was a lot of power.

Then his words hit me like an eighteen-wheeler.

"You were awake?" My eyes snapped back to his and narrowed at the guilty look that suddenly pulled on his unearthly handsome face. "How long?"

He shrugged and gave me a small, apologetic smile. It was such an Adriel thing for him to do that it tore at my insides. "Not long, just when your blood touched my tongue." His voice seemed to grow stronger and normal with each word he spoke. I think he could see the blatant fury brewing behind my eyes because he quickly continued. "It took me a while to gain all my senses back, I'm sorry. And my mind had to readjust after being—sent back like that."

I knew he meant 'rudely kicked out when those fucks snapped my neck' instead, but I appreciated that he didn't say it like that.

"And are you... like, okay?"

Those black eyes blinked at me, and he smiled again, like he found my complete awkwardness funny. "Yes Angel, I am okay."

"You do realize how fucked that is? Calling me that, right?"

He shrugged again but those arms seemed to pull me closer as if he were afraid I would take off at any moment. "Angels are beautiful, eternal. They are meant to keep peace and serenity. That's what you are to me. My angel."

"Oh." I didn't know what to say to that. When he was just human Adriel, he never really gave me a reason for the nickname. I always just assumed it was because that's what Raf said when we first met, like an inside joke. Then again, Rafael wasn't real, so it probably was him calling me that from the very beginning.

"So, what now?" I asked hesitantly as the fact that I was sitting on his very large lap suddenly entered my mind. That seemed to be a question I was asking a lot lately. I shifted uncomfortably, but those freakishly long arms tightened and didn't let me get very far. "Do you go all psycho and try to take over the world again?"

He raised a dark eyebrow, though I found it really hard keeping my gaze on his. "I told you I don't want that anymore."

"Right..." I rolled my eyes and tried to lean away from him. He wouldn't let me. "Because 'I'm all that matters now', yadda, yadda, blah, blah, blah."

"You are all that matters, and nothing has changed. We can still do whatever you want."

The hope that flickered in my chest was surprising, and I had to squish down the smile that wanted to pull at my lips. "You'll still leave, Deshua?"

The second his face fell and he looked away, that hope that surged in my chest died. "I can't."

"I knew it." I didn't bother keeping the disgust from my tone, and I tried to rip away from him, but those impossibly large arms refused to let me.

"It's not like that, Lark. I want to leave, I swear. I just can't."

"I don't believe you. You did before." I tried to push and struggle away from him, but the fuck head refused to budge.

"That was when I was human. Michael doesn't have restrictions on humans, but all Fallen can't leave where they fell. It's not allowed." His words came out as such a desperate plea that I stopped struggling against him.

"It's not like you haven't broken the rules before." I grumbled down at his strong chest. "You fell for a reason, right?"

He laughed, and the sound echoed around us. "Yes, I broke the rules, and do so quite often, but this is a domain issue I physically cannot overrule. Michael is stronger than all of us. His word is commanding rule. I can't leave in this body if he won't allow me." His words were soft, and he nudged his forehead against mine. It was such a simple, normal action between us that I felt my heart almost crumble at my feet.

"You can't just become human again and we can go?" I asked hopefully, even though I knew it was unfounded. Especially with how his gaze turned sad and guilty.

"I can look human again, and put my mind in one, but I can't be what I have been now that I'm awake."

"You can look like you did?" I tried not to sound as excited by that as I really was, but the thought of getting my Dri back was a little too tempting to ignore. He smiled, and even though it was soft and endearing, there was a sadness behind it that didn't sit well with me.

I blinked, and he was gone—or the angel/demon Adriel was. Now I was sitting on the lap of the man I had fell one hundred percent head over heels in love with. The one I gave everything to, the one that was a lie, and the one I watched die. I had no control over my own body, and I wrapped my arms tightly around his neck and squeezed with all my might.

"I am so sorry, Larkin." Adriel murmured into my hair as I buried my face into his neck and refused to let go. "I never meant for any of this to happen."

"Can we just... can we get off this thing please?" I mumbled before forcing my arms to let go.

He lifted me easily onto a sturdy looking piece of rock rubble, before jumping down after me. That dark pulsing power that had surrounded him significantly diminished as he switched back into human Adriel, but there was still an encompassing presence to him that dared anyone to try him.

Adriel groaned when his feet touched the floor, and I raised an eyebrow. "What?" He grunted as he stretched out his sore limbs.

"You try being asleep for five hundred years without waking up sore."

I didn't say anything but let him take my hand when he was done grunting and stretching. I looked carefully at his bare back as he guided me through the destruction. There was no trace of those ginormous black wings he had only minutes ago. No tattoo either.

"Where's your tattoo?" I asked as he lifted me over a boulder bigger than my car.

"It wasn't a tattoo." His hand slipped back into mine, like he was terrified I would disappear if he wasn't holding onto me. "Power leaves marks, especially when you have to shove through a piss poor spell to create four humans." I still wasn't okay with how nonchalant he was talking about all this power and creating bull, but I wasn't in the right state of mind to be okay with anything.

"So that wasn't real either?" Even though he could have taken that however he wanted, my voice was sad. Just another thing I loved that didn't exist.

He glanced over his shoulder at me, with those dark blue eyes that I loved, not the pitch-black ones that came to my dreams. "It was real, it just wasn't a tattoo." But no sooner had the words left his lips then those dark, intricate, black lines started snaking down his arm. I blinked, not sure I was seeing things correctly, but when my eyes opened again there was the tattoo. Exactly as I remembered it.

"Whoa..."

He smiled at the surprise, and slight awe, in my voice, before helping me over a fallen tree. "I'll do anything for you, Larkin.

Now that I have my body and all of my mind again, I can do almost anything. Change myself, change the town, anything. Just name it."

"Except leave."

Adriel's smile faltered and he looked away, but not before I saw the sad look crossing his handsome face. "If I could, I would in a heartbeat."

I sighed but didn't say anything else as the ground finally started to even beneath our feet. I believed him, even if it wasn't that great of an idea.

EPILOGUE

"What about Shorzin? And River, and Siena?" I asked uneasily as we headed closer and closer to the college's campus. Well, the part of it that hadn't been destroyed.

"I'll deal with them."

It was the way he said it, so assured and strong, that sent a chill down my spine. I was uneasy enough when human Adriel talked like that, but with angel/demon Adriel, it was a whole other ball game. The tone wasn't directed at me, but I still felt that sharp bite of fear. I didn't need to ask to know what he meant by 'deal with them'. It was already implied.

He didn't have to go looking for those crazy psychos though. By the time we cleared the chaos and reached the courtyard of the campus, Shorzin and his group were waiting, minus River and Siena. Jess still stood awkwardly behind their 'leader', though she looked both relieved and nervous at the sight of us. The professor did not look happy.

"Well, this is... unexpected." Shorzin's voice carried uneasily across the destruction of the mountain as Adriel pulled us to a stop a few safe yards away. Like before, he maneuvered me easily behind his back.

"I told you this wouldn't end well for you, Jemison." The way Dri talked, with that raspy old accent, carried around the entire courtyard. No one spoke against him, as if fear itself held their tongues. I didn't blame them.

"I had not realized she could wake you."

"She's not an idiot."

I stood a little taller as Adriel defended me but had to suck down my pride when I realized it was so not the time to be sassy.

"Look, yes, dramatic measures were taken, but you can not blame us. The town has been in peace for five hundred years, we could not risk that." I could sense when someone was trying to back themselves out of a corner, and Shorzin was trying hard. Suck ass, moron.

"You tried to kill my girl."

"The lock is the key. We could not let her wake you, though that obviously didn't go so well."

There was a brief pause between the two of them, though the tension strumming in the air was undeniable. "Close your eyes, Larkin." The second those words left his lips, Shorzin's group scattered. Like little rats running from the big bad cat, his group ran with all their might.

"No, Adriel, wait." I grabbed onto his arm as he took a slow step forward, like he wasn't at all concerned about the runners.

He glanced over his shoulder, one dark eyebrow raised in question as I ignored how nice his bicep felt. "They locked me up for five hundred years and tried to kill you—again."

"I know, I just—don't hurt Jess."

Both eyebrows raised at that, and his voice took on a scoffing incredulous tone. "The psychic?"

I nodded and let go of his arm to step behind him once again. "She's the only reason I knew how to wake you. I heard her, in my head."

Those dark blue eyes gazed over me curiously before softening. "Alright, I will not hurt her. You should still close your eyes." I knew better than to ignore him.

A part of me knew I should have stopped him, begged him not to hurt anyone, but another part wanted them gone just as badly. Shorzin killed me once and tried to again. Hell, I didn't even know how many times the guy's killed me, especially if Jess was right about that Angel of Death dude sending me back a lot.

'He knew the only way to really get my attention was for a soul to call to every part of my own—the dark and all.'

Then again, maybe I just wanted them gone.

I kept my eyes closed the entire time and had little idea what was going on. I was expecting to hear screams, shouts, something, but it was nearly silent. The only thing out of the ordinary was that pulsing dark power that streamed off demon Adriel. It seemed to surge through the air, wrap around my skin and sink into my brain. Then it slipped just as easily away.

I had no idea what Adriel did to Shorzin, or his group, but when he finally told me to open my eyes everyone was gone. Everyone except a horror-stricken Jess who was bent over and throwing up the contents of her stomach. Sympathy immediately racked through my chest, and I went to go help her, but demon/not-demon Dri gripped onto my wrist and stopped me.

I glanced over at him as those familiar blue eyes flickered from her to me. "She's still one of them. I don't want you near her."

I ripped my arm away and glared at his stupid handsome face. "She basically saved me, and you. I don't think she would have if she wanted me dead." I turned on my heel and walked over to the small girl. He didn't stop me.

"Hey, it's okay." I tried to sound soothing as I rubbed my hand awkwardly down her thin back. She had stopped vomiting but was still bent over dry heaving.

"He is... not good." Jess breathed heavily as her hands pressed against her knees. I frowned but stayed silent. I wasn't sure what to say. No, I didn't think he was good. They wouldn't have locked him up for centuries if he was ending wars and striving for world peace, but that didn't mean I could stop loving the guy either. Or demon, or whatever the fuck he was.

"It's alright." Were the only soothing words I could think to say as she stood back up and wiped at her mouth with the back of her sleeve. Those bright green eyes darted to Adriel standing a few yards away, watching us intently.

"You must know," She started softly, even though neither of us pretended like he couldn't hear, "I would have given anything to keep him locked away. If there was another choice, I would never have told you how to wake him."

"Why did you?"

Jess brought those creepy green eyes back to mine, and there was no denying the fear shining there. "You have more yet to do. I could not allow you to die."

I swallowed and tried to shove down the unpleasant shiver her words sent down my spine. Why couldn't I just live my life?

Why was there always some bullshit legend and creepy psychics telling me I had more to do? It also didn't help that my boyfriend was a crazy fallen angel who created vampires.

"I will leave now." Jess straightened completely, her eyes flickering uneasily to Adriel before at the desolate space around us. College kids were streaming out of the buildings now, though more than half of them didn't seemed surprised at the chaos. It made me wonder how much of the town actually knew all of this was real, and how many weren't human at all.

"There is much I need to discuss with what remains of the council."

A dark grumble sounded behind us, and I looked over my shoulder to see a dark, determined expression take over Adriel's face. I gulped and looked away. "Um, I wouldn't talk about that around him. He doesn't seem to like it."

Jess nodded, her face just as sickly pale as when I first walked up to her. "Noted."

She was barely a few feet away when Adriel was suddenly beside me, his dark eyes watching every step the psychic took. "That will have to be fixed." I had no doubt he planned on doing to the rest of the 'council' what he did to Shorzin.

"You can't kill everyone, Adriel."

"Sure, I can."

"I don't want you to." That had him grumbling quietly to himself and made that strong jaw tick shut. "You promised me you wouldn't go all psycho again, that you didn't want to. Prove it."

There was no mistaking that dark look that passed over those blue eyes. Then they softened and he let out a small sigh. "You're right. I don't want that anymore. I'll behave, I promise."

I wish I could believe him.

I knew what I had to do, and I knew he was not going to like it.

It had only been two days since everything happened, and even though we unload the SUV, all my stuff still sat packed in my room. Rafael wasn't there anymore, and when I asked Adriel about it, he just said she disappeared when they killed his human form. I tried not to show how badly that tore me apart.

We hadn't spoken much since then. He was always off 'handling situations' as he called them, and I sat all alone in that house thinking over everything.

Which wasn't a good idea on his part.

I sat waiting for him at the bottom of the manor's staircase, my last suitcase waiting beside me. I wasn't exactly sure what I was going to say, despite having rehearsed the words over and over again. I needed time to think, away from him. Even if I went somewhere else in Deshua, he would still be there, hovering over me. I had to get away. My world had been flipped completely upside down, nothing was real anymore. I needed time.

My stomach twisted in nerves the second the front door opened, and I stood shakily to my feet. "Hey, why are there a bunch of boxes in your car—" Adriel's words died on his tongue when those blue eyes landed on me, and my hand on my suitcases lever.

"No."

"I need time, Adriel."

He slammed the front door shut so hard the entire wall trembled. He shook his head, his now shaggy dark hair lying messy against his forehead. Adriel, my Adriel, the human one, hadn't morphed back into that ginormous demon since the day he collapsed the mountain. It only made this twice as hard.

"No. You're not leaving." His voice held that strong commanding tone he used to always use whenever he wanted me to do something, the tone that always made obey. I wouldn't let it now. I couldn't.

"It's too much. I need to think." I tried to keep my voice unwavering as I gazed over at those blue eyes, but it only sounded as strong as my heart—and that broke two days ago.

"Think here!" He took a step towards me, anger brewing behind that dark gaze. "I can even go away for a few days if that's what you want!"

"I—"

"Is this about Rafael? I can bring her back. I can give you anything you want, Larkin." He was pacing now, his human sized body walking back and forth in the large foyer.

My chest clenched at the mention of Raffie, and at how miserable he looked. The last thing I ever wanted to do was hurt him, but things were different now. We were different. I fell in love with a man that doesn't exist, no matter how much he tried to convince it was still him. And even if it was, I couldn't just look the other way and pretend I was okay with all of this.

"It's everything, not just Raffie. I can't be here. I can't be in this town, around all those freaks. I—I can't be near you right now, Adriel."

He stopped pacing then and turned to face me. The look on his face almost had me changing my mind. Almost. "You can't leave me." I didn't flinch away when he walked over and gripped at my upper arms, though the hard look passing over his eyes was a little frightening. "You're everything, Larkin. You can't leave me."

I let out a shaky breath and tried to steady myself. I hated upsetting him, I always have. He was the one person that could put me on top of the world and drag me under it just as fast. "You promised if this was what I wanted you would let me go." His hands tightened at my words, and even though he opened his mouth to say something, nothing came out. "It's what I want, Dri."

His jaw clenched shut but he refused to tear that dark gaze away from mine.

"I love you." Adriel's words were so soft, and sad that they actually brought tears to my eyes, tears I tried to shove away as best as I could. I was always strong, nothing growing up could phase me, but this whole experience tore down all those walls. I was weak.

"I can't do this right now. I need to leave."

For a moment, one, long, scary moment, I actually thought he would lock me in this house with some crazy demon magic and never let me leave. But then his hands loosened, and he let reluctantly go. "If that... is what you want." His words were hard, clipped, and those blue eyes would no longer look into mine.

"Thank you." It took everything inside me not to sigh in relief. I wouldn't be gone forever, just until I sorted out everything raging through my head. Just a little while.

I leaned up, pressed a soft lingering kiss to his cheek, and pulled away. It's not for forever. I tried to 'scream' in my head so he could hear, but he let out no indication that he did.

I grabbed tightly onto the handle of my suitcase and rolled it around him. Adriel didn't move, not one inch. Not even when I opened the door and carried the suitcase down those stone steps and into my car. I waited just outside my driver's door, convinced he would come out and try to stop me, but he didn't.

It felt like someone took that gardening shovel I had left in the flowerbed what felt like so long ago and tried to dig my heart out of my chest. A large part of me wanted to stay, to forget everything that has happened in the pass week, curl up in his arms and never leave.

He could make that happen too. I had no doubt he could wipe my memories if I asked, but I couldn't hide behind a façade. I loved him, with all my heart, and I probably always would. I just needed to sort everything out.

I was nearly out of Deshua, the middle of nowhere town disappearing in my rearview mirror, when something strange happened. I soon as I passed the city limit sign, I was suddenly driving through town square again. I had to slam on my breaks to keep from hitting a group of pedestrians crossing the walk-way.

They all shouted at me and raised their hands angrily as I sat wide eyed, staring in disbelief. "What the fuck...?"

What the hell was that?

I tried to leave again, but the same thing happened when I reached that sign. Then I tried again, and again, by the fourth time I was fed up, and I had a pretty good idea who the fuck was causing it.

I stopped just before the city limit sign, the town a mile or so at my back, with open country stretching in front of me. I slammed open my car, stepped out into the middle of the deserted road and turned towards the town. There he was, standing only a few feet away, his hands resting casually in his jacket pockets even though he looked more ready to fight than have a conversation.

"What the actual fuck, Adriel?" My voice was more of a snap than a genuine question and anger licked at the back of my neck.

"You're not leaving."

My breath hitched at how serious he sounded, at how dead-panned hard his voice was. "You promised."

His jaw grit shut, and those blue eyes flashed black. I could almost feel ice grow on my lungs as that dark energy surged through the air. "If you love me you wouldn't leave."

"If you love me you will let me go!"

He looked away at that, his hard jaw grinding together as if he were trying to reign in the anger so desperately wanting to escape. Then he was right in front of me, moving faster than I could blink, and his arms were caging me tightly to his chest.

"I don't—I don't understand, Larkin." He had backed me up against my car, his body nearly absorbing mine into him as his face pressed into my neck. "Why do you want to leave me?" His voice was so sad and heartbroken that I felt those tears from before enter my eyes. I closed them and sucked in a shaky breath.

"I have to." I whispered softly since I didn't think I could speak any louder. "It's the only way I can figure everything out."

Water officially fell down my cheeks when Adriel's hands wrapped in my hair and he pressed his forehead against mine. The black of his eyes had disappeared, but the white surrounding those blues had turned a veiny red. I had never seen him cry before, never, and he wasn't exactly shedding tears right then, but I knew what that red meant.

"I love you." He murmured against me, his eyes never leaving mine. "More than anything."

"I-I love you." My voice cracked as it came out, but he didn't care. His lips pressed against mine in a hungry lingering kiss that I didn't push away. I leaned into him, my fingers curling into his jacket as I kissed him back with just as much intensity.

"Come back to me." Adriel whispered softly against my lips when I finally pulled away. I didn't answer him, I couldn't. He was my everything, and I was leaving that all behind. I had to.

He didn't stop me from pulling away and getting back into my car. I sat there quietly for a minute, my hands like iron as they gripped tightly onto the steering wheel. Then I let out a shaky breath, buckled my seat belt, and drove pass the city limit sign. He didn't stop me.

I glanced in the rearview mirror when I was about a mile away, but Adriel was still standing there, watching. He stayed until Deshua, and that sign, disappeared in the distance.